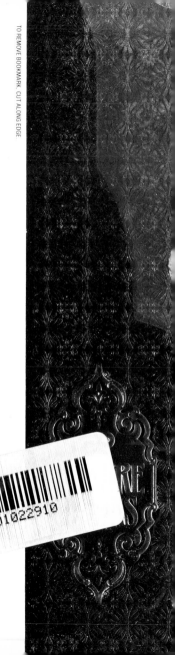

Dear Reader,
Your response to
my books has been
most gratifying.
Your cards and
letters mean more
to me than words
can say. It's your
support and
enthusiasm that
make the writing
so worthwhile.

All my roma...

Robin Lee (.

D1022910

LEISURE
BOOKS

ROBIN LEE HATCHER

PIRATE'S LADY

LEISURE BOOKS ∞ NEW YORK CITY

To my brother,
Rick,
and the three beautiful women in his life—
Joyce, Wendy, and Cheri.
We're separated by miles
but kept close by love.
I miss you all.

A LEISURE BOOK

Published by

Dorchester Publishing Co., Inc.
6 East 39th Street
New York, NY 10016

Printed in the United States of America

PROLOGUE

August 1849

The fetid smell of spoiled fish and rotting garbage, sewage and sea water lay heavy in the still night air. Black clouds, slung low to the earth, cloaked the moonless sky. The three men moved silently along the wharf, the light from the sailor's torch causing eerie forms to dance amid the stacks of crates and piles of sacks. Pairs of tiny yellow eyes captured and reflected the flickering glow, and a chorus of squeaks complained of the intrusion. One dock rat, plump and unafraid, stood on its hind legs, black nose twitching, as the men passed within inches of its scavenged meal.

They climbed into a small boat and rowed toward a ship anchored in the harbor. The steady rhythm of oars slicing the liquid surface melded with the gentle lapping of water against the ship's barnacled sides as they drew near. The first man to start up the rope ladder moved with caution. The two behind him scampered up with the ease of men who belong to ships and seas.

As the last man's feet touched the deck, the first said, "Show me the cargo."

"This way, milord."

They moved to the opening which led into the bowels of the ship. Several lanterns lit their descent into the hold.

"On your feet, you useless baggage," a sailor barked, his voice threatening. He used a boot to encourage quick obedience.

The young women, their hands tied behind them, struggled to rise, their legs catching in a tangle of skirts.

The leader's dark eyes moved slowly, studying each face, each figure with a merciless gaze. They were the usual lot, most of them common wenches, taken from the masses of the nameless, faceless poor that swelled the slums of London. A few might have claims to the middle class. Some were attractive beneath the dirt that smudged their faces; most were merely ordinary. Still, they would bring him a handsome profit.

His relentless study halted abruptly. The object of his attention returned his gaze with an unwavering glare, her round black eyes snapping in defiance, her chin raised proudly. He walked toward her, motioning to one of the sailors to bring a lantern closer.

She was a beauty. Her skin was creamy smooth over high cheekbones and a heart-shaped face. Her generous lips were rose-hued. A tangled mass of raven black hair fell over her shoulders, and he reached out to feel the rich texture of it. She drew back, a startled gasp slipping through parted lips. A smile twisted the corners of his mouth as he dropped his hand. His gaze traveled down from her face, taking in the costly traveling costume that clothed her shapely young body.

"What is your name?" he asked.

She remained silent, her eyes mutinous.

He turned to the sailor waiting expectantly behind him. "Where did you find her?"

"She's an American, milord. Just off the ship this morning and no one to meet her."

"You're certain of that?"

"Aye. We watched her for a long spell, sir, before we . . . ah . . . persuaded her t'join our little venture. She's not been missed, either. We've kept a sharp eye out."

"She's no common girl, White. She's a lady, and she'll be a virgin still. I'd wager on it. See that she stays that way during the voyage. Understand me, White?"

The sailor nodded. "Aye, milord. There'll not be one onboard that takes their pleasure here. I give my word on it."

"Tell Penneywaite that he's to get a premium price for this one. He'll know what to do with her." He looked at the girl one more time. There was fear behind her brave facade, but she was doing an admirable job of disguising it. "Once you're out to sea, move her to a cabin and let her bathe. Extra care here, White. Extra care. Get one of these wenches to act as her maid." His hand darted out to stroke her cheek as he looked into her ebony eyes. His voice was gentle as he said, "I wonder who you are, my lovely American. Pity you must leave England so soon."

Suddenly, he laughed aloud, the gentleness vanishing in the harsh sound. He turned on the heel of his boot, slapping White on the back and saying, "That one's worth a fortune, White. We'll both profit by your quick thinking this day." With long strides, he led the way out of the hold. His voice drifted back to the frightened, bewildered women. "You sail with the tide."

"Aye, milord."

One by one the lanterns were carried up the ladder, leaving the human cargo as much imprisoned by darkness as by the ropes that bound their wrists. The young women sagged back to the filthy floor, a few of them sobbing aloud, some huddling together for comfort.

Gabrielle Jackson was the only one to remain standing. She turned her face upward, seeking any slight breeze that might filter through the grid that now covered the opening of the hold. She was shaking violently. Two tears slipped from swimming eyes and traced damp paths down her pale cheeks.

"Oh, Grandfather," she whispered. "Find me, please." But there was no hope in her voice. She sank toward the stinking floor of the hold as she pleaded, "Tristan, help me."

1

A brisk wind filled the canvas sails of the *Dancing Gabrielle* as she sliced her way through the choppy waters of the Strait of Dover. Tristan stood alone near the bow, arms braced against the rail, his dark face wet from the salty spray that blew off the sea. His ebony eyes stared over the whitecapped waves toward the shores of England.

"Won't be long now, Captain," his first mate said as he stepped up beside Tristan at the rail. "All will be right, sir. You'll see. Captain Frost wouldn't let anything happen to her."

Tristan ran his fingers through his raven black hair, then shook his head. "You know, Whip, I don't know what I'm going to do first when I see her. Shake her or hug her."

Whip gave Tristan a good natured slap on the back, then chuckled as he moved off.

Tristan Dancing's eyes returned to the channel as his thoughts slipped backward in time. He remembered how Ella had pleaded with him to take her along on his last journey to

China. Their mother had died only two months before, and she hadn't wanted to stay with her elderly aunt. Tristan had always had a soft spot in his heart for his little half sister, but he had remained firm on this issue.

"The sea is no place for you, Ella," he'd insisted.

"Then take me to England to stay with Grandfather. Please, Tris. You know I can't stand Aunt Elvira." Her black eyes had filled with tears. "She's so spiteful. She's never forgiven mother for marrying my father."

But he hadn't relented and soon after had set sail for Foochow. She was gone when he returned. After Tristan read her note, the *Dancing Gabrielle* had sailed immediately for London.

Tristan turned his back to the rail and raised his eyes toward the sails above him. A slight smile turned the corners of his rugged mouth. The *Dancing Gabrielle* was his one true passion, and she had proven herself worthy of his pride this trip. They had crossed the Atlantic with great speed, arriving in England little more than four weeks after their departure from New York.

His smile broadened, showing a flash of white teeth, as he thought about his grandfather, the duke. How had he reacted to Ella's sudden appearance on his doorstep?

Tristan had only met his maternal grandfather once, when the Duke of Locksworth had visited her daughter and her family in America many years before. Tristan had been instantly drawn to the white-haired, old gentleman and had meant to return the visit many times before now. Somehow, something had always happened to change his plans. Now that both his mother and stepfather were dead, and with Ella already here, the only family he had left was in England. He had to admit to himself that he was glad Ella's impetuous nature had brought him here at last. Once he had assured himself that she had arrived without mishap, he could relax and enjoy the unexpected reunion with his grandfather.

Whip appeared beside him once again. "We'll be nearing the mouth of the London River before long now, Captain."

Tristan nodded and started walking toward the helm. Yes, it would be good to see Ella and his grandfather again.

Aldrich Phineasbury, sixth Duke of Locksworth, sat in a dim corner of the east room, staring up at the portrait of his daughter while he waited for his mysterious guest to arrive. As always when he thought of Felicia, his heart constricted in his chest. It was impossible for him to think of her as dead. Always she remained in his memory as the girl in the portrait, a beautiful blonde with startling blue eyes. Her gurgling laughter had filled the halls of Locksworth House and brought smiles to all the servants. Sometimes he thought he could hear it still, echoing through the lonely mansion.

He closed his eyes. He never should have let her take that trip to America. He should have kept her at home, safe from the charming wiles of that ship's captain. But he hadn't kept her at home. Felicia, his only child, had fallen in love with George Dancing on the crossing to New York, married him upon arrival, and remained in America.

Locksworth got up from his chair and left the east room, but his thoughts were still on his daughter and her family as he entered his study.

Perhaps Felicia would have come home with her young son after her husband died if Locksworth had gone to see her sooner, if he'd let her know that he loved her and forgave her for running away with the captain, but he'd been so hurt by her desertion of him for another man that he just hadn't been able to make himself go. And then it was too late. Felicia had married another American, her husband's half brother, Jonathan Jackson. The next year her daughter was born.

The duke reached for the note lying on his desk and read the missive once more. The handwriting was nearly illegible, but it was clear enough to know it was about his granddaughter, Gabrielle Jackson.

Little Ella. That's how he thought of her. She had been eight years old when they'd met for the first and only time. Eight years old and already a charmer. That was eight years ago now. She'd be a young lady by this time. Sixteen. The same age as Felicia when she'd left England for a visit to America.

The duke checked the mantel clock. The note had said he would be here at two. It was only one o'clock. Time seemed to be dragging. What could this man have to tell him about his American granddaughter? And why had he been so secretive?

"Milord."

Locksworth looked up at the butler. "Yes, Sims?"

"There's a carriage coming up the drive, sir."

"He's early. Well, bring him to me here, Sims."

The butler nodded. "Yes, milord."

Locksworth sat behind his desk, his back to the large window. He might be an old man, but he still knew how to take advantage of a situation. With the light at his back, his visitor would be unable to see his face clearly or read his expressions. Besides, the duke was not a small man. Old but not small. He would appear larger and stronger as a silhouette against the light.

He heard the footsteps in the hallway outside the study door. He saw Sims first as he held the door for their guest.

The man's tall frame filled the doorway. He was attired in tight black trousers and a black frock coat over a white shirt, his shiny top hat in his hands. His thick black hair, long and wavy, was tied back at the nape where it brushed his white collar. His face was bronzed by many days in the sun and wind. He exuded health and prosperity. He was not the sort of man the duke had expected to be the author of the note.

"Grandfather?" the fellow said, a smile turning the corners of his mouth.

"Good heavens!" The duke's eyes darted back to the man's handsome face as he rose from his chair. "Tristan? Tristan, my boy, is it you?"

Tristan crossed the room, tossing his hat

15

onto a nearby chair. Locksworth came out from behind his desk to receive the fond embrace of his grandson.

"Why didn't you let me know you were coming? I would have met you in London. How long are you staying?" Locksworth stepped back from Tristan, not waiting for him to answer his questions. "You've grown half a head since I saw you last. The sea agrees with you, boy."

"But you haven't changed at all," Tristan replied, still smiling.

"Don't try to flatter me. I know what time has done. Now, tell me. How long will you be staying?"

Tristan shrugged. "I guess that depends on Gabrielle."

"Ella? Is she with you?" Locksworth looked behind Tristan expectantly.

A heavy silence gripped the room before Tristan asked softly, "You mean she isn't here?"

"Here?" The duke's faded brown eyes returned to Tristan's face, meeting his ebony stare. "Why would she be here?"

"She left New York last June to come stay with you. I'd gone to China for a tea shipment and left her with Aunt Elvira."

"Last June? But, Tristan, she should have . . ." He fell silent. The note. He turned to the desk and picked it up, passing it without comment to his grandson.

Tristan scanned the scribbles, his face darkening. "If someone's harmed her, I'll—"

"Easy, lad. I think we'd best make some plans before our visitor arrives. It wouldn't do

16

to frighten him off until we know what he has to tell us."

When Sims showed the man into the study, it was Tristan who stood with his back to the window. Locksworth pointed to some chairs on the far side of the room from Tristan, and he and the man sat down.

The fellow's clothes were little more than rags but they were clean. The tattered hat he'd removed before entering the room was over one hand, and he twisted it nervously with the other. It was hard to guess his age, although Tristan was certain he wouldn't see thirty-five again.

"I believe you have word of my granddaughter," Locksworth began, his voice calm, his words precise.

The man glanced nervously toward the window and Tristan.

"You've nothing to fear from him," the duke said. "He's merely a friend of mine."

"You're sure no one will know I've been 'ere? Wouldn't do for 'is lordship to 'ear of it."

"No one will know. Now speak up, man, before I lose my patience."

"It's . . . it's your granddaughter, milord. She's been kidnapped, she 'as."

Tristan tensed and the man's eyes darted toward him again, sensing the threat in Tristan's taut muscles.

"How do you know this?" Locksworth inquired, encouraging the man to continue.

"I . . . I seen it wi' me own eyes, milord, though I didn't know who she was at the time."

"And how do you know now?"

The man shifted in his chair. "I think it'd be best if I told you me story." He waited for Locksworth's nod before he continued. "You see, milord, the wife an' daughter 'ad been ill and there wasn't enough work for the likes o'me. Not wi' only one good 'and." As he spoke, he removed the hat, revealing the stump beneath it. "When 'is lordship found me an' offered me work I could 'andle, I couldn't say nay. Not if I was going t'get a doctor t'help me little girl." He cleared his throat as he covered his bad arm with his hat again. "I know I shouldn't've done it, but what's done is done."

"And what is it that's done?"

"I get women for 'is lordship. Most of 'em are young girls from poor families like me own. Like as not their folks don't even miss 'em. Just one less mouth t'feed. Some want t'go." He paused guiltily. "Most don't."

Locksworth sat forward in his chair. "And just what does *his lordship* do with these women?"

Tristan ground his teeth, waiting for the man's slow reply, imagining the worst happening to his sister.

" 'e puts them on a ship an' takes 'em away." He swallowed, his Adam's apple bobbing in his narrow neck. "I asked one o' the sailors one time where 'e took 'em, and 'e said 'e sold 'em as slaves in the East."

Tristan gripped the window ledge, forcing himself to remain with his back to the window, while all the time what he wanted to do was to cross the room and choke the very breath from that miserable little man's body. He saw his grandfather glance his way, the old man's face drained of color.

"Why have you told me this?" Locksworth asked, his voice low. "And why do you think my granddaughter is among these women?"

"I was there when they took 'er. Snatched 'er right from the docks in broad daylight, they did. But they left 'er trunk, and I thought there might be somethin' in it me own could make use of so I took it 'ome wi' me. There was letters inside from you, milord. I thought about it a long while, I did, an' knew I couldn't be a part of it no more. So I wrote you that note to tell you I was coming."

Tristan couldn't stay silent any longer. "Who is this man, this lordship you speak of?"

Both of the men across the room turned their heads toward Tristan. The little man quaked visibly.

"I daren't tell you. Not while 'e could find me."

Locksworth spoke again. "Then what must we do so you will tell us?"

"Well, milord . . . if you could . . . if you could move me and me family from London. Maybe find me a position in the north somewhere—"

The duke stood. "Done. I'll have the lot of you on a coach out of London tomorrow. Now tell us. Who is behind this kidnapping?"

" 'e's known as the Englishman, milord, but I've learned 'is name." He stopped and swallowed hard, as if afraid to speak the name aloud. His eyes were large with fear.

"Well? What is it, man? Speak up!"

"Blackstoke, milord. 'e's called Blackstoke."

2

*She waited for him, leaning out the window of
her high-towered room. She could see his
approach, his black charger loping slowly, neck
proudly arched and thick mane and long tail
flowing in the wind. Her pulse quickened. He
was coming for her. Her love. Her life. She
turned from the window and raced down the
stone steps and out of the keep. She couldn't
reach him soon enough. She longed to feel his
strong arms around her. She yearned for the
taste of his sweet kisses. There! There he was.
Sitting so tall and straight in the saddle. She
could see his coal black hair and imagined his
twinkling black eyes. She held out her arms,
urging him to come faster. But though his steed
kept cantering, he covered no ground. In fact, he
was slipping backward, growing smaller.*

"No! No! Please don't leave me. Please!"

Jacinda sat up, her eyes flying open, her
heart beating rapidly in her chest.

That dream again!

"Lady Jacinda? Are you all right, miss?"

21

Her maid stood in the open doorway, a flickering candle in her hand.

"Yes, Mary. I'm fine, thank you. I'm sorry I woke you."

"No trouble, miss." Mary nodded good night as she backed out of the room, closing the door as she went.

Jacinda lay back on her pillows as she stared at the silver-edged shadows the moon was casting across her ceiling. She tried to will herself back to sleep, but she found herself thinking about the mysterious knight of her dreams instead. Who was he, and why could she never see his face?

"I would have thought I'd outgrown such foolishness," she whispered aloud, chiding herself. "That's what I get for reading so many of those silly novels. A head full of dreams."

Jacinda knew full well that there was no such thing as a knight in shining armor, riding in to carry her away to his kingdom of happiness. Love—the kind she was dreaming of, at any rate—was a fairy tale, nothing more. Great love, such as that were only found in books, not in real life. Certainly not in *her* life.

Jacinda rolled over onto her side, hugging a pillow against her breasts. She swallowed the lump that had formed in her throat and blinked away the sudden tears that swam before her gold-flecked, tawny eyes. Deep inside, her heart yearned for just what she believed could never happen, and she fought to stamp out that yearning for good, to be done with these childish dreams once and for all.

"It would never do for the viscount to know I dream of another man, whether he's real or just a vision," she reminded herself. "Not when we are so soon to be engaged."

She rolled onto her other side, seeking a place of comfort that was not to be found. Her mattress felt hard and lumpy. The room seemed cold. She wished she'd asked Mary to add more fuel to the fire before returning to her bed.

As Jacinda tossed and turned, the minutes of night stretched toward morning until, at last, she drifted into a troubled sleep, secretly hoping she would find the black-haired knight in her dreams once more . . . and that this time, he would reach her.

It was late when Jacinda opened her eyes again. Morning sunlight spilled through the high windows of her room. She sat up and threw off the bedcovers, rushing to her wardrobe to pull out a gown, paying little notice to which one it was.

"Why didn't Mary wake me?" she grumbled as she removed her nightgown and pulled the dress over her head.

She sat at her dressing table and reached for her brush. Her dark, flame-red hair, curly and thick and reaching to her waist, tumbled down her back in wild disarray. With quick strokes, she worked out the tangles the best she could, aware of each minute as it ticked away. Her mother would be in a royal temper. Lady Sunderland hated to be kept waiting for breakfast. Jacinda fastened her hair back with combs, knowing it would not merit approval, but it would have to do. She slid from her stool and hurried out of her room, silently cursing her maid once more for not waking her. Jacinda was in no mood for a lecture from her mother.

Lady Gwendolyn Sunderland looked up as Jacinda entered the dining hall. Her brown eyes flicked over her daughter, the critical glance noting any flaw in her appearance.

"Good morning, Mother," Jacinda said as she slipped into her chair.

"Aren't you feeling well, Jacinda?" Lady Sunderland asked.

"I feel fine."

"Then why are you so late this morning? And what are those circles doing under your eyes?"

Jacinda glanced down the table, meeting her mother's gaze. "I had a little trouble sleeping last night. That's all. And I'm late because Mary didn't wake me. In fact, I haven't seen her yet this morning."

"Oh, yes. Mary. I sent her on an errand. I naturally thought she would be back in time to attend to you, my dear." Lady Sunderland took a dainty bite of food and chewed slowly before continuing. "You know that your father is bringing Lord Fanshawe back with him this evening. It wouldn't do for him to see you this way."

Jacinda stiffened as she looked back at her plate. "Don't worry, Mother. I won't disappoint you. I will look my very best when Lord Fanshawe arrives."

"See that you do." There was a hard edge in her mother's voice. "I don't think you realize what a catch you're making, my dear. There are girls all over England ready to throw themselves into the sea because the viscount has chosen another for his bride. You should be honored that you are the one he chose."

"I know I should be honored," she replied.

"Jacinda, you must realize how much this marriage means to your father and me."

Jacinda did realize it. Her father, Lord William Sunderland, fifth Earl of Bonclere, had a fondness for gaming and gambling, a fondness that outstripped the income he derived from his estate. Over the years, the staff at Bonclere Manor had dwindled. The house in town had been sold. There were fewer horses in the stables and fewer hounds in the kennels.

Not that Jacinda cared for the manor enough to sacrifice herself for it. Bonclere had always seemed a cold place to her. And not just because it was drafty, though it was. The coldness went much deeper than that. There was no love in the house. Never had been. It would be no great sacrifice to leave, and as she was expected to marry anyway, Roger Fanshawe, the eldest son of the Marquess of Highport, seemed as acceptable as any man to be her husband.

"Jacinda?" There was suspicion in her mother's voice. "You're not about to do anything foolish, are you? You're not going to turn Lord Fanshawe down like you did the others?"

"I turned the others down because I didn't care a whit for them."

Lady Sunderland relaxed. "And you do care for the viscount," she said, satisfied.

Jacinda thought again of windblown black hair and snapping black eyes, of strong arms and passionate love, but she pushed the vision away. "Not particularly, Mother, but I won't turn away another suitor. I will accept the viscount's proposal of marriage and save Bonclere for you and Father."

"You needn't make it sound as if we're selling you." Her mother sniffed indignantly.

Aren't you? Jacinda wondered. She turned a searching gaze upon her mother. "Did you ever *love* Father?" she asked, wanting desperately to hear a different reply than the one she knew was the truth.

"Love your father?" Lady Sunderland laughed aloud. "Why, Jacinda my dear. What a strange mood you're in. Haven't I told you that marrying for love is not for us. One has a position to maintain and duty to family. One must think of these things when choosing a husband." She pushed her chair back, her satin skirts rustling as she rose. "Of course, if one's husband is truly disagreeable, one can always take a lover after an appropriate length of time. Naturally, one must be discreet. The Sunderlands would not like a scandal in the family." She paused behind Jacinda's chair and kissed the air above her daughter's head. "Now eat your breakfast. Then go to your room and lie down. You must rid your eyes of those shadows before Lord Fanshawe arrives. And dear, please take pains with your dressing. We mustn't let the viscount see you in an old dress like the one you're wearing." On that, she swept from the room.

Jacinda lay beside the deep pond, unmindful of the leaves that clung to her riding costume or that were tangled in her hair. She drew in a deep breath, letting the fresh scents of the forest draw out the tension that had filled her all morning long. Nearby, her white Arabian mare, Pegasus, grazed contentedly. A squirrel chattered in a tree overhead, and another replied from some distance off.

This was her favorite hideaway. She had discovered it when she was a child and, ever since, had come here when she had a problem and needed to think things through. It didn't matter if she found no solutions. She always felt better when she left.

And she *did* have a problem. Her father would be bringing Lord Fanshawe back with him from London. They would have settled the engagement and a date would need to be decided upon. Her parents, she knew, would hope for a short engagement period. And Lord Fanshawe? She suspected he would prefer an early wedding, too. But she wasn't in a hurry. Try as she might, she couldn't become excited about marrying the viscount, even though someday he would make her a marchioness.

She closed her eyes, remembering the first time she'd seen the viscount. It was at a supper at Lord and Lady Andover's last season. He had arrived late. She had heard the appreciative murmurs and followed the admiring gazes of the young women. There he'd stood in the door- way, his glance assessing each woman there with a practiced eye, until his gaze settled on Jacinda. She remembered the nervous feeling that had spread through her as he smiled. He was handsome—there was no denying that— with his dark brown hair and those deep-set blue eyes beneath heavy brows. He sported side whiskers and a fashionable mustache, the same umber shade of brown as his hair. He was tall with broad shoulders and a narrow waist, and when she'd danced with him later that same evening, she could feel the muscles in his arms. She was certain he wouldn't go to fat early. The whispers and jealous looks that flew among the young women and their mothers when it become obvious that the viscount had found a favorite had confirmed to her his popularity.

So why wasn't she as captivated by him as the others? She couldn't come up with a good enough reason to deny him his offer of marriage; yet denying him was exactly what she wanted to do.

"It wouldn't matter if I did deny him," she said aloud. "Father has already consented. I have no choice but to marry him."

She sat up and stared into the still pool of water, brown leaves shining up at her from the bottom. She shook her red mane, sending dried leaves flying, then rested her chin on her knees.

In her two London seasons, Jacinda had had more than her share of proposals of marriage—and a few proposals not quite so honorable. She was not an heiress, so it wasn't her title or future estate that caused prospective husbands, both young and not so young, to offer for her hand. It was her unusual beauty. Her abundant, dark red hair—the color of hot coals when a fire has burned low—was free of any orange or brassy shadings. Her eyes were tawny, almost gold in color, and they sparkled when she was amused. Her smiles, though infrequent, seemed able to brighten a room all by themselves, and gentlemen fell over themselves seeking to earn one of those rare smiles. Her complexion was ivory smooth, without freckles or blemishes. Her beauty drew men like bees to honey, each one vying for her approval.

But Jacinda was not impressed nor enticed by the attentions of her suitors. She kept waiting, kept hoping, that somewhere among them would appear the man of her dreams. But he never came.

Now the decision had been taken from her. Her father would give her no more choices. He had agreed with her denials of younger sons or gentlemen in circumstances too much like his own, but he would not be so foolish as to let her throw away one of the most eligible bachelors in all of England. Roger Fanshawe wanted her, and he would have her.

She forced herself to think about him again. For the past year, he had been constant in his pursuit. He had never made an improper gesture, had never even tried to kiss her. He had always been a perfect gentleman with her. In every way, the gentleman. Except perhaps in the way he looked at her. She would swear, sometimes, that he could strip away her clothes with his eyes. She shivered, wondering about the private life of a man and woman.

Suddenly her eyes filled with tears and she began to sob. Pegasus lifted her head from her grazing and nudged Jacinda with her muzzle as if to say she understood.

"Mother's going to be furious with me," Jacinda said with a sniff. She stroked the mare's soft neck. "I was told to get rid of the circles under my eyes, and instead, I'm making them red with crying."

She got up and brushed the leaves from her riding skirt, sniffing again. "I'd better get home if I'm going to be ready to greet Lord Fanshawe. I promised Mother I wouldn't disappoint him, and a Sunderland never breaks a promise." There was a hint of scorn in her voice as she finished. "Especially not to the great Viscount Blackstoke."

When the viscount entered the drawing room at Bonclere early that same evening, he was greeted by a vision of loveliness. Jacinda was wearing a gown of dark gold satin which nearly matched the color of her eyes. The bodice was low and her shoulders were bare, emphasizing the enticing whiteness of her throat. Her hair, too long to be worn parted in the center with curls over her ears, was gathered high on her head, then fell in a single cluster of curls down the back of her neck, the flaming tresses woven through with gold ribbons that matched her gown.

Blackstoke paused for a moment in the doorway, his eyes lingering on Jacinda before he crossed the room to greet her mother. Her tawny gaze followed him as he bowed before Lady Sunderland, murmuring expected compliments. Again Jacinda admitted to herself that he was handsome and that she should be honored he had chosen her for his bride.

He swung around and caught her staring at him. "My dear Lady Jacinda," he said as he walked over to her. "It has been much too long since I've had the pleasure of your company." He took her hand and bowed low over it, his lips brushing her knuckles.

"We are happy to have you at Bonclere, Lord Fanshawe," she replied, drawing back her hand. "As always."

He lowered his voice. "I'd hoped you would find it in your heart to call me by my given name."

"I . . . I wouldn't presume to be so forward, my lord. After all, nothing has been decided between us."

A shadow passed over his blue eyes, but he smiled as he straightened. "Then you should be happy to hear that your father and I have settled matters regarding our marriage. All we need now is to set the date."

"How wonderful!" Lady Sunderland cried.

Blackstoke paid her no heed. "And you, Jacinda? Do you think it's wonderful?"

She felt all the color drain from her cheeks beneath his watchful gaze. "I . . . I—" she stuttered, unable to find the right phrase. How could she answer him truthfully without displeasing him?

"Why, how to you think she feels?" Lady Sunderland interrupted, rising gracefully to her feet and coming to stand beside Jacinda's chair. "The girl is speechless with happiness."

Jacinda saw the stiffening of his jaw, and his eyes seemed to darken with repressed irritation. "Of course," he replied, turning away from Jacinda. "Sunderland, I'd take that brandy you mentioned on our way in."

While his back was turned, Lady Sunderland pinched Jacinda's arm. "For pity's sake, Jacinda, at least pretend to be pleased," she hissed into her daughter's ear. "You'll be the ruin of us yet."

Blackstoke turned with his glass in hand and raised it in a salute. "To my future wife.

31

The loveliest lady I have ever seen. May she be content beneath my rule."

Somehow she forced herself to smile, despite the feeling that she was being sucked into a black pit from which there was no escape.

The dream began as it always did, with her knight coming for her, with her running down the stairs to meet him, but this time she was certain he would reach her. This time he wouldn't slip away . . .

Suddenly, there was a hand on her arm, a strong hand pulling her back into the keep. She turned to refuse, but the protest died on her lips, quelled by Blackstoke's frigid glare. "You are mine, Jacinda. You belong to me." As the darkness of the keep surrounded her, she looked back toward the sunshine. He had reached the castle. For the first time, he had reached it. He waited, staring after her, seated on his black horse, waiting . . . but she wasn't free to go to him.

She would never know his love.

Jacinda sat on the window ledge, staring across the lawn that stretched before the manor. Blackstoke had left early, before daylight was more than a promise on the horizon. She had watched him go from this same window in her bedroom. She was relieved that she wouldn't have to face him again this morning. Last night had been dreadful enough. She had made him angry. Though he concealed it well enough, she could sense his displeasure, and it frightened her.

"What's wrong with me?"

May she be content beneath my rule. That's what he'd said. His rule. She was to be his servant. Her life would no longer be her own.

But is it my own now? she wondered.

No. Her life was her father's until she married, then it would be her husband's. It was that simple. It was a fact of life. Why couldn't she just accept it like other women did?

"Because I want to *give* my life to my husband, not have him take it from me." She pressed her forehead against the glass as she whispered, "Because I want to know love."

There it was. She wanted to know love. She could deny her dream forever, but it still expressed what she felt. She wanted to know love. But she never had and maybe she never would. She was to be married to a man who was little more than a stranger, a man who never shared of himself. He wanted her and meant to have her, but there was no love in his expressions toward her.

"It's not fair," she whispered. "It's not fair."

3

It rained for a week. The gray skies mirrored the heaviness of her spirits as Jacinda wandered aimlessly through the manor. She knew her mother watched her with disapproving eyes, but she didn't care. She couldn't muster the strength to pretend that she was happy. She had awakened this morning to golden sunshine spilling through her windows, and without a thought for breakfast, she donned her riding dress and hurried to the stables.

"Giles, saddle Pegasus for me please," she called as she entered the barn.

"Right away, miss," the groom responded.

She watched Giles lead Pegasus from her stall, his work-worn hands moving deftly as he brushed the mare's white coat, then lifted the saddle onto her back. As he worked, she stroked her horse's muzzle, whispering nonsensical sounds.

"Out mighty early, aren't you, Miss Jacinda?" Giles asked as he slipped the bridle over Pegasus' head.

"I couldn't bear to be inside another minute," she answered, pulling on her riding gloves. "If the rain hadn't stopped today, I would have gone mad."

The groom nodded in understanding, obliging her with a toothy grin. As she walked beside him, he led the horse outside, then helped her into the saddle.

"I may be gone all morning, Giles, but I promise not to bring Pegasus back overheated." With that, she clucked to her mare and they jogged down the long drive toward the road.

Once out of sight of the house, Jacinda gave Pegasus her head, allowing the mare to stretch out into a vigorous gallop, the ground speeding by beneath her pounding hooves. As the wind whipped Jacinda's face, the corners of her mouth turned up in a smile. She wished fleetingly that they could go on running like this forever but knew it couldn't be. Reluctantly, she eased her mount's pace back to a walk.

The air was pungent with the freshness of a spring morning after a rain. She could almost smell the new green of the trees and the wild grasses. The morning sun caressed the earth with its warming rays, glittering off the tiny drops of water that were left clinging to the leaves of bushes and trees.

Without consciously thinking about her destination, Jacinda soon found herself turning up the drive leading to Locksworth House. The massive stone structure spread out in a broad sweep. In the center, it was four stories high. In the wings, only two. She rode directly up to the front entrance where she was met by a young page who held her horse as she dismounted.

"Is the duke receiving this morning?" she asked the butler as she entered the house.

Sims, the head butler at Locksworth, nodded. "His lordship is always at home for you, Lady Jacinda." He led her into the east room. He bowed, motioning for her to be seated, as he said, "I'll let his grace know you are here."

Jacinda tugged at her gloves as she waited, feeling a little guilty for coming so early in the day. Yet she knew Sims was right. She would be welcome, no matter the hour. The Duke of Locksworth was her friend. No, even more than that. He was like a grandfather to her. He'd been the only constant source of affection she had known in her eighteen years. If she knew nothing else, she knew that Locksworth loved her as he would his own granddaughter if she were here.

She rose from her chair and wandered around the room, gazing at the portraits on the walls. There was one of the duke's wife, the Duchess of Locksworth, and another of the duke and duchess with their only child, Felicia, a beautiful blue-eyed blonde. She had died the winter before in America, and Jacinda knew her old friend still mourned his daughter's passing.

"Jacinda, my girl. What a pleasant surprise!"

She turned from the portrait. "Have I come too early, your grace?"

"No. No. Not at all. I'm an early riser, as I expect you are. Have you breakfasted?"

She shook her head, suddenly realizing she was hungry.

Locksworth grinned, his brown eyes twinkling. "Then come with me. We'll dine together."

The morning passed quickly in his delightful company, and Jacinda made no move to leave. Here her problems could be forgotten, even if only for a few hours.

Jacinda knelt on the floor of the nursery and leaned inside the deep toy box. "Here!" she exclaimed, drawing out a doll with golden curls. "This was the one. Ann. That's what I called her. She was always my favorite."

Locksworth sat near the open window, a tolerant smile on his lips. "You should have said something. I would have given her to you long ago."

"Oh, no." She gave her head a vehement shake. "Then I couldn't have come to visit her." She paused. "And you."

"Your pardon, milord." Sims stood in the doorway, a slip of paper in his hand. "A message for you, sir."

"Is it the one I've been awaiting?" the duke asked.

"Yes, milord."

Locksworth rose quickly. "You must excuse me, Jacinda. I've some business to see to." When she began to rise, he waved his hand. "No. Please stay. We'll have tea before you go." By this time, he had reached Sims and was taking the missive from the butler's hand, then they both disappeared into the hall.

Jacinda stared at the empty doorway, listening as the footsteps faded and she was left alone in the nursery. Alone on the entire floor, no doubt.

She got up and went over to the window. The view from this third story room looked over the vast expanse of lush green lawn that spread before the mansion. She opened the window and rested her elbows on the sill, then cupped her chin in the palms of her hands. She closed her eyes and imagined herself again as a young girl, playing in this very nursery. She sighed. How happy she'd always been here, pretending that the Duke of Locksworth really was her grandfather and Locksworth House her real home.

She opened her eyes slowly, gazing almost without seeing at the long drive that wound its way from the main road to the house. How long did she watch their approach without realizing they were really there? The steed's glossy black coat gleamed bright in the golden sunshine. His long tail flew out behind him, rippling like a sail in the wind. He was a magnificent animal, his beauty and strength clear even from this room high above. And the rider? Jacinda's glance shifted to him, and her heart seemed to skip a beat. It was him. It *was* him. The man in her dream. It had to be him.

Jacinda spun away from the window and hurtled herself out of the nursery and down the stairs. She had to see his face. She couldn't let him slip away without seeing his face. This time he wouldn't disappear. Sims was standing just inside the open door when she reached the entry hall. She paid him no heed as she flew by him, coming to an abrupt halt at the top of the stone steps leading to the drive. Her heart pounded in her ears as she stared at them. She still couldn't see his face. His back was toward her as he spoke softly to Locksworth, his head bent close to the duke, the coal blackness of his thick, wavy locks in sharp contrast to the older man's thatch of white hair. Then he turned, and he and the duke began walking toward the entrance. He looked up, saw her standing there, and stopped.

Her breath caught in her throat. He was even more handsome than she had imagined, but his eyes were just as she'd known they would be. Blackest ebony, capped by thick black brows. His face was tanned and clean-shaven with a square, determined jaw. She saw his eyes light with interest as a smile curved his strong mouth.

"And who is this, your grace?" he said, his voice deep and warm.

Jacinda felt a strange shiver running up her spine.

Locksworth grinned. "Ah, my dear." He lifted his arm toward her, motioning her down the steps. "Come meet someone very special."

She moved forward, knees trembling, her eyes never leaving the stranger's face and the warmth of his smile. Locksworth caught her hand and pulled her closer, then passed her hand to his visitor.

"Tristan, this delightful creature is my neighbor and very dear friend, Lady Jacinda Sunderland of Bonclere, daughter of the earl."

His eyes seemed to darken, if that were possible. "Lady Jacinda," he repeated softly. It was almost a caress. He lifted her fingers and brushed them lightly with his lips.

For a moment, she imagined him in shiny hauberk, sword at his side, war horse in full battle regalia standing behind him. Just like in her dream. No, better than in her dream. This time, he had reached her. He hadn't left without her. She could feel a warm color spreading from the neckline of her gown, moving up to stain her cheeks in a becoming blush.

"My dear," Locksworth said, "may I introduce Captain Dancing of the tea clipper, the *Dancing Gabrielle*."

"How do you do, Captain Dancing?" The words came out barely more than a whisper.

"Very well, my lady," he answered, a twinkle in his dark eyes. "Decidedly well."

Locksworth cleared his throat, then said to Tristan, "I have asked Jacinda to stay for tea. You'll join us, Tris?"

"Of course."

The duke took her hand and placed it in the crook of his arm, leading her away from the captain. But she could feel his eyes on her back as they entered the house.

They took their tea on the terrace, enjoying the balmy late September day. Jacinda had finally gained control of her wild imagination and was forcing herself to behave in a proper fashion.

"You're an American, Captain Dancing?" she asked as she poured the tea for the duke.

"Yes, from New York. But I'm not there very often. My real home is my ship."

"And how is it you know his grace?"

Tristan glanced at the duke before replying, "We met when he visited his daughter and family a number of years ago. He invited me then to come to Locksworth House. Now, at last, I'm here."

Her voice quivered with anticipation as she

asked her next question. "How long will you be staying?"

There was a flicker of something in his black eyes. Almost anger. Then his expression closed. His reply was terse. "I'm unsure."

"Have one of Mrs. Bitterli's crumpets," Locksworth inserted quickly, filling the awkward silence as he shoved the small serving tray in front of Jacinda.

She took one automatically, keeping her eyes on her plate. She didn't know what she'd done or said that was wrong, but she knew it was something awful. With a few words, she had driven the smile from his eyes and mouth. With the going of his smile went the warmth of the sun. She bit into the crumpet without tasting it.

"These are very good, your grace. You tell Mrs. Bitterli I said so."

Jacinda looked up as Tristan spoke. He was watching her, and there was an apology in his gaze that brought back the brilliance of the day, warming her to her toes. "Yes, your grace. Please tell Mrs. Bitterli how especially good her crumpets are today."

The terrace doors opened, and Sims stepped outside. "The Earl of Bonclere, milord," he announced.

Lord Sunderland's portly stomach preceded him onto the terrace. He wore a tight smile on his ruddy face as his hazel eyes settled on his daughter. "Your mother said I would find you here, Jacinda. Have you been pestering his grace all day?"

Locksworth rose from his chair. "Here now, Sunderland. Don't scold the girl. She's been ready to leave long ago, and I forced her to stay. Now that you're here, you must join us for tea also."

"Well—" the earl began, his eyes locking on the tray of crumpets, toasted to perfection. "I suppose Lady Sunderland can be made to wait a short while longer before we return." He pulled out a chair and sat down. As he spread preserves on one of several crumpets, he glanced at Tristan in silent question.

"Lord Sunderland, this is Tristan Dancing, captain of the *Dancing Gabrielle* which is in port in London. Captain Dancing, Lord Sunderland of Bonclere, Lady Jacinda's father."

Lord Sunderland nodded a greeting, his mouth full.

"We've been enjoying your daughter's company, Lord Sunderland," Tristan said. "Thank you for not stealing her away too soon."

Her father dabbed away some jam from the corner of his mouth before replying, "Well, sirs, enjoy it while you can. Come Christmas she'll be living in her new home with her husband." The earl's chest puffed up with pride. "Yes, she's made herself the best catch of the season, she has."

Jacinda wanted to die. She wanted to run away and hide rather than meet Tristan's gaze. Why did her father have to come here and spoil her day? Why couldn't she have had just this little while? Why couldn't she pretend for one afternoon that her dreams were coming true?

"Jacinda?" Locksworth touched her shoulder briefly. "Why didn't you tell me?"

She couldn't answer. She hadn't told him because she wanted to pretend it wasn't so, but she couldn't admit that in front of her father.

"Must be shy," her father said. "Can't believe she isn't out telling the countryside. Her mother certainly isn't keeping it a secret. Our daughter marrying a future marquess. Why, Blackstoke was coveted by every young lady in London, and he's asked for our Jacinda's hand."

"Blackstoke?" Locksworth and Tristan said in unison, their eyes turning on each other quickly, then flicking away.

Lord Sunderland reached for another crumpet. "Yes, indeed. Viscount Blackstoke himself. We wrapped up the arrangements last week. And I don't mind telling you, I didn't let our Jacinda go lightly, either."

At last, Jacinda looked up from her plate. With the practice of many years, she was able to wipe any trace of emotion from her face, steeling her heart against another rejection. But Tristan was still watching her with interest. He was even smiling at her. Still, it was a different smile than the one he had worn before. There was an odd light in his black gaze that made her feel uncomfortable.

"I'm not sure I care for this idea of yours, Tristan." Locksworth paced his study, hands behind his back and a deep frown furrowing his forehead. "I like this girl. She's like one of my own. I'm not sure I want her used this way."

"But what better way to gain Blackstoke's confidence than through her? I've spent the last week looking for a way to meet him. The man is too careful, too crafty to be found out that way. I don't want to wait months to find Ella. Even weeks will be bad enough."

"I suppose you're right," the duke responded, sagging into a nearby chair. "But, by heavens, Tris. I don't want Jacinda hurt. Do you hear me?"

"How could I hurt her? She's engaged to another man. I'm nothing to her. Besides, it's Blackstoke I want." His face darkened. "And *his* just dues will have to wait until I've brought Ella home from wherever he's sent her."

4

"William, Jacinda and I simply *must* go into London. We'll just have to let a house in town, that's all. There's no way around it. Our clothes are a shambles, and Madame Roget is too much in demand to come out here. We have far and away too much entertaining to be done before the wedding. We just can't make do with these rags any longer." Lady Sunderland slid her chair back from the table. "William, are you listening to me?"

Lord Sunderland nodded morosely. "Yes, dear. I'm listening." He sighed. "The way you're going, we'll be forced to ask for another advance from Blackstoke."

Jacinda felt her stomach tightening into a knot. With a murmured apology, she slipped from the table and left the dining room, her departure unnoticed by either of her parents. Her head was throbbing at her temples and behind her eyes. She had to get out, get some fresh air before she exploded. She grabbed a cloak and left the house, choosing to walk rather than wait for Pegasus to be saddled.

There was the telltale nip of fall in the morning air, and she filled her lungs with it as she pulled her cloak close around her shoulders. She forsook the road, cutting across the fields, the hem of her skirt soaking up the heavy dew still sparkling on the blades of grass.

'I don't want to go to London,'' she muttered. "I don't want any new clothes. And I don't want to marry Roger Fanshawe.''

But there was no going back. Even if she'd been brave enough to weather her mother's wrath, she couldn't back out now. Money had changed hands between the viscount and the earl, and the earl had just said that the money was near spent. Even now he was planning to ask for more. No. There was no way out of this marriage.

She heard the dog's barking and turned. Bounding across the field was a black and white collie, her long coat shimmering in the morning sun.

"Sable," she called in greeting, "what are you doing so far from Locksworth?''

The collie circled her several times before settling herself at Jacinda's feet, waiting for the expected strokes. Jacinda knelt beside the dog and ruffled her ears, then petted her tapered muzzle. Sable was the most beautiful of the Duke of Locksworth's prize collies, at least as far as Jacinda was concerned, and she was surprised that the dog had wandered so far afield. Especially since she'd given birth only a few weeks ago to eight adorable puppies.

"Hello."

Jacinda twisted at the voice, the sudden

movement causing Sable to jump off to one side. With a plop, Jacinda was sitting in the damp grass.

"I'm sorry," Tristan said as he dismounted. "Here. Let me help you up."

Jacinda accepted his hand. "Thank you." He drew her to her feet with ease. "I didn't hear you coming."

"How could you with all the noise Sable was making." Tristan grinned as the collie rubbed her muzzle against his hand, urging him to stroke her glossy coat. He obliged with a chuckle. When he looked back up at Jacinda, he asked, "If you're alone, perhaps you'd like to join us in our morning exercise?"

She should decline. It wasn't proper for her to be alone with him. Her mother would be furious. And Blackstoke? He wouldn't like it either.

"I'd love to," she replied, an uncertain smile stealing onto her lips.

They walked in silence, Tristan leading his horse behind them while Sable raced ahead, then doubled back to circle them before bounding off in another direction, sniffing out and giving chase to an occasional hare or squirrel. Jacinda laughed aloud as she watched the dog's antics.

"You have a lovely laugh, Lady Jacinda," Tristan said suddenly. "You should do it more often." There was that same warmth in his voice which she had heard the day they first met.

She stopped abruptly, her laughter fading. She was afraid to look at him, afraid he would see how starved she was for the words he spoke.

Was she imagining more to his simple statement than was there? Was it because she was being forced to marry Blackstoke, a man she didn't love, that she imagined something special between herself and this man?

She glanced around her, not knowing what to say, how to reply. Her eyes fell on Tristan's horse. "He isn't one of the duke's. Is he yours?"

"Yes. This is Neptune. A barb." He laid a hand on the sleek neck. "I bought him in Tunis several years ago."

"Does he always sail with you?"

"No," Tristan answered with a chuckle. "He's not all that fond of the sea. I brought him with me from home since I planned to be in England longer than I normally stay in any one port."

She couldn't stop asking questions. She wanted to know everything she could about him. "Why are you staying here so long? I mean, what makes this visit so different from your other stops around the world?"

The corners of his mouth hardened as his black eyes looked away, staring off across the field where Sable still scampered. "I'm between cargos," he replied, his words clipped. "I wanted a rest."

Jacinda felt an overwhelming emptiness as he withdrew from her. She began walking again.

Tristan's long legs brought him up beside her before she'd gone very far. "I understand your viscount has an interest in shipping, too."

"Lord Fanshawe?" She glanced at him quickly, then looked away again. "I've never heard him mention shipping."

"Perhaps I misunderstood. After all, you'd know him better than anyone."

She had an insane desire to laugh but suppressed it. She had to pull herself together. Ever since she'd seen Tristan riding toward Locksworth, she hadn't been thinking straight. Just a few weeks before she had been agreeable enough about marrying Blackstoke. Even when she'd privately railed against the unfairness of being given and taken in marriage with little thought for her feelings, she had accepted it as part of her life as a woman. She had told herself that her dreams of a knight in shining armor were foolish dreams, that such a love didn't exist. And then this captain had ridden into her life, and she'd thought of little else since that moment.

She gave herself a mental shake. "Yes. Of course. I know him better than anyone." She lifted her chin and turned a steady gaze on Tristan. "If you'd like, I'll ask Lord Fan... Roger... about it next time I see him. In fact, Mother and I will be letting a house in London soon. I should see him then. I'll ask him about it."

"No need for that, Lady Jacinda." Tristan seemed unaware of her inner turmoil or the sudden stiffness of her voice. "Besides, I'm hoping I'll get to meet him myself before I leave Locksworth. I'd like to be able to congratulate him in person on his choice of a bride."

Leaving Locksworth? When? she almost cried, but Sable's enthusiastic presence was thrust upon them as she ran up from behind, barking noisily, insisting that they pay her more attention.

51

"All right, Sable. All right," Tristan responded, patting her luxurious white mane. He looked back at Jacinda. "I'd better get her home to her pups. May I give you a ride to Bonclere first?"

Jacinda shook her head. "No," she answered, her voice a little strained by the constricting of her chest as she envisioned Tristan holding her in his arms while Neptune carried them off into the distance. Again, she gave herself a mental shake, discarding her fanciful thoughts. "No, I think I'll walk awhile longer. Good morning, Captain Dancing."

"Good morning, my lady."

Locksworth shook his head. "I don't know, Tris . . ."

"But it's a perfect plan, Grandfather. You offer them Fernwood so they don't have to let a house. You're a friend and neighbor. It's natural for you to do it. Then we go to London too. When Blackstoke calls on Jacinda, we'll be there. I drop a word here and there about my ship. It just might work."

"And if it doesn't?"

Tristan frowned. "Then we're no worse off than we are now."

"All right, my boy. We'll try it your way."

Locksworth's brougham traveled up the drive to Bonclere at a smart clip. As the driver brought the carriage to a stop, the footman jumped to the ground and opened the door for him. The duke stepped out, his brown eyes glancing up at the manor before he walked toward the entrance. The front door was opened by the butler before he reached it.

"Good afternoon, your grace," James said as Locksworth entered.

The duke returned the greeting as he handed his hat and walking stick to the butler, then asked, "Is Lord William at home?"

"Indeed, sir. He's just returned from the kennels. I'll let him know you are here." James showed him into the drawing room, then went in search of the earl.

It had been a long while since the duke had been to Bonclere. He wasn't overly fond of Lord Sunderland or his wife. If it weren't for Jacinda, he would have avoided the family altogether. He remembered so clearly the first time he'd met the little redhead.

Five years old and just learning to ride, her pony had run away with her, carrying her across fields and low-lying fences, her bonnet lost and her flaming tresses blowing wildly behind her. The duke heard her cries for help and gave chase, bringing the miscreant animal to a stop not far from Locksworth. Seconds later, the inattentive groom arrived. The duke gave him a suitable upbraiding for allowing the mishap to happen. Then he turned his attention to the child. Already fear had disappeared from her startling tawny eyes, replaced by curiosity. He'd lost his heart to her in that moment.

Locksworth shook his head at his thoughts, wishing he could have done more for Jacinda. The poor girl had grown up in a home bereft of warmth or any real feelings. He had seen so often the sadness in her eyes. She tried to hide it from him, pouring out all her stored up affections on him because her parents were too self-centered to accept her love or return it. The duke liked to think he had played a part in keeping the beautiful child from growing into a coldhearted woman like her mother.

"Well, Phiney! How good to see you." Lord Sunderland stopped in the doorway. "It isn't often we see you at Bonclere."

Locksworth grimaced at the nickname he hated. He'd never cared for it as a young man when his friends had used it. His dislike grew even greater when it came from a man he disliked even more. "Good day, Sunderland," he said as he turned to face the earl.

"Would you care for a drink?"

"Not for me, thank you."

Lord Sunderland motioned toward a grouping of chairs. "Well, then. Have a seat and tell me what brings you to our humble abode."

The duke wasn't about to prolong the discussion. He got right to the point. "Sunderland, you know how fast news travels, especially from one servant's quarters to another. I heard that Lady Sunderland and Jacinda will be going to London for a short stay and are looking for a house to let. I wanted to offer them the use of Fernwood. No point in you taking on an extra expense, what with your daughter's wedding and all to get ready for."

"Fernwood. I say, Phiney, that's awfully good of you. I—"

Locksworth got to his feet. "Then it's settled. I'll have Mrs. Charring see that the house is aired and ready for their arrival at any time." He began walking toward the door, then stopped and looked back at the earl. "I may be in town a few days myself in a week or two. I

Robin Lee Hatcher

54

trust they'll not be sorry for my company if I arrive while they're still in London."

"Mind? Why, Phiney, they'll be looking forward to it."

"Good. Well, I must be off." Locksworth stepped into the entry where James was already waiting with his hat and cane. "Good day, Sunderland." He hurried out the door before the earl could respond.

Jacinda and Lady Sunderland arrived at Fernwood, the duke's elegant town house on Green Street, less than a week later, just as dusk was settling over the city. Mrs. Charring, the housekeeper, greeted them, introducing the servants who would see to their needs during their stay, then disappeared into the back of the house, saying something about preparations for supper. Jacinda's last visit to Fernwood had been during the London season of a year ago when Locksworth had hosted a ball in her honor. But this would be the first time she had ever actually stayed in the house.

The dark-eyed maid, introduced by Mrs. Charring as Chloe, bobbed another quick curtsey. "If miladies would care to follow me, I'll show you to your rooms."

Chloe led the way up to the second story, opening first a door to a bedroom suite that faced the street. The decor was in shades of yellow. Two bright yellow, brocade wing chairs framed the fireplace, and a chaise longue was positioned near the window. Through a pair of open doors, they could see the canopied bed, the floor covered with a luxurious carpet.

"This is perfect," Lady Sunderland

announced as she entered the room.

"The bath is through that door, milady,"
Chloe said, pointing. "If you'd like, I can have
one drawn for you."

"Yes. See that you do." Lady Sunderland
tugged at her gloves as she walked over to the
window, dismissing them with her back.

Jacinda followed Chloe to the far end of the
hallway, a good distance from her mother's
suite, and was delighted when the door opened
to her rose-hued rooms. The windows of the
sitting room, facing east to let in the morning
sunshine, looked over the gardens of Fernwood.
The parquet floor was buffed to a high sheen. A
fire crackled on the hearth, drawing her toward
the friendly grouping of chairs around it. The
nearby wall held a bookcase filled with books.

"It's lovely," Jacinda whispered.

"Mrs. Charring said it was Lady Felicia's
room when she was a girl."

"Oh?" Jacinda turned to look at the maid.
"Perhaps I'd better take another room."

"His grace said you were to have *this*
room," Chloe replied firmly. She started to
back out of the room, then added with a shy
smile, "You must be very special to him,
milady." With that, she closed the door.

Jacinda sat on the edge of the chaise, placed
near the window. Countless times in her life,
she had wished she was the duke's granddaughter, and at this moment, the wish
returned. How different her life would be now.
Tears welled up and she closed her eyelids to
stop them from falling. Tears were of no use to
her.

"Well, he's not your grandfather," she said

aloud. "And your wife is *not* going to be different. It is the way it is."

She stood up again and went over to the bookcase, her fingers tracing over the backs of books. She knew many of the titles, especially the novels. She had filled many an empty hour, lost in the stories between such covers.

"You're a fool, Jacinda Sunderland," she spoke aloud again. "You've filled your thoughts with fantasies. With dreams of things that will never be yours. What makes you believe anyone could ever love you the way it happens in books?"

Unconsciously, her heart finished, *Few enough have loved you at all.*

Blackstoke sat behind his desk, staring at the message from White. His ship was lost in a storm on the return voyage. Most of the crew had perished on board, although a few, like White, had survived.

"Damnation," he cursed under his breath. The ship was no great problem. He could always buy himself another, although he would dislike the delay it would cause him to find, or even build, just the right one. But a crew, one that he could trust with his particular stock in trade, wasn't easily acquired. He cursed again as he got to his feet. That would all have to wait until White returned to London. He wouldn't have any time for it, now that Jacinda and her mother were in town.

He'd been pleased when he received word that they were coming to London for a week or two while Jacinda's trousseau was readied. Of course, her visit would be much more enjoyable if he didn't have to endure Lady Sunderland's unbearable presence too. He smiled to himself. At least there were only two more months before the wedding. Then he would take Jacinda with him to Highport Hall—or perhaps one of the other, more remote, estates—and if he had his way, he would never be subjected to Lord and Lady Sunderland's company again.

Blackstoke left his study, walking with quick steps through the hallways of Langley House, the Fanshawes' London residence. Jacinda had arrived in London the day before, and tonight he was joining her for supper. He paused before a gilt-framed mirror and straightened his narrow tie, then slipped into his coat. Setting his top hat over his dark brown hair, he went outside and entered his waiting carriage.

The clatter of hooves on cobblestones blended with the other evening sounds of London as the high-stepping pair pulled the fashionable landau through the streets. Blackstoke settled comfortably into his seat, letting his thoughts rush ahead to Fernwood and to Jacinda.

She was the most beautiful woman he had ever seen, with her golden eyes, fiery hair and ivory skin, and the viscount was a connoisseur when it came to the beauty of women. A man of wealth and title, such as himself, never lacked for the attentions of women—beautiful women, lonely women, married women. But when he had seen Jacinda at Lord Andover's, he had known she was the one to be called his wife. She was fresh, untouched. He had to own her. To possess her. Love never entered his thoughts, nor did he consider her feelings in the matter. The decision was one made between men, himself and Lord Sunderland. Her part was to be the willing bride, standing at his side, supporting him happily in whatever he did.

Now that the bargain had been struck, he was impatient for December to arrive. He was eager to make her his own in every way. He smiled in the darkness of his carriage, imagining the pleasures he would take from her on his wedding night, the night when he would brand her as his, the night when he would taste what no man had tasted before him. The past months had held many difficult moments for him. Times when he was alone with her, when he could have grabbed the opportunity to crush her to him and kiss her, but he had denied himself that pleasure, preferring instead to save that moment, savoring the anticipation that burned in his loins. He wanted her untouched, even by him, for their wedding night. When the suppressed excitement grew unbearable, he found himself a wench to relieve his desires, sometimes sampling the wares of his own ship's unique cargo.

That thought brought him back to White's message. He would have to do something about a ship soon. Each day of delay would cost him dearly. Not that he needed the money, although Penneywaite made the venture very profitable. It was just something he enjoyed doing. It was a challenge, an adventure with an element of danger. Some gentlemen preferred to hunt. Some liked to gamble. But his "shipping venture," as he called it, was his favorite sport.

The landau stopped in front of Fernwood.

The carriage door was opened for him, and he stepped down, straightening his frock coat as he walked toward the door. He was ushered inside by a tall, thin butler with inscrutable eyes. Lady Sunderland was waiting for him in the drawing room.

"Ah, my dear viscount. How delighted Jacinda and I are to have you joining us this evening. London seems so deserted this time of year. We were happy to find you still in town."

"Where is Jacinda?" he asked, dispensing with any pleasantries.

"She'll be down shortly. Please, come join me by the fire." She patted the sofa beside her.

Luckily for Blackstoke, he didn't have long to wait. Before he had even taken his seat, Jacinda could be seen descending the stairs. Clad in a full-skirted gown of teal satin, a delicate white shawl draped through her arms, she was his vision of feminine perfection. Blackstoke turned from Lady Sunderland and walked to the doorway to meet her.

"My dear, how good it is to see you," he said as he took her hand in his. "I hadn't hoped I'd have the pleasure again so soon."

"I hadn't expected it either," Jacinda replied without the smile he awaited. "Mother insisted that Madame Roget do my trousseau, and the madame wouldn't come to Bonclere."

Blackstoke led her into the drawing room. "You should have let me know. You could have stayed at Langley House."

Jacinda looked at him, her eyes startled.

The viscount laughed. "It would have been quite proper, my dear. After all, your mother would have been there to chaperone us."

A look of panic flashed across her features before she could smother it. Blackstoke felt a stab of irritation with her. Wasn't it time she showed her eagerness for his company? Wasn't it time she exhibited her joy at being chosen for his bride?

Jacinda sat down quickly in the chair nearest the fire. "His grace was most kind to offer us Fernwood. We're lucky to have such a friend," she said, sounding a trifle breathless.

"I'm sure." He stood behind her, placing his hand on the back of the chair. "But I think it's time you looked to me for help. Don't you, my dear?"

5

Madame Roget was a pinched-faced woman of inestimable years, buxom with a narrow waist and ample hips. Like a field marshal, she barked orders at her seamstresses and clients alike, expecting them to be followed immediately and to the letter. Jacinda thought her the supreme tyrant but was forced, reluctantly so, to admit that Madame Roget knew her craft as a dressmaker. She chose the perfect colors of cloth to compliment Jacinda's coloring, the perfect patterns to flatter her feminine form.

For five days straight, Jacinda and her mother had visited the French woman's shop, arriving early in the morning and remaining until they were dismissed late in the afternoon. Jacinda thought she must be going to have enough gowns and riding outfits and day dresses to last her the rest of her life.

At this moment, Jacinda was surrounded by a swirl of white satin and delicate lace. Madame Roget was circling her with a mouth full of pins and a thunderous frown scrunching up her forehead. She was mumbling something indiscernible.

Finally, pulling the pins from her lips, she cried, "This is all wrong. We must begin again. Brigette," she ordered her young assistant, "take it away."

Without a word, the tiny seamstress freed Jacinda, hauling away the basted gown. Jacinda sighed and moved to sit down in a nearby chair.

"What are you doing?" the madame cried. "Do not move while I am studying you! You will destroy the effect I seek to create."

"But, madame—"

"Quiet. Do you or do you not wish your bridal gown to be as it should?"

"But I'm so tired. Couldn't I just—"

Madame Roget poked her sharp nose toward Jacinda's face, her thin brows arched above nearly colorless eyes. "And I am not tired? Do you think this is not work for me as well?"

"Of course not. I just—" Jacinda began again.

"*Harumph*," Madame Roget snorted, then turned toward Lady Sunderland. "My lady, if I am to work, I must have the cooperation of your daughter. Is that understood? Speak to her." On that note, she marched out of the room.

"Honestly, Jacinda. Do you think you can act this way and get away with it? This is Madame Roget. Now you stand there until the madame is finished." Lady Sunderland leaned forward in her comfortable chair. "She's right, you know. This is work for all of us."

Jacinda wanted to scream. She wanted to throw on the nearest gown and go running into the streets of London. She didn't care what this woman designed for her wedding dress. She didn't care what it looked like. She just didn't want to be cooped up in this airless little room another moment.

But before she could form a suitable reply, Madame Roget returned, a facsimile of a smile on her thin-lipped mouth. "Ah, I know what it is I have been seeking. Please return next week, and I will have it ready for you to see. Now, you are tired, no? Why don't you go home, Lady Jacinda, and rest."

Jacinda balled her fists but kept them clenched tightly at her sides. All her life she had done her rebelling internally. It was impossible to break those habits now, as much as she might wish she could toss a snappy retort in the madame's direction. She turned away and entered a small changing room. With Brigette's help, she donned the emerald green dress she had worn from home that morning. As she dressed, her anger drained from her, taking with it the last of her strength. All she wanted now was to return to Fernwood and crawl into her bed and sleep.

"I will have the finished gowns sent to you this afternoon," Madame Roget was saying to her mother when Jacinda joined them again.

"Very good, madame. Until next week."

The ride home was made in a strained silence. Jacinda knew her mother was brewing another scolding about her behavior, but she hoped she could avoid it until later. As soon as the carriage door was opened, Jacinda was out and scurrying into the house and up to the warmth of her rose-colored rooms. She threw herself across the bed just as she burst into tears, pounding her fists on the spread in frustration.

As the tears dried on her cheeks, she drifted into a restless slumber, escaping into her special dream world . . .

Her grandfather, the Duke of Locksworth, kissed her cheek. "You're a beautiful bride, my dear." She turned toward her parents. They were gazing upon her with tenderness. "We love you so much," her mother whispered. "We're so happy for you," her father added. Jacinda hugged them, secure in the knowledge of their devotion to her, then she turned. The duke held out his arm for her, and together they walked down the aisle, her long white train trailing behind them. He was waiting at the end of the aisle, clad in his glowing armor. His smile caressed her. His black eyes twinkled with joy. There was love in the air, and it was all because of him. He loved her. He would always love her.

And then the wedding party disappeared, and they were alone in her bedroom. His fingers lightly traced over her shoulders and down her back before he drew her into his embrace. She was impatient for his kiss, eager for his touch. Tonight she would know love. Tonight she would know his love . . .

"Milady?" Chloe's hand touched her arm. "Milady?"

Jacinda opened her eyes reluctantly. They burned and felt swollen.

"Milady, I think I should help you dress for supper. It's getting late. His lordship will no doubt be here before long."

Jacinda got up from the bed and slipped out of her crumpled gown, letting it drop to the floor. She stepped out of it, then gave it a petulant kick with her foot.

"Here now, miss. Best wash your face. Then I'll help you with your hair." Chloe continued to chatter while Jacinda splashed cool water on her face and patted her skin dry with a soft towel. "Your dresses came from Madame Roget's, milady. I've put them away. My, but you'll have so many lovely clothes to wear for his lordship. I envy you all the parties and your wedding trip and all." She sighed, her hazel eyes growing dreamy.

"Yes. I suppose," Jacinda replied unenthusiastically.

"Would you like to wear one of your new gowns tonight, milady?" Chloe asked, eager to see her visiting mistress in one of them.

Jacinda glanced at the maid in the mirror, wishing she could feel as excited as Chloe about her new clothes—and the reason for them. A wry smile appeared on her lips, and she nodded. At least she could make Chloe happy by wearing one of the new gowns. "Why not?" she answered. "Go pick one out, Chloe. Any one you like." Her smile grew more genuine as she watched Chloe making her decision, a very lengthy pursuit.

Finally, the dark-haired maid returned with the gown of her choice. It was made of a deep Mediterranean blue satin. The lace corsage revealed the silk chemisette beneath. Her shoulders were bare above the satin ruffle that served for a sleeve, and the bodice was cut low enough to reveal the gentle swell of her breasts. Several taffeta petticoats supported the yards and yards of fabric that made up the skirt.

Once she had Jacinda encased in the tight corsage, Chloe began to work with her mistress's hair, drawing the flame-colored tresses into a mass of curls at the back of her head, weaving dark blue ribbons into the hair as she worked.

"There," Chloe said with satisfaction as she stepped back to survey her work. "Oh, how very beautiful you are, milady. His lordship must count himself a lucky man to have won your favor."

Jacinda wished Chloe hadn't mentioned Blackstoke. It put a damper on the pleasure her reflection had brought. But she had to agree with Chloe. She really did look beautiful in Madame Roget's creation.

"Thank you for your help," she said as she chose a simple pair of diamond earbobs.

"My pleasure, milady." Chloe opened the door to leave.

Voices drifted faintly into Jacinda's hearing. The viscount must already have arrived. Her mother would be irritated if she didn't hurry. She closed the jewel box without searching for a necklace, leaving her throat bare. Lifting her skirt with one hand, she hurried out of her bedroom and down the hallway.

As Jacinda reached the top of the stairs, Lady Sunderland stepped out of the drawing room. "There you are, my dear. I was just about to send for you."

"I'm sorry I'm late, Mother. I fell asleep."

"Quite all right, dear. Lord Fanshawe sent word that he'd been called away on business and won't be able to join us this evening."

"Oh?" Jacinda glanced into the drawing room. If Blackstoke wasn't here, then whose voices had she heard?

"But I have a delightful surprise for you," Lady Sunderland continued. "His grace has just arrived."

Jacinda's face brightened with a joyous smile as she fairly flew down the steps in her hurry to see her old friend. "Your grace," she began as she entered the drawing room, then came to a sudden stop as her eyes fell on the tall, black-haired man standing near the fireplace.

Tristan stepped forward and bowed over her hand before she scarcely knew what he was doing. "My lady Jacinda," he said in that deep timbred voice of his. "Your beautiful company makes the trip to London well worthwhile." His ebony eyes came up, pausing ever so briefly on the glimpse of cleavage above her bodice before meeting her gaze. His voice was hushed, meant only for her ears as he added, "Such beauty few men behold."

She felt warmth rising from her neck into her face. She'd heard more flowery, more gushing praise in her seasons in London, but she'd brushed the words aside, along with the goggle-eyed swains who spoke them. But Tristan seemed to be speaking a heartfelt truth. A strange knot formed in the pit of her stomach. Her mouth felt dry, and she was unable to make a reply come to her lips. *He's even more handsome than my knight*, she thought suddenly, and felt another rush of heat as she remembered her dream, his hands on her arms, his lips . . .

Locksworth came to her rescue as he stepped up to her, retrieving her hand from Tristan and brushing the younger man aside. "Don't pay any heed to that young buck, Jacinda. He doesn't know your heart already belongs to me." He kissed her white hand.

Jacinda dragged her gaze away from Tristan, realizing she'd been staring. "It's true, your grace," she answered in a whisper. "I do love you dearly." They were words she seldom said but meant from the heart. She kissed the old man's weathered cheek. As she stepped back from him, she found that some of her composure had been restored, and she was able to face Tristan with a calm smile. "Captain Dancing, will you be joining us for supper too?"

He nodded. "His grace has kindly invited me to stay at Fernwood while he conducts his business."

Staying? Here? Her heart thumped in her breast. She had never been one to swoon, but she felt distinctly light-headed at the thought. She walked quickly across to a chair and wilted into its support.

Lady Sunderland, who seemed to have missed the undercurrent of emotions, came toward Jacinda and sat down in a nearby chair. "Please, gentlemen. Do be seated. Mrs. Charring will let us know when dinner is ready." As the men took their seats, she looked at Tristan. "You were telling me about your ship, Captain Dancing. Do continue."

"I think I've told you all there is to tell,

Lady Sunderland. The *Gabrielle* is a fast clipper ship. One of the fastest. Someday she's going to make a name for herself. She can sail through the stormiest seas with ease." Tristan's eyes glowed with undisguised pride. "Perhaps while you're in London, you and your daughter would like to come see her."

"Well, I don't know," Lady Sunderland answered. "I don't much care for the docks. Not very pleasant, you know."

"I'd like to see your ship," Jacinda said softly. She didn't look in her mother's direction, certain she would find disapproval in those pale blue eyes. She couldn't bear it if her mother denied her wish.

"Lady Sunderland," Locksworth interjected before Jacinda's mother could speak. "Since you don't care to see Captain Dancing's ship and Jacinda does, allow me to escort her there. She certainly won't come to any harm while in my company."

"I don't know, your grace. It doesn't seem quite . . . well, seemly."

"Oh, Mother, let me go," Jacinda pleaded, feeling a rush of excitement. "I really would like to see the *Gabrielle*. I've never been on a ship before."

"Well . . . I suppose it can't hurt. Not if the duke will escort you. Perhaps Lord Fanshawe will be able to join you, too."

Jacinda's bubble of pleasure burst. "Yes. Perhaps he can," she echoed woodenly as thoughts of her intended intruded in her mind.

"That would be even better," Tristan said. "I'd like the opportunity to meet the viscount. When does he return?"

Whenever it is, Jacinda thought, *it's too soon*.

Tristan lay in his bed, staring up at the ceiling. The embers from the dying fire threw strange shadows above his head, but he didn't notice them. His thoughts were wandering far astray of this room.

He imagined her sleeping, her long hair, free of hairpins and ribbons, spilling across the white pillows. He imagined himself standing at her bedside, bending over to kiss the whiteness of her throat, stroking his hand through her silky tresses. Her eyes would flutter slowly open, and she would look up at him with those tawny eyes. Perhaps she would whisper his name.

Tristan sat up suddenly, giving his head a rough shake. He frowned into the darkness. He couldn't let himself become interested in Jacinda Sunderland. Beautiful, she surely was, but she was off limits to him. His only interest in her must be because of her engagement to Viscount Blackstoke. He needed her to introduce him to the viscount, to help him win Blackstoke's confidence, if possible. Nothing more. He didn't have the time for any complications. He had to find his sister.

Still, he couldn't stop himself from thinking about the lovely lady. Such an enigma. On one hand, she seemed quite self-possessed. So very sure of herself. So very aloof. And then he would catch a glimpse of the frightened little girl that still remained. He could sense her unhappiness, her loneliness. She had the most lovely smile, but its appearance was all too rare.

He wondered about the viscount. What was the man like with Jacinda? What drew a man like Blackstoke and a woman like Jacinda together? Did she love him? Did she give her smiles to him? Somehow, Tristan was certain that she didn't. If only things were different . . .

He rolled over on his side and punched his pillow into shape. It was best he stop thinking about her. He must have only one use for her. He needed her to help him find Ella. There could be nothing else between them.

This time he came to her on a ship, white sails billowing in the wind. He stood at the bow, one foot resting on the rail. He was wearing tight trousers, dark blue in color, and a white blouse that whipped about his broad chest. His black hair was caught at the nape of his neck, and a blue bandana was knotted around his forehead. His skin was darkened by the ocean sun. The ship was sailing toward the dock. He would reach her soon.

But a hand snatched her arm, hauling her away from the wharf, and she was helpless against it. She held out her free hand toward the sea, beseeching her black-haired captain to save her, but there was nothing he could do. Her captor pushed her into a dark carriage and carried her away.

She awoke with tears dampening her pillow. Her throat felt tight. Her heart ached. Her knight was gone, but in his place sailed a ship's captain. A stranger still, he held her heart, yet he would never be allowed to reach her. She knew his face, knew his name, and her pain was all the greater because of it.

Brushing the last stubborn tears from her cheeks, Jacinda threw off the covers and got out of bed. The bedroom seemed especially chilly this morning. She walked across the room and pushed aside the draperies. A dense shroud of fog had fallen over the city, hiding even the gardens from her view. The dismal scene seemed well-suited to the condition of her heart. She shivered again and let the curtains fall back into place.

Feeling in need of something warm and cheerful, she chose a salmon-colored day dress, the bodice decorated with tiny flowers and shiny ribbons. She ran a quick brush through her hair but let it hang loose, falling in gentle waves down her back.

Her bedroom door opened suddenly, and Lady Sunderland swept into the room. "Good morning, dear."

Jacinda twisted on her chair, surprised. "You're up terribly early this morning, aren't you, Mother?"

"Couldn't sleep. So much on my mind. I kept thinking of things that must be done. Your masked ball is less than two weeks away. And then, of course, there is still so much to do before the wedding."

"We needn't have the masked ball, Mother," Jacinda said as she swiveled back toward the mirror.

"Needn't have it?" Lady Sunderland exclaimed. "I never heard anything so ridiculous. Of course we must have it. It will be the social event of the season. Everyone who's anyone will be there. And not just for the ball, either. Why, your father is right now buying more horses for the hunts we'll have that week."

Jacinda sighed softly and began brushing her hair once more.

"I can't understand you, Jacinda."

I can't understand me either, she thought, staring at her reflection.

"You ought to be the happiest girl in London at this moment. All the years we've done with so little. You know how hard it's been. You've seen how much we've had to do without. Now you're to have the party we should have had long ago. And you'll have the biggest, most elegant wedding." Lady Sunderland shook her head slowly. "No, I just don't understand you."

Still without comment, Jacinda walked across the room and picked up her shoes, then sat on the bed while she slipped them onto her dainty feet.

Her mother scarcely missed a beat. "Quite a surprise to have the duke arrive with that captain in tow, wasn't it? Your father did mention that he might be in town while we were here, but I didn't expect him to bring anyone with him. I wonder what the viscount will think?" She looked at Jacinda with a peering glance.

Jacinda shrugged noncommittally.

"He *is* rather handsome—" her mother continued "—in a common sort of way. Of course, those Americans are mostly a common people." Suddenly her voice sharpened. "Jacinda, I want you to be on your guard around that man. I won't have him trifling with you. You have given your word to Lord

Fanshawe, and I wouldn't want it said that you hold your promises lightly. We have the honor of the family to protect."

"You needn't worry, Mother. I shan't forget my promise."

"Good," Lady Sunderland said with satisfaction. She rose to her feet and walked toward the door. "Well, I think I'll go down for breakfast. Are you coming, dear?"

"In a moment."

The door shut behind Lady Sunderland, and Jacinda stared at it, emotions teetering between rage and despair. *What have I besides my honor?* she wanted to scream at her mother. *Have I ever had your love? Have I ever had Father's love? When have you held me in your arms and cared about my feelings?*

"Is it too much to ask?" she whispered. "Is it too much to want someone to love me?"

When Jacinda descended the stairs some time later, there were no traces left of her inner sorrow. Whether she realized it or not, her ability to bounce back, to face life with a smile, was what kept her from becoming a bitter woman. That and her fantasies. Her ability to escape into a world of make-believe where she was loved and cherished.

But she didn't have to make believe with the Duke of Locksworth. When she entered the dining room, he was standing at the sideboard. He set his plate on the table and walked over to greet her, kissing her hand with aplomb.

"My dear," he said, "I was afraid you weren't going to join us this morning." Her stomach grumbled just then, causing him to chuckle as a light blush colored her cheeks. "Well, let's not keep you standing here. I can hear that you're hungry."

She laughed too. "As a matter of fact, I'm starving," she said, realizing just how hungry she was.

Jacinda followed behind the duke, filling her plate nearly as full as he did his own, then followed him to the table where Lady Sunderland was just finishing her morning meal. She felt a stab of disappointment when she realized Tristan was not there but managed to restrain herself from asking about him.

While Jacinda and Locksworth ate their breakfast, Lady Sunderland kept up a constant chatter, telling the duke all the latest gossip she had heard while in London. Jacinda paid little heed, having heard it several times already, and she suspected that he wasn't listening either. Every few minutes, she glanced toward the doorway, hoping she might see Tristan standing there.

As if he read her thoughts, the duke pushed his chair back from the table and turned her way. "Well, Jacinda, are you ready to see Captain Dancing's ship today? Tristan went down early this morning and is waiting for us. I think the fog is beginning to burn off, so we can go whenever you're ready."

"I'm ready," she answered eagerly.

"Good. You get your wrap and we'll be on our way."

Lady Sunderland glanced at Jacinda with a worried frown. "Perhaps I should join you."

"Don't be silly, my good woman," Locksworth protested. "You have already stated how you feel about the wharf. I promise to take good care of your daughter. There is no need for you to come out in this damp."

"I suppose you're right," her mother said, still sounding unconvinced.

Jacinda wasn't about to wait for her to change her mind again. She got up from her chair and hurried to her room to get her cloak. She was back downstairs as quickly as possible without running through the halls like a child. The duke was waiting for her by the door, and he held out his hand for her wrap and helped her into it.

"We will take tea at my club," he told Lady Sunderland as he opened the door, "so don't look for us until later this afternoon. Jacinda and I are going to make a pleasant day of it." He looked at Jacinda. "Aren't we, my dear?"

Her eyes twinkled with shared merriment, and she nodded.

Jacinda snuggled inside her wrap as the carriage made its way through the London streets, horses' hooves clip-clopping on cobblestones. She stared out the window, watching for a glimpse of ships at anchor, unaware of the duke's astute perusal of her.

By gad, he thought, *she's fallen for the young whelp.*

He'd known this plan wasn't a good one. He'd known Jacinda would get hurt. And what made it worse was he would like nothing better than for these two youngsters to end up together. He should warn Tristan again not to use her this way, but what else were they to do? They still had to find Ella and there seemed to be no other way to do it than through Jacinda.

And even then there was no guarantee.

He sighed. He was getting too old for this kind of intrigue.

6

Tristan strode the length of the *Dancing Gabrielle*. His black eyes swept over the other ships anchored in the river before returning to inspect his own vessel. The *Gabrielle* was a sleek clipper, built in Baltimore, ship-rigged with three masts carrying square sail. Her frames were of live oak and copper-fastened throughout, and her stern was sheathed with red copper. Her rails, companions and skylights were all made from Spanish mahogany. She was mounted with brass guns, six on each side. She was built for speed and had proven herself a trusty vessel more than once.

He felt a rush of pride as he paced the decks, waiting for his grandfather and Jacinda to arrive. This was his home, and he was eager to show it to them. He crossed to the rail and leaned against it, his eyes searching the docks for a sign of the duke's black carriage. The fog had lifted, and despite the dampness of the air and the cool fall breeze, it was going to be a grand day.

He spotted Whip, waiting on the dock, holding onto a rope attached to the dinghy. Besides being Tristan's first mate, Whip was a friend. True, he didn't know much about the wiry, blond-headed fellow before they'd met aboard ship—not where he came from, not even his real name. Yet Tristan would have trusted Whip with his life and had, in fact, done just that in the past.

He saw Whip raise his arm and wave at him, and his eyes moved away from the first mate and down the dock until he spied the carriage moving slowly through the jumbled mass of people and cargo that filled the wharf area during the daylight hours. The carriage stopped; the driver got down and opened the door. Tristan saw his grandfather get out, then turn and offer his hand to the lady inside.

She had come then, just as he'd hoped. He found himself smiling in anticipation. He knew he shouldn't be feeling this elated. It was, after all, just the next step in his plan to reach and gain Blackstoke's confidence. If she just weren't so lovely, so damned lovely . . .

He watched as Whip hurried toward the couple and introduced himself. He saw Jacinda's head turn toward the ship and wished he could see her face, wished he could see those golden eyes of hers, wondered if just maybe she might be wearing one of her rare and very special smiles.

"Tris, old friend," he whispered to himself, "you've been at sea too long. You're letting a pretty face get to you."

When the dinghy reached the ship, a rope sling was dropped down the side for Jacinda to

sit in and then she was hoisted up to the deck.
Whip and Locksworth climbed a ladder.

Jacinda was laughing when her feet
touched the solid boards of the deck. Tiny
splashes of color dotted her cheeks, and her
eyes sparkled with merriment. It made Tristan
feel as if he'd done something special for her.
He liked that feeling.

"Welcome to the *Dancing Gabrielle*," he
said, sweeping his arm in an arc to indicate the
ship that was his.

"Captain Dancing, it's beautiful." Jacinda
glanced up at the masts. "There are so many
ropes. What are they all for?"

"Over three hundred different ones, my
lady. Sheets, brails, braces, halliards, down-
hauls. And woe to the hand that pulls the wrong
one. Believe me, Lady Jacinda, the men who sail
with me know every inch of the rigging and
what to do with every one of those ropes, even
in a full gale." He took her arm. "Come. Let me
show you my home."

Tristan was pleased by the way Jacinda
looked at everything and listened to what he
told her. She wasn't being merely polite. She
actually seemed to be interested. He found himself telling her more than he had ever taken the
time to tell any other visitor to his ship.

As Jacinda peered down into the hold, she
asked, "What kind of cargo do you carry,
Captain?"

His glance met his grandfather's before he
answered, "Tea from China, cotton from
America." He paused, as if for emphasis, then
added, "But I'll take on just about anything if
the price is right."

"And what cargo are you waiting for now?"
"I'm not sure, my lady."

The duke's carriage pulled away from the club much later in the afternoon than they had planned. Jacinda glanced out the window to see Tristan waving good-bye, then settled back against the cushions to ride in silence on their way back to Fernwood.

It had been a glorious day. She was captivated by the *Gabrielle* and thought she would love to get to sail aboard such a ship one day. She shied away from acknowledging that what she would truly like would be to sail aboard this very *same* ship with this very *same* captain. She closed her eyes, remembering the way he'd held her arm in his, the way he towered over her, his black eyes so intense, his smile so warm. So much better than she had ever dreamed . . .

"Ah. Looks as though we have company at Fernwood," the duke said thoughtfully.

She opened her eyes and followed his gaze out the window as the carriage was brought to a stop. Blackstoke's landau waited at the side of the house. The whispery smile she had worn most of the day vanished. "Roger's returned."

Locksworth looked her way, and she read the understanding in his glance. She couldn't bear it if he felt sorry for her. She forced an even brighter, if artificial, smile back onto her lips. "Mother must be in quite a frenzy with Roger here and me away with such a charming gentleman as you, your grace. She'll have a hard time explaining how she let me go unchaperoned. Roger can be a very jealous man, I think."

"I would gladly face a hundred jealous men to be in your company, my dear." Though he tried to say it in jest, she heard the pity in his voice.

The door of the house opened just as the duke was helping her to the ground. She looked up to find Blackstoke and her mother waiting on the steps. "Roger," she called to him, trying to sound pleased, "you're back. If we'd known you would be here today, we'd have waited for you to join us." As she spoke, she hurried up the walk.

"I wish you had." His dark blue eyes studied her a moment, then he took her hand and kissed it. "Now, why don't you tell me about your day." He placed her hand in the crook of his arm and led her inside.

How different the way she felt when Blackstoke held her arm than when Tristan had.

"Well? Aren't you going to tell me what you've done with yourself all day?"

"His grace took me down to see Captain Dancing's ship."

Blackstoke's eyes seemed cold and hard, despite his slight smile. "Your mother told me that much, Jacinda. I had no idea you were so interested in ships."

"I've never given them much thought before," she replied, feeling a little defiant, but she couldn't keep the excitement out of her voice as she continued. "I had no idea a ship could be so interesting. Roger, they live in the smallest spaces. But the *Gabrielle* is clean and tidy. Even the hold where they keep their cargo. And the rigging. I've never seen so much rope in any one place in all my life. It's like a cobweb or a maze. I don't know how it can mean anything to them, but Captain Dancing says the men don't make mistakes, even in a gale."

"Captain Dancing . . . I don't think I've ever heard of him."

"He's a guest in my home," the duke interjected.

Blackstoke turned toward Locksworth. "A longtime friend, no doubt."

"No," the older man responded as he sat in a chair near the fire. "As a matter of fact, I only became acquainted with him on my trip to America a few years back." He paused. "No. More than a few years now, isn't it?" Again he paused, shaking his head thoughtfully. "He was just a second mate at the time, and I took a liking to the boy. Invited him to visit me at Locksworth House if he were ever in England. And here he is. Quite a surprise to me, I might add." He took out his pipe. "But a pleasant one. I'm enjoying his company."

"What kind of ship is this *Gabrielle?*" The viscount addressed his question back to Jacinda.

"He calls it a clipper. He says it's very fast, and he's terribly proud of it."

"Most interesting," Blackstoke muttered to himself. Glancing back toward the duke, he asked, "When will he be sailing with his next cargo?"

"Doesn't have one. Can't quite figure that out. Fine ship like that and a good crew too. He hasn't said as much, but I get the feeling he's looking for something that pays better than usual. Seems to need some extra money. Told Lady Jacinda just today that he'd ship anything if the price was right. Odd thing to say. Took me back a step, I don't mind telling you." He shook his head, then drew on his pipe. "I'd give him some help if he'd ask, but I don't want to offend by offering first."

"I'd like to meet him, your grace. Will he be joining us for supper tonight?"

"Sorry, Blackstoke. The captain said he was going to stay with his ship for a few days."

Jacinda drew in a tiny breath of disappointment. She hadn't known that.

"But," the duke went on, "I've taken the liberty of asking him to join me at Bonclere for your masked ball. I'll introduce you to him then."

"I'm looking forward to it."

Suddenly, Jacinda was very anxious for the night of the ball to arrive, the very same ball she had told her mother she wasn't interested in.

Tristan lay on his bunk, listening to the gentle lapping of water against the sides of the ship. He kept seeing Jacinda in his mind, thinking how beautiful she'd looked today—her face all aglow with excitement, the way her hair peeked out from beneath her saucy bonnet, the appealing whiteness of her slender neck. Again the thought came to him. *If only things were different.*

He tried to convince himself that she deserved the viscount. He was certain she wasn't in love with Blackstoke, yet she was going to marry him anyway. She was just like so many other women he had known. She was only after a title and money, and if she would marry for that alone, then she was getting what she deserved.

But Tristan didn't believe it, no matter how much he told himself he did. She didn't deserve the viscount, not if Blackstoke was all Tristan suspected him to be. Besides, he could sense her unhappiness. Maybe he should tell his grandfather to warn her. Give her a chance to be free of Roger Fanshawe before it was too late.

No. He couldn't. He'd been over this time and time again. Jacinda would have to take care of herself. If it weren't for Ella, Tristan never would have met Jacinda, and she would have married her viscount anyway. He mustn't let himself get involved with her. Soon he would be gone from England. It would be better that way.

7

Jacinda slipped from her bed at first light and hurried toward the stables. She wanted to be away from the house before the first of the guests started rising. She needed a moment by herself, away from the gossiping tongues and envious stares, away from Blackstoke's possessive hand on her arm. She needed a moment to breathe and to think.

They had been home only a few days from London when guests began to arrive. Her mother was in her glory, entertaining as she hadn't been able to in years. Likewise, Lord Sunderland was in fine spirits, riding to the hounds by day and playing cards late into the night. At least her parents were happy.

Jacinda gave her white mare free rein, and Pegasus carried her into the dense woods between Locksworth and Bonclere, picking her way toward the deep forest pool that was so often their destination when Jacinda rode out alone. She slid from the saddle, letting the reins trail on the ground as Pegasus grazed among the fallen leaves. She walked over to the water and stared down at her reflection on the dark surface as her thoughts drifted back to the previous evening.

They had spent the day riding to the hunt, and many of their house guests had retired early. Jacinda had gone for a stroll in the gardens, seeking refuge in the chilly evening darkness among the remains of autumn's flowers. Suddenly, Blackstoke had appeared at her side.

"You have a way of disappearing, Jacinda. Are you hiding from me?"

"Hiding? Why would I want to hide from you, Roger?"

He placed a hand on the small of her back as they began walking again. "My dear, you're to be my wife. As your husband, I will expect you to be near when I need you. And don't you think a few of our guests must be wondering at your lack of affection for your groom?"

"I don't know what you're talking about," she protested weakly.

He stopped and turned her toward him. He grasped her chin between his fingers, pinching the delicate skin, and raised it, forcing her eyes to meet his. "I have known many beautiful women, my darling bride. I could have been married many times over before now, but I was waiting for a woman worthy of me, a woman good enough to share my title and my wealth. I found her in you. Men will envy me because you are mine and mine alone, just as so many women envy you for your groom. I'll have what no other man has ever had or will ever have." His fingers tightened and his eyes hardened.

"You *will* remain at my side from now on, and you *will* show me the affection everyone expects you to. Do you understand?"

"Please. You're hurting me."

He released her, but he didn't move away. Instead, he pulled her close against him. His face just inches away, she thought he was going to kiss her. He had never kissed her, never even tried. She closed her eyes, hoping against hope that a kiss would change the way she felt about him. Suddenly, he laughed, his breath hot on her face.

"No, my lovely bride. I'll give you no samples of what you have in store. Be patient. It will be worth the wait."

She had flung herself away from him and raced into the house, taking refuge from him in her room.

The images of last night faded.

"I hate him," she whispered aloud, still staring into the dark water. "I'm going to marry a man I hate, and there's nothing I can do about it."

Jacinda sank to the ground at the edge of the pool. Her heart wanted to cry, but her eyes were dry. Perhaps she had cried too often in recent months and there were no tears left in her. Perhaps she would become like her parents. Perhaps her heart would harden, and she would stop longing for the love she'd never known. Perhaps it was already happening to her. She grabbed a stone from beside her and threw it into the pool, shattering the still reflection. She didn't want to see herself becoming hard and cold. That wasn't her. It wasn't!

The ripples couldn't triumph against the stillness that reigned in this forest hideaway. Slowly, the glassy surface returned, revealing not only the disturbed Jacinda, but a tall man astride a black horse at the edge of the clearing. Jacinda gasped and twisted around. Tristan's face was solemn as he watched her.

"What are you doing here?" she demanded as she got to her feet.

"I didn't mean to intrude," he replied, but he made no move to leave.

She looked down at her riding gown, covered with leaves and speckled with mud. She brushed at her skirts with a nervous hand. "You're not intruding. I was just about to leave. They'll be wondering where I've taken myself."

"I'm sorry we missed the hunt yesterday. Locksworth wasn't feeling up to it."

"He isn't ill, is he?" Jacinda asked, earnest concern in her voice.

Tristan dismounted and stepped closer. "No. Just tired." He smiled. It was that same warm, friendly smile he had worn the day she first saw him, the one that had made her heart pause in her chest. "He wanted to rest up for the masked ball tonight."

"You're coming too?"

"I wouldn't miss it," he answered.

She couldn't think of anything else to say and found herself staring mutely into his ebony eyes. She liked it when they looked at her like that. It made her feel almost giddy. She wished she felt that way when Blackstoke . . .

"I must leave," she said suddenly, a tinge of fear lacing her words. What if he were to find her here with Tristan? He would be furious. There would be an ugly scene. She moved toward Pegasus.

Tristan touched her arm. "Allow me." He retrieved the white Arabian and brought her to her mistress. "May I?" he asked, then lifted Jacinda onto the saddle with ease, his hands lingering just a moment longer on her narrow waist.

"Good day, Captain," she said, softly but firmly.

His hands dropped away, and he stepped back to let her pass. "I'll see you tonight, Lady Jacinda," he called after her as she urged Pegasus toward home.

Jacinda sat perfectly still as Mary drew a black line across her eyelid.

"There," the maid said with satisfaction. "You're done, miss, and I don't think anyone will guess who you are."

Jacinda turned to look at herself in the mirror of her dressing table. Mary was right. She didn't recognize herself.

Over her red hair, she was wearing a black wig which was bobbed at the shoulders. Her costume was a simple white tunic with a heavy gold collar around her neck and a gold girdle at her waist. Despite the high neckline, the tunic seemed to reveal more of her shapely figure than any of her truly daring gowns with their low necklines. Looking at herself, Jacinda felt more lighthearted than she had in weeks, perhaps months.

"Your mask, my lady," Mary said from behind her.

The gold mask covered her nose and eyes, with only narrow slits to see through. It had a filmy white veil attached to the bottom which succeeded in concealing the rest of her face from view.

"Are there many people downstairs yet, Mary?" she asked.

"Yes, miss. The house is nearly bursting at its seams."

"Then I'm going down the back way. I'll slip around to the front and come in as if I'm an invited guest. We'll see if anyone can guess just who the Queen of Egypt is." She laughed aloud. "Don't you dare tell a soul, Mary, or I'll never speak to you again."

"Not a soul, miss. You've my word on it."

Jacinda hurried down the hallway and out a side entrance, dashing through a spot in the hedge before she could be seen. She waited until there was no one about and then walked sedately toward the front entrance. Her heart was in her throat. Would she be recognized by the butler when he opened the door?

James, his face appropriately expressionless, bowed his greeting as Jacinda entered the house. As the occasion was a masked ball, he did not inquire as to her name nor announce her arrival, and Jacinda passed on toward the ballroom on silent feet.

The orchestra was playing a gay melody. Dancers whirled around the room in a varied array of costumes. The mood was festive, the air sprinkled with laughter. Jacinda smiled beneath her veil. She felt free of the constraints that had weighed on her so heavily of late. She was going to have a wonderful time tonight.

The moment she stepped into the ballroom, she drew the attention of men. Many of them she recognized even before they spoke. The identity of others were revealed by their voices. To each of their invitations to dance, she shook her head, her false black hair brushing her neck. Behind her mask, her eyes swept the room, looking for someone in particular. She recognized Blackstoke by his costume. He had told her he would be dressing as an Admiral in the Queen's Navy. But her gaze only lingered on him briefly, then moved on, still seeking.

"An Egyptian queen," said a voice from behind her. "What a prize for a pirate seeking treasure."

Jacinda turned quickly. He was indeed a pirate. A bright bandana was tied around his forehead. His white blouse was open at the throat, revealing a dark mat of chest hair over bronzed skin. His snug fitting black breeches were belted with a red sash, and an ebony-handled dagger hung at his waist. His arm darted out to capture her and draw her close. For a breathless moment, he gazed down at her with flashing black eyes, then he waltzed her out onto the floor.

Does he know who I am? she wondered.

And as if he read her thoughts, he asked, "Did you think I wouldn't know you, my queen?"

"Should I care that you do?" she whispered, meaning her question to be a haughty challenge, but failing because of the soft quiver in her voice.

He paused, as if considering the question. "I'm not sure if you should or not," he replied at last. After another long pause, he added gravely, "No, my queen, you would be better off not to care."

"Then I shan't, my pirate," she lied. It *was* a lie, for with each turn around the floor she knew that she already cared too much.

They danced one dance and then two . . . and then another and another. She could not pull away from his embrace even when she knew she should seek Blackstoke's side. He would be furious when he discovered she had been here all this time, dancing with another man when she should have been with him. But she didn't want to think of him nor of his thinly veiled threats of the night before. She wanted only to think of now, of being here in Tristan's arms.

The circling of the waltz brought them near the doors of the library, and Tristan twirled her through the opening. Without even a pause, he pushed the door closed behind them and kept dancing, whirling her into the soft shadows of the darkened room. Suddenly, he stopped, but his arm didn't release her. Instead, he drew her closer to him.

Jacinda felt dizzy, her breath coming in tiny gasps. But was it from the dancing or from the mere nearness of this man? She waited, certain he would lift her veil and kiss her. She wanted him to kiss her.

Then his arm dropped, and he stepped back from her. The very atmosphere around her seemed to change, charged with tension. "Lady Jacinda," Tristan said, his voice bold, "I have a favor to ask of you."

"A favor?"

"I've heard some rumors around the wharf that Lord Fanshawe might be in need of a ship. As you know, mine is available, and I need a cargo right now. Would you introduce us? Would you use your influence with him?"

"I'm sorry. I don't—" she began, confused and hurt.

"I'm afraid you're talking to the wrong person, Captain. The lovely lady has no influence with me. I'm my own master." Blackstoke suddenly stepped up beside Jacinda. "Perhaps you Americans do things differently than we do, but I suggest you leave the talking of business for when we men are alone."

Tristan bowed slightly. "Please accept my apologies, Blackstoke. I admit my error. I hope you will at least consider my ship."

"All right, Dancing. See me tomorrow morning. About eleven."

Tristan nodded as he stepped backward. "I'll be here." He tapped his forehead in a lazy salute, then turned and walked away.

Jacinda was left numb. Later she would feel the pain of his duplicity. Later she would rail against the injustice of his use of her for his own gain. Now she was left numb, mercifully free of feelings of any kind.

"Jacinda," Blackstoke said as he took hold of her elbow, "you've forgotten my warning."

"No, Roger. I didn't forget. I merely wanted to see what the captain had to say. That's all." Even her voice was void of any emotion. "I won't leave your side for the rest of the evening. I promise."

8

"Just how desperate are you for money, Dancing?" Blackstoke stood near the windows of Bonclere's library. The morning had brought black clouds, and large raindrops spattered against the glass behind the viscount as he spoke.

Tristan had thought about this meeting throughout the night, weighing every possible approach, every word he might speak, considering every angle. He had to be careful, yet appear confident. Now was the moment he'd been waiting for. He couldn't afford to make any mistakes.

His dark eyes returned Blackstoke's steady gaze. "If I don't make a generous profit this next trip out, I could lose my ship. If you know anything about sailors, Blackstoke, you know what it would do to me to lose the *Gabrielle*."

"Where did you hear that I might be in need of a ship? Do I look like a merchant?"

"Rumors fly around the docks, Blackstoke. And many gentlemen have interests in shipping."

Blackstoke nodded and took his seat behind the desk. "Sit down, Captain. Care for a smoke?"

Tristan shook his head.

"What if I told you my interests were slightly beyond the law. Would you still be interested?"

Tristan leaned forward, grinning. "I would ask you what it will pay. And nothing more."

"You're an odd sort to be such good friends with old Phineasbury." Blackstoke continued to watch him with a suspicious stare.

"I know a useful friend when I see one." Tristan shrugged and leaned back, throwing a leg over the arm of the chair.

Suddenly, Blackstoke laughed. "Rather sure of yourself, aren't you?"

The grin disappeared from Tristan's face and his eyes darkened. "I'm the best captain on the seas, and I've got a ship that can outsail anything afloat. I've bet my life on her before and I'll do it again. I won't ask any questions if you'll pay me enough to keep the *Gabrielle*."

"I'm not sure I approve of you, Dancing," Blackstoke replied, his laughter already forgotten. "You've been too friendly with the woman who's to be my wife, and you've taken advantage of your acquaintance with the duke. But—" He drew on his pipe, watching Tristan through the blue smoke that circled above him. "—I suppose your kind makes the best pirate."

"Pirate, my lord?" Tristan raised an eyebrow. "Is that what I'm to be?"

Blackstoke ignored the question. "You ready your ship, Dancing. Prepare for passengers. Twenty. Perhaps thirty."

"And my destination?"

"Constantinople."

"When do we leave?"

"I'll have to notify you about that."

Tristan checked his impatience. He didn't know if Ella was in Constantinople, and even if she were, he had no way to find her without Blackstoke's unwitting guidance. This was only the first step. He would have to wait until the viscount was ready to entrust him with more knowledge.

He nodded his agreement, then asked the question that was expected of him. "And what can I expect to benefit from this venture, Blackstoke?"

"We'll split the profits, Captain, and I assure you they will be very large indeed." He smiled. "You see, I can be quite generous."

Again Tristan nodded. Feeling that the interview was finished, he got up and stepped backward toward the library doors. "I'll send word to my first mate to gather supplies. I'll remain at Locksworth House until I hear from you." He bowed slightly from the waist. "A pleasure doing business with you, Blackstoke."

The viscount didn't acknowledge the remark.

Tristan opened the door and stepped out into the hallway. He was left with a bad taste in his mouth and wanted to put as much distance between himself and Roger Fanshawe as possible. If not, he had the feeling he would barge back into the library and try to choke the truth from the man's treacherous lips.

The gentle swish of skirts was his only

warning that someone was descending the stairs. He looked up, prepared to nod and be on his way, but he was stopped by the look in her tawny eyes. Anger and hurt warred with each other, but Jacinda was doing her best to hide both emotions.

"Lady Jacinda," he said, his eyes sweeping over her strawberry-colored gown. "How beautiful you look today."

She didn't deign to reply.

How he'd wanted to kiss her last night. He would have kissed her if Blackstoke hadn't suddenly appeared in the doorway. And then what would he have done? He had no room in his life for a woman now. Especially not *this* woman.

"I trust you've finished your business with Lord Roger?" Jacinda asked, her voice cool.

Gads, she was lovely. And proud, too.

"Quite successfully, thank you," Tristan answered.

He thought of the way she'd felt in his arms last night as they'd waltzed around the ballroom. She'd fit into his arms as if made for him. He also remembered what they'd said. He'd warned her not to care, and she'd said she wouldn't. It was best left that way.

"Well, I must be on my way." Tristan placed his hat on his head.

Jacinda smiled thinly. "I wouldn't think of detaining you, Captain Dancing. Good day." She continued down the stairs and swept past him without a backward glance.

Tristan felt a twinge of regret for what he sensed could have been between them, but he didn't have time to dwell on could-have-beens.

With a firm step, he went outside and mounted his black barb, then sent the stallion cantering down the drive.

Jacinda was relieved when Blackstoke finally left Bonclere. The strain of the past week was telling on her nerves. It was bad enough that she had discovered she despised the man who would be her husband. Now, on top of that knowledge, there was the constant ache in her chest to contend with. The pain had been with her ever since the night of the masked ball, ever since the moment Tristan had left her in the library with Blackstoke, left her knowing she had been a mere pawn to him and nothing more.

She no longer dreamed of the knight in shining armor coming to carry her away nor did she dream of an imaginary ship's captain. But now she wished the dreams back. It had hurt less to have a faceless dream lover than to feel this pain of rejection, rejection by a man she hardly knew, yet wanted to know so very much.

With Bonclere emptied of guests, Jacinda thought she would find respite from her tormented emotions, but it wasn't to be. Her mother gave her little time to herself. There was too much to be done before her December wedding, a wedding that would be *the* event of the year as far as Lady Sunderland was concerned.

Often, Jacinda found herself slipping out the door and hurrying toward the tables with thoughts of a brisk ride on Pegasus, but then she would imagine where her ride would take her. As inevitably as the sun rising in the east and setting in the west, she would have ended her ride at Locksworth House. So she would turn around and return to her mother's domain, submitting herself to one more round of fittings and endless chatter on how fortunate she was to have been chosen as the bride of Viscount Blackstoke.

But there came a day when she could resist the temptation no longer. She was obsessed with thoughts of Tristan. Time had worked its healing magic. Those moments of rejection were forgotten. She remembered only the way he'd looked at her that first day at Locksworth House, that brief feeling of intimacy when they were beside the forest pool, the way his arms had held her firmly against him as they waltzed around the ballroom of Bonclere Manor. She wanted to see him one more time. Just one more time. It might be her last memory of happiness before she wed Blackstoke.

She dressed carefully, donning her most attractive riding dress of emerald green. The saucy bonnet had a golden plume on one side and was tied under her chin with a satin ribbon. Her black leather boots had been buffed to a high sheen. She checked her reflection in the mirror and was pleased with the final results. Eagerly, she left her room and went to the stables. Once mounted, she forced Pegasus to maintain a sedate walk, savoring with delicious anticipation the moment she would see Tristan again after so many days.

"I love him, Pegasus," she said aloud, stroking the silky white neck of her mare. "I don't even know him, but I'm in love with him."

She looked out over the verdant countryside, blinking back the wetness that threatened her tawny eyes. Loving him made no difference. Even if he loved her in return, it wouldn't help. She would still have to marry Blackstoke. It was settled. Too much money had changed hands. Too many promises had been made. Too many people were counting on this marriage. She hadn't the strength to fight them all. There was no escaping Blackstoke.

"Then I shall treasure this next hour all the more," she whispered as she nudged Pegasus into a jog.

As she turned off the road, Jacinda saw the duke coming down the drive in his carriage. She brought Pegasus to a halt and waited for him to reach her. Locksworth tapped his driver on the back with his cane, and the carriage stopped beside her.

"My dear, what a nice surprise. I was wondering when you would call on me again. I've missed your visits."

"I'm sorry, your grace. I've been so busy." She couldn't stop herself from glancing toward the mansion, wondering where Tristan was. Now that the duke was leaving, she would have to leave too. She wouldn't get to see him after all.

"Well, I won't scold you for your neglect. I must say, I've been a trifle busy myself. But now that Captain Dancing has left—"

"Left?" she cried, her head snapping back toward the duke. "He's gone?" She realized before the words were out of her mouth that she had revealed too much. With great effort, she smoothed the panic from her features and controlled her voice. "I'm sorry I hadn't the chance to bid him farewell." She glanced down at her gloves, missing the older man's satisfied smile.

"Well, he's not gone from England yet. He's in London, preparing to sail. I believe his business here is finished." He sighed dramatically. "I don't suppose I'll have the pleasure of his company again for many years. I'll miss the boy. Brought a bit of life to the old place."

"In London?" She looked up, a spark of hope bringing color back to her cheeks.

"Yes. On his ship. At least, I think so. He could sail any day. Perhaps even today."

London. He was still in London. It wasn't too late to see him one last time. She could go to London and wish him well. She could leave at once. It wasn't too late to be able to reach the city before nightfall if she left right away.

"I can see you were on your way out, your grace, so I shan't keep you any longer." Jacinda turned her mare's head around. "I promise to visit again soon," she called over her shoulder before cantering away from Locksworth House and the grinning duke.

Tristan glanced up at the sky. There was heavy cloud cover. It would be a dark night, no moon to offer any illumination even should the clouds blow over. Blackstoke had chosen the time wisely.

He began pacing the deck again, his hands behind his back. Tristan had heard from Blackstoke just two days before and had come to London at once. His cargo was to arrive tonight. He would sail for Constantinople as soon as he was loaded. He went over everything again in his mind. He had all the supplies he would need to feed the women. He had made their quarters as comfortable as possible. He had taken his officers into his confidence, explaining carefully the risks they were taking. If they were caught, no one would believe their innocence. They would probably all hang. He'd given them a chance to leave before they left port. None had chosen to accept. The rest of the crew had sailed with him on many voyages. He trusted them to obey his commands, no matter how outlandish.

"Well, Captain, it'll be a good night to slip from port."

Tristan looked over at Whip, then back toward the docks. "That it will," he replied.

Whip followed Tristan's gaze toward shore. "When do you think they'll come?"

Tristan shrugged. "Anytime after dark."

"The men are feeling impatient. They're ready to sail. We're lucky we haven't lost the lot of them, as long as we've been in port."

"I know."

"It's 'cause they respect and like you. Not many captains earn those feelings from their men."

Tristan glanced back at his first mate. "They may all wish they jumped ship before this is over. I sometimes wonder if this was such a good plan."

"Don't seem to have had much choice, Tris."

"Have we sent word to Danny?"

"Aye, but we'll get there near as fast as our message. Still, if anyone can help us with those Turks, it's Danny O'Banyon."

Tristan nodded and began walking again. Whip remained where he was, watching his captain with concerned eyes. He would be glad when this night was over.

Jacinda cursed herself for bringing the carriage. If she had ridden Pegasus, she would have been in London long before. And to make things worse, she was ashamed of the way she'd upbraided the driver while he was trying to fix the wheel. It hadn't been his fault, after all, that another carriage had forced them off the road.

She leaned forward and peeked out the window. Night was already falling around them. Would she arrive too late? Had he already sailed down the river to the sea?

"Poor Jake and I'll be put out from our positions once Lady Sunderland finds what we've done," Mary muttered, shaking her head.

"Oh for heaven's sake, Mary. Quit your fussing. I've told you I shan't let Mother do any such thing." Jacinda turned away from the window to look at her maid. "It was I who made you come to London with me."

"If only your mother had been at home. She would've told you this wasn't the thing to do. And now we're so late. What will the Fitzgeralds think of us?"

Of course, Mary didn't know that their immediate destination was the wharf. Jacinda had whispered those instructions to Jake the last time they had stopped. He hadn't bothered to argue with her, not with that determined gleam in her eyes.

The carriage came to a halt. Jacinda was already pushing the door open before Jake could jump down from his seat.

"Lady Jacinda, we'd best not stay here," the worried driver said as she took his hand to step out of the carriage. "It's too dark to find any one ship. And we've no idea where it might be anchored."

"Nonsense," she answered stubbornly. "We've come this far." She glanced around, frowning into the darkness. "I was here just a few weeks ago. I'm sure I can find it."

Mary poked her head out. "Jake, what on earth are we doing here? You get Lady Jacinda to the Fitzgeralds at once. This is no safe place for her."

Jacinda turned on her maid. "I told Jake to bring me here, and I'm not leaving until I find Captain Dancing."

"Oh, miss—" Mary's voice faded to a shocked whisper as she sank back into the carriage.

"Go on, Jake. There must be someone you can ask directions from. I'll wait right here while you find out the way to Captain Dancing's ship." She folded her arms in front of her for emphasis.

Jake answered with a slow nod. "I'll do it, m'lady, but you'd best get back inside. Wouldn't do for the likes of these dock rats to see you."

"All right, Jake," she agreed. "I'll wait in the carriage."

He held the door for her, waiting to make certain she was safely enclosed inside before starting out, reluctantly, on his errand.

Jacinda glanced at her maid, bathed in the soft glow of the carriage lantern. Mary's eyes were closed and her lips moved in a silent prayer. Jacinda would have smiled, except for the nagging fear that had begun to creep into her own thoughts. Perhaps Mary was right. Perhaps she didn't belong here. It was dark, and she didn't have any idea where Tristan's ship might be ... or even if it were still here. He might already have sailed from port. She began to imagine strange sounds. She would have looked outside but was afraid of what she might see.

Time seemed to stand still as the two women waited for their driver to return. The air inside the carriage was terribly close and stuffy. Jacinda tried several times to think of something to say to ease the tension that filled the small compartment, but the words wouldn't form. Finally, she closed her eyes so she wouldn't have to look at her own fears reflected in Mary's eyes.

"Well, what have we here, mate?"

Jacinda's eyes flew open, and she found herself looking into a bearded face with a leering smile.

"It's a lady, come t'see us."

Another face joined his at the carriage door. This man, heavier than the first, had a white bandana tied over his dark hair. A scar ran the length of the left side of his face. A low whistle hissed through his thick lips. "She's a beauty, she is. What d'you think, Sam?"

"I think we'd be thanked by his lordship, is what I think."

It had taken Jacinda a moment to gather her wits. Now, she raised her chin to a haughty height and looked down her nose at the two sailors. "I believe you are amiss, gentlemen.

Please remove yourselves and close the door or my driver will see that you regret your impudence."

They laughed. Not a pleasant sound.

Suddenly, the bearded man, the one called Sam, grabbed her wrists and yanked her out of the carriage. He shoved her into the bigger man's arms, then went after Mary who had shrunk as far from the door as possible. Jacinda struggled to free herself, to no avail.

"Release me," she demanded, then called, "Jake! Jake!"

"If you're meanin' that fellow in the fine livery who was walking around here, you can save your breath, m'lady. He's having a bit of a nap. I think he'll sleep a long time."

"Jake," she whispered. They had hurt Jake, and it was her fault.

Gathering all her strength, she pulled back her foot and kicked her captor in the shin. He yelped and let her go. The second his hands loosened their hold, she was off and running through the darkness, stumbling over unseen objects that were strewn in her path of flight. She could hear the angry cries of her pursuer and tried to run even faster, but her skirts hindered her speed and she knew the big man was hard on her heels.

His hand clamped onto her arm, jerking her off her feet. He pulled her around. "I'll teach you t'kick at me," he growled, raising a fist.

She closed her eyes just before he struck her. There was an explosion of yellow light against her eyelids and then she slipped into oblivion.

9

Jacinda moaned and raised a hand to touch her throbbing jaw.

"M'lady?"

She opened her eyes but could see nothing but utter darkness. "Mary?" she whispered in return. "Where are we?"

"On a ship, m'lady."

"A ship?" She tried to sit up but sank back to the floor with a groan. Sharp pains shot up into her head and tiny stars flashed in the darkness. Her thoughts were foggy. She knew she shouldn't be on board a ship, but she couldn't remember how she'd gotten here or why her head hurt so.

Mary's hand reached out and touched her. "Are you ill, m'lady?"

Jacinda touched her jaw again. "No. Not ill, Mary. But I seem to have hurt myself somehow."

"Those men. Those dreadful men—"

Men. Yes, there had been a man with a beard. He'd chased her.

"Oh, Lady Jacinda, whatever are we t'do? We should have gone straight to the Fitzgeralds. Lady Sunderland will send me packing, she will."

With a flash, it all came back to her—the ride to London, the dark docks, the strange man yanking her from the carriage, her fear as she ran, and the burst of pain when he struck her.

"Oh, Mary, hush up," she snapped, fear making her irritable. "We've got more to worry about than your being without a position."

Jacinda sat up, cringing beneath the pounding in her head. She stretched out her arm until her fingers touched the wall, then braced herself and stood up. She swallowed back the bile that stung her throat as a new wave of dizziness washed over her. Leaning her forehead against the dank wooden slats, she waited for the feeling to pass. In the meantime, she forced herself to think. She had to keep her wits about her, for both of their sakes. Mary, it seemed, would be no help to either of them.

She could hear the lapping of water and felt the gentle sway of the ship, but she didn't think they were moving. That meant they were still at anchor. They were still in London. Perhaps if she cried for help . . .

A door was thrown open, and a harsh yellow light spilled across the floor.

"Git in wi' ye!" a voice cried.

Jacinda saw a girl pushed before the light. She stumbled and fell into the hold. Before Jacinda could reach out to help her, another young woman was shoved forward, followed by another.

Mary scrambled to her feet and clutched

Jacinda's arm. "Whatever is happening, m'lady?" she whispered in terror.

As more women were shoved into the small room, Jacinda replied, "I don't know, Mary."

"Let go o' me, ye bloomin' limey. I'll see ye in 'ell, I will," a girl shouted as a man pushed her into the now crowded enclosure. She swung wildly, striking the man several times before he backhanded her, sending her sprawling across the floor, landing near Jacinda.

A deep male voice said, "That's the lot, Captain. Good luck with 'em." Then the door closed, dropping the inhabitants back into inky darkness.

There was a breathless hush. The throbbing in Jacinda's jaw seemed even worse. She closed her eyes as she pressed her hands against the sides of her head.

"I'll find me a way t'kill that bloody bastard, I will." The words were uttered near Jacinda's feet.

"Are you all right?" she asked, kneeling down in the darkness.

"I'm right enough, but I'd be better if I was out of 'ere."

"Where are we?" Mary asked in a frightened whisper. "Where are they taking us?"

"I bloody well don't know, but I think it's safe t'say we ain't none of us goin' t'like it."

Jacinda agreed silently. She settled onto the floor next to the feisty, foulmouthed girl, feeling a little stronger. "What's your name?"

"Ida."

"Hello, Ida. I'm Jacinda Sunderland and this is Mary." It seemed quite ludicrous to be sitting here in the black of night, a prisoner on board a ship, surrounded by strangers, introducing herself as if she were at someone's afternoon tea party, but she felt the need to form a link with someone else and Ida was the closest at hand.

"You weren't with the rest of us," Ida said matter-of-factly.

"No," Mary answered. "*Lady* Jacinda and I were taken from her carriage."

"Lady, is it now?" Ida's voice was skeptical. "Have ye been 'ere long?"

This time Jacinda answered. "No. At least, I don't think so. I was unconscious." She rubbed her jaw as she spoke.

Suddenly the ship lurched. Mary fell against Jacinda. Jacinda fell against Ida. The room itself seemed to gasp as the women captives drew startled breaths. They could hear feet hurrying across the decks overhead. Commands were shouted and replies were made.

"Guess that means we're leavin' London," Ida said, voicing the thoughts of all the women in the dank hold. "Might as well get some sleep. It'll be mornin' before they think of us again."

Surprisingly enough, Jacinda did sleep. She was awakened by the creak and thud of the door as it was thrown open. She blinked at the unaccustomed light that spilled from the lantern into the crowded hold and raised an arm to shield her eyes.

"Captain wants you all on deck," a sailor ordered.

Jacinda glanced toward Mary, then toward

Ida, sharing their trepidation. What was it that lay in store for them?

"Let's go," the man in the doorway barked.

She pushed herself up. Her muscles ached from sleeping in a cramped, seated position all night. Her jaw still throbbed from the punch her captor had dealt her. Her bladder demanded relief. The air in the hold was stuffy, and she knew she would be glad to draw a clean breath once she reached the deck.

Taking Mary's hand, she hauled her maid to her feet. "Come along, Mary," she said, pulling them into line as the women captives filed out of the room.

Jacinda paid no heed to the narrow passageway or to the unaccustomed roll of the ship. Her eyes were locked on the patch of blue sky she could see at the top of the companionway. For the moment, that was all she wanted, to reach the fresh air and see the sky.

Jacinda stepped onto the deck, pausing for a deep draw of brisk sea wind. She felt a moment of joy at the awesome sight. All that could be seen beyond the ship was sea and sky. Puffy white clouds dotted the blue expanse, and white caps spotted the dark green sea.

"Move on. There's others what want out from below."

A hand shoved at Jacinda's back, and she stumbled forward, into the huddled mass of women gathered on the deck. The gnawing fear returned. What was she doing here? What did these men mean to do with all these women? She glanced around her. Except for herself and Mary, her fellow captives seemed to be women of the poorest class, some of them in dire need of a bath, most of them dressed in little more than rags, all of them young, and many of them beautiful.

"They're all here, Captain."

Jacinda craned her neck to see around the girl in front of her and felt herself go pale. She grabbed Mary's arm to steady herself. He was wearing a bulky coat against the cool wind and a hat covered his black hair. He stopped in front of the tight group, a frown knitting his brows.

"Whip, have one of the men bring up some blankets for these women before they all freeze."

"Aye, Captain."

Jacinda hadn't even noticed that it was cold until he spoke.

"Ladies—" He paused, as if unsure what to say. His eyes began to move slowly over them. "I am the captain of this ship. I will try to make your voyage as—" The words died in his throat as ebony eyes locked with tawny gold.

No one moved. No one spoke. Even the ship seemed to cease swaying as it plunged through the ocean waves.

"Good lord! Jacinda," he whispered. Suddenly his face mottled with rage. "What on earth is she doing here?" he bellowed at his first mate. "Get her out of here. Take her to my cabin."

His anger was almost a physical presence. Jacinda stepped backward, seeking a place of safety, but there was no place to run, nowhere to hide on board the *Dancing Gabrielle*. An enormous sailor grabbed her from behind.

Instinctively, she lashed out at him. "Let me go. Take your hands off of me."

The giant of a man waved off her flailing arms as if she were no more than a pesky fly. "I beg your pardon, my lady," he said. With a sweep of his arm, he threw her over his shoulder like a sack of meal and headed aft toward the poop and the captain's cabin.

"M'lady!" Mary cried, following after her mistress.

"Spar, take that woman with you," Tristan ordered.

Jacinda lifted her head, once again meeting his stormy gaze. She ceased struggling and let her head drop forward against the giant's back. As bad as things had been, knowing that Tristan was her captor made everything so much worse. The last shreds of her dreams, her precious dreams, lay in ruin.

She was carried into his tidy cabin and gently set down onto the bunk. Mary sat beside her, and together they perused their new quarters. Of course, it was not the first time she had seen this room. Tristan had brought her here when she visited his ship just a few weeks ago. She remembered how hungrily she had looked at each nook and cranny, memorizing each item as if it would help her to know more about the man. Now that same room had become her prison.

Jacinda's gaze returned to move up the length of the sailor who had carried her here. He looked even bigger inside the cabin. He was several inches over six feet tall with a barreled chest and thickly muscled arms. A furry mustache adorned his upper lip, but his head was free of hair and shiny smooth. His skin had been darkened by the sun and had the look of tanned leather. He watched her with what seemed sympathetic hazel eyes.

"Why are we here?" she asked, hoping she hadn't misread the look he gave her.

"Captain Dancing will have to tell you that, my lady." His voice was deep, matching his size to perfection, but it was warm and unthreatening, and she was surprised by his polished speech. "Please excuse me." He moved toward the door, then glanced back at the two women. "Don't try to leave the cabin. No one disobeys the captain." He bent down from his lofty height and slipped through the doorway.

Jacinda stared at the closed door as if looking for the answer to a difficult puzzle. She was frowning and, every so often, shook her head as if to clear it. This didn't make sense. None of it made any sense. Tristan couldn't be doing this. Not to her. Not to all these women. There was a logical explanation. There had to be.

Tristan paused at the companionway, then glanced back down the length of his ship. The women were being taken below, not to the lower cargo hold where he had placed them last night while Blackstoke's men were aboard, but 'tween decks where he had made a steerage compartment as comfortable as was possible for a ship not made for passengers. Though he couldn't tell them the truth, he had tried to assure the women that they would be returned to England unharmed. He only asked that they obey orders and keep out of the way of the men. "Pretend this is a pleasure cruise," he had told them.

But what about Jacinda? Why was she among them? Had Blackstoke sent her to spy on him? Was she involved in the trafficking of white slaves to the bazaars and harems of Constantinople?

He descended the steps and went toward his cabin where he pushed open the door and stepped inside. Jacinda and her maid were seated on his bunk, an arm around each other. Her face was still pale, and he noticed for the first time the ugly bruise that marred the delicate skin along her jaw. Her fiery hair was tumbling down her back and spread over the shoulders of her emerald green gown. She watched him with the wary eyes of a mistreated puppy; he had to resist the impulse to gather her tenderly into his arms and kiss away her fears.

"Lady Jacinda, you are an unexpected guest."

She pulled free of Mary, a splash of color returning to her cheeks as she protested, "I am not a guest, Captain Dancing. I am a prisoner. I demand that you return me to London at once."

"I'm afraid that's impossible. Our course is set." He closed the door behind him before moving across the cabin. He removed his hat as he approached the bunk.

Jacinda lifted her face toward him. "Why have you done this, Tristan?"

There was so much hurt in her voice, so much disillusionment. He swore beneath his breath, damning the fates that had brought her into the midst of this, damning himself for feeling the way he did when she whispered his given name, something she had never done before. Again he resisted the urge to hold and comfort her.

"Why is of no concern to you, my lady. Believe me, you were the last person I would have wished aboard for this voyage, but I promise to return you to Viscount Blackstoke as early as possible and without undue harm, I trust." He reached out and touched the blue-black mark on her jaw. "How did this happen?"

His words had hurt, more than she would allow herself to show. She jerked her head away from his touch. "*That*, Captain Dancing, is of no concern to *you*," she snapped, using his own words against him.

He was glad to see her fight returning to her. He grinned, and saw that it made her even more angry. He bowed. "As you wish, Lady Jacinda." He pulled out a chair from the table in the center of the cabin and straddled it, crossed his arms along the chair's back, then leaned his chin on his forearms. "Whip is clearing the next room for me. You and your lady's maid may remain in my cabin. I'm afraid I'll have to ask you to stay in here the better part of our journey. You'll be safer."

"I'd rather be with the other women."

"No, my dear, you wouldn't. Trust me in that."

"Why should I trust you?" she cried with a burst of blazing anger. "You've betrayed me. You've betrayed his grace. The duke was your friend and you pretended to be his. Just what sort of man are you?"

His smile vanished. He hated to have her believing the worst of him. He was certain now that she didn't know the truth about Blackstoke. She hadn't come here to spy on him. Somehow those filthy blokes had snatched her and thrown her in with the wenches from the slums. Perhaps the same way they had taken Ella.

He stood quickly, knocking over the chair. His mouth was grim as he said softly, "I'm not as bad as you believe me to be. I hope someday you'll understand what has happened here and forgive me, but there's nothing I can say to you now to change your mind." He pulled his hat back onto his head and strode across the cabin floor. As Spar, the giant sailor, had done before him, he turned at the door and said, "Don't leave this cabin until Whip comes for you. I can't tolerate disobedience on board ship. Not even from someone as lovely as you."

After closing the door, Tristan climbed the steps up to the wheel. Standing behind it, the crisp wind in his face, he tried to banish her face from his mind. He had thought he would be leaving her behind in England. He had thought he would be able to forget her on his journey to Constantinople. He had thought that his search for Ella would drive away his feelings for Jacinda. He had been wrong. Even now, he wanted to hurry down to his cabin. He wanted to burst through that door and tell her the truth, tell her that it was Blackstoke who had taken these women from their families, tell her why he was using the *Gabrielle* this way. But, of course, he wouldn't. He couldn't. Too much was at stake.

10

The *Dancing Gabrielle* pitched forward, then reared back, throwing Jacinda from the bunk. In the darkness of the room, she was helpless to protect herself as she rolled across the floor to smack into the cabin wall. The sounds of shrieking wind and pounding waves as they washed over the ship sent icy shards of fear coursing through her.

"M'lady!" Mary screamed in the night, heightening the sudden terror that had awakened her.

Jacinda tried to stand and was sent crashing back across the room. Her foot caught on the table leg, and she flew, head first, into the bunk, then fell back to the floor.

"Merciful heavens! We're going to die!" Mary cried.

Jacinda clutched at the blankets at the edge of the bed as the *Gabrielle* shuddered beneath the tons of cascading, foaming ocean that threatened to sweep the ship from the surface and press it to the bottom of the sea. Struck by the unexpected squall, the *Gabrielle* had broached and was in danger of swamping.

Fear clutched at Jacinda's stomach as sea water rolled across the floor. "We've got to get out of here," she yelled above the rage of the storm. She struggled to her feet, grasping the wooden side of the bunk as the ship breached a swell, then fell abruptly forward. Overhead, she could hear the creaking of the masts and knew they must soon come tumbling down to smash the cabin into kindling.

In the dark, the two women clasped hands. Mary struggled out of the bunk, and together they fought their way against the storm toward the cabin door, feeling their way along the wall, hanging onto anything that would give them balance.

"Perhaps we should stay here as the captain said," Mary said as they reached the door.

"I'm not staying in here!" Jacinda jerked open the door. "Stay if you like." She stepped into the corridor and rushed toward the companionway, Mary on her heels.

A giant wave thundered over the deck just as they reached the top step, drenching them as it shoved them harshly back against the poop deck wall. Jacinda sputtered and coughed, blinking her eyes against the sting of salty sea spray. Above the noise of the storm, she could hear men shouting to one another, and she thought she could see dark forms moving across the deck, bending into the wind and gripping a safety line as they waited for another wave of white foam to crash over them. Again she choked on the sea water that filled her mouth and nostrils.

"Lady Jacinda, we must go back!" her maid cried. She tugged at Jacinda's hand, trying to pull her mistress back toward the cabin.

"No!" Panic-stricken, Jacinda jerked free just as the *Gabrielle* twisted in a new direction. She felt herself sliding across the deck and heard herself screaming. Her arms stretched to find a handhold, anything to keep her from disappearing into the frothing, watery doom that surrounded them. Miraculously, her arm crooked around a rope, and she grasped it with a determined strength she didn't know she possessed.

She looked up, water streaming down her face. It was a memory from which she would never be free, a picture etched on her mind for eternity. In the dark night, when there was so little else she could see, the image of Mary being carried overboard by the white, broiling surf was as clear as could be.

"Mary!"

She let go of the rope.

"Mary!"

But just as a rolling wave would have swept her into the same fate as her maid, a strong arm locked around her waist and pulled her close against a firm, male body.

"Mary," she whispered weakly as her eyes closed against the harshness of the night. Her body went limp, though she didn't faint at once. She felt herself being half-dragged, half-carried into the cabin before merciful oblivion took hold.

It was a horrible monster, a dragon,

breathing icy fire, watching her with malevolent blue eyes. She was trapped against a wall, unable to move, unable to flee. She was doomed. She cringed before the beast, awaiting her death. Shouldn't his breath be hot? Shouldn't the flames be burning her even now? Yet she was cold, and she shivered uncontrollably. Then she heard his shouts of encouragement. She looked beyond the dragon's back and saw him galloping toward them, his lance forward, prepared to do battle. She wasn't doomed. She was saved. The dragon wouldn't swallow her up. She waited for him to slay the blue-eyed dragon. The battle was fierce. The ground shook beneath her feet, rolling and swaying with great fury as her fearless knight battled the monster. But her faith in him never wavered. He would not fall to defeat. And when the dragon fell, the earth was still once more. Her knight turned away from the beast, removing his helmet as he came toward her. She was safe . . . She was safe . . .

It was still dark when Jacinda awoke. Something was very strange. She wasn't sure at first what it was. Then she noticed the silence, the eerie calm that enveloped the cabin. Next she became aware of the strong arms that held her close. Her face was nestled against his chest. Her breath caught in her throat as she lifted her head. The bristle on his chin scraped her cheek. Somehow, even in the darkness, she knew he was watching her with those ebony eyes of his. Instinctively, she drew closer to him, seeking the warmth of his body. As she did so, she tipped her head back even further and closed her eyes again.

Tristan's mouth sought hers, brushing lightly across her lips, then hovering just above her in breathless restraint. She shivered, waiting. His hand moved up from her back to cup her head and support her neck as he drew her forward to taste his kiss once more. This time his lips demanded a response. A strange warmth spread through her, beginning where his mouth touched hers and moving through her until it seemed to scorch her very soul.

He released her lips and traced tiny kisses across her cheek, then smothered his face into her damp hair. "Jacinda," he whispered. "Thank God you're safe."

Safe. Yes, she was safe here in his arms.

He kissed her earlobe. "I thought I'd lost you. When I saw you falling across the deck—"

The warmth of his embrace vanished as the horror of the night's storm flashed again in her mind. "Mary," she whispered in anguish. She pushed at his chest, shoving at him. "Get away from me. Get away from me."

Tristan tried to keep her close.

"Let go of me, you murderer," she cried loudly.

His arms dropped away, and the room was filled with a stunned silence. Finally, he spoke, his voice low. "I saved your life."

Jacinda scrambled over him and out of the bunk. She hugged herself as she backed up until she touched the far wall. "You didn't save Mary's life. She wouldn't be dead if you hadn't brought us here. She'd still be alive if we were in London. You killed her as surely as if you'd pushed her overboard yourself."

Enough light from early dawn was

beginning to creep in through the cabin window to let her see him stand, his back rigid. "And why were the two of you out of the cabin? Whose idea was that, Lady Jacinda?" His words seemed cruel, all the more so because they hinted at the truth of her own guilt.

"You'll be caught and hanged for her murder. You kidnapped us. Do you think our absence won't be noticed? Viscount Blackstoke will see that you pay dearly for your part in all of this."

"Ha!" His laugh was harsh. "How naive you are, Lady Jacinda."

With a sudden movement, she grabbed a tin plate from off the floor and threw it at him. He deflected it with his arm. His look was grim as he glared at her in silence.

"It *is* your fault," she insisted. "You killed Mary, and I'll see that you pay for it."

"And my reply is the same as before," he answered with icy calm. "Who led the way out of the cabin when I had told you both to stay inside? Tell me, what part did you play in her death? Was it because of you that she was washed out to sea?"

His questions cut like a knife.

With a few quick steps, he had crossed the cabin and was pinning her arms to her side. "I'm sorry about Mary. I'd bring her back if I could. Do you think me a monster that an innocent girl's death doesn't trouble me? I would choose that no one ever died under my command, but the sea is a harsh taskmaster." He paused a moment, studying her hate-filled gaze before adding, "If I had it to do over, I think I would have reached for her instead.

You, Lady Jacinda, are an added problem I don't need." With a little shove, he released her and stalked out of the cabin, slamming the door behind him.

Jacinda reached out quickly for the table and sank into the only chair still standing. Hot tears scalded her eyes, but she blinked them back as she gritted her teeth.

"I'll make you pay for this, Tristan Dancing," she swore aloud. "If I die trying, I'll make you pay."

She didn't know how long she sat there, but slowly her anger faded, turning into dazed exhaustion, an exhaustion caused as much by strained emotions and shock as by physical fatigue. She was unaware of her own chattering teeth and the violent shivers that swept over her at intervals. She stared with a dull gaze at a deep groove in the surface of the table, while in her mind the horror of Mary's death replayed itself with torturous accuracy of detail.

The cabin door protested its opening with a baleful creak. Jacinda glanced up with unseeing eyes. Spar's bulk filled the doorway, but she seemed to look right through him.

He stepped inside. "The captain sent some dry things," he said, watching her closely.

Jacinda let her gaze fall to her sodden green riding gown. She had donned it with such care just . . . was it really only two days before? She had worn it for him. The emerald color was so good with her red hair. Her hair . . . She reached up to touch it. It lay snugly against her scalp, tangled and matted. Tears surfaced again, this time falling to streak her pale cheeks.

131

Spar picked up a chair from the floor and set it upright near her own. He sat, dwarfing the stick of furniture. "You lost a friend. I am sorry."

"It's my fault," she whispered in anguish. "I made her go outside with me."

" 'Tis no one's fault, my lady. The sea claims who she will."

Jacinda looked up as she blinked away fresh tears, seeing him clearly for the first time. On his rugged face, she read sympathy and an offer of friendship. She swallowed the persistent lump in her throat.

Spar held out the clothes. "There's not much that's dry after last night's storm. These aren't fancy, but they're clean and dry. You'd best change. You look as if you've already taken a chill, I fear."

"Thank you." Jacinda accepted the bundle.

"I'll come back to help you clean up and dry things out," he promised. He rose above her, granting her a smile.

"Thank you," she repeated softly. She watched him as he crossed to the doorway and left the cabin.

Jacinda laid the clothes on the table, then began to unbutton the bodice of her dress. Her fingers refused to move quickly. They were stiff with cold. At last she stood and let the green gown crumple into a pool of fabric around her feet. She reached out for the clothing Spar had left for her and was surprised to discover not a dress but a shirt and trousers, plus a warm looking coat. Though not what she had expected, they were dry, just as he'd said, and so she slipped into them. The warm, long sleeved shirt fit snugly over her rounded breasts, and the trousers felt foreign on her long, shapely legs.

Following a quick knock, the door opened. She turned with a gasp, feeling exposed in her new attire. Her hand flew to the top of the shirt in a protective gesture.

Spar grinned at her. "Now you look like a sailor," he said, then added, "I thought you might like these." He placed a pearl-handled brush and matching mirror on the table between them.

"They're beautiful, Spar." She picked up the brush and stroked its cool back, enjoying the elegant feel of it. She looked up at the giant of a man, her tawny eyes widening in question. "Why are you being so kind to me?"

"Because, my lady, you are caught in something beyond your control. Because you have lost your friend and are in need of another."

Jacinda responded to his sympathy and was angry at herself for it. Turning her back on him, she began brushing her hair with fierce strokes. "You're a strange one to be friends with that . . . that pirate," she ground out between clenched teeth.

"The captain is no pirate."

"No?" She whirled to face him. "Then explain to me what I'm doing here. Explain to me why Mary is dead."

In answer, Spar shrugged and shook his head. He walked back to the cabin door and opened it, stepped outside briefly, then returned with a bucket, mop and rags. "There's work to be done," he said as he placed the bucket on the floor near her bare feet. "Put on your boots."

He didn't wait for her response but turned and began picking up the few items that cluttered the floor. Tristan was a neat man and most of his things were locked up in their respective drawers and closets. Spar placed a candle holder, plate and cup, and one ruined book on the table, slid the chamber pot into a cupboard near the bed, and then took up the mop and began swabbing the floor.

Jacinda watched him as he worked. She distrusted the way he made her feel. She had no need of this man's friendship. He had an obvious allegiance to Tristan Dancing, and that in itself was enough to make him her enemy. She stiffened her back and lifted her chin, new resolve adding a spark to her eyes. She would not succumb to tears again. She would not feel sorry for herself. She would not trust a single soul on board this ship. She might be a prisoner here, but she would survive—and without anyone's help either.

She crossed the room and jerked the mop from Spar's hands. "I'll do it."

"As you wish." His mustache twitched as he suppressed another smile.

"I'd prefer to do it *alone*."

Spar nodded. "As soon as I can, I'll send a boy with something for you to eat."

She would have liked to tell him to keep his food, that she wasn't hungry, but her stomach was complaining even now. Between the unaccustomed rolling of the ship and the pain in her jaw, she'd had little appetite the previous day. Now her hunger was returning.

Once again, Spar left the cabin, closing the

door behind him. It was then she heard the click of the key for the first time. Her eyes widened as she dropped the mop and walked to the door. She tried to open it. As she'd suspected, her exit was barred.

"Lock the door, for all I care, Captain Dancing," she whispered stiffly. "I've seen your ship, and I have no wish to see it again."

She returned to her mopping.

Tristan stood at the helm and watched the men at work. They had been lucky. The storm had done little damage to the *Dancing Gabrielle*, but it was as close to being swamped as Tristan had ever been or ever hoped to be. They'd been blown far off course, and it would take them a day or two to make up the lost time.

He glanced up. A serene cerulean sky floated overhead, almost mocking the memory of the raging storm that had buffeted them throughout the night. The winds were light. The deep blue-green of the sea rolled and crested with a steady rhythm before the bow of the *Gabrielle*. The ship sliced through the waves with ease.

Spar stepped onto the main deck. He turned and looked up at the captain and shook his head mutely, then proceeded on down the deck, disappearing into the forward deckhouse which housed the galley and quartered twelve seamen. Tristan's hands tightened on the wheel. He knew his friend was trying to make things easier for Jacinda, but from the look of him, she wasn't cooperating.

Blast the girl! Why did she have to complicate his life so?

But he wasn't truly angry at her. It was the confusion of his own feelings for her that left him frustrated and angry. From that first moment she had appeared on the steps at Locksworth House, she had occupied his thoughts. What was it that made her so important to him? It wasn't just her beauty. He had seen many beautiful women, though few he would call her equal. No, there was more to it than that.

There was something special about her, something his grandfather had seen long before Tristan had arrived to see it himself. An eagerness for life. A desire to love and be loved. An inner strength that held her up when everything and everyone else had failed her. He knew the way she felt for his grandfather and was warmed by it. He had seen that lost look in her eyes, the sadness that she tried to hide from the world. She seemed vulnerable and too willing to abide by the wishes of others. But she was going to marry Roger Fanshawe even though she didn't love him—a fact Tristan continued to remind himself of every time he thought about her—so he'd tried to convince himself that she deserved Blackstoke and whatever he brought her.

He might even have succeeded in believing he truly felt that way about her had he been able to leave her behind in England. Now she was here, just footsteps away from him. She'd been hurt and bruised by her captor. She had witnessed her maid being washed out to sea. She was cold and afraid, and Tristan wanted nothing more than to comfort her, than to hold her in his arms as he had last night.

He closed his eyes, remembering . . .

He had been at the wheel, fighting against the storm, yelling orders at his seamen above the wind. From his position at the helm, he couldn't see the doorway leading out of the cabins beneath the poop. It wasn't until he saw her sliding across the deck toward the side of the ship that he knew she had left the relative safety of her room. With a shouted command, he gave the wheel to Whip and struggled against the merciless, broiling sea. He almost didn't reach her in time. He saw Mary carried away on a monstrous wave. He saw Jacinda let go of the safety rope and heard her call Mary's name. Another second and he would have been too late. His arms captured her, drawing her back from the ocean's jaws. He carried her to the cabin and left her tucked tightly in her bunk, a prayer on his lips that she wouldn't awaken and leave again. Then he returned to his post at the wheel.

After what seemed an eternity, Tristan entered the sodden cabin. Water rolled back and forth across the floor, but the worst of the storm was over. They were out of danger. He stepped to the side of the bed and gazed down at her. The lamp in his hands shook from his own fatigue, making the light waver over her damp skin. He reached down and moved aside a stray lock of hair from her cheek. Her arms were clutched tightly against herself and she was shivering.

Tristan blew out the lamp and lay on the narrow bunk beside her. He gathered her into his arms, sharing what warmth was left in his own body. He placed a soft kiss on her temple, then drifted into a deep slumber of his own.

She was still wrapped in his arms when he awakened just as first light was tinging the interior of the cabin. Tristan knew a peaceful joy he hadn't felt in many months, perhaps years. He watched her sleeping and hoped selfishly that she wouldn't awaken for a long time. When she opened her eyes and turned her face up to him, it seemed the most natural thing in the world to kiss her. And she returned the embrace, returned the kiss. If it hadn't been for the memory of Mary . . .

Tristan shook himself from his reverie, cursing under his breath. He couldn't afford to go soft in the head over her. She was a lady, the daughter of an earl. She had a destiny of her own. A ship's captain—and one she suspected of being a pirate besides—could not be part of that destiny. It was better that she go on hating him. Better for both of them.

11

Blackstoke reclined deep into the richly padded chair and drew on his cigar. Pursing his lips, he exhaled, watching as the pale blue smoke drifted toward the ceiling of his library. He smiled to himself. White's report was most satisfactory. Captain Dancing had left with his cargo of thirty-seven women without mishap, and a ship had been purchased to replace the one lost. By the time Dancing returned, White would have put together a crew of the right sort for this line of work, and Blackstoke could send Dancing on his way.

Blackstoke's gaze dropped to the crackling fire on the hearth as his grin broadened. Now all he had to think about was his wedding to Jacinda. Just three more weeks and she would be his bride. His and his alone. No longer would she be able to skitter away from him, feigning shyness. He would show her that he was lord and master, and she would be his willing servant. Remembering the way she had looked upon returning from Captain Dancing's ship, he swore silently. By damn, she *would* be his willing servant. If he had to beat her into submission . . . He chuckled, the momentary anger disappearing as he imagined stripping the clothes from his lovely lady and laying the lash to her delicate flesh. Yes, he thought, he would enjoy that.

He tossed his cigar into the fireplace and got to his feet. Perhaps he needed a little feminine entertainment to take his mind off Jacinda. Now that the ship was out of the harbor, he had little else to occupy his mind.

"Milord?"

Blackstoke turned toward the door. "Yes, Smithens," he replied to his manservant. "What is it?"

"Lord and Lady Sunderland are here, milord. They've asked to see you."

"Is Lady Jacinda with them?" Again he imagined her bare flesh.

"No, milord."

He sighed, his fantasy vanishing. "Ah, well, I suppose I shall have to see them. Bring them in, Smithens."

"Yes, milord."

Blackstoke returned to his comfortable chair near the fire and sat down. He reached for another cigar and was lighting it when Smithens showed the earl and his wife into the room. He gave them a languid perusal, noting Lady Sunderland's pale face and her husband's heightened color.

"My friends, what an unexpected pleasure." He waved a hand at the sofa across from him. "Please sit down."

"I'm afraid this is no pleasure for us, sir,"

Lord Sunderland began.

Blackstoke cocked an eyebrow and waited.

"We've come to demand you do right by our daughter. Call her here this moment."

"Your daughter?" His glance darted to Lady Sunderland. This was no jest. "What makes you think Jacinda is here?"

Lady Sunderland's face lost any remaining trace of color. "Are you saying that she's not?"

"Of course she isn't here. What made you think she would be?"

Lord and Lady Sunderland exchanged worried looks. When they turned in unison to gaze at Blackstoke, it was in strained silence.

Blackstoke felt his alarm changing to anger. "What made you think she would be here?" he asked for the third time.

"My lord, she left Bonclere last week with her lady's maid. Her note said she would be visiting the Fitzgeralds. But when we came to London this morning, we learned she hadn't arrived at their home. They hadn't even expected her. We thought . . . we'd hoped she had come here."

"Good heavens, man!" Blackstoke exclaimed. "You mean she's disappeared?"

Lady Sunderland touched her husband's hand. "Perhaps she's gone to Fernwood," she suggested. "You know how fond she is of the duke."

Blackstoke got to his feet at once. "Smithens," he yelled, "get my carriage."

"We can take ours," Lord Sunderland offered as he rose.

Blackstoke cast the earl a withering glance before marching out of the room in silence. He

141

grabbed his cloak from his manservant as he hurried out the front door into the cold night air to wait impatiently for his carriage to be brought around. He clenched his teeth, seething inside. She'd run away rather than marry him. That's what she'd done. The ungrateful chit. Well, she wouldn't succeed. He would find her and bring her to heel. No woman would spurn him. Especially not the woman he wanted. He would find her and make her understand that, once and for all.

The Duke of Locksworth was dozing beside his own fire when he was awakened by voices in the entry hall. He heard Mrs. Charring's angry protest just before Blackstoke burst into the drawing room.

"All right, Locksworth. Will you send for her or must I go after her myself?"

Locksworth blinked his eyes, clearing his throat as he straightened in his chair. "What, by heavens, are you babbling about?"

"You know what. I'm here for Lady Jacinda. Now send this woman for her."

"Jacinda? But she isn't here."

Blackstoke turned as if he meant to carry out his threat of finding her himself.

"Fanshawe," the duke said in a clear voice as he rose to his feet. "I give you my word. Jacinda is not at Fernwood."

The viscount turned around once more. His blue eyes searched the older man's face. Locksworth opened his mouth to ask why he'd thought she would be there when a new commotion sounded in the hall. He glanced toward the door as Jacinda's parents hurried into the room.

"I say, Locksworth. Is she here?" Lord Sunderland inquired.

The duke shook his head. "I think we'd best sit down and find out what's going on." He waited for the others to comply, then took his own seat. He listened with growing apprehension as Lord Sunderland explained why they had come.

"Missing nearly a week? But she came to see me at Locksworth House. She never said a word about coming to London, not even when I told her—" He stopped abruptly, remembering the way she'd looked when he'd told her Tristan was in London and readying his ship to sail.

"Told her what, Locksworth?" Blackstoke demanded.

The duke gathered his thoughts before replying. "When I told her I was coming to London to see Captain Dancing off," he said, the lie slipping smoothly off his tongue.

"He's gone, is he?" Lord Sunderland asked. "It's just as well. I don't care much for his sort."

"I rather liked him," Locksworth responded. "Unfortunately, I didn't arrive in time to bid him farewell. He'd already sailed." He looked back at the viscount. "Regardless, I'm surprised she didn't tell me she was coming to London once she knew I would be here. Perhaps her decision was made suddenly."

"Oh, William, what are we to do?" Lady Sunderland cried. "The wedding is only weeks away. I won't be able to hold my head up if we don't find her in time. What an ungrateful daughter you sired, to leave us in such a mess."

The three men turned to look at her askance.

"Well, it's true," she protested in a shrill

voice. "She has always been a difficult child. Always dreaming. Always wanting what she couldn't have. Never caring what her parents have had to do without. I wouldn't put it past her to agree to this engagement just so she could disappoint me by running off at the last moment."

"Shut up, Gwendolyn," Lord Sunderland growled harshly. "This is beneath even you."

The duke cleared his throat once again, then said, "I think we'd better notify the authorities. There may be trouble afoot."

"I'll send my driver," Blackstoke said as he got to his feet.

Locksworth watched him go, then glanced back at Jacinda's father. "Did you happen to bring her note with you?"

Jacinda lay on the bunk, wrapped in the coat Spar had brought her, topped by three woolen blankets. It wasn't enough. She couldn't stop the shivering. She thought of forcing herself out of bed to add to the fire in the small stove, but she just didn't have the strength to do it. For several days she had managed to hide her growing illness whenever Tommy, the young fo'c'sle boy, came to her cabin, bringing her a meal or taking away the dishes. She hadn't seen Spar or Tristan since the day after the storm. Tommy had offered several times to take her for a walk on the deck, saying it was by permission of the captain, but she always refused.

She heard the rattle of the tray outside and tried to rise. She couldn't let Tommy see her this way. She managed to sit up, but a sudden swell of blackness threatened to sweep over her and she sank back onto the bed. She turned her back to the door as she heard the key turning in the lock.

"Miss?" Tommy said uncertainly as he entered the room. "I've brought you somethin' to eat."

"I'm not hungry, Tommy. Take the tray away."

"Captain won't like it."

"I don't care what the captain likes," she snapped, but her voice carried no real conviction. She was too weak to sound angry.

"Miss?" Tommy stepped up behind her.

She felt his small, work-roughened hand touch her shoulder. "Go away." She closed her eyes.

His hand moved to her forehead, then was drawn away quickly. "You're burnin' up," he whispered.

Before she could respond, he had dashed from the room.

I should get up, she thought. I can't let him see me this way. I should get up.

But she didn't get up. She hadn't the strength. Instead, she succumbed to the chills that shook her body as the fever raged.

Spar brushed a hand across his bald head as he turned to face Tristan. "She's very sick, Tris. You'd better bring one of the women up to help take care of her. I don't think she'd like to have one of us doing for her."

Tristan read the concern in Spar's hazel gaze. The man was as good as any doctor Tristan had ever seen. He trusted the big seaman completely. "Will she . . ." He stopped himself. "How bad is she, Spar?"

"She's weak, Tris. Very weak. I should have checked on her before this. She was shaking like a flag in the wind last time I was in here, but I thought with the coat I brought her and a fire in the stove . . ." His voice trailed off into guilty silence.

Tristan laid a hand lightly on the big man's arm. "She hid it from Tommy. She would have done the same with you." He turned away, crossing the cabin to the door, then glanced back toward the slight figure on the bed. "I'll bring up a girl."

As he stepped onto the deck, he was met by the chilling wind that filled the *Gabrielle*'s sails. He cursed it, while at the same time wishing it would carry them more quickly toward the Mediterranean and a warmer clime. He hunched his shoulders, drawing his coat closer as he hurried toward the hatch.

When Tristan entered the makeshift steerage compartment, more than a score of heads turned to look in his direction. Some of the women were seated on benches near the long table in the center of the room, others on the tiered bunks that lined the walls. With a captain's sharp eye, he noted that they had bathed and were wearing new clothes. The room had been swept clean. It was free of the stench of vomit and fear that had filled it the morning after the storm.

His dark gaze moved slowly around the room until he found the girl he was looking for at the end of the table. Her bright orange hair made her easily distinguishable from the others. She was tiny, but her green eyes were full of spunk. When he had checked on the women a few days ago, she had asked about the fine lady and her maid. She had seemed genuinely concerned, and so he sought her out now to help with Jacinda.

Tristan walked toward her. She waited for him, a look of curiosity on her face rather than the fear he had read in many of the others. He stopped before her.

"I need your help," he said.

"Mine?" A shadow of suspicion darkened her face. "What for?"

"It's Jacinda. She's ill."

"The lady? What's wrong with 'er?"

"She's taken a chill. Her fever's raging."

" 'aven't we all got problems? Is she worth so much more t'ye than the rest o' us? Tell 'er snippy lady's maid t'care for 'er 'erself."

"Her maid was washed overboard in the storm," he told her in a grim tone. Then he reached out and clasped her wrist, his eyes pleading with her. "Please help. You asked about her the other day. You must care a little."

The girl lowered her eyes. "I'm sorry I said what I did, and I'm sorry about the girl. I wouldn't've wished it on 'er, even though she was a mite snippety. You take me t'the lady, and I'll 'elp ye care for 'er."

"Thank you," he said softly.

As Tristan turned, his gaze was drawn across the table to a pair of sultry gray eyes set in a dark, sensuous face. The woman leaned forward, exposing a generous view of her full breasts. "If you need any more help, Captain, I hope you'll call on me." A smile curved her mouth as the tip of her tongue made a slow sweep of her lips.

"Thank you. I'll do that, miss," he replied, but there was no return smile for her. He hadn't the time or the inclination to make use of the kind of help she was offering. He glanced back at the redhead waiting behind him. "Come with me."

Tristan strode across the room, not checking to see if she followed. He hurried up the ladderway and down the deck toward the captain's cabin. When he pushed open the door, he was surprised by the darkness. While he was gone, Spar and Tommy had hung canvas over the windows, hoping to block out the wind and hold in the warmth. The stove had been stoked, and heat was making a valiant effort to combat the cold that crept through every crack or crevice. Tristan stepped across the threshold and opened his mouth to introduce the girl to Spar, then closed it as he realized he'd never asked her for her name.

Spar was sitting in a chair beside Jacinda's bed. He turned at the sound of their entrance. His eyes flicked from Tristan to the girl waiting behind him, then he motioned to her to come forward. She obeyed quickly, her own gaze turning toward the still form buried under blankets on the bunk.

"She's not lookin' well, is she?" she asked softly.

"No, she isn't," Spar answered. "Will you help me?"

"I'd be obliged to."

"I'm Spar."

"Me name's Ida."

Spar nodded, then pointed to a bowl of water lying on the table. "Her fever's raging,

Ida, and she's still racked by chills. I don't know what to do, to tell you the truth, but for now I'm trying to keep her warm and stop that infernal shivering. If you could just sit with her, wipe her brow, keep an eye on her—"

"I'll do it," Ida replied. "Don't ye worry. I'll take good care o' the lady, and I'll send for ye if there's need."

Spar got up from the chair and walked over to Tristan. He placed a hand on the captain's shoulder. "Come on, Tris. You've got a ship to run. You can't stay in here all day."

Tristan nodded, but his eyes remained on Jacinda.

"Tris?"

"I'm coming, Spar." He pulled his gaze away from the pale face beneath the flaming hair. "I'll be back, Ida. Take good care of her."

"I will, Captain. I promise."

The black horse loped slowly toward her, carrying the knight in shiny mail. She waited for him impatiently. He stopped the mighty charger just inches away from her. The horse tossed his head and snorted. She could see his black eyes staring at her intensely through the visor of his helmet, and her heart quickened. He dismounted and stepped closer. His hands lifted his helmet from his head. A hood of mail hid his ebony hair from view. She reached up and slid the hood back. His arms circled her and she was drawn into his embrace, surrendering willingly to his kisses.

It was hot. So hot. She couldn't move. Her throat burned. Water. A drink of water.

He wore a bright bandana around his

forehead. The skin of his pirate's face was tanned brown by the sun. He flashed her an encouraging smile as he walked toward her. The sun beat down on the deck with merciless intensity. She felt as if she were on fire. She tried to plead for water, for something to drink, but her throat was too parched and she couldn't speak. But he seemed to understand. "Get well, Jacinda," she heard him whisper. Then he placed a cool cup to her lips.

Cold. She couldn't get warm. If only she could get warm. Another blanket. A fire. Anything to make her warm again. She would never be warm again.

There were people everywhere. The church was filled with people, and all their eyes were turned upon her. Strains of music, haunting music, reached her ears. She was walking forward. She wanted to stop. She wanted to turn and run away. The church was so cold. She shivered. Why was it so cold? What was she doing here? Why were they watching her so? Then she saw him at the end of the aisle. Blue eyes watched her. Cold blue eyes beneath heavy brows. That's why the church was so cold. His eyes. This wasn't the right man. Not those cold blue eyes. So cold. So cold.

She was smothering. Too many blankets. Too much weight holding her down. She hated to be held down. Too hot. So hot. And she hurt. Her body ached so. Held down. She was smothering.

You are such an ungrateful child, Jacinda. You must marry well, Jacinda. Love has nothing to do with it, Jacinda. You owe it to us, Jacinda. You're the envy of every young lady in England,

Jacinda. You'll be the ruin of us yet, Jacinda.

Water. She was so thirsty. Just a sip of water.

"Drink this, Jacinda. That's it . . . Get well, love. I mustn't lose you. I can't lose you. Get well, Jacinda."

12

Tristan leaned on the oak rail, watching the ebb of the sun's reign. It rested on the edge of the world, a giant yellow ball, cut in half by the ocean's horizon. Then it slipped slowly from view until all that remained was a golden hue to glaze the watery surface. The smattering of clouds changed from white to purple, from pink to pewter, and suddenly the day was gone.

"Captain?" Tommy had stepped up behind him. "Whip says you're to go below and eat, sir." He shifted nervously, looking down at the deck, then back at the captain.

Tristan turned to look down the length of the ship. He could see his first mate at the wheel and knew the man's brows were knitted in a concerned frown. "Oh, he does, does he?" he responded, irritation and fatigue making his words harsher than he meant them to be. "And do you think a captain should follow a first mate's orders?"

The boy's eyes grew wide, and he shook his head vigorously.

Tristan sighed and gave the boy a weary smile. "All right, Tommy. I'll do as you say. And," he added, "Whip's right. I do need to eat."

Tommy grinned.

"Will you join me?"

"Me, sir?"

Tristan's smile grew more earnest. "I'd like your company, Tommy."

"Aye, Captain. I'll join you then."

"Good boy." Tristan turned toward the galley. "Anything good waiting for us?"

"Not since Spar's been taking care of the lady," Tommy answered honestly.

Tristan nodded, but his thoughts were no longer on the meal awaiting him. If he'd had his way, he would have turned on his heel and gone to his cabin to check on her. He'd been with her much of the day, just as he had been the day before and the day before that. He knew Spar was worried, and so his own worry had doubled.

"The fever's got to break soon, Tris," Spar had told him this morning, "or we'll lose her."

Tristan sat at the table in the forward deckhouse. In the galley, Edward Shaw, a young apprentice seaman, filled a plate, and Tommy brought it to the table. Tristan looked at the unappetizing food—thick pea soup, boiled salt pork, and hard tack. There were better provisions to be found on the *Gabrielle*, but young Shaw had few skills as a cook. Tristan forced himself to take a bite, chewing the tough meat for a long while.

The men must be about to mutiny, he thought as he swallowed.

Sailors had to have iron stomachs to

survive at sea. It was difficult to keep food fresh for long, and a cook could whip up some mighty strange concoctions in the galley. Officers might get the choicest of what was on board, but the conditions were the same for everyone. Weevils got into the rice. Maggots grew fat in the flour. Butter could melt and reset itself several times during a voyage. But despite the difficulties involved in keeping it fresh for any length of time, Tristan had always prided himself on providing his men with the best food possible. This wasn't it.

Tristan managed to take a few more bites before shoving the plate away. A young hand reached and slid the plate back again. The captain looked over at the fo'c'sle boy. Tommy's eyes never wavered this time. His look was bold and firm.

"As you wish, Seaman Tom," Tristan said lightly. "I'll eat every last bite." He would have added *even if it kills me*, but Edward Shaw stepped into the doorway between the quarters and the galley at just that moment, and Tristan was forced to swallow his disparaging remark. Instead, he reluctantly lifted another fork full of peas and pork into his mouth.

He ate in silence, doing his best to think of nothing. If he thought of the food, he would refuse to eat it. When at last he was able to push away the clean plate, he looked over at Tommy again. The boy's eyes were at half-mast, and his head jerked as he fought to stay awake.

Tristan threw his leg over the bench and stood up. Touching Tommy's shoulder, he gently said, "Off with you, Tom. You've had a long day."

Once the boy was gone, Tristan shrugged into his jacket again, then went back on deck. He walked toward the bow and looked out over the figurehead. A crescent moon had risen, frosting the black ocean with silver whitecaps. Above, the clouds of white canvas billowed and shook in the song of the wind. Below, he could hear the sucking of the wash around the hull as it piled high, whipped into boiling eddies. A fine mist sprayed his face, and he licked the salty taste left on his lips.

"Tris."

He turned. "What is it? Is she worse?"

Spar shook his head. "About the same." The big man stepped closer. "Are we close to land?"

Tristan was alarmed. "We can be . . . if that's what she needs."

"I think it would be a good idea."

Tristan had planned to avoid the British port of Gibraltar, wanting to slip through the straits under cover of darkness. If he put in there, he risked discovery of the women captives on board. They had been treated well and his reasons for taking them—at least in his own mind—were justified. Still, the women had been taken against their will, and his entire crew's lives depended upon his caution. But if that's what Spar thought he should do, he would have to do it, risk or no risk.

"We might consider Madeira," Spar suggested, seeming to read Tristan's thoughts. "The climate is mild and there's no garrison."

Tristan headed laft, tossing back over his shoulder, "If the wind holds, we could be there tomorrow."

* * *

There was something very strange about the way the sunlight filled the room, but Jacinda couldn't figure out what it was at first. She had to close her eyes against its brightness several times, then try again. That was it. It seemed *too* bright. She left her eyes closed.

Next she noticed the singing of birds. I must be dreaming, she thought. No. That *was* a bird.

She opened her eyes again, slowly this time. It wasn't just the brightness of the sunlight. The walls were white. They hadn't been white before. This was a different room and there was a window with a bird singing outside and . . . and the ship wasn't rolling. She wasn't on the ship. A flash of panic forced her to try to sit up, but she immediately fell back onto the bed.

"Here now. Let's not have you doing that." Spar's large form appeared above her.

She lifted a hand toward him. It felt as if there were weights tied to her wrist. She touched the collar of his shirt, making sure he was real and not a dream.

"Take a sip of this, Jacinda." He held a cool cup to her lips while he braced her neck with his other hand.

The water felt deliciously soothing to her throat, and she drank until it was empty. When she was finished, Spar gently laid her head back on the pillow.

"Where are we?" she asked, the words coming out in a hoarse whisper.

"We're in Madeira. It's an island in the Atlantic." He sat down beside her. "I don't want you to talk anymore. I want you to sleep."

"I've been ill?"

157

"You've been very ill."

Jacinda nodded wearily. Her eyes obeyed him, fluttering closed even as she might have spoken again.

The sunlight had weakened when she awakened the second time, but she could feel more strength in herself. This time when she raised her head, she recognized Ida's orange locks as she dozed in the chair next to Jacinda's bed.

"Ida?" she croaked.

The girl's head popped up. " 'ello there, milady. Nice to 'ave you back with us, it is."

Jacinda tried to smile and felt the skin on her lips cracking. She winced as she touched them with her fingers. "I'd like something to drink," she said.

" 'ere ye go. Gave us a right scare, you did, miss. And I'm glad t'see ye've cheated the grim reaper. I thought ye was 'is more'n once, I did."

Jacinda drained the cup as Ida chattered. When she was finished, she pushed herself up against the wall. The effort weakened her for a moment, but the room righted itself quickly, and she knew she was getting stronger by the minute.

"Would ye eat somethin', milady? I can bring ye a good beef broth. It's a strong sight better than the biscuits an' salt pork we were 'avin' on the ship."

Jacinda nodded.

"Ye don't try t'get up while I'm gone," Ida warned her. "I'll be back in no time."

"I won't," Jacinda promised.

Ida was as good as her word. Jacinda had

scarcely had time to give the plain, white room a perusal before she was back with a tray. On it was a steaming bowl of soup, the rich fragrance drifting ahead to spark Jacinda's hunger. Ida placed the tray on Jacinda's lap and handed her a spoon.

"Have you been taking care of me?" Jacinda asked.

"Not me, milady. I've just done what Spar 'as told me t'do."

"Spar?"

Ida's green eyes brightened. "That 'e 'as. I've never seen the like. 'e's a doctor or my name's not Ida Spencer. 'e's taken good care of ye, and there's none can say otherwise."

Spar a doctor? She couldn't deny what Ida had told her, yet it was difficult to think of the giant seaman as a healer rather than a pirate. And pirates were what she considered every man aboard the *Dancing Gabrielle*.

"Where are the other women, Ida?"

"Still on the ship in the harbor. It's only me that's come ashore."

"Is everyone . . . are they all right?"

Ida smiled and chuckled. "All right? I'd say there's none of us that's been better. I was mad enough t'kill the bloke that dragged me there." She paused thoughtfully. "An' I may still if I ever see 'im again. But we 'ave enough t'eat and clothes t'keep us warm. An' there's not a one of us 'avin' t'lay on our backs t'feed ourselves." She looked at Jacinda and reddened. "Beggin' your pardon, milady."

Jacinda suddenly remembered the night she first met Ida and the scornful way she had accepted the news that Jacinda was from the titled gentry. "Why did you choose to come take care of me?"

"I didn't choose, milady. Least not at first. It was the captain that came for me when the fever first came on ye."

"The captain?"

"I'd asked about ye before, and 'e remembered me. 'e's worn 'imself thin, takin' care of the ship and ye too."

Jacinda's heart skipped a beat or two. She felt a trifle flushed and wondered if she were still feverish. "The captain took care of me?"

" 'e's been more'n a little worried, milady. 'e'll be 'appy to see ye doing so well, 'e will."

"Will he be back today?" Jacinda asked, glancing at the fading light falling through the window.

" 'e will."

Jacinda touched her hair. It felt limp and snarled. Her fingers moved to her lips again, feeling the chapped, cracked surface. "Ida . . . I would like to take a bath."

"A bath? I don't know, milady. Spar went back to the ship and I don't . . ."

"A bath, Ida. Surely that's not too much to ask." She straightened on the bed and threw off the light covers. "If you won't see to it, I will."

Ida jumped to her feet and raised her hands to stop Jacinda from rising. "I'll do it, milady. Just don't ye get up until I'm back."

Jacinda sighed and settled back against the pillow. "I promise, Ida. I won't move until you return with the bath water."

A peaceful silence blanketed the town as Tristan walked toward the cottage where

Jacinda and Ida were staying. An occasional voice rose and fell. A dog barked in the distance. Another answered from the other side of the village.

Tristan's pace was hurried. Spar had told him that Jacinda was doing much better, but he tried not to let himself expect too much. Still, there was a new spring in his step, and he whistled a few notes as he walked along. As he neared the small cottage, he could hear voices coming from the kitchen in the lean-to at the back of the house. He recognized Ida's as being one of them and the other as belonging to the old woman who had rented them her spare room. He checked his step only a moment before proceeding into the house through the front door.

He paused at the door to Jacinda's room, muttering a quick wish for her to be awake, then opened the door slowly. No candle flickered, no lamp was lit, but there wasn't any need for either of them. The moonlight streamed through the window, bathing the room in a soft white light. In the middle of the room was a small round tub, and seated in it, with her back toward him, was Jacinda, her wet hair piled high on her head.

"Ida, hand me the towel, please," she said as she rose from the tub.

Tiny drops of water captured the glow of the moon as they traced glittering paths down her delicate skin. Tristan was held mesmerized by the sight of her—her long neck, narrow waist, round hips.

"Ida—" She turned, her arm stretched out to receive the towel, and froze.

His eyes were drawn to her breasts, round and firm, the rosy tips taut from the sudden coolness of the air after the warmth of the bath water. They beckoned to him, begged him to come nearer, to touch, to caress, to kiss. He took a step forward and heard her sudden intake of breath. He raised his gaze. Her tawny eyes seemed to burn with a light of their own. They were wide—with wonder, with surprise, with a myriad of emotions he couldn't begin to understand.

He picked up the towel from the chair and held it out to her. She hesitated. So still. Like a statue, the statue of some Roman goddess standing in the midst of an ancient garden, her cool marble flesh aglow in the moonlight. Not a real woman, but the image of man's ideal woman.

Then she took the towel, and he knew she was real. Her fingers brushed his, the touch seeming to sear his flesh. It was only her eyes that kept him from grabbing her, from crushing her against him, from drinking in her beauty with his lips against hers. Desire pulsed through him, pounding in his brain, throbbing in his loins.

Jacinda hugged the towel to her breasts, not so much hiding her body from him as teasing him with subtle camouflage. She seemed afraid to move, afraid to breathe. Her tongue licked lightly at her dry lips. She swallowed.

"Jacinda," he whispered.

He saw her lips quiver and knew he was losing control.

"Jacinda—"

The towel slipped from her fingers and fell into the tub. For a moment, his gaze was drawn back to her breasts, then lifted to her face once more. As he took the step that brought him to her, she leaned forward. His arms embraced her, revelling in the softness of her skin. With tender ecstasy, he kissed her, his tongue playing lightly with her lips. He controlled the urgency of his desire, savoring the feel of her body close to his, relishing the sweetness of her kisses. His shirt grew damp where her breasts pressed against him.

He released her mouth, raising his head so he could look at her again. She watched him with those same wide, confused eyes. Yet she didn't pull away. He could see her pulse beating in her throat and bent to kiss it.

"Tristan—"

She crumpled in his arms so suddenly she nearly slipped through them as she fainted. He caught her and swept her feet off the floor, carrying her to the bed. He laid her down with care, cradling her head while he drew the pillow under it. As he pulled the blanket over her naked body, he studied her beautiful face. The desire to make love to her ebbed but not the desire to hold her, to shelter her in the tenderness of his love.

He straightened and stepped back from the bed. What he wanted could never be. She was a lady, the daughter of an earl. She was the friend of lords and ladies, dukes and marquesses, perhaps even royalty. She lived in a manor house surrounded by acres of lawn, flowers, and trees. He, on the other hand, was a sailor, the captain of a clipper ship. The *Gabrielle* was his home, and the sea was his life. His friends were the men who scampered like monkeys up the masts, the men who set the sails, who swabbed the decks, the men who sweated in the hot sun of the tropics and froze in the frigid air of the Atlantic, the men who did it all because, like Tristan, they loved the sea. In Jacinda's eyes, he was nothing more than a pirate, a kidnapper and a thief. Could he ask her to share that life, to be a pirate's lady?

No, he couldn't ask it. He reminded himself, as he had so often in the past, that it would be better for them both if she went on hating him. Even if his deceit could be forgiven, even once she knew the truth about him, about Blackstoke and Ella and all the other women captives . . . No, he couldn't ask it. It would be better for her if she returned to England and married a viscount. Although it wouldn't be Viscount Blackstoke. That much he promised himself.

He turned and left the cottage.

Jacinda's eyes fluttered open. She sat up, glancing quickly around the room. She was alone. While she slept, the moon had continued its path across the night sky, and now only a pale blue-white light remained to filter through the window and illuminate her small room in the cottage.

She pressed her fingers against her lips. Had he held her, kissed her, or had it only been another of her dreams? She looked down at her bare breasts. Her skin tingled as she remembered being crushed against the hardness of his body. Or had she just imagined it?

The door opened, and Jacinda turned in expectation, but it was only Ida. She leaned against the cool wall and covered herself with a blanket.

"Sorry I was gone so long, milady," Ida said, setting the lamp she carried on the chair near the door.

"Ida?" Jacinda said softly. "Have you seen Captain Dancing this evening?"

"No, and surprised I am, too. I was sure 'e would come."

"Then I *was* dreaming," she whispered, again bringing her fingers up to touch her lips.

Only she knew it couldn't have been a dream. He *had* been there, he *had* kissed her, held her against him and whispered her name. She'd been frightened and enraptured at the same time. Those feelings still lingered. They were too real. Such things couldn't be dreamed.

But if he'd been there, why did he leave when she fainted? Why didn't he stay with her? Would he steal a kiss and leave? Yes—if she meant nothing to him.

"I pray I *was* dreaming then," she said softly, tears rising in her eyes.

"What's that?" Ida asked. She came over to the bed, peering down at Jacinda. "Are ye feelin' poor again? Maybe I'd best get Spar."

Jacinda reached out quickly and grabbed Ida's wrist before she could move away. "No. No, I don't need Spar." She released Ida and slipped down onto the bed.

"What's troublin' you, then?"

Jacinda turned her face toward the wall. "Have you ever had a dream, Ida? Have you ever dreamed of something so often that it became real to you?"

Ida was silent for a long time, giving the question serious consideration. "No. Don't think I ever 'ave."

"I have."

"Care t'tell me about it, milady?" Ida sat down on the edge of the bed and touched Jacinda's shoulder.

Jacinda turned her head again so she could look up at Ida. The girl looked years wiser than Jacinda felt at the moment. Perhaps it would help to tell someone else. Her gaze fell to her hands, folded in her lap, as she began to speak. "I've had a dream for a long time, Ida. I've been dreaming of this dark knight on a black horse. He was coming for me because he loved me. And I loved him." She envisioned him riding toward her and whispered, "Oh, how very much I loved him." She fell silent.

Ida waited patiently for her to continue.

"He was going to take me away to a place where I would always be happy. He was good and handsome and kind, and he would never hurt me or displease me. For a long time, he'd never quite reach me, but I kept waiting for him. I knew some day he would make it." She raised tawny eyes to meet Ida's gaze. "And then I saw Tristan, and it was him. He was my knight. I thought . . . I thought—" She shook her head, swallowing tears. "But he wasn't the same. He's lied to me. He's not good and kind," she finished bitterly.

Ida laid a hand over Jacinda's clenched fist. "But you love 'im anyway."

"No!" Jacinda exclaimed. "No, I don't love him. He's nothing like the man I've always dreamed I would love."

"Of course not," Ida said, sounding firm. "That's 'cause 'e's a real man, and it's a lot more fun lovin' a real man than somebody you've dreamed up."

"How can you stand up for him? Look at what he's done to you."

" 'e's not done ill t'me, milady."

Jacinda clamped her lips tight and turned her back toward Ida once again.

"We come from different worlds, ye and me," Ida said softly as she rose from the bed, "but we're both women. We both want t'be loved by a man we can love in return. Seems t'me ye need t'quit dreamin' and start lovin' before ye lose your chance. No real man's perfect, milady. Only in dreams is they perfect . . . and then they're naught but air."

Jacinda didn't reply. She heard Ida move across the room toward the other narrow bed. Then the lamp was turned down, and the room returned to darkness.

She lay still, a soft breeze entering through the window to brush her skin. Ida's words played over and over again in her head as she passed through a sleepless, dreamless night.

13

"I don't have time for excuses, boy," Tristan growled at Tommy. "If you can't get your work done, at least stay out of the way."

"Easy, Tris. It wasn't the boy's fault."

Tristan threw a heated glare in Spar's direction before storming out of the galley. He marched toward the helm, glowering at anyone who dared meet his angry gaze. He stepped up behind the wheel and grasped it tightly with both hands, watching as his knuckles turned white while he concentrated on calming himself.

Finally, he raised his eyes toward the sleepy village. The fishermen had all returned from the sea with their catch. The farmers had finished tilling the soil. The women had fed their families, and evening was spreading its gray cloak overhead, signalling the end of the day. All was at rest.

All except Tristan. He began pacing from starboard to port and back again.

By thunder, we'll sail tomorrow or heads

will roll, he thought. She's not going to keep us here any longer. She's well enough.

"She's well enough," he repeated, aloud this time.

He smacked the palm of his hand against the rail. If she was well enough to take a cart ride around the island, she was well enough to travel, and that's just what they were going to do. He'd listened to Spar for too long. He had to get to Constantinople. He had to find Ella. He'd wasted too much time on Jacinda Sunderland already. He wasn't going to waste any more.

"Tommy!" he bellowed.

The young fo'c'sle boy came scurrying into view, his expression anxious.

"Tell Spar I want Lady Jacinda and Ida on board this ship tonight. We sail in the morning."

"Aye, Captain."

As soon as Tommy had disappeared into the galley, Tristan left the helm and went to his own cabin. He stopped just inside the door. With Jacinda returning to the ship, he would have to move into the next room again.

"I should put her in steerage with the others," he muttered as he went to the table and pulled out a chair to sit on.

Why not put her with the others? It's where she'd said she wanted to be. The women didn't know anything more about their trip than Jacinda did, and once they reached Constantinople, Jacinda could be brought back to him before the others were taken off the ship. She wouldn't learn anything from them which she might let slip to Blackstoke, accidentally warning him before Tristan could see a noose slipped around his vile neck.

The door to his cabin flew open with a crash. "What the devil's the matter with you, Dancing?" Spar's large frame filled the doorway. "Barking at Tommy. Now ordering the lady back on board. I've told you she's not ready yet."

"She's ready. I heard about her little jaunt today. Running around the island in that little cart. Probably flirting with all the natives."

Spar stepped quickly to the table. He was as angry as Tristan, and his hazel eyes flashed as he glared down at him. "You know what your problem is, Tris? You want that lady. I daresay you're in love with her but you haven't the gumption to do anything about it. Well, you needn't make the rest of us suffer for it. These men are all risking their necks to help you and your sister, just because they're your friends." He poked a finger into Tristan's chest. "Now give that some thought." Without waiting for a reply, he spun around and left the room, slamming the door closed behind him.

The sudden silence was deafening.

Tristan dropped his head into his hands, his elbows resting on the table. Perhaps Spar was right. Perhaps he'd better think a few things through.

Jacinda dressed quickly that morning in a simple white blouse and long, colorful skirt, a gift from one of the village women. She tied her curly hair back at her nape, then covered it with a white scarf. Moving softly so as not to awaken Ida, she opened the door and slipped out of the room.

It was still early. Daylight was just beginning to caress the peaks of the Paul de Serra mountains that rose to the north of the island village. A balmy breeze blew off the ocean. A rooster crowed in the distance, breaking the silence that had greeted her. Suddenly, the sun crested the watery horizon, spilling its yellow light through the narrow village streets.

"Pretty, isn't it?"

Jacinda gasped and whirled around. Tristan was seated on a bench, leaning back against the whitewashed wall of the house.

"What are you doing here?"

"Waiting for you." He straightened as he offered her a tentative smile. "I thought you might like to go for another ride today."

"In the cart?"

Tristan shook his head. "If you're up to it, I can get us some horses to ride."

Hesitantly, she returned his smile. "I . . . think I'd like that," she replied.

He pushed himself up from the bench. They stood, looking at each other, while the village awakened around them. Finally, his grin broadened. "I'll get the horses. Wait here."

She watched him hurry off down the winding street until he disappeared from view. Then she sat down on the bench he had occupied only moments before. She felt a little weak but wasn't sure if it was because of her recent illness or because of Tristan or, perhaps, because of both.

For three days she had waited to see him, but he hadn't come. Sometimes she still wondered if she could have dreamed his appearance while she was bathing. The longer he stayed away, the more she'd thought it was all part of her vivid imagination. Still, she had longed to see him, hoping that Ida had told her the truth, praying that Tristan did care for her. The past three days had also given her plenty of time to take Ida's advice to heart. She wasn't going to long for her dream lover any longer. She was going to find out what it really meant to love a man, and now was the time to do it. She wasn't in England any more. Her parents weren't there to tell her she must marry a man she feared and despised. She was free at last to discover for herself about living and loving. She was ready to take some risks.

She heard the clip-clop of hooves and looked up as Tristan rounded the bend in the street, leading two saddle horses behind him. They weren't much to look at, not much more than ponies really. She got to her feet. A smile lifted the corners of her mouth in greeting.

"The old man didn't have a sidesaddle. Do you mind riding astride?"

Jacinda shook her head. "I don't mind at all."

Tristan held her hand and led her toward the shaggy roan gelding. Cupping his hands, he offered her a boost, lifting her with ease onto the saddle. She straightened her skirts as best she could, but there was no hiding her trim ankles from view. She caught Tristan watching her intently and flushed in embarrassment. He turned away and mounted his own little horse, then led the way in silence out of town.

They followed a dusty road through the sugarcane fields, the orchards and the vine-yards, winding their way across the island until

the road stopped abruptly. A cove lay below
them, the green-blue water calm. A short
stretch of white beach was just visible beyond
an outcropping of rocks.

"Shall we?" Tristan asked, glancing her
way.

Jacinda nodded.

He lifted her down from her trusty steed;
then, keeping her hand in his, he led her down
the rocky hillside to the sandy shore. Jacinda
found her eyes fastened to the back of his loose-
fitting linen shirt. The breeze blew the fabric
against his broad shoulders, molding it to his
muscled arms. She longed to reach out and
touch his back, to feel the strength of him.
Shocked by the train of her thoughts, her eyes
fell away, coming to a halt on his hard sculpted
thighs beneath the tight black breeches. She
stumbled over a rock.

"Oh!"

Tristan turned to break her fall, his arms
locking around her. Her heart was pounding in
her head.

"Oh." The word was little more than a sigh
as it slipped between parted lips.

Ebony eyes locked with hers. Staring into
their dark depths, a kaleidoscope of memories
flashed in her head—Tristan at Locksworth
House the day she first saw him; Tristan by the
forest pool, his eyes warm and caring; Tristan
in his pirate's costume, waltzing with her at
Bonclere; Tristan holding her in the moonlight,
kissing her lips, caressing her bare back.

She knew he must be able to read her
feelings in her eyes. She saw him swallow as he
stepped resolutely back from her. His square

jaw stiffened. "Be careful," he warned as he turned to lead them the rest of the way down the hillside.

Jacinda blinked back the sudden sting of tears.

When he stopped on the beach and turned toward her again, he was wearing a tender smile. "Do you mind sitting in the sand?" he asked, the warmth of his voice shedding a ray of sunshine into her heart.

She shook her head, speechless.

They sat beside one another, both of them staring in silence at the peaceful waters of the cove. Jacinda fought the urge to look at him again, afraid to reveal any more of her private feelings than she had already, afraid that he would turn away from her once again. Following Ida's advice was not without risk.

"I'm sorry I've brought you here." Tristan's voice was low but clear.

"No," she answered quickly. "No, it's beautiful. I'm glad we came." Her heart was thundering in her ears again.

"I didn't mean here, to this beach. I meant here, away from England. I'm sorry about Mary and . . . and about everything. I never meant to involve you like this. I never meant for you to get hurt."

Now she turned to look at him. His handsome face was truly troubled. His eyes remained locked on some invisible point in the distance. Her hand rose to touch his cheek, but she drew it back, clutching it with her other hand. "Never meant to involve me in what?" she asked softly. "What is it you're doing here? Why have you taken these women?"

175

"I can't tell you, Jacinda." His gaze shifted to meet hers. "I can only ask you to trust me. Will you trust me?"

Trust him? Why should she trust him? What had he ever done to make her trust him?

"Yes," she whispered. "I'll trust you, Tristan."

His hand—his calloused, wind-chapped hand—stretched out to cup her cheek. "Lord, you are beautiful." He spoke softly, almost reverently.

She was aware of the gentle lapping of water against the shore. The morning sun was warm against her skin. The twitter of birds drifted down from the trees on the ridge above them. Above all else, she was aware of his fingers as they traced a path down from her cheek, caressing her throat, stroking her arm. She shivered, but not from the cold. When his hand cradled her breast through her thin white blouse, she drew in a sharp breath but didn't pull away, couldn't pull away. Hot blood coursed through her, setting her body afire. She continued to stare into the black depths of his eyes and felt as if she were drowning in them. Her lips parted slightly, and she moistened them with the tip of her tongue.

Slowly, ever so slowly, he leaned toward her. His mouth grazed hers with agonizing tenderness. She closed her eyes and waited breathlessly. Waited without knowing what she waited for. A deep yearning cried out from somewhere deep inside her, begging to be quenched. Teardrops slipped from beneath dark lashes and rolled slowly over ivory cheeks.

Tristan pulled back from her. She knew he

was looking at her, watching her with that searching gaze of his, but she didn't open her eyes, couldn't bear to open them. She could only wait . . .

She felt his breath on her cheek, then she felt his lips kissing away the tearstains, moving from side to side. For a moment, she could do nothing. She could scarcely breathe as a myriad of strange and new emotions flooded through her. Then she leaned forward, her hands creeping up to curl around his neck.

Tristan's arms wrapped possessively around her, crushing her taut breasts against the broad plain of his chest. His mouth returned hungrily to hers, drinking deeply of the sweet taste of her kisses. A primal groan sounded in her throat as her fingers twisted through his shaggy black mane.

He lowered her gently to the sand. His kisses moved down her throat. His mouth pressed hard against the throbbing vein in her neck, then moved on to the gentle swell of breasts above the flimsy blouse.

"Tristan," she said, her voice sounding hoarse in her own ears.

He paused.

"Tristan?" she whispered again, desire and uncertainty warring in her chest.

"Trust me, Cinda," he said, ever so softly.

She looked into his stormy black eyes, bright with passion, and knew she could do nothing else but trust him, for her heart wouldn't do otherwise. "Yes," she answered into the breathless hush.

His kiss, though still tender, held a new fire, a new demand. She sensed it without understanding and responded to it. She tried to pull him closer, seeking to satisfy the yearning that burned in her veins.

Tristan's hands moved skillfully over her body, titillating, enticing, thrilling, frustrating. She was scarcely aware of the moment he drew her up from the beach and led her to the grassy shade that bordered the rocky hillside. Deftly he removed his shirt, spreading it on the ground beneath her. Then, with tender care, he undressed her. She resisted the urge to hide herself from the caress of his gaze as he lowered her to the ground.

Her eyes were fixed on his face. She was half-afraid to let her gaze wander as he shed the rest of his clothes. Then he was beside her on the ground. His mouth resumed its path of discovery. She closed her eyes, a moan sounding in her throat as his lips brushed first one breast and then the other.

As he rose above her, his kisses returned to tease her lips. He whispered her name, then lifted his head and stared down at her in silent question. Did she trust him?

"Yes," she answered aloud, feeling as if she would soon explode with wanting him.

They came together in a sudden fury. Jacinda's cry of mingled pain, surprise, and joy was muffled against his throat as she clung to him, thinking briefly that they would always be a part of each other from this moment on.

And then she abandoned all thought, succumbing to the heights of ecstasy to which his touch was taking her.

The sun warmed the sand around them.

Jacinda wanted to purr like a contented cat. She opened her eyes. She lay curled up beside him, nestled in the crook of his arm. He still slept, and she watched the even rise and fall of his bare chest, intrigued by the dark matt of short black curls. Her gaze moved tentatively lower, stopping when she spied the ugly white scar that ran from just below his last rib around to his back. Without thinking, she reached out to touch it.

"Happened on my last trip to China," he said. "I had a difference of opinion with a drunken sailor."

"You might have died." It frightened her to think of it. "I might never have met you." That was even worse.

With a quick sweep, he pulled her over to lie across his broad chest. He growled with pleasure. She drank in the gleam in his eyes, feeling warmed to her very soul. The cold fear that had invaded her with the dark thought of his death vanished.

She laughed, a throaty, seductive sound, though she was unaware of it. "You seem to have recovered completely from your wound, good sir."

"Completely, lady fair."

His hand behind her head, he drew her mouth down to his. His tongue played lightly with her lips for a moment. She returned the kiss in kind, enjoying the tingling sensations that surged through her. Suddenly, he rolled to his side.

"We'd better get back to the village. Ida will have a search party out for the two of us." His eyes perused her lovely nakedness. "And I think you might feel a little embarrassed to be discovered by my men in your present state of undress."

She felt the blush spreading up to warm her cheeks, but it wasn't from the thought of discovery. It was from the flush of desire—a totally new and wonderful feeling—which his gaze had renewed.

Tristan stood and held out his hand to bring her to her feet. "Come," he commanded.

He led her across the white sand and into the water. Slowly he washed her silky skin.

"You are so beautiful, Jacinda," he said in a husky voice.

She couldn't answer. Her reply seemed caught in her throat. She prayed he could read her feelings, her love and devotion, in her eyes. She hoped he could see that she thought him beautiful too.

He dipped quickly into the salty water, washing himself, then once again took her hand, this time leading her back to their discarded clothing. Without comment, Tristan kicked aside his shirt, now stained by her virgin blood.

Heat rushed into Jacinda's face, and she dropped her eyes. Suddenly shy and embarrassed, she wanted desperately to be covered again. While he donned his breeches, she hastily pulled on her skirt and blouse, tugging at the low neckline that seemed to reveal too much cleavage.

Tristan reached out to stay her hand. "Don't. You look wonderful." His hand moved to her hair. He brushed it lightly with his fingertips. "Sand," he whispered.

That crazy pounding had started up in her

head again. Her knees trembled. Things were happening so fast. She was no longer a girl. She was a woman. She loved this man. She belonged to him. In the shade of these cliffs, with the lapping of the sea in her ears, she had given herself to him. Her life would never be the same again, and she discovered she was afraid.

"Come on," he said, his words rumbling up from deep in his chest. "We have to get back to the ship. We sail in the morning." He took her hand to lead her up the hill.

Jacinda balked, and he turned back to look at her. "Where, Tris?" she asked, her voice quivering. "Where is it we're going?"

"Constantinople."

"Constantinople," she echoed.

He stepped back toward her, sensing her uncertainty, her fears. He lifted her chin, forcing her to meet his steady gaze. Once more he asked it of her. "Trust me, Jacinda. A little longer."

Jacinda sighed and leaned her head against his chest. Yes, she would trust him. Even if he took her to hell and back, even if that's what loving him took, she would trust him.

14

The Duke of Locksworth stared solemnly at the lawn outside the window of the east room. The day was darkened by heavily burdened rain clouds, and the trees and bushes drooped with the chill of late autumn. The scene suited his mood.

If only he knew for certain about Jacinda. He had written a brief missive to Tristan's contact in Constantinople, but it would be weeks before he would hear back from this Danny O'Banyon fellow, if he received any answer at all. In the meantime, he could only hope that she had left with Tristan on the *Dancing Gabrielle*.

He turned away from the window and went to stand before the portrait of his wife Ellen, himself, and their daughter.

"What is it about these ship's captains, Felicia?" he asked the image of the beautiful blonde. "First I lose you to George Dancing, and now I'm losing Jacinda to his son."

There was no mistaking how Jacinda felt

for Tristan. Locksworth was certain she had followed him to the docks that fateful day. Now if he could only be positive she had left with Tristan. If it weren't for the discovery of Jake's beaten body, the duke would have felt some certainty that she was safe with his grandson. As it was, he could only hope.

He sank into a chair and continued to stare at the family portrait. "I'm getting old, Ellen. Too old. I've lost too many loved ones. I won't be able to bear it if anything happens to either one of them." He closed his eyes. "Dear God," he whispered, "keep them safe."

Lord Sunderland arrived, shivering from the cold dampness, in answer to Blackstoke's summons. Smithens showed him into the library where Blackstoke awaited him.

"Is there word of my daughter?" he asked as he entered the room.

Blackstoke made no reply. With a wave of his hand, he motioned for Lord Sunderland to be seated near the fire.

"What have you learned, Blackstoke?" the earl demanded.

"I called you here to ask the same thing," he replied, his tone more chilling than the weather. "What have *you* heard from her?"

Lord Sunderland sputtered. "Heard? Why, I've heard nothing? Good heavens, man. She's missing. How would I hear from her?"

Blackstoke rose from behind his desk. His mustache twisted as a nerve jumped at the corner of his mouth. His steely blue eyes bore into Lord Sunderland with merciless regard. "I'm not so sure she's missing, Sunderland. Yes, the body of that servant of yours was found, but he could have been in London for any reason. He needn't even have been driving her that day. And there's been no sign of her carriage, of Jacinda, or of that maid of hers."

"Is that meant to give me comfort?" her father protested.

"On the contrary, my dear sir. It's meant only to warn you." Blackstoke sat down in a chair near the fire and repeated the motion for the earl to do likewise. His countenance darkened as he bit back his anger.

"Warn me?" Lord Sunderland echoed, his face blotching. He sat down. "Whatever are you talking about?"

"I'm telling you that you have taken money from me. A very ample sum, might I remind you. For that sum, I was to marry your daughter, a daughter who is now missing without a trace." He leaned forward. "Sunderland, I warn you. Your daughter had better return in time for our wedding, or I'll see you in ruins."

Lord Sunderland was sweating. He patted his forehead with a handkerchief. "See here, Blackstoke. My daughter may be lying dead this very minute, and you're threatening me. I'll return your filthy pounds, if that's what you want."

"Will you now? And once that's done, which I am all too certain you would be unable to do even if you were so inclined, is that when Jacinda would miraculously reappear, saved from the jaws of some terrible fate? No, I will give you until our wedding day to produce her, Sunderland. It's not the money I want. It's her."

Blackstoke got to his feet and started for the door. "Two weeks, Sunderland," he added without turning around.

"I say, sir. You're being unreasonable. I don't—"

Blackstoke whirled and stopped him with a frigid glare. "I don't want excuses. Just tell Jacinda that she has no choice in this matter and make her behave like an obedient daughter should. Good day, Sunderland." With that, he left the room.

Jacinda stepped on board the *Dancing Gabrielle* and immediately felt the eyes of everyone on deck fastened on her. She glanced nervously at Tristan. Could they all see the changes in her? Did they know what had happened on that beach yesterday?

"I was wrong, Tris."

Jacinda turned toward Spar's voice.

The giant grinned at her. "I told the captain you weren't well enough to leave the island yet. Seems I was wrong. I've never seen anyone who looked so well. Welcome back, my lady."

An attractive blush colored her cheeks. *He knows*, she thought. "Thank you, Spar. If I'm well, it's because you took such good care of me."

"Anyone could have done what I did," he answered.

Tristan's hand touched the small of her back. "Well or not, I think I'll see Jacinda to her cabin before we sail." He steered her aft. "I wouldn't want you doing anything to tire yourself," he whispered in her ear.

Her blush deepened as she remembered his

ardent lovemaking the previous morning and her own response. And he didn't want to tire her?

Tristan led her down the companionway toward his cabin. He paused and opened the door, moving back so she could enter first. Her eyes swept the sparsely furnished but comfortable cabin before she stepped inside. Jacinda was awash with strange feelings. The memories she retained of this room were not pleasant ones. She had started this voyage with this room as her prison cell. From here she had led Mary to her death. She shivered.

"Cinda?"

"I'm all right," she responded, moving into the center of the captain's cabin. Her fingers traced the surface of the table, then brushed the back of the chair while her gaze slipped to the bed.

"I'll move my things into the next cabin," Tristan said softly from behind her.

"No, Tris." She turned around. "Please don't."

His dark eyes scrutinized her face. "Are you sure? No one need know what happened yester—"

"I . . . I'm not ashamed of what happened," Jacinda said firmly. She tilted her chin in a defiant gesture. "And I won't hide it from anyone."

Tristan's smile was tender as he gathered her close against him. "Lady Jacinda—" he began.

"Just Jacinda," she interrupted. "I have no title aboard this ship." Her heart was thumping loudly in her breast. "I'm just a woman." Her heart in her eyes, she added in a near whisper, "Your woman, Captain Dancing."

His mouth covered hers, arresting anything further she might have said. She melted against him, helpless to resist. His arms tightened around her. When he released her lips, she gasped for air and opened her eyes.

His voice was ragged with checked desire. "Jacinda—"

A throat cleared in the passageway outside the cabin. "Excuse me, Captain."

Tristan released her, and she felt bereft even though he only moved inches away.

"We're ready to sail, Tris," Whip said from the corridor.

Jacinda could see the first mate fighting to keep his features in check, politely ignoring the heated scene he had interrupted.

"I'm coming," Tristan told him before turning back toward Jacinda. "You rest. I'll be back soon."

Loralie watched the captain and his red-haired wench come on board. She was hidden in the shadows of the galley. The crew had been more lenient while they were anchored in Madeira, allowing the women more freedom on the ship. Loralie had learned that if she was careful and sat quietly out of the way, she could stay on deck for long periods of time without even being noticed. She had even done some exploring in the cabins, including the captain's, when he had gone ashore.

Her gray eyes followed Jacinda as Tristan led her below, his touch both loving and possessive. *A lady? Bah!* Loralie recognized the signs. They were lovers. Jacinda was no better than her. It should have been Loralie lying in the comfort of the captain's bed, not that pampered, hothouse flower. She clenched her hands in the folds of her skirt, feeling the angry knot twisting in her belly. It was always that way. Women like *Lady* Jacinda took everything away from the Loralies of the world, just because they were born into the moneyed and titled class. How she hated them!

Loralie closed her eyes, suddenly surrounded by memories from her past. She was fourteen again and working in Lord Mosley's house in London. She had grown up in the kitchens, but her eyes always watched the way the lord and lady lived, and a hunger for a better life possessed her. She worked hard on her speech, erasing the accent of the poor, working class as she mimicked the Mosleys and their frequent guests. She studied how the ladies walked and how they dressed their hair. Loralie was beautiful and she knew it, and as she began to blossom into a woman, she made certain Lord Mosley knew it too.

She might have been satisfied just to be his lover; after all, she wasn't the first maid he'd deflowered nor would she probably be the last. But Loralie was too smart for that. Through careful manipulation—teasing, taunting, sometimes even threatening—she became more important in his eyes. Soon she was moved to a town house of her own. She had jewels and fine clothes and even her own maid. By the time she was eighteen she almost believed the lies she told others, that she'd been born to the gentry.

And then, without warning, Lord Mosley

turned her out, taking back the jewels, the clothes, everything. Perhaps, if it had been because Lady Mosley had found them out, Loralie could have dealt better with the betrayal, but it wasn't because of his wife, she was to learn later. He had taken another lover, a lover from his own class, the youngest daughter of an earl. Loralie, Lord Mosley informed her, was just a whore, but he was in love with the Lady Beth, a young woman of refinement and class, something Loralie would never have.

Some day, she had sworn, it would be she who replaced a lady in a gentleman's heart. She, Loralie, would prove she was just as good. No, she would prove she was better.

The memories scalded her, leaving a bad taste in her mouth. She opened her eyes as she got to her feet.

Perhaps here was her chance, she thought. She had heard it whispered that this Jacinda was also the daughter of an earl. Perhaps her time had come at last to have revenge. A smile touched her generous mouth. Of course, it wouldn't be a hardship to share the captain's bed, either. He was a very handsome man.

Still smiling, she slipped unnoticed below deck.

Tristan stood at the helm, his sharp eyes watching the active seamen. Sails were hoisted by means of block and gantline until the bunt was well above the yard. On the yardarms, seamen spread the sail and tied the head to the jackstay, then unfurled the canvas sheets. The sails snapped smartly as the gust of wind caught them, then curled in fine white arcs against the blue sky. Tackle creaked overhead and rigging hummed. Waves boiled before the bow, sending a salty spray across the decks of the *Dancing Gabrielle* and into Tristan's face.

He breathed deeply, enjoying the feel of wind and sea on his skin as they left the Madeira Islands behind. The *Gabrielle* clipped through the rising waves with a steady, comforting rhythm. Tristan smiled.

"Do you know what you're doin', Captain?" Whip had slipped up beside Tristan in his usual quiet manner.

"What?"

"With the lady. You're takin' quite a risk."

Tristan grinned. "No risk, Whip. She doesn't know it yet, but I'm going to ask her to marry me when we get back to England. When this is all over and I have the right to ask her, I will."

The short blond man at his side shook his head. "Aren't you forgetting that she's engaged to the man who took Gabrielle?" He placed a hand on Tristan's arm. "Don't forget why we've come on this mission."

The grin vanished, a dark scowl replacing it. "I haven't forgotten. But that has nothing to do with Jacinda. She doesn't love Blackstoke. She loves me."

The first mate observed Tristan for a long moment, then turned to walk away.

"Whip."

He stopped and looked around.

"It isn't her fault about Ella."

Whip nodded grimly. "I suppose you're right, Tris. Sorry I put my nose where it don't belong."

* * *

Jacinda opened the cabin window and stared out at the rolling green surface. It looked very gentle this morning, not at all like the angry sea that had nearly swamped the ship her second night on board. The wind was light, blowing in a fresh scent to caress her cheeks. She leaned her chin on her arms and closed her eyes.

He loved her. He hadn't told her so, but she knew it was true. Could this really be happening to her? To her, docile Lady Jacinda, dreamer extraordinaire? She tried to imagine herself telling her mother that she was in love with Tristan Dancing, a mere ship's captain, an American no less. Lady Sunderland would forbid it, would demand that she marry Roger Fanshawe as promised.

"But I won't," she whispered. "I won't be made to marry that man."

A rap sounded at the door. Her heart quickened, hoping it was Tristan.

"Yes."

The latch raised and the door opened. Spar leaned over to pass through the opening. "I came to check on you."

"Check on me?" she echoed, wondering where he thought she might go. "As you can see, I'm still here."

He laughed. "No, I meant your health."

"I feel wonderful."

Spar pulled out a chair from the table and drew it close to the bed where she was seated. He studied her face, then felt her pulse.

"You *are* a doctor, aren't you?" Jacinda asked suddenly. "Ida said you were."

"I was. I gave it up to come to sea. I'm the cook on the *Gabrielle*. Most ship's cooks are known as Slushy, but I was too big for that nickname, so they dubbed me Spar. I guess they figured if a mast snapped they could use me in its place."

"But the cook?" Jacinda couldn't believe it.

"Yes, and a good one too," he said with mock huffiness.

"But why, Spar? Why would you want to give up something so important as being a doctor? Look what you've done for me."

Gruffly, he replied, "You made yourself well because you wanted to live."

"No, Spar." Jacinda knew there was more to her recovery than that. "You offered friendship when I first came on board. Then you saved my life. Now won't you let me be *your* friend? Won't you tell me what happened to bring you to this ship?"

The sailor rubbed a hand over his shiny head, then met her questioning gaze with clouded hazel eyes. "I had a fine practice in a small town in Pennsylvania. Gentle people. Farmers mostly. All of them friends. I was married to a wonderful woman. Kind and sweet and delicate. And tiny. Just a wisp of air next to me. But she loved me."

"I'm sure she did."

"Mary Rose was so pleased when she told me she was going to have a baby." His eyes fell to stare at his burly hands. "Those months were so happy while we waited. But something went wrong. The baby was turned and too big for her. I tried everything I knew how to do but—" His voice dropped to an agonized whisper. "But I

193

couldn't save her . . . or the baby."

"Oh, Spar. I'm so sorry." She laid a hand on his shoulder.

The big man straightened in his chair. "There wasn't much point in being a doctor if I couldn't keep my own wife and child alive. So I signed on with Tristan and he made me a cook. If the men get sick, I help when I can, but I'm not a doctor anymore."

"Thank you for telling me." Jacinda blinked away a tear, then asked, "How long will it take us to reach Constantinople?"

Spar was surprised. "He told you?"

"Yes."

"Two or three weeks."

"And how long will we stay?"

"As long as it takes for Tris to find Ella."

"Ella?" She spoke softly, feeling suddenly empty and afraid. "Who is Ella?"

Spar's expression was one of discomfort. "I thought you said Tris told you."

"He told me we were going to Constantinople. Nothing more." She leaned forward, pleading with her eyes. "*Who* is Ella?"

Spar shook his head. "I'm sorry, Jacinda. I cannot tell you if Tris has chosen not to. I'd be betraying his confidence. I've already said too much."

"He must love her very much if he would travel half way round the world and kidnap a shipload of women just to find her."

"Yes. He loves her very much." Spar placed a hand on her shoulder. "But it's not what you're thinking, my lady. Tris will tell you when the time is right. You'll have to trust him until then."

Trust him. Trust him. It's what Tristan had

said too.

If he *was* in love with this Ella, where did that leave Jacinda? Yet, if she loved him as her heart said she did, wouldn't she trust him no matter what? Perhaps this Ella *was* a woman from his past, but Jacinda was the woman of his present, of his future. She wouldn't give him up. She wouldn't step aside. But she *would* trust him. She would do anything she had to do to prove her love.

Spar stood suddenly. "I don't think you need any more rest," he said, changing the subject. "I'd recommend a stroll up on deck, my lady." He offered his arm, and Jacinda took it.

They walked through the narrow corridor and up the companionway. Jacinda paused to take in the breathless view as soon as her feet touched the main deck. For the first time she was able to take in the magnificent view of the ship in full sail. She had thought the stark masts with their complex maze of rigging beautiful when she had first visited Tristan's ship in the harbor in London. Now, with every piece of canvas spread to catch the wind, the view was spectacular. She could understand what made a man choose the sea, if only for this single moment.

"Hello!"

She turned toward Tristan's voice. He was standing on the poop, his hands on the wheel, his feet straddled in a mariner's stance. The wind was tugging at his long black hair, and his shirt was molded against his chest. A second wave of appreciation washed over her. He was even more breathtaking than the ship.

"Bring her up, Spar."

Spar's hand beneath her elbow, Jacinda

climbed the steep steps leading up to the poop deck. Her eyes never left Tristan as she moved toward the back of the ship. She thought she'd never get enough of the sight of him, feet splayed to accommodate the roll of the ship, his bronzed hands gripping the giant wheel, his black eyes catching the water's reflection of the sun.

Tristan's arm went around the back of her waist, and he drew her close to his side, though his gaze was still locked on the horizon. Jacinda found it difficult to pull her eyes away from his bronzed features. Spar wasn't even missed when he returned to his galley.

"We've a good wind. We should reach the strait in three days if she holds."

"Will we stop in Gibraltar?"

Tristan shook his head, still not looking at her. "It's too dangerous with—" He stopped abruptly.

"With the women on board," she finished for him.

He nodded.

Without forethought, she began, "What are you—" She stopped, biting back the question. When he turned his head to look at her, she reached over and placed her fingers over his lips. "I don't want to know what you're going to do with the women. I don't want to know why we're going to Constantinople. I just want *you* to know that I love you. I trust you, Tristan Dancing. That's all either of us needs to know."

She leaned her head against his shoulder and watched as the bow of the *Gabrielle* cut through the ocean waves, speeding them toward the Mediterranean.

15

The wind was calm. The Mediterranean Sea was like a mirror, reflecting the image of the *Dancing Gabrielle* without flaw or crease. Frustrated, Tristan could do nothing but wait for the wind to rise.

The women passengers were up on deck for the first of their twice-a-day strolls. Some of them flirted with idle seamen; others leaned against the rail and stared across the glassy water. Tristan chuckled when he spied Spar on the forecastle deck, listening to Ida's chatter. Even from this distant viewpoint, he could read the adoration in her stance, but it seemed his oversized friend was blind to it.

He turned away, leaning his forearms on the starboard rail at the stern. Below him, in his cabin, Jacinda was sewing one of his shirts. She had insisted she was going to do it that morning, and so he had left her there, needle in hand. He smiled to himself, savoring the memory of her seated on the bed in that flowing silk nightgown he had given her. He had found it in one of the chests of clothing they had taken on board with the women. The pale yellow fabric barely concealed the rosy tips of her breasts, but her flame-red curls tumbled freely over her shoulders, camouflaging her cleavage, as if to make up for the gown's inadequacies. It had been all he could do to make himself leave the privacy of their cabin.

"Pleasant thoughts, Captain?"

He turned his head to the side to find one of the women standing not far down the rail. He remembered those sultry gray eyes from their previous meeting. She walked toward him, each movement deliberately sensuous. She shook her heavy chestnut hair as if to throw it back from her face, yet it remained unchanged, tiny curls hugging her forehead.

"Pleasant enough," he replied, still smiling.

"I've hoped we'd have a chance to meet again."

"Have you now?" He cocked an eyebrow.

She ran a fingertip in a lazy sweep across her collar bone, drawing his eyes with it. She took a deep sigh, her generous breasts straining the muslin blouse. "I'd hoped we might get to know each other better."

He drew his eyes back to meet hers. "Unfortunately, a captain has little time to socialize."

"What a pity." She pouted, laying her hand on his chest.

"If you'll excuse me now, miss . . ."

Her voice was low and throaty. "The name is Loralie, Captain. I hope you won't forget it."

He nodded his head, then moved to step around her just in time to see Jacinda pause at the edge of the poop deck. Her eyes darted from Loralie's hand to Tristan's face; they widened in an unspoken question. Loralie followed his gaze, turning around to face Jacinda. Once again she shook her shaggy mane of dark brown hair, this time in a symbolic challenge. As innocent as she could be at times, Jacinda understood the action. Her gold eyes sparked as she walked toward them. Tristan put another pace between himself and Loralie as Jacinda neared, stopping just out of arm's reach.

"I finished mending your shirt," she said to him, her eyes still fixed on the intruder.

Loralie looked at her blandly. "Oh, do you do the captain's laundry?" Her gray gaze shifted to Tristan. "How nice that you can have a maid on board."

"I am not his maid." Jacinda's voice was cool, but it wavered slightly. She stepped to Tristan's side, placing an arm around his waist.

"How nice for you both," Loralie replied, unrattled. "Good day, Captain." Her look promised much as she perused his chiseled face before her gaze slid idly over his chest. A smile curved her full mouth as she turned and walked away, unhurried.

"Who is she?" Jacinda asked softly, turning her head to look up at him.

"Just one of the passengers." He could tell she would like to ask more. The courage that had fired her eyes when she had faced Loralie was doused by uncertainty. He brushed his lips against the tip of her nose. "She is no one, Jacinda my love." His arms tightened around her waist. "Why don't we go back to our cabin? You could show me what a good seamstress you are."

She nodded, a tentative smile lighting her face. "Yes. Let's go back to our cabin."

The door burst open without warning.

"Sir!" Tommy cried. "There's a ship approaching and she's flying no colors. Whip says you're to come up, sir."

The boy was gone before Jacinda was clear awake.

Tristan scrambled from the bed and pulled on his breeches. "Stay here," he ordered as he rushed out of the cabin.

It took her a moment longer to realize the ship was moving again. She glanced out the window above the bed. The clear blue canopy that had greeted them that morning had disappeared behind dark, broiling clouds, and a strong wind had risen to catch the canvas sails.

Jacinda slipped out of bed, picking up her clothes that were strewn across the room, clothes that had been discarded in haste an hour or more ago. She dressed quickly in the peasant costume she had acquired in Madeira. She gripped the side of the bed as the ship swung suddenly to port, nearly toppling her to the floor. She could hear men shouting and feet pounding across the decks.

What was happening? She started toward the door but stopped herself as her hand touched the latch. Wasn't that why Mary wasn't here now? Because Jacinda hadn't listened to him when he told them to stay in the cabin? She backed away from the door, moving carefully until her legs touched the side of the bed. She sat quickly, her eyes locked on the cabin door, and waited.

The glass to his eye, Tristan watched the frigate approaching with growing apprehension. "She's got several rows of gunports, Whip. I think we can assume she's unfriendly. She'll be within firing range soon."

"We can't outfight her," the first mate replied.

"Then we'll have to outrun her. Full sail, Whip. Fly everything but my nightshirt." He paused, then threw the man a grim smile. "And you can have that too if it'll help."

"Aye, Captain." Whip shouted orders, and the waiting seamen scrambled to obey.

As more sails unfurled, the *Gabrielle* jumped forward, but not before the other ship opened their ports on their starboard side.

"There's men at the guns, sir!" came a startled warning.

Tongues of orange fire spewed from the side of their assailant. Billows of white smoke rose in the air. Within seconds, spouts of water erupted at the *Gabrielle*'s side as the shots riddled the ocean. The clipper ship pitched in the unruly sea, straining with the wind to evade the deadly guns.

"Return the fire!" Tristan ordered, though he knew his weapons were no match for the battle ship that threatened him. He could only pray that the *Gabrielle* could outdistance them before their aim proved true.

Another volley was fired from the frigate. Chain shot shattered a rail and part of the forecastle deck, and another tore a hole amidships. Splintered wood flew through the air, spearing the thigh of one unlucky sailor. He screamed in startled pain. Tristan saw Spar dash across the deck to carry the man inside. Then his gaze shifted across the water, waiting breathlessly for the next round to bombard his ship.

"We're pulling away," Whip yelled at him above the noise, and Tristan saw that it was true.

The other ship followed, firing another round. Tristan could hear the shot whizzing overhead. If it hit the mizzenmast or tore the sails, they were lost. He waited, but there were no sounds of splintering masts or burning canvas. He muttered a quick prayer of thanks as he saw the next volley fall harmlessly in the ocean off the port quarter.

"Check the damage, Whip," Tristan ordered. "Send someone to look in on the women."

He wanted nothing more than to hurry below to his own cabin to check on Jacinda, but his place was at the helm until the *Gabrielle* was out of danger. He glanced behind them. The frigate was still following them, although she was falling steadily behind. Without a belly full of cargo, his sleek clipper flew before the wind, outrunning the danger of the frigate's guns.

He raised the glass to his eye once more. Still no flag flying. Still no reason for the attack, an attack that had lasted mere minutes but had seemed an eternity.

It wasn't long before Whip had returned to the helm. "The women are all right, sir. Frightened and a bit shaken up, but none of them is hurt. We've lost one man and have three more wounded, one rather badly I fear."

Tristan grimaced. "And the ship?"

"We'd best put in for repairs as soon as we can. A storm'd near drown us with that hole in her side."

"All right, Whip." He jerked his head behind him at the trailing vessel. "Keep an eye on her. I'm going below for a minute."

"Aye," his first mate replied, taking the glass from the captain.

Jacinda was sitting on the bed, staring out the window, when he entered. She turned at the sound of the door. "Are we out of danger?" Her voice quivered, though she tried to hide it.

"Yes."

She dropped her feet over the edge of the bed. Her eyes seemed terribly round in her pale face. "Was anyone hurt?"

"Yes," he answered again, moving closer.

Her eyes scoured him from the top of his head down to his feet. "Are you?" she asked in a small voice.

"No."

He pulled her up from the bed and nestled her against his chest, breathing in the fresh scent of her hair, offering her comfort as he drew the same from her.

"I don't think I'm a very brave soul," Jacinda whispered into his shirt. "I was so frightened."

"Everyone was frightened, though most wouldn't admit it."

She looked up, blinking away the tears that swam in golden pools, ready to spill over dark lashes. She sniffed. "I'd like to help, Tristan. Let me help Spar care for the wounded."

"I don't—"

"I need to do something. I can't just stay

hidden in this cabin, counting the minutes until you return. Let me help, Tristan." She sniffed again. "Please, Tristan."

He laughed low. "How can I deny you anything? Come on. We'll see what Spar needs."

The main deckhouse had been converted into a surgery. When Tristan opened the door, Spar looked up from the table. He stared at Tristan a moment, then shook his head. Tristan's gaze shifted to the sailor lying on the table. Blood was everywhere, and there was no mistaking the severity of his injuries. His arm was missing below the shoulder.

Jacinda shouldered her way past him. "Spar, I've come to help." Her gaze also took in the grisly scene, but it didn't stop her. She swallowed hard and her face paled dramatically, but she took a determined step toward the table. "Tell me what I can do."

Spar measured her with a steady gaze, then jerked his head toward two men in beds against the wall. "See what you can do for those two. You'll find some bandages on the other table."

Jacinda nodded and moved to obey.

"Tris," Spar said in a low voice, "I could use your help. You'll have to hold him still. I've got to staunch this wound before he bleeds to death."

Tristan looked at the sailor again. "Are you sure he's still alive?" he asked as he stepped closer to the table.

"For a little while," Spar answered bitterly. "Long enough to feel the agony." He drew Tristan's gaze. "What'd you bring her here for? This is no place for a lady."

"She wanted to help. It's important to her, Spar."

"Well, if she can handle this, there's more to her than just beauty." Then, face grim, he ordered, "Hold him tight, Tris," and he picked up the hot instrument.

They left the unfriendly frigate behind them in the misty sea. Tristan would have preferred to race on with the fresh breeze at his back, but the dark clouds were threatening to unburden themselves and he didn't relish the thought of sinking any more than the thought of capture. They set course for shore where they discovered, quite by accident, a deep water inlet. A stretch of land, laden with tall trees and rocky hillsides, curled around to conceal the cove from view. It seemed a good place to make the needed repairs. Before making his final decision, Tristan sent Whip with several able seamen to scout the surrounding area. It appeared deserted, and the *Gabrielle* dropped anchor in the cove.

The storm arrived as promised. Rain fell in violent sheets. Beyond the peninsula, the sea churned and waves roiled. Aboard the *Gabrielle*, the men and women settled in to wait out the storm.

16

Spar carried Stu Adams from the ship himself. He had watched the young sailor dying by inches throughout the night. Now he would bury him. By rights, a fellow who'd begun his life at sea as a fo'c'sle boy when he was a mere nine years old should have been buried at sea, but they couldn't wait until they left this cove. That might be several days.

Spar carried the body up the inland hillside, picking a spot which overlooked the blue-green sea. He laid the corpse under a nearby tree and began digging a suitably deep grave. The earth was heavy with rain water, and his heart was heavy too. He knew he'd done all he could to save Stu, but the knowledge didn't make him feel any better, didn't stop the *whys* that filled his mind.

" 'e wasn't very old, was 'e?"

Spar looked up. Ida, her orange-colored curls ruffled by the breeze, was standing on the hillside, her green eyes solemn.

"Not much older than you," he replied.

Ida lifted her skirt as she moved up the hill. "Ye're a good doctor. I've watched ye, I 'ave. Ye did all ye could."

"Aye, all I could." His throat thickened. "But it wasn't enough. It's never enough." He threw down the shovel and picked up the body, wrapped in canvas sailcloth. He eased the shrouded remains into the dark, earthy-smelling hole.

Ida knelt across from him. "The lady told me about yer missus."

Spar swallowed the lump that had formed in his throat.

"I 'ad a babe once. Loved 'er, I did, but she weren't long for this world."

"I'm sorry." He looked across the grave at her. She was staring into space with a bitter-sweet smile on her lips, and he knew she was remembering the child she'd lost.

"A girl, she was, and pretty too, with hair like mine. She only lived five days, but they were the best five days o' me life." Tears overflowed from emerald orbs.

Spar cleared his throat. "You're young. You'll have more children."

"No." She shook her head violently. "What 'ave I t'give 'em if I did? A dirty room in London while their mother's out whorin' t'feed 'em. It's best she died when she did. I'll not 'ave more."

"There's other ways to make a living," he suggested gently.

Ida laughed. "Look at me. What else am I t'do? It's all I've ever done. They don't 'ire girls like me t'cook and clean. No decent man would 'ave me in 'is 'ouse."

Spar took a good look at the girl. He'd

talked to her often enough when he was caring for Jacinda, and he'd visited with her a time or two on board the *Gabrielle* since leaving Madeira. But he didn't think he'd ever really looked at her. She was cute with her carrot curls and the sprinkle of freckles across the bridge of her nose. She was tiny. He would wager she wouldn't even reach his chest if they stood side by side. She probably wasn't even half his thirty-eight years.

"You can start over," he suggested gravely.

Her reply was soft, barely audible. "Seems that's what I'm doing. Wherever the captain's takin' us, it's a new start for me."

Perhaps he should tell her the truth, that in the end she would be back in England. That if she wanted to make a new start she would have to do it there.

He shook his head and stood up. He reached for the shovel and began dropping earth back into the hole. He didn't like the direction his thoughts were going. He didn't need to complicate his life by taking the likes of Ida under his wing. She would have to look out for herself.

The storm was gone, and sunshine once again kissed the earth. While the men worked to repair the ship, Tristan allowed the women to be taken ashore. Jacinda, along with several of the others, wandered far enough back in the trees to discover a fresh water pool. It made for a perfect bath.

Jacinda shed her clothes and slipped into the clear pool, relishing the feel of the cool liquid against her flesh as she swam to the other side. Her long red mane grew heavy, pulling at her head as she submerged to swim back across beneath the surface. She came up, gasping for air as she shook the water from her eyes.

"You won't hold his interest for long, you know." Loralie sat on a rock in the water, watching Jacinda with a malevolent gaze.

Jacinda was taken aback by the look.

Loralie splashed water onto her throat and let it trickle through the deep crevasse between her voluptuous breasts. Her skin was a golden hue, and even Jacinda could see that her brazen good looks were seductive. A man would have a hard time resisting such charms as Loralie possessed.

Jacinda sank back into the water, feeling suddenly inadequate beside such earthy beauty.

Loralie laughed, that deep self-possessed laugh which Jacinda already hated. "I see you understand me."

"I understand you." Her shyness was temporarily forgotten, a surge of anger giving her courage. "But you're wrong about Tristan. He loves me."

"Oh, love," Loralie drawled, proclaiming the emotion utterly worthless just by the tone of her voice. "Men get over that silliness very easily."

"Not Tristan."

"Even your precious Tristan." Loralie stood and stretched with feline grace. She was totally unashamed of her own nakedness. In fact, by her very stance, she proclaimed her pride in her physical attributes. And she obviously knew just how to use them. She stepped onto shore and unhurriedly pulled on her clothes. She shook her wet hair, dragging her fingers through it to loosen the stubborn snarls. She glanced back at Jacinda, a sly smile turning up the corners of her generous mouth. "Enjoy the comfort of the captain's cabin while you can, dear lady. When I replace you, you may have my cot in the hold." She laughed as she turned to walk away.

Jacinda bit her lip in repressed rage. *You'll not replace me*, she thought to herself. *I'd scratch out your eyes before I'd let that happen.* But she didn't feel quite so sure of herself as she would have a few moments before.

She heard laughter coming from across the pool, this time the carefree laughter of people enjoying themselves. She turned. Ida and another girl about her age were splashing each other with water, giggling and screaming. She looked over her shoulder once more, but Loralie had disappeared from view.

"Good," Jacinda muttered, then dove back into the pool and swam toward the others.

Loralie returned to the ship alone. She had no need for the company of women. She had caught the eye of the captain. Now, while Jacinda was still ashore, was the time to make sure he more than noticed her. Now she must make him remember her.

She descended the steps leading to his cabin. Softly she knocked on the door. She was in luck.

"Come in."

Tristan was bent over the table, a map spread across it. He looked up, lifted a surprised eyebrow, then straightened, allowing

211

the map to roll closed.

"I was hoping to find you here, Captain."

"What may I do for you?" he asked politely.

She closed the door and moved across the room to stand before him. "I think you know what you can do for me, Captain." She smiled suggestively, lowering her voice as she added, "Better yet, I think you can imagine what I can do for you."

Tristan put his hands on her shoulders and gently but firmly pushed her back from him. "Thanks for the offer, Loralie, but I'm not interested."

"You *are* a gentleman, aren't you, Captain? But gentlemen need—"

The door opened. "Tristan, I—" Jacinda stopped, her mouth agape as she observed Tristan's hands on Loralie's shoulders.

"Why don't you go away and come back when the captain and I are finished?" Loralie queried with a smirk.

Jacinda's face went white, then turned red. "Get out!"

Loralie glanced up at Tristan, her smile fading into a seductive pout. "Do you want me to go, Captain?"

Tristan opened his mouth but had no chance to speak.

"Get out!" Jacinda's hand on Loralie's arm spun her around. "And don't come back or I'll—"

Loralie jerked her arm free. "You don't frighten me, *Lady* Jacinda." On her tongue, the title became an insult. "You have no claim here."

"Why, you—" Jacinda raised a hand to strike her.

212

Tristan grabbed Jacinda's wrist. "Enough!" Stormy black eyes glared at Loralie. "I'd like you to leave," he said evenly. "Now."

"I want only to please you, Captain. I'll go since that is your wish." Softly, she added, "Until later, Captain." She brushed past Jacinda and left the cabin, still wearing a confident smile. She knew those two would be exchanging heated words as soon as she was gone.

"How could you?" Jacinda cried. "How could you protect that . . . that—" She couldn't say it.

"Me? I didn't ask her here, but I couldn't have the two of you brawling in my cabin."

"So instead you encourage her?" Her fists were clenched at her sides. Oh, how she'd longed to hit that woman.

"I *didn't* encourage her," he protested, his own temper rising.

"No? Well it was a cozy scene I interrupted. When were you going to kiss her?"

"Wait a minute. I wasn't going to kiss her. I was just—"

Tears scalded Jacinda's eyes. "Is she going to be next? Tell me. Tell me!" In anger and fear, she struck out at him, hitting his chest with her fists, once and then again and again.

Tristan stopped her by pulling her against him, trapping her arms against his chest. "Cinda! Cinda, stop it."

His mouth ground down on hers, smothering her tirade. His own anger made the kiss seem harsh. She fought against him, whimpering.

"Cinda, please," he whispered in a ragged

213

voice as he drew his mouth away from hers. "Listen to me. I love you. There'll be no other women in my bed."

She ceased her struggles. Large golden eyes turned up to meet his. "You . . . you've never told me."

"Never told you what?"

Softly, "That you love me."

He held her head between his hands. "I haven't? I thought you knew."

"I knew," she replied in a whisper, "but I guess I needed to hear you say it." More tears slid down her cheeks. "Say it again?"

"I love you, Cinda." He kissed her, slowly, sweetly, tenderly. "I love you."

The men worked swiftly to repair the damage done to the *Gabrielle*. The voices of the women enjoying themselves in the crystal pool carried easily through the air to their ears. A few of the men grumbled, knowing they would be welcomed by some of their special passengers; however, the captain had laid down strict rules. There were to be no dalliances, no slap and tickle beneath the stairs. They were to be treated with respect. The men who kept a lookout for any trouble were on their honor to avoid looking in the direction of the bathing women. It wasn't an easy order to obey.

They'd been in the cove for two days and the repairs were close to finished. While Tristan worked beside his men, Jacinda decided to go for another swim. It was the middle of the afternoon. The day was warm, pleasantly so, and most of the women were lying down for naps. But Jacinda didn't feel like sleeping. Not wanting to disturb Tristan in the middle of his work, she poked her head into the galley and told Spar where she was going, then slipped over the side of the ship and into the waiting boat as if she'd been doing it for years.

Her bare feet sank in the sandy shore. She loved the sensation. It made her feel light and carefree and happy. She paused and looked back at the *Gabrielle*. Somewhere in the belly of the tall ship, Tristan was working. He had probably thrown off his shirt, and his chest would be glistening with sweat. The thought of it made Jacinda's stomach tingle.

Lifting her skirts up to her knees, she began running through the sand. It was like being a little girl again. No, it was better. She had Tristan to love and to love her back. She hadn't had that as a little girl. She had never known such freedom.

The pool welcomed her into its blue depths. She had always loved to swim, although the forest pool in England was not nearly so clear and blue. Her mother had never approved of swimming, but Jacinda had slipped away to her private retreat as often as she could in the warmer summer months while she was growing up. And this water felt all the more special because she knew that back home the weather would be cold and damp.

She swam back and forth, sometimes underwater, sometimes on the surface, enjoying the heavy tug of her wet hair. Finally, refreshed and exhilarated, she crawled up onto a rock at the water's edge and began combing her hair. Pulling the red mane forward over her shoulder, she caught a glimpse of her reflection.

She paused, examining the nude woman with a critical eye. In the back of her mind was the image of Loralie as she stretched and shook her chestnut locks. How did she compare with Loralie? Not well, she decided, slipping back into the water so she didn't have to compare herself any longer.

But the uncertainties continued, spoiling her afternoon swim. She felt a deep yearning to see Tristan again, to read his love for her written in the inky black depths of his eyes, to know the touch of his hand as he gently caressed her hair, to feel his warm breath on her cheek as he whispered words of endearment.

She scrambled out of the water and reached for her clothes. She didn't try to dry off first. She pulled the white blouse over her head, not realizing how it molded itself to her damp breasts. She stepped into her skirt and began walking while she fought with the button at her hip.

"What's this?"

The deep male voice surprised her. She jumped backward with a gasp.

"Well if it ain't the captain's doxy." Large brown eyes leered at her, and the sailor chuckled.

She felt a sudden dread. "Excuse me, sir," she said, sounding more confident than she felt. "I was just returning to the ship." She stepped to the side to go around him.

His hand shot out to touch a nearby tree, stopping her passage. "Why? You ain't been missed." His gaze slid slowly downward.

She followed the direction of his eyes. The

white fabric was nearly transparent when wet, and it clung to her breasts like a second skin. Jacinda gasped again, her arms moving to shield herself from his view.

"No call t'be unfriendly. I can give you anything the good captain can." The sailor's grin vanished. His eyes seemed to burn with an unnatural light.

"Please," she said, her throat tight, "let me pass."

"Not yet." He stepped toward her. "Not yet."

She turned, poised for flight, but his hand gripped her arm like a vise, spinning her around. Harsh lips pressed against hers, the dark stubble of his chin scratching her face.

"No!" she screamed, but the sound was muffled by his mouth.

While one arm pinned her against him, the other hand moved to her breast. She squirmed, fighting to free herself. He chuckled again. With a jerk, he rent her blouse down the front, eliminating the last of her flimsy protection. He squeezed the tender flesh. She tried again to scream but again the sound was drowned.

In a panicked, reflex action, she drew her knee up sharply, jabbing his groin with a strength she didn't know she possessed. He yelped and released her. She spun and fled back toward the pool, the only way open to her. She didn't dare look behind her for fear she would see him on her heels. The bushes grabbed at her feet, trying to trip her. The tree limbs reached out to scratch her face and blind her eyes. She could hear him crashing through the bramble behind her. She gasped for air, screaming in her mind but lacking breath to call for help.

The hand slammed down on her shoulder, arresting her flight. Driven by stark fear, she turned with nails bared, clawing at his face. She heard his cry of rage just before his hand swung up to strike her alongside the head, knocking her into the once still pool. Before she could gain her footing, he was in the water with her.

"You'll not fight me, you worthless wench," he growled before pushing her beneath the surface. He let her up, coughing and sputtering, then shoved her under once more. Then up again. "You'll not refuse me what he's been getting." And again he pushed her down.

Jacinda couldn't struggle any longer. She was drowning. He had won. She was helpless.

He pulled her up by the scruff of the neck. She coughed and choked and gulped for air, the world tumbling before her eyes. Her assailant was a mere blur. He hauled her unceremoniously toward shore where he pushed her down. He straddled her, hands on his hips, a triumphant laughter spilling from his throat as he loosened his breeches. Her ears rang, muting the ugly sound, and she closed her eyes against the sight of him. She sobbed, her world a living horror.

"Arrgh!"

The cry of rage split the air as a body catapulted into the clearing, tackling the sailor and knocking him to the ground. Before Jacinda could comprehend what was happening, her bruised arm was grasped once more and she was dragged to her feet. Suddenly, she was scooped up into strong arms and carried away from the pool.

"No," she whispered, wanting to fight but unable to.

"Lady Jacinda, are you hurt?" Hands touched her face, her arms, probing carefully.

"Don't." She shook her head and raised her arms to protect herself.

She was lowered back to the ground, her back against a tree. The hands released her. Something was placed over her naked breasts.

"Stay put."

What was happening? It was a moment before she understood that Spar had pulled her to safety. It was Spar who had covered her. Her thoughts began to clear along with her vision. Spar was already hurrying away from her, and her gaze followed his movements.

Tristan had her assailant pinned to the ground. Again and again, his fist struck the man's face. There was blood everywhere. Was it Tristan's?

"Enough, Tris. You'll kill him," Spar shouted.

"I mean to kill him," Tristan snarled in reply. "Do you hear me, Jacobs? I mean to kill you, you son of a whore."

In his fury, Tristan had the strength of two men, but Spar's strength was still greater. He grabbed the captain's arms from behind and locked them with his own; then he hauled him away from the unconscious Jacobs.

"Stop it," Spar demanded as Tristan struggled against him. When Tristan didn't obey, he spun him around and pushed him backward into the water.

Tristan came up with a roar as he stumbled toward shore. "Get out of my way."

"No." The giant's reply was soft, but there was no denying he meant to defy his captain.

"Spar—" Tristan warned, black eyes flaring.

Jacinda pushed herself up. Her knees quaked beneath her as she came forward, clutching Spar's shirt in front of her. "Tristan." She choked his name through a sob.

His head turned. She saw his emotions run the gamut, changing from deadly rage, to surprise, to fear, to sorrow. She felt sullied. She wanted to hide from his searching gaze, yet she needed him to hold her, to comfort her, to tell her all would be right again.

"Tristan," she repeated softly. Her vision blurred as tears spilled over, but she kept walking.

Spurred forward by her painful cry, soft though it was, he was out of the water and gathering her into loving arms in a flash. He crushed her to him, not in the passionate embrace she had known of late but one of protection. "My love. My Cinda," he crooned. "Hush, love. I'm here. I'm here."

17

"Keelhaul him."

Whip and Spar exchanged a look of dread.

"Tris—" Whip began.

"I want him keelhauled." Tristan's look was deadly earnest.

"Listen, Tris—" Whip tried again.

Tristan stood up and braced himself against the table with his knuckles as he leaned forward. His voice was carefully restrained. "Am I the captain of this ship? Now I want my orders carried out." He shoved the chair out of the way as he turned to cross the cabin.

Whip and Spar looked at each other again.

"You try," Whip said with a futile shake of his head.

Spar got up from the table and approached Tristan. The captain's glance warned him not to speak. Spar raised a hand. "Hear me out, Tris. Please."

Tristan turned a rigid back toward his friend but waited silently.

"I understand your anger with Jacobs.

What he did was—" What word could describe what both Tristan and Spar felt? "What he did was reprehensible and he should be punished. But you've always been a fair captain to sail under. If you resort to torture, you'll lose these men."

Tristan's stance remained tense.

"Fair or not, the men have a legitimate gripe about these women. You've made them hands off while Jacinda is sharing your bed."

"I plan to make Cinda my wife," Tristan snapped in protest.

Spar shook his head. "They don't know that. Besides, it makes no difference. They just know you're enjoying what they'd like to."

Tristan's voice was ragged as he asked, "Do you know what Jacobs did to her? He nearly drowned her. He was going to rape her. You're asking me to let him get away with it."

"No," Spar answered honestly. "I'm asking you to be fair in your punishment." He turned his head, looking back at the first mate for help.

"Spar's right," Whip said, getting to his feet and following the other two across the room. "I'm fond of the lady. You know that. But you've got to do your thinkin' with your head on this, not your foolhardy heart."

The two men waited as their captain continued to stare out the cabin window. The silence lingered, one agonizing minute following another.

Suddenly, Tristan slammed his palms against the window frame. "Damn!" he swore. "I wanted to kill him." His head drooped forward toward his chest as he drew in a long breath; then he turned around. He straightened as he did so, his expression rock hard. "Thirty lashes." There was a steely glint in his eyes as they moved back and forth between the two men across from him. "Fair enough?"

Spar nodded.

"Fair enough," Whip answered.

"Tomorrow morning." Tristan turned back toward the window. "At sunrise."

Jacinda lay huddled on the bed. She felt cold and bereft without Tristan's arms around her. She shivered. She tried not to think about what had happened. She tried to tell herself it wasn't so terrible. She hadn't been harmed, not really. He hadn't violated her. She was all right. But she didn't believe any of it. She wasn't all right. It had been terrible, more terrible than she could have imagined. He had, indeed, violated her. Perhaps he hadn't succeeded in raping her, but he had violated her nonetheless. Another dry sob shook her body. She hadn't any tears left to shed. She had cried them out hours ago.

Where was Tristan? Why had he left her for so long? What was he doing? Did everyone on board know what had happened? Shame washed over her.

The door opened. She shrank back on the bed, drawing a startled breath as she pulled the blanket up to her eyes. Tristan stepped inside. His gaze darted toward her, then he turned and closed the door.

He can't bear to look at me. She closed her eyes against her fresh misery.

The bed creaked beneath his weight. He lay down, reaching with an arm to draw her against him. He kissed her hair. "You'll not be bothered by Jacobs again," he said harshly. "Not Jacobs nor any man aboard this ship."

"What . . . what have you done?" she inquired, afraid to know.

His anger made him stiff. The warmth and protection she'd felt earlier were missing. "He'll be punished in the morning."

"Punished?"

"Thirty lashes. You'll be expected to be on deck. Everyone will be there." Tristan's arm tightened around her, frightening in its strength. "I should have killed him." He bit off each word with bitter intensity.

A fresh wave of tears rose in her eyes. She had thought she could cry no more, yet she wept again. "It . . . i-it . . . was m-my . . . m-my fault," she choked out between sobs. "If o-only . . . I . . . I h-had st-stayed on th-the sh-ship."

"No. You're wrong. It wasn't your fault." He kissed her hair again. His arms relaxed, yet felt more like a safe haven. "Please don't cry, Cinda. Please."

She sniffed, trying to stop the tide.

"Don't cry anymore. All will be right. I promise I'll make it right."

She laid her head against his chest and closed her eyes. She wouldn't think about the ugliness of this day any longer. She would think only of Tristan's love.

At sunrise the next morning, the ship's crew, from captain down to fo'c'sle boy, stood on the deck of the *Dancing Gabrielle*. The furled sails were splashed with a pink hue. The inlet was still. No birds sang. No fish jumped. The world seemed to wait in dreadful anticipation.

Jacinda was there. She stood alone, off to Tristan's left and a step back. Most of the other women had come up on deck, too, and had gathered behind her. She could hear their whispers, but she didn't turn to look at them. She felt too stiff to move. Her eyes burned from the tearful, sleepless night just past.

She sensed the sudden tension that rippled across the deck as Jacobs was brought forward. With trepidation, she forced herself to look upon her attacker. His face was swollen and his eyes were blackened from Tristan's pounding, yet he wasn't cowering with shame before his fellow shipmates. His walk was sure and unafraid.

"Read the charges, Fielding," Tristan said.

Jacobs gaze shifted from the captain to Jacinda as Fielding obeyed. Jacinda didn't hear a word. She was paralyzed by the sailor's hate-filled glare. He continued to stare at her even as he was led to the iron grating set against the shroud. Fielding told him to remove his shirt, which he did without hesitation or complaint. His eyes only released hers when he was forced to turn around so his wrists could be bound to the iron bars.

I'll feel better when you're punished, she thought. *You deserve it. I'll feel clean again when this is over.*

"Proceed, Fielding," the captain ordered.

Jacinda looked at Tristan. From the side, his face seemed to be an expressionless mask, but she, who was just beginning to learn the many facets of this man she loved, could read the strain beneath his taut cheekbones.

"It's her own fault," a woman whispered, just loud enough for her to hear. "Flaunting herself before a man like that. What does she expect him to do? It's her that should be flogged."

Was that what everyone thought? A chill spread through her. She let her eyes move over the assemblage and imagined accusations in every male face on board. *The captain's doxy*, they seemed to say. *'Tis her own fault.*

She heard the singing of the whip as it whistled through the air, then the sudden crack as it met with Jacob's back. Her eyes were drawn involuntarily toward the ship's shroud. The cat-o'-nines had left red welts across the sailor's naked flesh. The whip was drawn back through the mate's hands, then sent sailing through the air again. The muscles in Jacob's back jerked, and his arms bulged as he tightened his hand hold on the iron bars. Again and again, the cat-o'-nines was released with cruelty against the sun-browned flesh, laying it bare as often as it raised angry welts. Never in her life had Jacinda witnessed anything so cruel, so terrible as this punishment. Not even what Jacobs had done to her seemed deserving of this fate.

As he'd done each time, the mate ran the whip through his fingers, but now he was squeezing out blood. Jacinda felt a wave of nausea wash over her. Without thinking, she stepped toward Tristan, placing a hand on his arm. "Make him stop," she said hoarsely.

His head jerked around and he met her gaze with cold black eyes. "Get back, Jacinda."

"Please. It's enough."

Every eye was on the captain and Jacinda, every ear trained to catch their conversation. Even the mate wielding the whip had paused in indecision.

"I want you to stop." Her fingers tightened on his arm as her voice grew louder. "Stop it. Stop it."

"Go below, Jacinda," Tristan said evenly, his tone brooking no argument. "Now." Without waiting to see her obey, he turned his back to her. "Proceed with the punishment."

Surprised, Jacinda remained only long enough to hear the cat singing toward Jacobs, then she whirled to leave, but she was halted once again, this time by Loralie's triumphant gaze.

Go below, Jacinda, the dark beauty mouthed, mocking her.

Humiliated and confused, she fled to her cabin.

They left the cove under full sail later that morning. A fresh breeze carried them forward at a brisk seventeen knots.

Jacinda had not seen Tristan since she'd left the deck with hot tears on her cheeks. She had waited in their cabin, certain he would come to apologize to her, certain he would comfort her once again. But she continued to wait alone. She'd considered going up on deck to seek him out but had known she didn't dare. Not after the way he'd spoken to her. Not after the way they'd all looked at her. She cringed. What had she become in the name of love?

It was nearing supper time before the cabin door opened and a weary, taut-mouthed Tristan stepped inside the room. Jacinda stood up, every bit as weary. So many conflicting emotions warred within her breast. She was angry because he hadn't listened to her, hadn't stopped the flogging. She was hurt because of the way he'd looked at her, the way he'd ordered her out of sight. She was filled with shame when she saw herself as she imagined she was seen by others. *Well if it isn't the captain's doxy.* She'd heard that phrase repeating in her mind too often this day.

When the silence became more than she could bear, she asked, "Why wouldn't you stop?"

"I'm the captain of this ship. My word is law."

She recalled Jacob's tattered back. "He was bleeding. He'd learned his lesson. It was enough."

His eyes darkened. "And the other men? Would they learn if I weakened?" His voice raised. "This isn't a nursery, Jacinda. If I don't maintain control—"

She shook her head. She didn't understand. How could Tristan be so harsh? Was this man the same as the one who held her tenderly in his arms at night, who rained kisses over her body, who whispered words of love and teased her body into ecstasy? Was this Tristan?

"You knew what the verdict was last night," he reminded her solemnly.

"I didn't understand what it meant," she protested. "Besides, I was hurt and afraid."

The cold edge of steel filled his voice. "And what he did to you? Does it seem less violent to you now than it did yesterday?"

"No," she whispered.

He came toward her. He held out his hands, palms up. "I would have killed him with these if it hadn't been for Spar. I'll never forget what he did . . . and what he almost did. You may have forgotten, but I won't. I can still see you, lying on the ground, half-drowned, your dress torn, and him standing over you."

She shivered at the memory.

"I had to make sure no one thought they could treat you that way ever again," he finished.

"I haven't forgotten," she said softly, her anger temporarily dimmed, "but maybe the others are right. Maybe I've brought this on myself. It's because I've become your . . . your—"

Tristan reached quickly to put his hand over her mouth, stopping her from speaking. He shook his head, his eyes demanding that she forget the thought.

She pulled away. "It's true, Tristan. I know what they're thinking. I told you I wasn't ashamed. I didn't care that they knew I shared your bed. But look what it's done. Look what it's doing." She stepped back from him. "I think you should put me with the other women."

"No."

"It's either that or losing your men to more envy and bitterness, isn't it?"

He didn't answer.

"Well, isn't it?" Jacinda stiffened her spine. "I *want* to be with the other women."

"No."

Tawny eyes flashed. "Am I your prisoner once again? Will you keep me against my will?"

Anger erased all reason. "If I tell you I'm sick of being the captain's doxy, will you release me? If I tell you I don't want you touching me after I've seen how you treat these men, will you set me free?"

As soon as she'd spoken, she regretted it. She began to reach out with her hand, to touch his arm and tell him it wasn't the truth, she didn't want to leave his cabin or his bed. But he had turned away from her and was walking to the door before she could speak.

"There's no need for you to leave this cabin, Lady Jacinda. I won't trouble you again. I'll remove myself to the next room."

The door slammed behind him.

Jacinda had never realized how large a bed could feel when it was occupied by only one. She spent a sleepless night, tossing and turning beneath the covers, wishing she could call back the words that had sent Tristan slamming out of their cabin. She wondered if he was spending the night staring at the darkness, unable to sleep, just like she was.

She replayed the scene in her mind often, puzzled by her actions. It was so unlike her. She had spent her life submitting meekly to what others wanted, finding her escape from things she didn't like in her dreams. When she'd been hurt or angry, she'd always hidden behind cool reserve and kept silent. What had happened to her to make her speak that way to Tristan?

She got up on her knees and pushed aside the heavy curtains that draped the windows. Silvery moonlight glittered on the crests of the breaking waves. She leaned against the window pane and stared out at the sea, her confusion pulling and tugging inside her just like the pull and tug of the ocean's tide.

"Maybe I'm not me anymore," she whispered.

The thought came to her suddenly, and she considered it a moment. Yes, she was a different person now than she had been as little as six months ago, even three months ago, but for good or bad, she wasn't sure.

Would you rather be back in England, getting ready to marry Roger? she asked herself. You would always know exactly what was expected of you. You wouldn't have to worry about ships with cannons or storms or vile sailors or floggings. You could live in a beautiful manor and give fancy dress balls. You could have servants taking care of you and plenty of good food . . .

And I wouldn't have Tristan either, she thought in reply.

She pushed away from the window and slid off the bed. "I'd rather have Tristan," she said aloud as she lit the lantern.

On bare feet, Jacinda padded across the room and opened the door. She peeked out into the corridor. Nothing stirred. No one was about. She turned her head toward the adjoining cabin and spied the light beneath Tristan's door. He was still awake. Her hand on the latch, she drew a deep breath, trying to calm her racing heart. Then she opened the door and went in, closing it quickly behind her as she leaned back against it. The lantern was turned low, but she could see his form beneath the blankets on the bed.

"Tristan, I need to talk to you."

He didn't answer. Maybe he was asleep after all.

"Tristan? Please let's talk." She swallowed. "I was wrong to tell you what to do in front of everyone. I know that now. It doesn't change how I feel about the flogging, but I'm sorry for what I did." She took a step forward. "Mostly I'm sorry about what I said. I don't care what anyone else thinks of me. I don't want to be without you. I love you. Will you forgive me?" She waited, scarcely daring to draw a breath.

The blankets shifted, then were tossed quickly aside.

"A very pretty speech, but you've wasted it on me." Smug pleasure lit Loralie's face. She sat up, then pulled her knees close to her naked breasts. "The captain had to go up on deck, but he should be back soon if you'd care to wait for him."

Jacinda didn't believe it. She must be seeing things, hearing things. This couldn't be real.

Loralie laughed. "I told you you couldn't hold his interest. You really shouldn't be surprised. It's only natural that he should turn to me when he tired of playing with you."

Everything that had gone wrong in the last few days seemed to peak in this one dreadful moment. Jacinda's initial urge to turn and flee in tears was quickly overruled by a white hot rage such as she'd never known. She lunged across the room, her fingers reaching for the cascading chestnut hair. With a violent jerk, she pulled Loralie from the bed. In the next instant, they were tumbling on the floor. Jacinda reacted instinctively as Loralie attacked with teeth and nails, fighting back with fury. Loralie was more experienced in physical confrontations, but Jacinda's wrath gave her added strength.

Suddenly Loralie jabbed Jacinda's eye and rolled away from her. Blinded by pain, Jacinda struggled to her feet, not sure where Loralie would strike next.

"You fancy harlot. I'll teach you," Loralie warned before she pounced.

Still holding her blind eye, Jacinda dodged the attack, swinging around to thrust Loralie across the room headfirst. Loralie's cheek struck the sharp edge of the stove, and she cried out as she fell to the floor.

Jacinda gasped for breath, waiting for Loralie to get up. She watched as Loralie's fingers came up to touch her face. Loralie looked at her hand, then swung around toward Jacinda. Her cheek and fingers were covered with blood. A nasty gash was bared below her left eye.

"You'll pay for this," Loralie cried, getting to her feet. "You'll—"

The door flew open with a crash. Tristan stepped into the room, his gaze darting quickly from the disheveled Jacinda to the naked, bleeding Loralie. "What the devil is going on here?" he demanded.

"Your lady came calling on us, love," Loralie replied, "and I had to tell her her services were no longer needed."

With a despairing cry, her anger faded, Jacinda pushed past Tristan, tears replacing rage.

Tristan continued to stare at Loralie a moment longer, then realized Jacinda had fled. "Get out of here," he snarled at Loralie before following after Jacinda. He reached her cabin door before she could lock it against him. "Let me in, Cinda," he said softly, his hands against the door.

"No! Go away." She fought back the tears. "I trusted you. Even after everything that had happened, I trusted you. I came to tell you I was sorry, that I was wrong, and look what I find. You and that . . . that . . . Loralie."

Tristan gave the door a firm push. It flew open before him as Jacinda backed away from it, taking refuge behind the table.

"You didn't see me and Loralie," he insisted. "You saw Loralie."

"Would you rather I'd found you there together?" she asked with a stricken look on her face. "Do you wish I'd found you . . . found you—" She choked on another sob, feeling hysterical.

Tristan closed the door behind him, then moved toward her. His eyes pleaded with her to listen to him. "It wouldn't have mattered when you'd come, Jacinda. I haven't been in that room all night. I've been on deck."

She wanted to believe him. With every fiber of her being, she wanted to believe him.

"I didn't know Loralie was there." His hand touched her shoulder. "I swear."

"But she—"

His fingers tilted her chin, forcing her tawny eyes to look at him. "I've been on deck all night." His free hand brushed a tear from her cheek.

"But she said—"

"I swear," he whispered, his lips brushing her forehead.

"Oh, Tris." Tears threatened to spill again, but were stifled by the strength of his embrace. "I don't know what to believe anymore." Her words were muffled by his shoulder. "I only know I love you."

"Then know I love you too. We'll forget about Loralie and whatever happened in there tonight. I love you, Jacinda."

Soft kisses brushed the top of her head. She could feel his heart beating next to her own. Her arms wrapped around his torso, holding on for dear life. They stayed like that for a long time, until her tears had dried and she felt safe again, until thoughts of Loralie had faded from her mind.

Finally, Tristan spoke. "I'm sorry, Cinda. I'm sorry for what I've done to you. If only you were still in England, none of this—"

She shook her head while tightening her hold around his chest. "No. If I were still in England, I'd be marrying Blackstoke and would never have known your love."

"Blackstoke," he echoed softly, pulling back from her. His ebony gaze searched her face as she looked up at him. "What of Blackstoke?"

"I despise him."

"But you would have married him."

"Yes."

"Why?"

Jacinda shook her head once more. "How can I explain it to you? It didn't matter then. I had nothing but my dreams. What difference if

I lived with Blackstoke as my husband or with my parents at Bonclere? My father agreed to the match. I was expected to marry and marry well. A future marquess was indeed a great catch for the daughter of the Earl of Bonclere. I had no reason to refuse my father's wishes." She leaned her head against his chest once more. "I hadn't the strength to defy him."

Again he kissed her hair. "And what of now?" he asked softly. "I doubt your father will approve of a mere American ship's captain when he was counting on a marquess. Do you have the strength to defy him now?"

She stepped back from him, golden eyes flashing. "I have the strength to defy anyone who would keep us apart. I don't care if my father approves or not. I'll give him no choice. Unless you discard me yourself, I will be at your side."

"As my wife?"

She was caught offguard, left speechless. His wife? He wanted to marry her. She had hoped but . . .

Tristan wore a tender smile but his eyes were serious. "I would never discard you, my Cinda. I've become too used to your fiery beauty. I grow cold when I'm away from you even for a short while. You will marry me, won't you?"

"Oh yes, Tristan. Yes."

He drew her back into his arms. His mouth melded with hers in a kiss with a scorching heat of its own. As their lips parted, he whispered, "Cinda, my love, my flame."

All else was forgotten as he stirred the fires of their love once more.

18

On a mild winter's day, the *Dancing Gabrielle* travelled through the pleasant waters of the Aegean Sea and into the Dardanelles. The strait was forty miles long, as wide as four miles, and lined with watchtowers for the defense of the capital of the Ottoman Empire. At the other end, the Dardanelles opened into the Sea of Marmara. They were nearly at journey's end.

The night before their arrival in Constantinople, Tristan ordered veils and long, black robes distributed among the women with strict orders they were not to appear on deck without wearing them. Jacinda slept restlessly that night, Tristan missing from her side, and upon awakening, she slipped into the black garb of the Kurdistan women and hurried onto the main deck.

Constantinople, the only city in the world astride two continents, spread over a series of hills, unfolding its splendors to those on board Tristan's ship as she sailed in the Golden Horn. To the right rose the Christian quarters, many of the homes distinctly European in their architecture. On the left stood the old city, a maze of wooden houses, long palaces, elegant kiosks, and the pink cupolas of the old Byzantine churches. Mosques and minarets were sprinkled throughout, spheres reaching for the sky. At the far end of the old city, they could see the domes of the Seraglio, the Sultan's imperial residence.

Jacinda couldn't help feeling a twinge of excitement and curiosity at her first glimpse of this foreign city. She leaned against the rail, wrapped in her dark robes, a cool breeze tugging at the fabric while overhead the wind danced in the topsails. She wanted to ask Tristan what she was seeing, where they were going, what was happening. She cast a covert glance back at the helm.

Tristan was at the wheel, a furrow of concentration on his brow as he talked with Whip. In honor of their arrival, he was wearing a black frock coat, an elaborate waistcoat beneath, and tight black breeches. His hair was tied at his nape with a ribbon, though his captain's cap kept most of his dark locks hidden from view. She thought he looked terribly handsome and wished she dared join him at the helm.

With a sigh, she turned her gaze back on the eastern city, but her thoughts went to the previous evening.

He had stood in the doorway of their cabin, the black veil and robe over his arm, contemplating her with serious eyes. "Jacinda, I won't be able to share this cabin with you until we leave Constantinople."

"But why—"

He raised a hand as he shook his head. "I've asked you before to trust me. Now I must ask you to obey me." He entered the room and closed the door behind him. "Our mission here is a dangerous one."

Jacinda rose from the bed where she'd been seated, embroidering a handkerchief for Tristan. "I don't understand, Tristan."

"It's better that you don't." He laid the black garments on the table and came over to her, taking hold of her upper arms with his strong, tanned hands. "You mustn't leave this ship, Jacinda. You mustn't talk to anyone other than those on board. Can you do this for me?"

"But—"

"Can you, Jacinda?"

"If that's what you want, Tris, but I still don't—"

He folded her into his arms. "It's what I want." He kissed her soundly. "You must be kept safe." He released her and reached for the robe and veil, passing them into her hands. "As a woman, you must keep yourself hidden from view. Something to do with their Moslem religion, and they're very strict about it. When you go on deck, be sure to wear these."

Feeling uneasy, she forced a fleeting smile. "Not very pretty, are they?"

Tristan echoed her smile with one of his own. "You'd look pretty in anything."

"Tris?" She touched his jaw lightly with her fingertips. "What is it you're not telling me?"

He caught her hand in midair. Slowly, he turned it, kissing her palm, then folded it between both his hands. His eyes seemed to bore through her as he spoke softly. "Not all things are as they seem, Jacinda. Remember that. And . . . trust me just a little longer."

Sunset splashed pink hues over the city, and with the falling of night's veil, the air chilled. Tristan waited on the deck of the ship, scanning the harbor for a familiar figure. He prayed Danny would show up soon.

Years ago, before Tristan had his own ship, he and Danny O'Banyon had sailed together, young men out to discover and conquer the world. Only Danny decided to conquer Constantinople, the center of power in the Ottoman Empire. He had been bewitched by the exotic essence of the East. Through the years, he had built a successful trading business in the Christian quarters, but he had also made many friends among the Moslems. Danny and Tristan had kept in touch, though it had been a long time since they'd seen one another. When Tristan learned that Blackstoke was sending him to Constantinople, he'd thought of Danny at once. If anyone could help him find Ella in this city, it was Danny O'Banyon.

Tristan began pacing the ship from bow to stern. He was alone on deck. His men were having their supper in the galley, and the women were eating in their quarters. Jacinda would be having a solitary meal in their cabin. He cast a wishful look toward the poop, then shook his head. He mustn't weaken.

At last he spied a tall, thin shadow moving along the wharf toward the *Gabrielle*. It was Danny. It had to be. Tristan didn't believe there could be two men built just like his friend,

Danny O'Banyon. Nearly six and a half feet tall, his frame appeared to be little more than skin over bones; however, he had always been possessed of surprising strength. Danny raised an arm in a wave of recognition as his foot touched the gangplank, and Tristan motioned him on board.

They shook hands in warm welcome. Tristan's eyes flicked over his friend's angular face with its hawk-like nose and high forehead. "Come with me," he said, leading his visitor to his temporary cabin. "I was afraid you didn't get my message. I was beginning to think you weren't coming." Tristan opened the door and squired Danny inside.

"I thought it best I come after dark. I've had a lad watching these waters for signs of this ship for days. I'd not have missed you."

They sat at the table in chairs opposite each other. Tristan removed his cap and ran his fingers through his hair. "You know what's brought me here. Can you help? Have you been able to make arrangements?"

"That I have, Tris. Word will be spread that you have women on board to be sold as a group. The auction will be by invitation only. I have arranged for a friend of mine, a Jew with family in England, to be there. His name is Abraham. Abraham Ben-Chayim. He is a wealthy man, and no one will be surprised at whatever price he is forced to pay."

Tristan nodded.

"Tell me," Danny continued. "Do you have any special beauties among them?"

He thought immediately of Jacinda. "Only one, but she won't be with them."

"Why not?"

"I'm going to marry her."

Danny's eyes widened in amazement. "Marry! Well now, and I wouldn't believe it. Captain Dancing taking himself a bride. I'd like to meet this girl."

"Sorry, Danny. She doesn't know what's going on here. I think it best to keep her hidden until we're safely out of this port."

"As you wish," Danny said with a shrug. "Now. About the others?"

After a thoughtful moment, Tristan nodded. "Yes, there are several beautiful girls among them."

"Any of them virgins?"

Again he thought of Jacinda, of the beach on Madeira, of golden sun shining on warm sand. He shook his head. "I'm not sure, Danny, but I don't think so." He blinked away the memory. "You won't be selling these girls to replenish the sultan's harem."

Danny leaned back in his chair. His brown eyes stared at the table as he rubbed his pointed chin. "It's just as well. If Penneywaite is to believe this auction, the buyers will have to be allowed to . . . ah . . . inspect the merchandise."

"Would you like something to drink?" Tristan offered suddenly to change the subject. He wished there was some way he could avoid the auction, especially this aspect of it, but knew he couldn't.

"That I would, Tris. It's hard to find a draft in this country."

The captain rose from his chair and went to the side board where he poured them both a glass of beer. Coming back to the table, he asked, "What about after the auction? What are your plans?"

"Abraham will take them to his home for a week or so. Then they will be placed on one of his ships bound for England. They'll be told what would have happened if you hadn't rescued them, and we'll compensate them for their troubles."

Tristan nodded. "You've planned well, Danny." He lifted his glass. "Here's hoping it goes just as smoothly." They drank together. His glass empty, Tristan set it on the table and leaned toward his friend. His eyes darkened as he asked the question that had tormented him throughout the long journey.

"I'm sorry, Tris. I've learned nothing. Perhaps in a few more days."

"But do you think she's here?"

"I think there's a good chance. Penney-waite's been holding auctions here for a long time. I suspect he's supplied by his own pirate vessel in addition to his partnership with the Englishman. If Ella was among the women brought here, she was likely sold to someone here in the city, where the wealthiest pashas live. Penneywaite doesn't let them go cheaply. Not the pretty ones, and you've always told me how pretty your little sister is."

Tristan rubbed his forehead with the tips of his fingers. "I've got to find her, Danny."

Danny placed a hand on Tristan's shoulder. "We will, my friend. I promise."

Seated on her cot, Loralie picked up the mirror again, touching her cheek beneath her left eye. There was going to be a scar, despite

Spar's attention to the wound. Oh, she knew the redness would fade and the puffiness would diminish, but still there would be a scar. Her beauty was marred and it was all because of that earl's daughter. Well, Jacinda wasn't going to get away with it. Somehow, someway, Loralie would even the score.

Tristan waited in the long, narrow room. A tiled stove stood in a corner, a fire glowing inside. Thick, colorful carpets hung on the walls. In the center of the room was a low, round table surrounded by silk cushions in hues of blue, red, and green.

"So! The Englishman sends me another cargo at last." Penneywaite bustled into the room. He was a short, bulbous fellow of about fifty with a shock of graying hair and a ruddy complexion. His eyes darted over Tristan. "And you're the American?" He waved toward the cushions. "Sit and let's talk. Tell me what you've brought for me."

Tristan sat down before responding. "I haven't brought anything for you."

Penneywaite's face reddened, and his eyes looked as if they would pop out of his head. "What? See here. The Englishman's note tells me you're carrying another load of women for me. What has happened to them?"

"Nothing has happened to them. They are just not for you." He smiled confidently. "I'm arranging to sell them myself."

"You must think me a fool—"

"On the contrary, Penneywaite. But I wouldn't have you thinking me one either. I'm splitting the profits of this venture with Black-stoke—"

Penneywaite shook his head and waved his hand frantically. "Please. No names. The walls have ears. Just call him the Englishman."

"The Englishman," Tristan corrected with a solemn nod of his head. "As I was saying, the Englishman and I are sharing the profits from my attractive cargo, and I intend those profits to be large. Very large, indeed." He smiled again. "Now, if I can arrange a profitable sale, who's to complain?"

A black servant entered the room, carrying a coffee tray, a sliver of steam rising from the silver pot. The men fell silent while the servant poured the thick brew, lacing it with cream before passing a cup to each of them. With a bow, he left the room as silently as he had come.

Penneywaite stirred his coffee, his bushy gray brows knotted together and his lips pursed in concentration. "I don't like this, American. It isn't how we do business."

Tristan shrugged, then sipped his coffee. "You haven't any choice, Penneywaite. It's how *I'm* doing business."

For several moments, they studied each other across the table. Tristan waited patiently, feeling confident. Penneywaite's gaze wavered, then dropped to his coffee. His fingers fidgeted with the rim of the cup.

Tristan leaned forward. "Of course, I understand you must have an interest in this venture so you will want to be present to see that you and the Englishman aren't cheated. I'm going to have a private auction on board my ship and sell these girls as a group." He rose from the cushions, holding his hat in his hands. "I'll send word once the sale is arranged."

"Wait a minute, American," Penneywaite

blustered as he scrambled to his feet. "What makes you think anyone would want the lot of them?"

"If that's the only way I'll sell them, they will buy." He placed his hat on his head. "Good day, Penneywaite. I'll find my own way out."

Spar bent down as he stepped into the steerage compartment. His eyes traveled slowly around the room until he spied the carrot-orange hair. "Excuse me, ladies," he mumbled as he hurried toward Ida.

She looked up at him, surprise written in her green eyes. She hadn't seen him since the morning of Jacobs's flogging. The mood aboard ship had been a dark one that day. Loralie had been vocal in putting the blame for it on Jacinda and had continued to cause trouble ever since. Ida knew that Spar had cared for her injury, but Loralie had always gone to the galley to see him. Ida had watched for Spar every chance she had, but he never seemed to be around. She'd missed him sorely.

"May I speak with you, Ida?" Spar asked. "Alone."

She glanced from side to side. "There's no alone 'ere."

"Come with me." He took her elbow and brought her up from her cot.

She felt dozens of pairs of eyes watching them leave the room. She glanced up at Spar, towering so high above her, and felt a rush of pleasure. Whatever he needed to talk to her about, she was glad of it. It had brought them together for at least a little while. Spar led her into the bowels of the ship, to the hold where she and the others had spent their first night on the *Gabrielle*. Lighting a candle, he opened the door for her, and they stepped inside. Ida glanced quickly around the dank room while Spar set the candle on a barrel near the door.

"Ida—"

She turned toward him.

"I'm not much for words, Ida Spencer. I'm a simple man." He took a step toward her. "I'm not much to look at and I have little enough to offer a woman, but I've grown fond of you. If you'll have me, I'd like you to do me the honor of becoming my wife and going back to America with me."

"Marry ye?" She couldn't believe it.

His face fell. "I was wrong to ask. I'm sorry."

Ida reached out and grabbed his hand. "No, Spar. I'm pleased that ye asked. I can't believe it, is all. Look at me. Would ye be takin' the likes o' me for a wife?"

"I know what you've been," he said tenderly, reaching out to touch the bright curls on her head, "but all that would be behind us in America. We could start over again, you and I. Dr. and Mrs. Nathan Spears."

"Nathan?"

"My name."

Then she smiled. "Ye said doctor."

"Aye, that I did. If you'll marry me, Ida, we'll both make a new start."

Of all the things she might have guessed as the reason he'd brought her here, this one would never have occurred to her. Marry him? Go to America? She wanted more than anything to say yes. "I couldn't marry ye, Spar. Ye'd be

ashamed o' me. People would know me for what
I am, and they wouldn't let ye care for them
because o' me." But then she smiled. "And ye're
wrong about bein' not much t'look at. I find ye
most handsome, Dr. Spears."

Spar lifted her up off the floor in his
powerful arms, hugging her tiny frame to his
broad chest. "I knew you'd agree."

"But Spar, I haven't—"

He kissed her, and she weakened.

"Spar, it just wouldn't—"

He kissed her again.

"Aye, Spar. I'll marry ye, and 'eaven 'elp us
both."

The next kiss left her quivering, and when
he returned her feet to the floor, she thought
her knees would refuse to hold her.

"Now I must tell you what I promised I'd
tell no one." He held her chin in his palm, tilting
her face upward. "I do this because I couldn't
bear to face you later if I didn't."

"Can it be so bad as all that?" she asked,
frightened by his grim countenance.

"It can, Ida, but you must swear to me
you'll tell not another soul, not even the Lady
Jacinda. I'm trusting you not to give all away."

"I swear, Spar. Now tell me."

19

Something was going on. Jacinda could feel it. The air seemed to hum with tension. She longed to go on deck, but Tommy had brought word that morning from Tristan; she was to stay below all day. She could hear footsteps on the poop and longed to throw open her window to see if she could catch a word that would give her a clue to what was going on. But the cold winter wind blowing in from the Black Sea forced her to keep the window closed.

She sensed that the final scene in some mysterious drama was about to be played out, and the conclusion would have a powerful effect on the man she loved. Whether he wanted her there or not, her place was at Tristan's side.

She dropped the needle and fabric onto the bed. "I'm not going to stay here another moment," she said decisively. "I'm going to find out what's going on."

Jacinda started for the door, then stopped suddenly and turned around. She might disobey Tristan's order to remain in her cabin, but she would at least wear the odious black clothing. She donned the robe quickly, then threw the ankle-length veil over her flaming red hair. Not only couldn't anyone see in, she could barely see out.

She opened the door cautiously, listening for voices. On silent feet, she left her cabin, moving carefully toward the companionway leading to the main deck. Two steps up, she paused and peered outside.

The afternoon had turned gray with dark clouds, clouds heavy with unleashed rain, and the wind rattled in the riggings and masts overhead. As she watched, two Turkish gentlemen boarded the ship. Whip was there to greet them before guiding them toward another companionway, this one leading into the main part of the ship. She continued to wait, wondering if there were any more men waiting to board.

When the coast was clear, she stepped up onto the deck and glanced around. Not another soul was in sight. It gave her an eerie feeling, standing alone on the main deck, the ship creaking in the wind. Despite the fact of land only a gangplank away, she felt deserted. Holding the hindering skirts out of her way, she hurried after Whip and the strangers.

Muffled voices drifted from deep within the ship to tease her ears, drawing her closer to the mystery of that day. She recognized the deep timbre of Tristan's voice, though she couldn't understand his words. She moved on, holding her breath.

It was surprisingly easy to slip into the cavernous storage room and hide behind some crates. The corner was dark, and she had a brief thought of ship rats scurrying around behind her, making her want to head for daylight, but she forced herself to remain still. She wanted to know what was going on.

Tristan had asked her to trust him. And she did. She did trust him, but she was tired of waiting for answers. She wanted to know and understand. Everything about this journey was a mystery to her. Though her own presence might be due to chance, there was a reason why the other women were here. There was a reason why Tristan had brought the *Dancing Gabrielle* to Constantinople. And there was a reason why Whip had been ushering Turks aboard. She was going to stay here until she had her answers.

She peeked around the crates, her eyes growing more accustomed to her dim surroundings before traveling toward the light at the other end of the room. Tristan stood in a far corner, his arms crossed in front of him, a grim set to his mouth and chin. Whatever was going on was not to his liking. Her gaze moved on, stopping on the group of Turks. There were about ten or twelve of them, all of them turbaned and sporting beards, many of them attired in obviously costly fabrics. They spoke amongst themselves, glancing often toward the doorway.

When the tall man leaned forward to enter the room, Jacinda drew back further into her corner, startled by his appearance. He was clad in a long silk robe under a sleeveless caftan of black and burgundy. On his head he wore an enormous turban. In every way, his clothes proclaimed him a man of the East, yet she would swear he was not. His sharp jaw was clean-shaven in contrast to the other men waiting in the room. He looked down his hawk-like nose with alert brown eyes. She sensed the tension in his thin frame, yet on the surface he appeared totally at ease.

The visitors fell silent as he moved toward them. She heard him speak a greeting, though she couldn't understand the words. Then he turned toward Tristan.

"Captain," he said, "are you ready to begin?"

"Let's get this over with," Tristan said impatiently. "And make it worth the trip, Danny O'Banyon."

"I will do my best, sir." He grinned as he turned around and raised his hand, motioning someone forward.

Jacinda turned her gaze once more toward the door. For a moment, no one appeared. Then, to her amazement, a woman stepped through it, clad in a revealing silk outfit. Before she could believe it, another woman stepped into the room, followed by another and another. They were all there. All the women aboard the *Gabrielle*, all of them wearing shimmery trousers and filmy blouses and sheer veils across the bridge of their noses.

"Don't be afraid, Bridget. I promise it'll be all right."

Jacinda recognized Ida's whispered encouragement as she pushed a dark-haired girl into the room.

The last to enter was Loralie. She paused just as she entered the glow of the lantern's light. She turned an indolent gaze upon the men gathered in the room, then moved confidently, sensuously, to stand with the others.

For a moment, Jacinda forgot that anyone else was there. It was only Loralie whom she saw. Loralie with her sultry beauty. Loralie with her generous breasts and ample hips. Loralie taunting her. Loralie mocking her.

Then the tall fellow in the black and burgundy caftan began to walk among the women, every so often bringing one of them forward to stand in front of the others, turning them this way and that while he talked in a foreign tongue. Interspersed with his monologue, an occasional word was tossed from one of the men.

How long did this go on before it began to dawn on her what was happening? She watched and listened but nothing made sense. Then, as the Turkish visitors began speaking more often, always with only a word or two, their voices rising in intensity, she began to understand. Her tawny eyes widened and she shook her head, denying the thought. Not this. Surely not this.

Suddenly the room grew quiet. The man called Danny turned toward Tristan. "Ben-Chayim has made you a rich man, Captain Dancing, and you will no longer have to care for this colorful cargo."

"Good," Tristan said. "Tell him to get them off the ship before nightfall."

"Very well, Captain."

I don't believe it, she thought. I won't believe it.

Not all things are as they seem, Jacinda. Remember that. And ... trust me a little longer.

Loralie stepped toward Danny, placing a hand lightly on his arm. "Do I understand that someone here has bought the lot of us?"

He looked her over but made no reply.

"Shouldn't he know that there's another woman the captain's kept hidden for himself?" She smiled. "We wouldn't want to cheat him, now would we?"

"What's this?" A short, fat man with a red nose and gray hair stepped forward from the back of the room. Jacinda hadn't noticed him before now. He'd been hidden in shadows, just as she had been. "Captain, are you trying to cheat the Englishman?"

Tristan shot Loralie a deadly glance before responding to the question. "The woman she speaks of was not among those sent with me, Penneywaite. In fact, she's my wife."

"That's a lie!" Loralie protested. "They may live like man and wife, but there's been no clergy to join them. He singled her out the first morning on this ship and has kept her in his cabin ever since."

Penneywaite stepped closer into the light. "I would like to see this woman for myself."

"I'm afraid not," Tristan replied.

"We wouldn't want it said that you were cheating your partner, now would we, Dancing? Let me meet your . . . ah . . . wife."

Heart in her throat, Jacinda slipped from her hiding place and out of the room. She ran through the corridors, the cursed black robe snatching at her ankles, trying to trip her. The veil hindered her sight, making her race a treacherous one. With no time for caution, she scrambled up the stairs of the companionway and across the deck toward the captain's quarters.

Still feeling as though someone were breathing down her neck, she tossed off the Kurdistan attire. She ran a hasty brush through her loose hair, then picked up a piece of embroidery and settled into a chair at the table. She was none too soon.

A knock preceded his voice. "Cinda, there is someone here who would like to meet you. May we come in?"

"Of course."

The door opened, and Tristan ushered in the short, gray-haired man, followed by Danny. "My love, may I introduce Mr. Penneywaite and Mr. O'Banyon, fellow citizens of the British Isles."

"How do you do, gentlemen." She nodded to each. "Please, do sit down. May I get you some tea?" She motioned toward the other chairs. "I'm afraid my husband's quarters aren't very large, but we find them comfortable enough for just two." She blushed as she turned adoring eyes on Tristan. Luckily, he was standing behind the other two men, or else they would have seen the surprise on his face as she spoke her pretty speech.

Penneywaite was studying her with undisguised appreciation. "It's an unexpected pleasure to meet an Englishwoman with your great beauty in these parts. Most captains leave their wives at home." There was a trace of suspicion in his tone.

Jacinda could almost see him counting the sum she would bring on the auction block. She had a difficult time quelling the shiver that started up her spine. "I'm afraid he would have left me behind, Mr. Penneywaite, but I smuggled myself aboard so I could be with him. We've been married such a short time, you see." She rose from her chair and slipped an arm through Tristan's, squeezing it against her as she gazed up at him. "I'm afraid he was terribly angry with me at first, but there was nothing he could do." She smiled a secret smile. "He forgave me in time."

Danny chuckled knowingly. "I'm sure that he did, ma'am. I think I'd forgive you anything myself."

Jacinda acknowledged his statement with another smile and a slight tilt of her head.

Tristan finally managed to stir himself. He freed his arm from her grasp and placed it casually over her shoulders. "Would you care for that tea my wife offered, or would you like something stronger?"

"Sorry, Dancing," Penneywaite said as he stood up. "I must be getting back to my house. I still have much work to do today. You will call on me tomorrow?"

"Of course."

"And bring your lovely bride. I'd love to talk with her of England."

Danny rose too. A single step brought him before Jacinda. "Mrs. Dancing, I can't tell you what a pleasure these brief moments have been." He kissed her hand, then looked at Tristan. "You're a lucky man, Captain."

Tristan's arm tightened. "I know," he said softly, looking at Jacinda. Then he followed the two men from the cabin.

Jacinda sat down on the edge of the bed,

her knees too weak to hold her. As soon as the door closed behind them, she felt as if she might fall apart. She couldn't believe anything she had seen happening, let alone her own part of it. What was Tristan involved in? What was *she* involved in? Could any of this really be happening to her? She hadn't even ever *dreamed* such things! Yet the longer she sat there, the more she believed it really was happening. And, even more to her surprise, she discovered her shaky knees were due as much to excitement as to fright. Perhaps even more so.

The door burst open, Tristan's frame filling the doorway. Jacinda jumped up from the bed, her heart hammering wildly in her chest. He would know of course that she'd disobeyed him. He would know that she'd left this cabin and witnessed the auction.

"Why?" he asked, walking toward her.

"Why?" she echoed.

"Why did you do it?" His ebony eyes seemed to pierce right through her, seeing into her soul. She couldn't tear her own eyes away from him. They were locked together by a gaze. Tristan's hand reached out to grasp hers. "Why?" he asked again, even more softly this time.

"Because I love you, Tristan."

"Even after what you saw?"

Her heart skipped a beat. "Not everything is as it seems," she answered, quoting the words he'd spoken on the beach at Madeira. "And I will trust you a little longer . . . and forever."

The last was hardly more than a whisper as he drew her into his arms, crushing her against him. His face brushed against her hair. He murmured her name again and again. A wonderful feeling possessed her as she understood his need for her. Not just a physical need but an emotional one. Their love went beyond the joys of a marriage bed. It bound them together more securely than any vows spoken over them by a priest. She hadn't lied when she'd called him her husband. It was true. More than she could have guessed at the time.

His mouth sought hers in a tender kiss, then he stepped back from her. "Cinda, it's time I told you the truth."

20

Tristan looked lovingly down upon Jacinda. She
was waiting, waiting for him to at last tell her
what was happening. And the telling was long
overdue. He should have told her on the beach
on Madeira. He'd started to tell her on the ship
the day they sailed from the island, but she had
silenced him. He'd been so moved by her total
trust, he hadn't wanted to spoil the moment
with revelations. But if not then, he should have
at least told her when he asked her to marry
him. Yet he hadn't told her even then, and still
she trusted him. Now he must tell her.

"Sit down, Cinda. Please."

She obeyed.

"The story is a long one. I want you to sit
quietly and hear me out."

She nodded.

"My name is Dancing, but my mother's
name was Phineasbury. Felicia Phineasbury,
daughter of the Duke of Locksworth."

Jacinda let a small gasp escape her. Her
eyes widened, but she said nothing.

"I was returning from Foochow when my sister, Gabrielle, decided to come to England to see Grandfather. I followed after her, but she'd never arrived. Ella was kidnapped in London."

"Ella! She is your sister?"

"Yes. That's what we call Gabrielle. My ship is named for her. Why?"

Her smile was tender and joyous. "Nothing. I'm sorry I interrupted. Go on, please." Her smile vanished quickly. "Oh, how terrible! She was kidnapped?"

"Yes. In London. The duke and I learned that she'd been taken to be sold into slavery by a man known as the Englishman." He paused for a moment. Should he tell her that Blackstoke was the Englishman? No. This was one thing he would not tell her. The pleasure of his revenge would be his and his alone. She needn't know that she had nearly married the man who had taken his sister. "We knew that much but not where she might have been taken. Somehow I had to find out. So we let it be known around the docks that I would carry *any* kind of cargo, that I was desperate. The ploy worked, and I was hired to take on these women to be sold in Constantinople."

"But, Tristan—"

He raised a hand, silencing her. "I informed my friend, Danny O'Banyon, that we were coming and asked him to help me and explained what I was doing. The man you saw, the one who bought the women. He is going to ship them back to England within a week or two. They will never know slavery and will be compensated for their time at sea."

"And Ella? Is she here in Constantinople?"

Tristan sat down beside her, his hands clenched as he stared at the floor. "I don't know. I pray she is, for I don't know where else to look. I know that Penneywaite handles auctions for the Englishman frequently. If anyone can lead us to Ella, it must be him."

Jacinda's arm slid around Tristan's back and she laid her head against his shoulder. "Don't worry, Tris, we will find her. And I'm going to help any way I can."

He turned, looking deep into her tawny-gold eyes. Her love for him was almost frightening. Could he ever live up to such devotion?

"We must have a plan," Jacinda whispered to herself.

Tristan took her face between his hands and drew her toward him for a kiss. "The first thing we're going to do, my love," he told her softly, "is see that what you told Mr. Penneywaite and Mr. O'Banyon was not a lie. We are going to find a man of the cloth and I'm going to make you Mrs. Tristan Dancing. Will you do me the honor, Lady Jacinda?"

"Tris," she replied, "I've been your wife in my heart for such a long time. I will happily be your wife in truth."

She wore the emerald green riding gown that she had worn especially for Tristan so many, many weeks before. As Jacinda arranged her flaming tresses in a mass of intricate curls atop her head, she thought of the hours she had stood in Madam Roget's salon, surrounded by yards and yards of lace and satin, her mother harping on every detail for the grand bridal gown. Yet that dress had meant nothing to her. But then, neither had the groom. How much happier would be her memories of this gown and this day.

She gave herself a final once-over in the small mirror, then turned to pick up the spray of pale flowers Spar had brought to her not long before. Later, she would think to ask him where he had found them on such short notice and in the midst of winter. For now she could only think of his thoughtfulness and be grateful.

With a fluttering heart, she opened the cabin door. "Please come in, gentlemen."

Tristan was waiting in the corridor with the Reverend Taylor, a friend of Danny's from the Christian quarters, Danny himself, Spar, and Whip.

Tristan was wearing his dress uniform and looked as handsome as she had ever seen him. For a moment, as he moved into the room, she had a fleeting vision of her gallant knight riding up to the castle. She saw him smile as he vaulted from his shiny black charger, then he gathered her into his arms. The daydream vanished, and she realized it was Tristan who was holding her. Tristan, the real man, the man she would love . . . 'til death did them part.

He was so much better than a dream.

Penneywaite sent his coach for Tristan and Jacinda early the following afternoon. Shrouded through her dark veil, the streets of the city seemed, perhaps, even more exotic than they were. Still, her first real glimpse of the city was exciting.

Penneywaite's home was a grandiose stone

structure with many pillars and large windows. Inside, it was elegantly decorated with rich carpets and jeweled statues. The servant who greeted them at the door led them through a long hallway, past many closed rooms, and into a dining room with a crystal chandelier and a long mahogany table with many straight back chairs surrounding it. The room was entirely English in decor, a departure from the Eastern influence they had seen elsewhere.

"Ah, my friends, you have arrived." Penneywaite bustled into the room, all smiles. "Welcome. Welcome to my home." He turned toward Jacinda. "Please, Mrs. Dancing. Remove those terrible black things and let me see how beautiful you are. There is no need for them inside my house."

She did as he asked, willingly shedding the robe and veil. She was wearing a dark red dress which Danny had brought to her as a wedding gift the previous day. The fit was surprisingly accurate, but she hadn't asked him how he'd known. With it, she was wearing the diamond necklace and earbobs which had been her gift from Tristan. She had worn them at Tristan's request, but Penneywaite's open stare made her wish she'd left on the black robe.

"You are the loveliest woman to ever visit my home, Mrs. Dancing," he told her.

"Thank you, Mr. Penneywaite."

"Please. Please. Where are my manners? Do be seated." He clapped his hands and a servant appeared. "We shall dine at once, Abdul." While he waited for their supper to be served, Penneywaite said, "I must tell you I continue to be surprised that a lady such as you would subject herself to such a miserable journey, Mrs. Dancing."

"It is not so miserable when one shares it with her husband," Jacinda replied sweetly.

"Ah, yes. Yes. I see." He turned his head toward Tristan. "And you, sir? Will you be coming again to Constantinople?"

"I don't know, Penneywaite. This has been a very profitable venture, but it could be even more so if I didn't have to share those profits with the Englishman."

Penneywaite's forehead lifted in surprise.

"My wife knows all about my cargo. We need have no secrets from her."

Again the fat man looked at Jacinda. "Really? Now that is a surprise. And what is it you think of your husband's business dealings, Mrs. Dancing?"

"I disapprove, sir, but it was only this one time. Besides, my husband assures me that their lives will be no worse here than they were in England. Or wherever else they might have been from."

"Speaking of which," Tristan said, leaning across the table toward Penneywaite. "Do you think there would be a market here for American women?"

"Women are women," Penneywaite answered with a shrug.

"Tristan, really. You told me you wouldn't consider doing this again."

"Did I? Oh, yes, I did." Tristan smiled at her. "But dear, if their lives are no worse off than before, why shouldn't we profit from it? Someone will."

"How do we know their lives are no worse

off? Have we seen how they live? I was only echoing what you told me." She twisted her hands in her lap, staring down at them with tearful eyes.

Tristan turned toward his host once more. "How about it, Penneywaite? Can you let me meet one of these girls you've . . . ah . . . found a home for here? An American, perhaps, since that would be my stock in trade. If my wife could see that they are not mistreated, perhaps her objections would cease."

Penneywaite glanced back and forth between the husband and wife. "An American? Well, I don't know if I've ever . . . No, wait. I did have one American girl. Several months ago. A beauty as I recall."

"Wonderful!" Tristan exclaimed. "When can we meet her?"

"Oh, you could never meet her, Captain."

Tristan's eyes clouded. "Why not?"

"Because you are a man, and she belongs to the harem of a pasha."

"A pasha?" Jacinda repeated.

"It's a title of honor, Mrs. Dancing."

"I see." She turned toward Tristan. "Are you seriously considering bringing women from America to this place?"

He shrugged, then nodded.

Jacinda turned again toward Penneywaite. "*I* am not a man, Mr. Penneywaite. Could you arrange for me to meet this American woman?" She showed him a resigned smile. "If my husband is going to insist on embarking on such a venture, I would feel much better if I knew these women were well treated, as my husband says."

"I will speak to Halidah Pasha, Mrs. Dancing. I will do what I can."

"Thank you, Penneywaite," Tristan interjected. "You are very tolerant of my wife's whims. I'm sure you can understand why I can deny her very little."

"Yes, indeed, Captain. I can certainly understand."

She sat on the pile of cushions, idly strumming her tanbur. Her legs, tucked beneath her, were clad in sheer, lavender silk pantaloons, and she wore a matching bodice trimmed in purple velvet. A wide, silver girdle set with tiny amethysts circled her waist. Purple and silver brocade slippers encased her petite feet. Held by a simple silver clasp, her shiny hair fell straight down her back, then spread over the pillows behind her.

"You are very sad tonight, my little flower."

Ella's fingers fell silent as she looked toward the doorway. Halidah Pasha had entered quietly and was sitting on a chair just inside the room. She shook her head, swallowing the tears that threatened to fill her dark eyes.

"You torture yourself with memories of another life. Will you not turn your face to the future?" His voice was gentle, his words concerned.

"I cannot forget."

Halidah rose and came to stand over her. He stretched out his hand and stroked her ebony tresses. Then, without another word, he turned and left the room. She was alone again.

Ella left the tanbur on the cushions and went to stand on the terrace overlooking her private gardens. She shivered in the cool wind that blew down from the Black Sea, but she didn't go back inside. Instead, she sat on one of the marble benches and continued to stare at the star-studded sky.

"Oh, Tristan," she whispered. "Will I ever see you again?"

She had told Halidah that she couldn't forget, and it was true. Though the faces were blurring, the emotions her memories evoked were as strong and as painful as ever. How she longed for her home in America. How she longed to hear Tristan's voice as he teased her. Even old Aunt Elvira had lost some of her spitefulness when she entered Ella's thoughts.

How had all of this happened to her? What was she doing here, a prisoner in this strange land?

Drawing her feet up onto the bench, she nestled her face against her knees and clasped her arms around her legs. How had this happened to her?

The journey had been long and frightening. Even after she was taken to a cabin and allowed to live in an element of comfort compared to the other captives, it was a nightmare. But nothing that happened on the journey prepared her for the shock awaiting her in Constantinople.

She still had hopes that Tristan would find and rescue her, even once they arrived in this strange, foreign city, but those hopes were quickly dashed when the captain brought her a sheer, peach-colored robe and veil and ordered her to put them on. Then she was taken to stand before a group of dark-skinned, turbaned men with trimmed beards and peering eyes. While they ogled her body, so clearly exposed beneath her flimsy attire, and discussed her attributes and flaws in a tongue she couldn't understand, she was forced to wait helplessly for her fate to be decided.

Her first sight of Halidah Pasha was in that room. When the bidding was finished, he rose and motioned for her to follow him. When she didn't immediately obey, the captain gave her a rough shove in his direction. As she left the cabin, another girl was brought in. There was a brief exchange of trepidation as their eyes met, and then she was taken from the ship.

He was patient with her. Surprisingly so. She had expected rape or worse, not the gentle persuasion Halidah used to bring her to his bed. He could speak English and had, in fact, served his sultan as an ambassador to England in the past. He was no more than thirty-five, perhaps younger, and he was handsome. He treated her with gentleness and affection. Despite herself, she grew fond of him. And yet her feelings for her gentle master didn't affect her loneliness for her home, her country, and her family.

The weeks became months. She was housed in a beautiful, cream-colored marble palace with elegant furnishings and servants to care for her. Her clothes were encrusted with rare gems, and she dined on rich foods. Still she was a prisoner and longed for her freedom.

Would Tristan ever find her?

21

"Halidah Pasha is a very powerful man. He lived for a time in England as an ambassador and speaks English quite fluently." Danny looked out the window of the captain's cabin, staring at the other ships floating in the harbor. "I've met him once, but I've never been to his palace."

"Then you don't know if there's some way we can get Ella out?" Tristan asked.

"If she's even Ella," Jacinda gently reminded her husband.

Danny returned to the table and sat down across from Tristan and Jacinda. "The first thing to do is get Jacinda inside, let her see Ella and let her know that you're here and trying to free her. Perhaps Jacinda will see a way to sneak her out once she sees where Ella is kept."

"And if not?"

"Then we'll have to come up with a different plan, Tris. Besides, we don't even know at this point if Penneywaite will be able to arrange an audience."

Tristan's fist hit the table, causing the other two people in the room to jump. "*Damnation!* How can I be this close to her and unable to help?"

"Darling," Jacinda said, wrapping her fingers around his arm, "you knew it wouldn't be easy. We must be patient just a little longer."

Jacinda felt awkward and a little frightened as the veiled litter traversed the narrow streets of Constantinople. The six black Nubians carried the litter, with her inside it, with ease. The pasha had sent the litter for her early that morning. Alongside them, Danny rode on his white horse, his colorful robes flowing over the animal's rump. The litter stopped and was lowered gently to the ground. Danny dismounted and pushed the curtains aside, motioning for her to disembark, which she did quickly. The marble palace stood like a pale jewel amidst a grove of tall trees. Jacinda followed Danny up the steps toward a side entrance.

"Remember to keep quiet unless you're spoken to, Jacinda," he warned her. "This entrance is for women and leads to the harem. Penneywaite has arranged this meeting as a favor, but there are apt to be spies to hear what you say. Be very careful. Servants have big ears, and sometimes so do the walls. I won't be there to help you."

Beneath her black veil, Jacinda nodded. Excitement and anxiety knotted her stomach. She wouldn't fail Tristan.

Danny returned to wait beside the litter while Jacinda was admitted into the small waiting room just inside the double doors. It was here the local female vendors could come to sell their wares to the women of the pasha's household. It was also here that Jacinda was led away by a swarthy eunuch through a private anteroom which opened upon the rooms of the harem. The eunuch stopped at the fourth door and opened it for her, showing her into a nicely proportioned private salon.

Seated upon varied-colored cushions was a young woman close to her own age. Jacinda would have known her as Tristan's sister without ever being told. Ella had the same raven-black hair and expessive ebony eyes as her brother, though where Tristan was tall and muscular, Ella was small and petite.

Ella rose from her cushions. "Remove your veil and let me look at you."

Jacinda obeyed.

"I was told you wanted to meet an American who lived in this country. Why would you want such a thing? Who are you?"

Jacinda felt a strange, prickly sensation, a feeling that she was being watched. She remembered Danny's warning. She stepped closer to Ella, raising a finger to her lips quickly, then dropping it, hoping Ella would understand her warning. "My name is Jacinda Dancing."

Ella's face paled. "Why have you come here?"

"May we sit down? I am weary."

"Of course. Perhaps you would like some tea?" She flicked her wrist toward a curtain at the end of the room.

Jacinda saw the curtain move and heard

footsteps retreating. She longed to ask if they were now alone but held her tongue. She settled onto the cushions near the fireplace. A warm fire glowed on the hearth, chasing away some of the strangeness of the room. She watched her sister-in-law as she sat down close by.

"Please," Ella said, "tell me what has brought you here."

"My husband is a ship's captain. He came to Constantinople from England with a cargo of women to be sold here. I am very much against this trading in human beings, but he is considering doing it again, this time with American women since he is himself an American."

The servant returned with their tea, and Jacinda paused in her tale until she had retired once again. She could see Ella's hand shaking as she lifted the cup to her lips, but Jacinda had to continue with her story in case there were extra ears hidden to hear what she had to say. Surely Ella would know that Tristan wouldn't do the things she was saying. Surely she would know that they were here to rescue her.

"I have been assured by Mr. Penneywaite that the women who are brought here are no worse off than they were in England or America, but I wanted to see for myself." Her eyes held Ella's gaze as she asked, "Can you tell me what it's been like for you?"

"I have not been ill-treated. I was lucky to have the pasha choose me for his harem. All masters aren't so kind." Tears welled in ebony eyes. "But I fear my heart will break from missing my own home, my own family. I long to see my brother and my grandfather again."

Jacinda discovered there were tears in her

own eyes.

"Come. Walk with me in the gardens before you must leave." Ella placed her teacup on the low table and rose gracefully to her feet, then extended a hand to Jacinda. She slipped her arm through Jacinda's and led her outside. "Speak quickly and softly. Is Tristan really with you? Are you really his wife?"

"Yes. To both your questions."

"What will he do now?"

"I don't know, Ella, but he has come to free you, and that is what he will do. You must wait patiently while we devise a means of escape. Can you help us?" She cast a quick glance over the tall wall that surrounded the gardens. "Is there any way out of here?"

"No. There is no way out except the way you entered."

"Then that is how you shall leave."

Ella shook her head sadly. "Perhaps you should give Tristan my love and then leave me here. Perhaps it would be better if I remained."

"You mustn't say that," Jacinda protested, stopping in the middle of the path.

"You don't understand. I think . . . I'm quite certain I'm with child."

Jacinda's hand flew up to cover her mouth, muffling the gasp she couldn't contain. Her eyes darted quickly around the private gardens, but she saw no one else about. "Ella, are you sure?"

"I think so." Ella began to cry. She didn't make a sound, only the silent tears streaking her cheeks gave her away. With a little encouragement, she laid her head against Jacinda's shoulder. "What am I to do?" she whispered.

Jacinda didn't know what to tell her. She patted her thick black hair and stroked her back, but she was without words. She felt so inadequate at this moment. And what was she going to tell Tristan? *Should* she even tell him? She knew he was growing impatient to take her from this place. What would he do if he knew his little sister was pregnant by this infidel?

"If Halidah finds out about the baby, there will be no more hope of escape. I will be taken from here until after the baby is born."

Exasperated, Jacinda hissed, "What kind of man is he?"

"He's never been unkind to me, Jacinda. He's been gentle, and he is troubled by my sadness. I believe he loves me in his own way. He paid a great price for me."

It surprised Jacinda to hear Ella's defense of her master.

"Perhaps, if things were different, I could have learned to love him too." She pulled away from Jacinda and began walking once again.

"Ella, you can't mean that."

Round black eyes turned to gaze at her. "Oh, yes. I can mean it. Jacinda, I was so frightened and alone. He could have been an ogre. He could have done anything with me he wanted. He could have tied me in a bag and thrown me into the river. After all, I am only a woman. But he was kind to me."

"But love him?"

"I said if things were different." Ella shook her head sadly. "If we had met in America or in England. If he were a Christian and not a Moslem. If he believed in only one wife." She dropped her gaze to the path in front of her. "But these things can never be. I can never be happy here, and I can never love him with things as they are."

Jacinda was silent for a long time before asking, "And what of the child?"

"I will love him fiercely. But he must not be born here." She grasped Jacinda's arm. "I must get away from here. I must get away from here soon."

"Tristan won't fail you," Jacinda promised.

Ella wiped away her tears and led the way back toward her salon.

"Ella, you must be ready to leave at a moment's notice. We may not be able to give you any warning. I don't know if I will be able to come back, but don't give up hope. We won't leave you here."

Ella watched the door close behind Jacinda, leaving her alone once more. Hope and despair warred in her heart. Tristan had found her, but was there any way he could free her? She fought the tears that rose so easily and so quickly to her eyes. It seemed she had done nothing but cry for the past several months of her life. She despised the helpless feeling that overwhelmed her.

"Oh!" she cried in frustration, picking up a porcelain vase and hurling it across the room. It smashed into the wall, breaking into a thousand pieces.

"What's this? Has my little flower grown teeth?"

Ella whirled around, finding Halidah standing in the terrace doorway. He was smiling at her, his amusement crushing the last of her self-pity, leaving only the anger that had caused her to break the vase.

"The Englishwoman, she is good for you," he said as he entered the room. "There is color in your cheeks again. Will she come again?"

"She said she would, if you would allow it."

"I will allow it if it will make you happy."

"Oh yes, my lord. It would make me happy. Very happy."

Halidah's hand cupped her chin, lifting her face toward his. "I will do all I can to make you happy, my flower of delight. This I promise."

"I cannot be happy as long as I'm a prisoner, my lord."

He sighed. "You Americans are a strange people," he said as he held her against him.

"Perhaps, my lord," she agreed, closing her eyes.

Tristan was pacing the deck, anxiously awaiting her return. She spied him from her litter and felt a sudden quickening of her heart, wanting to urge the slaves to move faster toward the ship. She could hardly wait to tell him about Ella. When he saw her approaching, he ran down the gangplank. He whisked her out of the litter as soon as it touched the ground and nearly dragged her onto the ship.

"What's wrong?" she asked as he pulled her down the companionway toward their cabin.

He stopped abruptly. "That's what I want to know. I thought you were never coming back. Do you know how long you were gone?"

"No, I—"

"Hours. And here I waited, not knowing

what was happening."

A tender smile brightened Jacinda's mouth. "You needn't have worried about me, my love. Danny was with me. I came to no harm." She stood on tiptoe and kissed his cheek.

"And Ella? She is Ella, isn't she? How is she? Is she all right?"

"Yes, Tris, she's Ella and she's fine. Really she is. She's unhappy because she wants to be with you, but she is truly all right. Now, if we can get into our cabin, I'll tell you all about it." She looked over her shoulder. Danny was looking down the companionway. "You'd better join us, Danny," she called to him. "We're going to need your help."

Jacinda was nestled in his arms, snuggled against his side. A fire in the stove warmed the cabin, but it was the warmth of Tristan's body that stayed the chill of night.

"We've got to get her out of there. And soon," he said, not for the first time that evening.

"We'll think of something, Tristan." She rolled up onto her elbow, throwing her other arm across her husband's chest. "I'll do anything I can. You know I will."

His arm pulled her on top of him. "I've risked you too much already. I want you stay on the *Gabrielle* from now on."

"No! You need me, Tristan Dancing. I won't be shoved aside to darn your socks and wait. I want to help. She's my sister too, you know."

In the darkness of their cabin, he kissed her, a warm chuckle sounding in his throat. "You're grown too bold, my love. What's happened to the compliant lady who meekly agreed to marry the man her parents chose for her?''

"She was never compliant, dear pirate mine. She was merely a prisoner of herself. You have set her free."

"Saints forgive me," he whispered, burying his face in her hair, allowing himself to forget, for just a little while, the problems that would face him again with the coming of day.

Danny led the bent older woman onto the *Gabrielle*. The city had been given a brief respite from the cold winds that had buffeted it in recent weeks, a balmy breeze coming to take its place. Jacinda and Tristan were in the galley and met with Danny there.

"This is Wilona. She has solved our problem."

Jacinda and Tristan turned their eyes upon the shriveled woman. She must have been at least fifty years old. Her hands were gnarled and her hair gray. There were dark circles under her colorless eyes, eyes that spoke of pain and sadness. They turned to exchange wondering glances. How could this woman solve their problem?

"Sit down, Wilona," Danny told the woman, pulling out a bench for her. "Tris, the pasha has agreed to let Jacinda visit Ella one more time. It may be the last time. If he discovers she is expecting his child and moves her to one of his other palaces as she said he would, we might never find her again. And according to Jacinda, there's no way in or out of her rooms except through the harem. That's how Wilona can help us."

"I'm afraid I still don't understand," Tristan said, looking once again at the old woman.

"Mr. O'Banyon?" Wilona asked in a soft voice. "May I explain?"

"Of course."

She turned toward the captain. "If your wife were to take Christmas gifts to your sister, she would need a servant to help her carry them in. The pasha would understand the gifts. He has lived in your country. When she left, the servant woman would leave with her. Only it wouldn't be the servant woman. It would be your sister. The servant woman would be left behind." She looked at Jacinda. "I would like to be that servant woman."

"But, Wilona, what would they do to you when they found out?"

"They would kill me."

Jacinda looked at Tristan, horrified. "Tris, we can't allow that! We—"

"Please, Mrs. Dancing," Wilona interrupted, "let me finish. They would kill me if they had the chance. But you see, they won't. I would already be dead . . . by my own hand."

Tristan reached across the table and touched Wilona's misshapen hand. "I'm afraid we still don't understand, Wilona," he said gently. "Besides, why would you want to do this for us?"

"Captain Dancing, I was brought here as a very young girl. I've been a slave to these people for many, many years. My masters have seldom been good to me. I have an unfortunate face that brings no pity. I have learned to hate these Turks." She paused, fighting tears. "Mr. O'Banyon purchased me nearly a year ago. He has offered to send me to England, but I doubt my family would be pleased to see me after all these years. That is, if anyone is even still alive. Besides, I am dying. It's a very slow and painful death I suffer from, and I long to be free from the pain.'' She let out a deep sigh. ''When I heard Mr. O'Banyon discussing the problem with one of his trusted friends, I knew this was something I could do to repay him for his kindness. And more than that. It was a way for me to strike a blow against a Turk and be free of my pain, all at the same time.''

''It could work, Tris,'' Danny said when Wilona had fallen silent.

''I don't know, Danny. We're asking this woman to die for someone she's never even met. It just doesn't seem right.''

''No, sir,'' Wilona objected. ''That's not what you'd be doing. You'd be letting me die in peace. You'd be doing me as great a favor as I'd be doing you. Please, Captain Dancing, let me do this, for both our sakes.''

22

There would be a tree in the parlor at Bonclere and a yule log on the hearth. She imagined the gray skies that might bring a flurry of snow to whiten the ground on Christmas morning. If she were home, she would drape the bells on Pegasus's saddle and take the mare for a wild ride through the countryside, dressed in her fur-lined cloak of red wool. She did it every year, over the mild protests of her parents— mild because the neighbors always enjoyed it and said so.

Jacinda lay awake, waiting for the coming of day. Christmas day. How very different this one was compared to those that had gone before. She moved her hand until her fingers touched Tristan's back.

"Merry Christmas, Cinda," he whispered, rolling over.

"I didn't mean to wake you."

"You didn't. I've been lying here thinking."

"About today," she added for him.

"Yes. About today." His arm reached out to

draw her closer to him. "Are you sure you want to do this?"

"I'm sure, Tris. Besides, it's the only way."

Tristan pressed her head against his shoulder. "I know. But there's so much risk."

"There's risk in our just being here," she replied, then kissed his throat. "It's Wilona that bothers me," she added softly. "She's going to die."

"At least she'll die quickly," Tristan said, hoping to comfort, but failing. He traced feather-light kisses across her forehead. "She's doing it for Danny." He paused, then added, "Just as you're risking your life for Ella."

She lifted her face so she could look into his eyes. For Ella, yes. But mostly for him. She would do anything for Tristan.

He understood. He could read it all in her gaze. With a sudden fierceness, he crushed her against him, whispering into her hair, "God keep you safe, Jacinda, my love."

"He will, Tristan. He will."

The late morning sun cast a warm glow upon the marble walls of the palace, belying the chill of the December winds that whistled through the streets. Jacinda climbed the steps, for once thankful for the folds of the black robe that hid her from the view of men. Wilona followed behind her, her arms laden with packages.

As before, Jacinda was led through the long hallway of the harem and let into the spacious salon. Ella was nowhere to be seen when Jacinda and Wilona entered. Removing her veil, Jacinda glanced out at the gardens, then settled onto the cushions near the fire. Wilona sank onto a cushion at her side. They didn't have long to wait.

Ella entered the room, her arm linked with Halidah's. She was laughing, and there were pretty splashes of pink on her cheeks. Her black eyes twinkled with mirth. Her raven hair was woven through with strings of jewels, and her fingers glittered with rings. Her costume was made of white silk, trimmed with silver and turquoise.

Jacinda was astonished to see Ella looking so beautiful. In fact, the happiness written on her face caught Jacinda so much by surprise that she forgot she was unveiled. Then the couple stopped, and Jacinda found herself looking into Halidah Pasha's slanting black eyes, and she was left breathless by the intensity of his gaze.

He smiled. "I saw many beautiful women when I was in your country, Mrs. Dancing, but none with hair the color of yours."

With a tiny gasp, she dropped her eyes to her lap, leaning her head forward.

"Don't worry about your veil," he said. "I have lived in your country and grew accustomed to seeing women without veils."

Jacinda looked up again as Halidah and Ella joined her near the fire. She was unnerved by the strangeness of the situation. Seeing him with Ella—and her smiling and laughing and showing affection for him—confused Jacinda and made her uncertain what she should do next.

"As much as I would like to stay with you, my little flower, and get to know your charming friend, I will leave you to your little celebration." He kised Ella's palm. He paused before Jacinda, his gaze frankly admiring. "I hope I will see you again."

Jacinda stared, neither confirming nor denying his statement. Her voice was caught in her throat; her heart hammered in her ears. She watched him walk across the room. When the door closed and they were left in silence, Jacinda turned. "Ella—"

She shook her head. "He doesn't know it, but I've been saying good-bye," she said softly. She leaned forward, whispering, "I wasn't mistaken, was I? You are taking me away from here?"

Jacinda was alarmed. She suspected prying ears behind every curtain and door.

"Don't worry. There is no one about."

"How can you be sure?"

Ella smiled knowingly. "I just know. Now tell me. What are your plans? How are we to leave?"

"You'll change places with Wilona and leave with me."

Ella's dark eyes grew wide as she turned to look at the servant woman who was sitting silently across from them. "But Jacinda, when they find out—" She stopped. Her head spun back toward Jacinda. "They'll kill her. First they'll force her to tell them where I've gone and then they'll kill her."

"They won't have a chance," Jacinda responded. "Wilona will already be dead." It was her turn to look at Wilona. "She wants to do this, Ella. Wilona hasn't long to live. It's her way of thanking Danny for rescuing her after so many years as a slave. He found her and bought her and offered to send her back to England. But when she heard him talking about you, she volunteered to help us."

Ella's eyes teared. "How can I allow her to do this?"

"You must, miss," Wilona said, rising from her cushion. She walked over and knelt on the floor before Ella. She wasn't a pretty woman, and the ravages of pain had stolen what little good looks there had been, leaving her with a pinched mouth and a wrinkled brow. She took hold of Ella's hand. "Please, let some good come from my dying."

"But, Wilona—"

"I can't bear to live with it much longer. Maybe I'll be free to smile again." She pulled a vial from the folds of her robe. "I'm told it's very quick, miss, and painless, too."

Jacinda took Ella's other hand. "We must do it, Ella. It's our only chance."

At last, Ella nodded.

"Will the pasha return?"

"No. I won't ever see him again."

Jacinda squeezed her hand. "Are you sorry? You seemed so . . . so happy when you were with him."

The mistiness in Ella's eyes turned to tears again. "No, I'm not sorry. The happiness we might have shared if things were different—" She shrugged. "It couldn't happen here."

Danny stood on the poop with Tristan, both of them ignoring the winds that blew through their coats while they waited for Jacinda's litter to return. The sailors were all in their quarters, but they too were waiting. Anxiously waiting.

The morning had crept past with dragging feet. Each sound Tristan heard made him start. He expected to hear shouts of outrage at any moment, expected to see an armed force of Turkish soldiers falling upon his ship. He cursed himself for allowing Jacinda to go into the city without him. He should have done something himself. He shouldn't have risked her. Any number of things could have gone wrong. She might not even make it out of that place alive, let alone with Ella.

"Tris."

He turned toward Danny.

"I'm leaving with you."

"Leaving?"

"I'm going back with you. I'm finished with this country. That is, if you'll take on another passenger."

"But, what about your house here? Your business? Won't it ruin you to leave so suddenly?"

Danny shook his head. "I'll lose some, but I'm nothing if not a shrewd businessman, my friend. My wealth is in England."

"You're welcome anytime aboard this ship, Danny O'Banyon. Wealthy or not." Tristan clasped right hands with his friend and slapped his shoulder with his left.

Jacinda and Ella left the palace in mid-afternoon. The walk through the halls and out to her litter was the longest, most torturous walk Jacinda had ever taken. She had to force herself not to rush, especially once the door was opened and she could see the litter with the black slaves waiting to carry them to safety. Then there was the moment, after she was in the litter, when she glanced back at the palace and had a sudden vision of Wilona lying on Ella's bed, wearing Ella's clothes, surrounded by the sheer curtains, drinking the deadly potion.

The litter moved steadily through the streets toward the docks where the *Gabrielle* was moored. The two veiled women didn't speak to one another. Both seemed to be afraid that any sound from them would bring the world crashing in on them.

At last, just when Jacinda thought she might go mad from her screaming nerves, the litter was lowered to the ground. The curtains were moved aside, revealing the beautiful tall ship in all her glory. Jacinda led the way up the gangplank, still not daring to speak to Ella. Moments after their feet alighted on the deck of the ship, the gangplank was pulled up, the ropes cast off, and the *Gabrielle* moved away from the docks of Constantinople. Jacinda took Ella down to the captain's cabin. They removed their veils, golden eyes meeting ebony ones in a look of shared apprehension. They sat down in opposite chairs at the table and waited in continued silence.

The door flew open before Tristan. The two young women were seated at the table, their hands folded before them. He paused, his eyes feasting first on Jacinda, then moving to Ella.

She rose slowly from her chair, black eyes glittering with repressed tears. "Tris," she whispered.

He stepped toward her. Suddenly, she was in his arms, her face pressed against his chest. He'd nearly forgotten how tiny she was. "Ssh. Don't cry. You're safe now."

"I thought I'd never see you again," she said, sniffling.

Tristan caught one of her tears with his finger, then kissed her forehead. "Didn't you know I'd find you? Even if it took me a lifetime."

Ella gave him a tremulous smile. "Yes, I knew."

Tristan hugged her again, then turned with her at his side toward Jacinda. She was still sitting at the table, her own cheeks wet with joyful tears. Tristan held out his free arm toward her, and she hurried to join them.

He closed his eyes. "No man was ever as rich as I," he said softly, holding the two women close against his sides.

The door opened behind them.

"May we join you?"

The trio turned. Framed in the doorway were several familiar faces—Whip and Spar and Danny.

"Move over, ye bloody baggage. 'ow's a body t'get by ye?"

Jacinda's face lit with joyous surprise, even before the bright orange crop of curls was seen. "Ida!"

"It's me, milady," she said, elbowing her way past the three men.

The two women hugged each other. "How on earth did you get back on the *Gabrielle*?" Jacinda asked. "I thought Ben-Chayim had sent everyone back to England."

"And leave the man what says 'e'll marry me? Not a chance."

"Marry?" Jacinda's surprise turned into glee as her gaze moved to the doorway. "Spar. Is she telling me you've had sense enough to propose marriage?"

"That she is, Jacinda." Spar and the others entered the cabin. "And I'll tell you more once I've feasted my eyes on this one," he said as he reached out to touch Ella's cheeks with his massive hands.

"Oh, Spar. It's so good to see you."

"Not near what it is for me to see you, little Ella."

They hugged each other, Ella nearly disappearing beneath his arms.

"You've had enough time with her," Whip protested, shoving at Spar. "Let off, you mangy sea dog, before I have you thrown overboard."

Spar just laughed as he stepped back, allowing Ella to turn toward the first mate.

"Look at you," Whip said in awe. "You've grown even more beautiful than before. I'd never've thought it was possible."

"Oh, Whip," she sighed, giving him a big hug. "If you only knew how good you look to me."

A throat cleared. "And might I meet the lady?" a gentle voice asked.

Ella turned again. As tall as Spar, the man gazing down at her was thin to the extreme. Warm brown eyes watched her above a long, sharp nose. "You must be Danny O'Banyon," she said, offering her hand. "You've had much to do with gaining my freedom, I believe."

He took her hand and kissed the backs of

her fingers. "I was glad to help, Miss Dancing."
He smiled. "Would that I had done it sooner."

Tristan pushed his way back to his sister's
side. "All right, everyone. You'll all have time to
talk to Ella later. For now, she's mine. Clear
out."

"Aye, aye, Cap'n," Spar said with a mock
salute. "We'll be rescuing you from him before
long, Ella." He put his arm around Ida. "Come
on, mates. Let's leave them in peace."

23

Penneywaite was dragged into the palace of Halidah Pasha between two towering eunuchs and left to wonder at his fate in a small mauve-colored room. He didn't have long to wonder.

The pasha entered the room. His dark face was impassive, except for his eyes. They flashed with suppressed rage. "What do you know of my American flower?" he asked as he stopped before the trembling man.

"My lord, I don't know anything. I've no idea what you're speaking about."

"She is missing. She left with the English-woman. The one *you* asked me to allow to visit."

Penneywaite blanched. "My lord, I assure you, I know nothing of this."

"I want her back, Penneywaite. Her *and* the Englishwoman. I want them *both* returned to me."

"But . . . my lord pasha, I—"

Halidah's hand fell onto his shoulder. "Do not make the mistake of thinking I will hear any excuses. Find them and return them to me. Or you will not live to regret it."

"I . . . I will find them, my lord. I'll go at once."

The pasha released him and stepped backward. "Go." His voice was low but clear. "And do not think you will escape me should you fail."

Penneywaite hurried out of the palace, fear giving speed to his bulk. The pasha was not making idle threats. Should he fail to bring the women back, his life would be worthless. But what were the chances of finding them now?

He settled into his carriage, beginning to calm himself. He had no time for panic. He must think clearly or he was doomed.

My own ship is in the harbor, he thought to himself. I will follow after them. Should I find them, I can bring them back myself. Should I fail, I simply won't return.

Since the chances of his never returning were equally as high as those of his coming back a hero with both women in tow, he would have to hasten to put his things in order. The pasha would be having him watched; he knew it with certainty. He would have to spirit his wealth out of Constantinople with great care and shrewdness.

He thumped on the front of the carriage. "Hurry up," he barked at the driver, impatient to reach his home.

Fluffy clouds were stained pink and violet, announcing the coming of dawn. As the sun prepared to rise, the colors deepened, violet blending with purple, pinks bleeding into reds. With majestic certainty, the sun ushered in the day. The kaleidoscope of colors held tenuously to the sky for a breathless moment, then quickly faded. The clouds were once more a pure white, the sky once more cornflower blue.

Tristan watched the sunrise from the stern. He breathed deeply of the salty air, a smile curving his mouth. Never had he felt such contentment as he felt now. He was married to the woman he loved. His sister was returned to the safety of her family. His ship was coursing through the water with her usual good speed, bound for England and a joyous reunion with his grandfather. All was right with his world.

"Morning."

Tristan turned. "Didn't expect to see you so early this morning, Danny," he said with a good-natured chuckle. "You were in your cups last night."

Danny ran his hands through his rumpled hair, grimacing. "There was cause for celebration."

"That there was, my friend."

The Irishman stepped up beside the captain. His brown eyes traveled up to the top of the mainmast as his head bent backward. A low whistle slipped through his teeth as he brought his gaze back closer to the deck. "I'd forgotten how beautiful a ship looks with her sails unfurled." He rubbed his hand along the wheel. "She'll take us to England in a hurry."

"She will at that, Danny. And I'm eager to get there." Tristan's smile vanished. "I've a score to settle with a certain viscount."

"Viscount?"

"The man behind Ella's captivity. Viscount Blackstoke."

"Blackstoke . . . The heir to the Marquess of Highport? I've heard of him."

"The same," he muttered with a scowl. His eyes widened. "Danny, you mustn't mention his name around here. Jacinda doesn't know he is the Englishman."

Danny shrugged. "Why would it matter?"

"Because she was engaged to him."

"Engaged!" Again he whistled. "I'm not sure I understand, my friend. She's your wife. I saw you marry her myself."

"It's a long story. Just promise me you won't tell her about Blackstoke. I'll tell her when the time is right." He looked beyond the bow of the ship, scanning the horizon. "It's the only thing I've kept from her, but I just couldn't tell her."

"As you wish," Danny agreed. He walked to the railing and leaned against it. "What are your plans now, Tris? Are you going to stay in England or return to America?"

"I'm not sure."

"Going to keep sailing?"

Tristan grinned, feeling a little sheepish as he replied, "I think I might like to stay ashore with Jacinda for a while. This crew could get along without me for a time."

"And Ella?" Danny asked gently. "What's she going to want to do?"

"I don't know. She's not the little girl I left in America. She's seen too much. She's been hurt and frightened. She's going to need time." He didn't mention the baby. He didn't want to think about Ella's pregnancy.

"I'll do whatever I can to help."

"Thanks, Danny."

* * *

Jacinda had watched the same sunrise from the windows of the captain's cabin. She was still wrapped in the warm blankets of their bed, glad to know that with each passing hour they put more distance between them and the exotic city of Constantinople. As strange and beautiful as it had been, she would be glad to see the familiar shores of England once again.

Of course, her return wouldn't be entirely joyous. Her parents probably thought her dead by this time. Her return would be a shock. Even more so when she told them that she was married to Captain Dancing. It would help, she admitted to herself, when they learned he was the grandson of the Duke of Locksworth. Roger was another story. She shuddered when she thought about telling him of her marriage. He would be furious.

"But I don't care," she whispered, curling her arms around a pillow and closing her eyes.

She couldn't believe how perfect her world had become, especially now that the nightmare of Constantinople was behind them. Ella was safe, and they were all headed home.

Safe. But it would be a long time before this was all forgotten. There would be Ella's child to remind them. It was going to be so hard for Ella to return. Nothing would be the same for her again.

Jacinda threw off the bedcovers. She washed quickly, then pulled on a warm woolen dress she had purchased in the Christian quarter. She gave her red mane a quick brushing before hurrying out of her cabin, pausing only a moment before knocking on the door next to her own.

"Ella? Are you awake?" she called softly.

"Come in, Jacinda," came the reply.

She opened the door and peeked inside. Ella was seated on her bed, fully clothed, a blanket wrapped around her for extra warmth. She looked as if she hadn't slept a wink.

"How are you this morning?" Jacinda asked, entering the room to sit beside her sister-in-law.

Ella turned a woeful gaze toward Jacinda. "I'm frightened," she whispered.

Jacinda's arm encircled Ella's shoulders. "Of course you are," she replied, "but there's no need to be. You're going home."

"I should have stayed behind."

"Ella, don't say that. It would break Tristan's heart."

Tears sparkled in black eyes, then trailed down pale cheeks. "But don't you see? I'll be an embarrassment to him. This is a bastard child I carry, Jacinda."

"No one need know that." Jacinda's arm tightened its hold. "We'll tell them you're a widow. That Tristan had come to visit you, and when your husband died, he persuaded you to return home with him."

Ella choked back a sob. "No one will believe it."

"Of course they will," Jacinda replied indignantly. "They wouldn't dare not believe it."

Ella stared at her for a long time. Then, slowly, she smiled. She sniffed and wiped away the tear tracks on her face. "You're right. Even I believe you when you say it."

"Good girl. Now, how about some breakfast. I'm famished."

"Me too," Ella said with a laugh. "Let's see what wonderful fare Spar has prepared for us."

They hurried from the cabin and up onto the main deck. The brisk wind whipped their long hair into flight about their heads but neither paid it any heed.

Jacinda glanced back toward the helm. The watch had changed and a seaman stood at the wheel. Tristan and Danny were leaning against the rail, deep in conversation. She smiled to herself, thinking how handsome her husband looked.

And he's mine.

"My brother's a lucky man," Ella said, interrupting her thoughts.

Jacinda turned, shaking her head. "No. It's me who's the lucky one. I came so close to never knowing happiness."

"We're none of us guaranteed it, are we?"

"No," Jacinda answered, sobering. "We're not." And again she turned to look toward the stern and the source of her happiness.

We're none of us guaranteed happiness.

The thought lingered in her mind throughout the day. Every time she looked at Tristan, every time his fingers touched her arm or his lips brushed her hair, every time she heard his laughter, she remembered Ella's words again.

They were six in number when they sat down for their evening meal—Tristan and Jacinda, Spar and Ida, Danny and Ella. Whip had the watch and couldn't join them, leaving them an even number for supper. Jacinda let her gaze move slowly around the table, noting the shy glances shared between Spar and Ida; recognizing Ella's uncertainty with Danny, a stranger, yet the man responsible for her new-found freedom; sensing Tristan's own pleasure in being surrounded by family and friends.

The table was covered with a white table-cloth. Silver candlesticks bedecked the surface, the candles flickering softly, casting a warm glow upon the participants. The food was fresh and delicious—chicken and veal and beef, vegetables and fruits, breads and pastries, delectable wines. Spar had outdone himself, finding the finest in Constantinople, and every-one savored the meal, knowing that soon enough they would return to the often unsavory meals that were the norm aboard ship.

The meal was leisurely, the conversation mellow, a contrast to the previous evening when there had been jubilant celebration. They talked of the future, Spar and Ida sharing their plans to go to America where Spar would resume his practice as a physician. Danny ad-mitted he thought he might like to go to America, too. He'd been gone from Ireland too long for it to be home. He needed a new challenge. All the while he spoke, his eyes kept drifting toward Ella, a spark of hope in their umber depths. Ella softly admitted she wanted only to see her grandfather. Later she would decide what it was she would do with her future. Someday, she confessed, she would go home to America.

Tristan turned loving eyes on Jacinda. "I want only one thing," he said, speaking to her alone. "To spend the rest of my life with my lady Jacinda." He took her hand and raised it to his lips.

She felt a warm flush rush to her cheeks as her heart quickened. "You're my knight in shining armor. You're the captain of my heart. You're the pirate, and I the pirate's lady."

The room was breathlessly still. Suddenly, the others began to applaud.

Spar stood and lifted his glass. "To Tris and Jacinda. To long life and happiness."

"Hear, hear."

"Hear, hear."

Jacinda's color deepened. She'd forgotten anyone else was even there, she'd been so caught up in Tristan's loving gaze. She'd been unaware that others would hear her words of endearment, words she had often felt but never spoken aloud.

Tristan grinned at her. "I'll remember your words to my death." Then he kissed her, and neither heard the cheers of their friends.

24

Contentment made them careless. After many days without seeing another ship, the threat of pursuit seemed nonexistent. Tristan allowed himself to be persuaded to stop for two days, mooring near a white, sandy beach where the *Dancing Gabrielle* and her passengers could bask in the balmy winter weather that continued to bless their journey. The three women went ashore early the morning they were scheduled to resume sailing to pick wildflowers for the supper table, but when they stumbled upon a secluded pond, Jacinda felt a sudden wave of fear.

"Let's go back to the ship," she said, turning away. "Something's wrong."

Ida's hand stopped her. "Jacobs isn't here," she reminded gently, understanding Jacinda's apprehension. "The captain put him off the ship in Constantinople. Remember?"

"I know. I just have a terrible feeling." She turned around, lifting her chin. "You're right. I've nothing to fear. Let's get those flowers."

Holding the hems of their gowns with one hand, they filled their skirts to overflowing with the other. Flowers in winter. It seemed impossible. Their spirits rose as the morning waned, and when they started back toward the beach, their laughter preceded them.

Suddenly, just as the sound of gunfire reached their ears, a hand snatched hold of Jacinda's hair, jerking her back into the trees. She screamed as she tried to wrench free.

"Hold still an' you won't be hurt," a deep voice growled at her.

She turned, her arms swinging wildly at her assailant. She caught him below the eye, and he let go, more surprised than hurt. She didn't wait to see what he would do next. Holding up her skirts, she scrambled away from him, her feet sinking into the white sand, slowing her flight. She couldn't see Ida or Ella. Then she realized the dinghy was not on the beach. With only a moment's pause, she turned and ran for the brush, seeking a place to hide among the trees and foliage. Her heart thundered in her ears so loudly, she didn't know if the man was behind her or not. She only knew she must hide.

She raced into the trees, branches whipping at her face, bushes snatching at her feet. He was behind her. She could hear him now. Even above the sound of cannons exploding.

Cannons! Tristan!

Jacinda turned quickly in a new direction. She had to get back to the beach. She had to know what was happening. Tristan was on board the *Gabrielle*. She must reach the *Gabrielle*.

Suddenly another man appeared before

her. His grizzled face leered gleefully as his arms clamped around her, lifting her off the ground with ease. She struggled to no avail.

"Let me go," she cried, tossing her head back and striking out with her legs.

He laughed at her, then dropped her in an ignoble heap at his feet. "See if you can hang onto her this time," he told the first man when he caught up with them. "I'm going after the others."

Jacinda twisted around, hoping for a chance to run again, but her captor wasn't taking any chances. He made a quick grasp for her wrist, knotting a thong tightly around the tender flesh. He jerked her free arm behind her and bound it against the other.

"Who are you? What do you want?" she demanded, hiding her terror.

"Shut up," he growled as he turned away from her, peeking through the lush growth toward the ocean.

A battle raged just beyond Jacinda's view. She wriggled onto her knees and inched forward until she too could see beyond the once peaceful beach.

The *Gabrielle* was trapped. The men were returning the frigate's relentless fire, but her strength was in her speed, not in her cannons. Before Jacinda's eyes, the mainmast was blown in two. The top wavered, then began a slow motion fall toward the deck. Flames licked at her starboard side.

"Tristan!"

Hell reigned aboard the *Dancing Gabrielle*. Men and pieces of men lay across the decks of the once proud ship. The air was filled with their moans and their curses, along with the crackle of fires and the explosion of the cannons.

Tristan continued to shout orders to his men, those who were still able to obey, but there were too few against the frigate's mighty guns. He glanced quickly across the ship, spying Spar as he bent over a wounded seaman. He'd sent Whip below to try to put out some fires. When he first saw the frigate's approach, he'd sent Danny for the women. They hadn't returned.

"Dear God, keep her safe." He heard the creak and snap of the mast overhead. "Look out!" he cried, his voice hoarse but loud enough to warn those near by.

Men who could scattered out of the way. Those who couldn't prayed for a quick end.

Suddenly Spar was beside him. "We've got to surrender, Tris."

"No. We'll die fighting if we must." He ground his teeth. "We'd die anyway."

Spar grabbed his shoulder. "Look around you. Could it be worse than this?"

Tristan jerked free and returned to his cannon. "As long as Jacinda's safe—"

"And what makes you think she is?" Spar yelled at him over the cannon's boom. "Look at the beach."

He turned and ran across the deck, jumping over splintered wood and tangled masses of canvas. There she stood, her red tumble of hair covering her face and shoulders, her arm held by a tall man in sailor's garb. As Tristan watched, the man shook her, forcing her to look up at the crippled clipper. Then he slapped her.

Tristan growled as his hands gripped the rail. He would have thrown himself over the side of the ship if Spar hadn't stopped him.

"You can't help her that way. They'd kill you before you reached shore. They might kill her too." He loosened his hold. "Think, Tris." Then he turned away, hurrying back to attend to the wounded and dying.

Helplessness scalded him, burning through his veins like a paralyzing poison. He was trapped, trapped and helpless. There was no saving his ship. There was no saving his men. Worst of all, he couldn't save Jacinda. He cursed himself for being every kind of fool. He should never have stopped. He should have pushed the ship to her limit to be out of these waters and safe in England.

But surrender?

With a yell, he turned back toward the guns. He wouldn't surrender. He wouldn't watch these men, his friends, be butchered before his eyes or sold into slavery. The only hope he had of saving Jacinda was in saving the ship first.

Smoke and steam filled the air. Choking hot fumes burned the hair in his nose and stung his eyes as he prepared to fire another volley. Suddenly, the deck beneath his feet seemed to explode into a million pieces. He was in flight, then crashed with agonizing force against the water pump. His world darkened, and for a moment, he was oblivious to his surroundings.

His ears rang as he hauled himself to his knees. Blood ran into his eyes, but it was the pain that blinded him. Nausea dulled his senses, making him slow to understand what was happening around him. He struggled to his feet, wavering uncertainly on shaky legs. He tried to reach out for the pump to steady himself, but his arm hung limply at his side, refusing to move. His left hand touched his right shoulder and came away red.

Then a new cry arose. Blinking away the blood that streamed down his forehead, he saw the planks linking his ship with the frigate and the corsairs pouring across. He reached for the pistol tucked in his belt and stepped forward into the fray. His eyes locked with his target, and he fired. Tristan had the satisfaction of seeing the man fall before he too crumpled, unconscious, beside his foe.

Penneywaite stepped onto the deck of the *Dancing Gabrielle*, wrinkling his nose at the acrid smell that lingered in the air. Moisture glistened on his forehead, and he dabbed at it with a handkerchief, then placed it against his nose to filter the stench of battle.

The survivors were gathered together on the forecastle deck. He moved toward them at a ponderous speed, wearied by the dangerous excitement of the day. He climbed the narrow steps and paused to survey the pitiful lot. The captain was among the survivors.

"You should have stuck to your plans to bring American women *to* Constantinople, Captain, instead of trying to take them away." Penneywaite shook his head. "Very foolish, my friend. Very foolish."

Tristan glowered but kept silent.

Penneywaite laughed, then let his eyes

move on. The big man attending to the wounded would bring him a good price in the slave market, but most of them were worthless to him. At last his gaze reached the women. There were two of them—Mrs. Dancing and a girl with carrot-orange hair, a freckled nose, and defiant green eyes.

"Where is the American girl?" he demanded.

The pirate standing between the two women shrugged his shoulders. "We couldn't find her. Last we saw, she was swimming toward the ship. Must've drowned, more'n likely."

"Drowned!" He patted his forehead again. The pasha had demanded he return with both women. Now what was he to do? He pointed at Jacinda. "Put her in my cabin."

With a low growl, Tristan started to his feet but was stopped by a heavy foot in his chest. The corsair raised an arm to strike him.

"Tristan!" Jacinda cried, trying to break free of her captor.

Penneywaite stopped the seaman from delivering the blow, then looked at Tristan. "I advise you not to cause trouble, Dancing. It won't go well for her if you do." Penneywaite grinned. "You had a fine ship. It's a shame."

Before Jacinda could be led past him, Penneywaite reached out and touched her hair, still smiling. His plan was shaping in his mind. He would keep her alive as a safety measure. Once he reached England, he would send her back to the pasha as a gift. Surely a woman as beautiful as this one would more than replace the American Halidah had grown so fond of.

"Go on. Take her to my cabin and lock her in." He turned toward the rest of his men. "Tie them up. Make sure they can't get free. Then search the ship for any valuables. When you're finished, set fire to it." He started to leave the forecastle deck but stopped at the top step and turned. "I'm sure the Englishman will regret losing your services, Dancing. I'll tell him of your tragic accident."

"I'll find you, Penneywaite. Harm one hair on her head, I'll find you and tear you apart, piece by piece, even if I have to come back from the dead to do it."

Penneywaite laughed at Tristan's threat as he waddled down the steps and returned to the victorious frigate.

The sun hovered over the western horizon. Jacinda was released from her cabin and dragged up onto the deck in time to see the *Gabrielle* torched. A scream rose in her throat and was strangled there.

As soon as Penneywaite was satisfied that the flames would continue to burn, he ordered the sails of the frigate unfurled. The bow of the ship was turned westward. As the sun sank into the Mediterranean, the burning *Gabrielle* became only an orange light against the black sea.

Why didn't she faint? Why didn't she cry? Why didn't she scream? But Jacinda was incapable of any emotion, any action. She was wrapped in numbness, a safe cocoon, protecting her from the horror of feeling. When she was led back to the cabin, she sat obediently on a chair, unaware of her surroundings and

unafraid of her future. Even when Penneywaite
let himself into the cabin and came to look
down at her, that same lascivious grin on his
fleshy mouth, she was unmoved.

"What a rare delicacy you would be. It's no
wonder the pasha wanted you so badly. I'm
sorry I can't keep you in England with me." He
shrugged. "But—"

"You're taking me to England with you?"
she asked in a daze.

"Only for a short while, my dear Mrs.
Dancing, and then I'm sending you as a gift to
Halidah Pasha."

"The pasha?" It was as if she were waking
from a bad dream. The numbness began to fade,
and she was keenly, painfully aware of everything she saw and felt. Despite the agony in her
heart, her mind began to comprehend what
Penneywaite had been saying to her. "But why
send me to the pasha when you could ransom
me?" England. She must stay in England.

"Ransom you? To whom?"

"To my parents, Lord and Lady Sunderland. My father is the Earl of Bonclere." She
needn't mention that he was the penniless Earl
of Bonclere. "Or to my friend, the Duke of
Locksworth. Surely you know of him?" She
hesitated, then added in desperation, "Or even
to Viscount Blackstoke of Highport Hall. We
were engaged to be married. I was kidnapped
from the docks of London just before our
wedding." Tears welled but she fought to keep
them from falling. "They'll pay a fine ransom.
Any of them will."

"Does the Englishman know you were with
Dancing?" the fat man asked, incredulous.

"How would he? He doesn't know me. Just who is this Englishman?"

"You don't know?" Penneywaite's eyebrows arched, and then he began to laugh, the flesh on his belly jiggling wildly. "Oh . . . what a marvelous surprise, my dear lady." He turned toward the door. "I am going to be a very rich man," he chuckled to himself as he left the cabin, locking the door behind him.

And then she was alone. She wished for the numbness to return. She didn't want to think. She didn't want to feel. She didn't want to remember. But remember she did. The sight of the burning ship was branded on her mind. She would never be free of it. Neither would she be free of her last sight of Tristan, his arm torn and bleeding, dried blood crusted on his forehead, his face blackened by soot.

"Tristan," she whispered.

The pain that spread outward from her heart . . . Could she die from such a pain? She hoped she could. Her reason for living had disappeared in an agony of flames.

25

Jacinda lay on her bed, unmindful of the rise and fall of the ship as it plowed through the rough Atlantic. She didn't know if it were day or night. She hadn't any perception of the passing of time. Since the day the *Gabrielle* went up in flames, she'd stopped caring about such things. She ate without tasting her food. She awoke only to lie on her bed, staring blankly at the ceiling. She saw no one except for the boy who brought her meals and returned to remove the tray.

She heard the turn of the key in the door but paid it little heed. The boy would leave the tray on the table and soon she would be alone again. Sometimes she wondered why she even bothered to get up and eat. Wouldn't it be easier just to ignore the food? Just not eat and wait for death?

"So, the captain's doxy is all alone." The door closed.

Jacinda felt an icy fear trickling through her veins as she turned her head.

"You remember me, don't you?" He stepped into the light from the lantern. "You'd not forget me."

She sat up, her head spinning. He'd grown a beard since she'd last seen him, but she recognized him at once. His brown eyes were glazed with the same hatred she had seen in them before he was lashed to the shroud aboard the *Gabrielle*.

Jacobs removed his hat and tossed it onto the table. "I knew you wouldn't forget me."

"What are you doing here?" she asked breathlessly.

A twisted grin showed a glimpse of teeth before he replied, "As luck'd have it, I signed on the *Tiger's Queen* in Constantinople. I'd no idea it would be such an exciting journey." Jacobs straddled a nearby chair, staring at her all the while. "Did you know I helped torch his ship? Did you know I nearly blew his head off?"

Jacinda covered her ears and closed her eyes. "Stop it."

"Why should I? If the captain hadn't taken such a fancy to you, you think I'd be here now? I'd have had an afternoon of fun and none of us would've been the worse for it." He laughed, a low, guttural sound. "Well, he'll not come t'your rescue now, miss. There's not a soul on board this tub who'll care what happens t'the likes of you."

"You can't mean to do this," Jacinda whispered.

"Oh, but I do." He stood and began removing his blue checkered shirt. He shrugged it off, revealing a chest thickly matted with dark hair. Then he turned around. His back was crisscrossed with ugly scars. "Look at them, miss. You put these on my back."

She had to get out of this room. She had to find help. Someone would help her. Someone had to help her. She inched her way off the side of the bed. "I tried to stop him."

Jacobs spun around. "Don't go leavin' just yet, my pretty one. I have plans for the two of us."

She could sit there, begging with him to free her or let him use her. She could scream, hoping that someone would come to her aid. Or she could fight for herself. "Do you think I would let your filthy hands touch me?"

"What choice d'you have?" He pulled a dagger from his belt, the blade shining in the lamplight.

"Your threats mean nothing to me, Jacobs." Suddenly, she darted away from the bed, placing the table between them.

He laughed again. "Seems t'me you tried t'fight me the last time." He kicked the chair out of his way and leaned his hands on the table. "In case you don't know it, you're between the wind and water. There's no escaping me this time." With a sudden thrust, the table toppled over. His knife clattered to the floor, sliding across the room, but he paid it no heed. Jacobs moved toward her slowly, a smile playing on his mouth.

Jacinda felt panic pressing in upon her from all sides. She could already imagine his hands around her throat. She remembered the agonizing moments beneath the water when her lungs screamed for air. "No!" She dodged under his arm as he grabbed for her. Her fingers touched the door.

But before she could turn the handle, his hands were gripping her shoulders and wrenching her away. She stumbled and pitched headfirst across the room, falling to the floor near the bed. She twisted around and started to rise, but once again, he was there too soon. He pushed her back. Her head thumped against the hard wooden floor.

"Let me tell you what I'm going t'do," he whispered as his fingers tightened around her throat. "You're going t'like it, miss. You're going t'beg me for more before I'm done with you."

Then his mouth was covering hers as his hands groped with her gown. She beat at him with her fists, but he waved them off as he would a pesky fly. She could hear him chuckling in his throat, and it sickened her. She was losing.

Will the nightmare never end? Isn't it enough that Tristan is dead? Must I suffer this too?

Her arms fell to the floor in defeat . . . and the fingers of her right hand touched the cool metal of the knife where it lay on the floor beside her. Without a moment's hesitation, her hand tightened around the grip.

"That's better," he uttered in her ear. "Don't fight me. Just enjoy."

Her hand raised above his back and plunged with every ounce of strength she possessed, driving the knife into his back all the way to the cross guard.

Jacobs sucked in air as he rose above her on his knees. His eyes were wide with surprise and pain. His hands reached behind him, grappling for the protruding weapon. She listened in stunned horror to the gurgling noises his open mouth released, watching as his face began to turn purple. Still reaching for the knife, he managed to rise to his feet. With jerky, slow-motion movements, he turned and stumbled toward the door.

Jacinda looked at her right hand. It was covered with blood. Her stomach turned, and she clamped her mouth shut against the offending bile that rose in her throat. Clutching the side of the bed, she pulled herself to her feet as Jacobs neared the door, but it opened before he reached it. He stood, wavering, one hand outstretched in a plea for help.

"What are you doing here?" Penneywaite's outraged question ended the breathless silence of the room.

And then Jacobs crumpled in a heap at the obese man's feet.

Penneywaite's gaze lifted from the dead man to meet Jacinda's. "Did he harm you?" he demanded.

She shook her head.

Penneywaite swung around, barking at the man standing just behind him. "Sedgewick, throw him overboard. And put a guard outside this door. If anyone touches this girl, he's a dead man. I want that understood by every man aboard this blasted ship. They're free to do their wenching with other captives. Not this one."

As Sedgewick dragged the body out of her cabin, leaving a red stain across the floor, she remembered the knife. The knife. She should have kept the knife.

"There's even more to you than I'd thought, Lady Jacinda," Penneywaite said thoughtfully.

She turned her attention his way once more.

He chuckled. "Yes. The Englishman will be well pleased with me, I think."

Fury spread through her like fire, ignited by his mockery. "Watch yourself, Penneywaite. There may be another knife within my reach."

For a moment, that silenced him. Then he began to laugh even harder as he closed the door behind him.

She was in England. Snow covered the ground outside, and a cold wind blew through the halls of Bonclere. No, it wasn't Bonclere. She didn't know this place. She was being led down a long, dark hallway. At the end was a lighted room, the door thrown wide open. He was waiting for her there. She wanted to turn and run, but a hand gripped her arm. She looked to the side. It was Penneywaite, and he was laughing. He was laughing but she couldn't hear him. She couldn't hear anything but the thundering of her own heart in her ears. Suddenly she felt a strange calm washing over her. She wasn't afraid. She didn't even want to run. She had to know who awaited her. She had to see his face. She had to know who had killed Tristan. Yes, he had killed him. He may have been safe in England, but it was still he who had killed Tristan and all the others, and she had to know who it was. Then she was going to see him dead. She was going to see him dead by her own hands. The room drew nearer. The light grew brighter. She was about to learn the identity of the Englishman . . .

Jacinda came awake with a jolt. Her pulse hammered at her temples. She'd almost seen him. If she could have slept a moment more, she would have known who he was.

Dry-eyed, she stared into the darkness of her shipboard prison room. "I swear before all I hold dear, I will kill this Englishman. With my own hands, I will kill him."

Blackstoke waited for him in a dingy little inn outside of London. His anger at Penneywaite's summons increased as the minutes of afternoon ticked by. If it weren't for the mysterious wording of the note, he would have ignored it altogether, but he couldn't deny his curiosity. Why had Penneywaite returned to England? And what was this surprise gift he said he'd brought back with him? Well, it had better be good news. Blackstoke was in no mood for games.

The door was flung open. Snow entered in a flurry before the rotund guest. Voices stopped momentarily as heads swung round to view the new arrival, then returned to their noisy hum. Penneywaite shook the white crystals from his cloak as he walked toward Blackstoke.

"Good evening, my lord," Penneywaite wheezed as he tossed his cloak on a bench. "Innkeeper! An ale here."

"You're late."

"Sorry. It's this weather. Awful stuff, you know. I'd forgotten how miserable it could be in England in the winter."

Blackstoke watched Penneywaite settle his bulk on the bench across from him. The man had grown even fatter than when he had last seen him several years before. His shock of hair was more gray than Blackstoke remembered, and it stood straight up, as if he had experienced a great surprise.

"What's brought you back to England, Penneywaite?" he asked at last, tired of waiting for an explanation.

"Ah, that's a long story, my lord." He smiled secretively.

"I haven't time for a long story."

Penneywaite leaned forward and in a near-whisper said, "I think his lordship would be wise to hear what it is I have to say."

Blackstoke ground his teeth together in irritation but remained seated.

The serving wench brought Penneywaite his ale, and the man took a long draught of the dark liquid. He sighed as he set the mug on the table between them. "That's another thing they're without in the East, my friend. Good ale. There's nothing like good English ale." He leaned his elbows on the rough-hewn boards of the table. "Let me begin."

"Please do."

"Your new captain, the American, arrived with his cargo, all safe and sound. He was a shrewd fellow, this American. He made us all a considerable sum of money. But I didn't trust him."

Blackstoke frowned. "Why not?"

"Please." Penneywaite smiled again. "Don't make me get ahead of myself. As I was saying, I didn't trust him." He took another drink, draining the mug, then motioned for another. "He said he intended to start his own shipping business in America. In direct competition with you, my lord."

"He what?"

Penneywaite wagged his finger at the viscount. "But of more interest to you is the woman he saved from the auction block. An Englishwoman." He paused expectantly. "A beautiful, red-haired woman with golden eyes."

Blackstoke placed his palms on the table and leaned forward, his teeth clenched and his eyes narrowed.

"Luckily I was able to save her when Captain Dancing's ship sank. You didn't know his ship sank, did you? A pity. All were lost except for her."

"Where is she, Penneywaite?"

"Of course, when I learned she was a good friend of yours—you were to have been married, I believe—I brought her directly to England. Do you know something funny, Blackstoke? She doesn't know who the infamous Englishman is, the Englishman who was behind her own kidnapping."

Cold fury chilled his veins. "Where is she?"

"Oh, she is quite safe."

"Take me to her," Blackstoke demanded.

Penneywaite shook his head. "I'm sorry, my lord. You must understand that I have sustained tremendous losses because of my sudden departure from the East. And for reasons I don't care to discuss, I can never safely return to Constantinople." He let out a long, heavy sigh. "My, my. It is sad, indeed."

Blackstoke looked around the common room of the inn. There was an occasional glance from the peasants who surrounded them, but nobody seemed to be paying any real attention, no one was eavesdropping. Still, he'd have preferred this conversation to be taking place in more privacy, especially since what he wanted to do at this moment was throttle this blob of fat sitting across from him.

It was Penneywaite's turn to lean forward. "You'll not find her on your own, my lord."

"What is it you want?"

"I think we can arrive at a fair sum." Penneywaite grinned broadly.

"Before we discuss that, I have some questions. Was she harmed in any way?"

"No."

"You're sure she wasn't auctioned off to one of those heathens? She's still a virgin?"

Penneywaite's pause was infinitesimal. "No, my lord. She was never sold to anyone. I believe the captain knew her identity and made certain she was kept safe from harm. Perhaps he also intended to ransom her."

"And the American and his crew? You're sure they're all dead."

"All of them, my lord. It's a shame, is it not?"

Blackstoke leaned back against the wall, peering at Penneywaite with distrustful eyes. Inside, his anger raged. How dare this man try to blackmail him, using Jacinda to fatten his pockets? Hadn't he made the man rich enough, sending him shiploads of women to auction to the Turks? And another thought nagged at him. Was Penneywaite telling the truth? Had Jacinda come through this unscathed? Would she be worth the price Penneywaite would ask?

"Your bride," Penneywaite said suddenly.

"She is truly the most beautiful woman I have ever seen. It is no wonder men from every corner of the world would pay anything for her. The price I could get for her in an auction. Fit for the sultan himself. Perhaps she's not worth it to you. Perhaps I should take her east again. Hmmm. Now that's a thought."

"How much, Penneywaite? I'll pay your price."

"Five thousand pounds . . . for a start."

26

Jacinda was taken off the *Tiger's Queen* in the middle of the night and whisked away in a carriage under cover of darkness. She shivered in the thin cloak provided, the cold dampness of the isle seeming to seep into her bones. They drove away from London, ignoring the lateness of the hour, and arrived at their destination in midmorning.

The cottage was surrounded by dense trees and hedges, well-hidden from view of the road. The few windows were boarded over. It looked as though it had been deserted for a long, long time.

Penneywaite led the way into the cottage, sniffing at the musty odor that lingered inside. He motioned for the man holding Jacinda's arm to take her to the bed that was set near one wall. "Untie her," he said as he continued to look around.

Jacinda's gaze followed him, hatred burning in her eyes. Hatred was all she had left to give her strength. Hatred and her determination to find and kill the man she knew only as the Englishman.

Sedgewick left the cottage and returned with a pail of water and a basket of food, then he went out once more and returned again, this time with a lantern.

"Bring in the rest of the blankets," Penneywaite told his underling, and Sedgewick skittered away to obey. At last, Penneywaite turned his attention back to Jacinda. "I'm afraid you can't build a fire, my lady. Someone might see it and come to investigate. But we'll leave you plenty of blankets to keep you warm. You'll not freeze before someone comes for you."

"Who?" she asked. "Who will come for me?"

"Whoever will pay the highest price, my dear." He grinned. "Perhaps it will be the Englishman himself. Now that's a moment I would like to see. Or perhaps it will be your parents."

Not *her* parents. She would surely starve if it was left to them. She thought of Blackstoke. She hoped it wouldn't be him. She didn't want to be beholden to the viscount. But the duke would help her. If Penneywaite approached him, the duke would pay the ransom. Jacinda glanced around her bleak surroundings. "How long will I be here?" She hated herself for asking, even more so because of the tremor in her voice.

He ignored the question. "There is water in the bucket and bread and dried fruit in the basket." He smiled at her again. "And don't bother to try to escape. It's pointless. My men have done their job well." He walked toward the door, pausing there only long enough to say, "Farewell, my lady. It's been a pleasure." Then he stepped out the door and closed it behind him.

There was a moment's silence before the pounding began as the door was boarded shut. Jacinda jumped up from the cot and hurried across the small cottage room. She pulled at the door, but it was locked against her already. She was trapped. Although she was free of the ship, she had merely exchanged one prison for another.

She walked over to one of the windows and tried to open the shutters. It was useless. With a sigh of resignation, Jacinda returned to the cot to wait for the pounding to cease. Once the men were gone, she could try to force an escape. Now, even if she succeeded, she would just be apprehended again.

This time they met at Blackstoke's choosing, both time and place. He had ridden to Viridian, a small manor to the south of London. No one in his family had lived in or even visited Viridian for years, perhaps decades. The manor house stood like an empty shell, its dark windows watching over the deserted yard. The stables stood empty. The pasture grasses grew long, undisturbed by horses or sheep or cows. All was silent except for the whistling wind.

It was early morning, the sun just a promise in the eastern sky, when Penneywaite drove up toward the house. He was alone except for Sedgewick, his driver. Blackstoke was waiting for him near the stables. The two men eyed each other warily as Penneywaite approached Blackstoke.

"Have you brought the money?" Penneywaite asked as he stopped a few feet away.

"I have, but you'll not have it until I know Jacinda is safe and well."

"Then you'll not see her. I get my money first."

Blackstoke took a step backward. "Let's get out of the wind," he suggested as he turned and entered the stables, leaving Penneywaite to follow him in.

Penneywaite didn't trust the viscount. He had worked with him too many years for that. Blackstoke only cared about one thing—himself. Penneywaite knew he would have to be on his guard if he was to outfox his opponent.

"Tell you what, Penneywaite. I'll give you half your money. Then you take me to Jacinda. Once I know she's alive and unharmed, I'll give you the rest."

Penneywaite frowned but agreed. "All right. I'll agree to that, but if you try to trick me out of the rest, you'll regret it. My men are waiting near my cottage." He saw Blackstoke's eyes spark with interest. *He thinks I've revealed something useful.* But, of course, he couldn't have. Penneywaite had never met with Blackstoke at his childhood home, nor had he ever told anyone of his humble beginnings. The lady's whereabouts were still a secret from the viscount.

"One more thing, Penneywaite." Blackstoke's features hardened as he peered at the man opposite him. "You've promised me she's a virgin still. If I find otherwise, you'll be the one to regret it."

Penneywaite smiled easily. Actually, he was certain she was *not* a virgin. After all, hadn't he seen her in the captain's cabin? Hadn't she claimed to be his wife? But why tell this man? The captain was dead. Anyone who had known the two were married, if they actually had been, had perished with the burning ship—except for the lovely lady in question herself. By the time Blackstoke might learn of the deception, Penneywaite would be long gone from the shores of England.

"I haven't lied to you, Blackstoke. She was never auctioned, and the American captain kept her apart from the other women. Once she was on my ship, I saw that she was guarded day and night."

Blackstoke nodded as he turned to cross the stables, entering a stall. When he came out, he was carrying a sack. Penneywaite could feel his heart quicken in his chest. Five thousand pounds. He would go to America. New Orleans, he thought. A good place for a new start. Maybe he would buy a plantation. Yes, a plantation and a well-bred wife. He'd become a respectable member of society. Surely if Blackstoke could pass for such a man, so could he.

"Penneywaite." Blackstoke's voice drew his attention from the sack. "I don't like those who cross me."

The gun exploded. Penneywaite jerked backward, surprise and pain twisting his face as he fell to the stable floor. His ears hummed as the pain spread through his body. He heard another shot and knew that Sedgewick had fallen victim to the viscount, too.

Blackstoke came to stand over him, grim satisfaction lighting his dark blue eyes. "You shouldn't have tried to blackmail me."

Penneywaite was dying, dying quickly, and he knew it. He mustered his draining strength to form his reply. "You'll never . . . find her . . . Blackstoke. She's . . . hidden well."

"I'll find her. You gave your secret away. Do you think I don't know you grew up in Kent, in a cottage in the country? A cottage you bought once you had the resources to do so? I'll find her."

His vision was blurring, but he could still see the viscount's satisfied smirk. Penneywaite wanted only one thing before he died. To see that smirk fade when he learned his bride was no longer a maiden. "Black-stoke . . . I . . . lied. I lied . . . about—"

Blackstoke leaned down closer to hear the words as they faded to a whisper.

"She's . . . not—"

"What's that, Penneywaite?"

"She's . . . not—" But the words wouldn't come. Life was spinning away from him. He wouldn't have the satisfaction of seeing Blackstoke's expression. His last conscious thought, however, was knowing how enraged the viscount would be when he did learn the truth. He died with a grin on his face.

"Cinda, my love." His fingers caressed her hair as she stirred on the bed beside him, nestling against the smoothness of his bare skin, enjoying the feel of his hard, muscled body against her own flesh. Desire burned in the pit of her stomach. She ached for him to take her. "Tristan," she whispered in return. "I love you." But suddenly, before he could speak, she dis-

*covered they were no longer in the privacy of
their cabin. They were on deck and it was
littered with men writhing in pain. Penneywaite
was there and he was laughing. Laughing.
Laughing. A horrible sound. She was led away,
torn from Tristan's side, surrounded by the
laughter as she watched with horrified eyes as
the* Gabrielle *began to burn. The orange and
yellow flames licked at her barnacled sides and
raced up the masts to engulf the furled canvas
sails. And throughout the horror, she could see
him, standing on deck, watching her, caring for
her, even as he was dying.*

"Tristan!" She sat up, reaching for him.

The dreams. The dreams. Damn the
dreams! Why must she be haunted so? Why
couldn't she forget? Why must she continue to
be tortured, even in her sleep?

She wondered if it were day or night. It was
difficult to distinguish between the two in her
shuttered world. She got up from the cot,
hugging one of the blankets around her, and
turned up the lantern. The oil would soon be
gone and she would be without light. She went
to the nearby window and began pounding at
the boards with a broken leg from the stool.
How many days had she done this? How long
had she been a captive in this room?

The water was stale and nearly gone. The
remaining crusts of bread had begun to mold.
She was growing weak from the hunger and the
cold. Reason told her she wouldn't survive
much longer. Had the Englishman refused to
pay Penneywaite's price? Why would he, after
all? And if Penneywaite had approached her
parents? Even if they had the money, would

they pay it? She wondered. Besides, would death be so terrible? Without Tristan, was life worth living? She dropped the wooden leg and returned to her cot. It was better, perhaps, to simply resign herself to death and await its coming.

You should be ashamed o' yerself, Jacinda Dancing.

She looked across the room. "Ida?"

Look at yerself. Sittin' there, feelin' sorry for yerself. Would ye not rather get even with the man who killed us?

She straightened on the cot. She could see her so clearly, standing near the cold hearth, her orange curls wet and hugging her scalp. "But, Ida, there's nothing I can do. I'm trapped. I'm tired. I don't want to live without Tristan."

Do you want me t'feel sorry for ye too? If it was me, I'd find the bloke who sent us t'the bottom of the sea, and I'd see 'im dead meself.

"But—" Jacinda began again, but there was no one there. Ida was gone. She lay back and closed her eyes. "I've tried, Ida. I've enough hate inside me to kill him. But now I'm tired and there's no escape and I'd just as soon die. I don't want to live without him," she finished in a whisper.

Find the man who killed us, Jacinda. Find the man.

Find the man. Find the man. Find the man.

She heard the canter of hooves, faint and distant. Was she dreaming again? Would he come to her in her dreams? She closed her eyes, waiting for his vision to appear before her.

But no. It wasn't a dream. They were real and they were coming closer. She could lie there, quietly, and let them pass. She could stay here and die. Or she could do what Ida said. She could find Tristan's killer. She could find the Englishman. She could find him and make him pay for what he had done, for what *they* had done—the Englishman and Penneywaite.

Jacinda threw off the blanket she'd been holding so tightly around her and hurried toward the door. She pounded on it with what little strength she had left. "Please. Help me," she cried. "Please. I'm trapped in here. Stop. Stop." Even in her own ears, her voice was weak. No one could possibly hear her over the pounding hooves on the road.

Then she heard voices. The horses stopped. "This is it," she heard someone call.

"Yes! Yes, I'm in here," she whispered, her face pressed against the door.

She heard the wood splinter as the boards were pried away. She stepped back from the door, shaking, her fists clenched at her sides. "Hurry. Please hurry," she pleaded.

The door burst open. Sunlight spilled into the room, blinding her with its unaccustomed brightness. Two silhouettes stood framed by the doorway.

"Jacinda," the shorter man said.

There was a strange buzzing in her ears. The room tilted precariously. "Father?"

And then she toppled forward, arms catching her just before she struck the floor.

She was spinning, turning, tumbling, falling deeper and deeper into a black pit. But a voice was calling to her, coaxing her back toward the light. It seemed such a long way to go. It would be so much easier to just keep falling. Yet she reached out, trying to stop her flight into darkness. She chose to live.

"Aye, an' there's a good girl. Open your eyes, miss. That's a love. You've 'ad us frightened, you 'ave, miss. Come on now. You won't disappoint ol' Mrs. Shipwick, would you now?"

Jacinda's eyes fluttered open. "Mrs. Shipwick?" she asked hoarsely, her vision of the old cook blurred.

"Aye, it's me, love. Such a scare you've given us. 'Ere now. Drink this." She held Jacinda's head and pressed a cup to her lips. "Come on now. It's some o' me best soup, it is. Just like when you was a wee nipper and were feelin' poor. Didn't I always bring it t'you me-self?"

Jacinda sipped the warm broth obediently. When at last she laid her head back on the pillow, she closed her eyes with a sigh. "How long have I been here, Mrs. Shipwick?"

"Four days, miss, and long ones they've been." She squeezed Jacinda's hand.

"I don't remember what—"

" 'Ush now, love. You must rest. You can remember later. There's your family all waitin' t'see you well again." Mrs. Shipwick's cool hand smoothed Jacinda's brow, then stroked her hair. "You sleep, miss. When you wake again, you'll feel better. I promise. 'Ush now. Don't argue. Back t'sleep with you."

Sleep. Yes, she was tired. She would sleep. Sleep. Sleep . . .

* * *

Jacinda stretched, enjoying the warmth of the room. She could hear the friendly crackle of a fire on the hearth while rain spattered against her window. She snuggled down deeper beneath her quilt. She turned onto her side and reached out beside her, but the bed was empty. Empty? Where was he?

"Tris!" His name was torn from her lips as she bolted upright in bed, the horror of remembering dispelling the contentment she had felt upon awakening.

Mrs. Shipwick flew out of her chair and gathered the panicked girl in her arms. Sobs racked Jacinda's chest as she accepted the old cook's comforting embrace.

"Tris . . . Tris . . . Tris." She continued to whisper his name, longing for relief from the pain that rent her heart in pieces.

"Oh, miss. Don't cry, love. Mrs. Shipwick's 'ere."

"I loved him. I loved him so."

"Of course, you did. There now. Lovin's the best thing in the world, my girl."

"But he's gone. He's dead, and I'll never see him again," she cried into the cook's bosom.

Mrs. Shipwick patted Jacinda's head. "And aren't you glad you 'ad the chance t'love 'im while 'e lived, miss? You're lucky to 'ave loved someone at all. None of us is promised it."

We're none of us guaranteed happiness.

Wasn't that what Ella had told her? Yes. Mrs. Shipwick was right. She was glad she'd had the chance to love him. She'd been happy with him. She would never lose those memories. She dried her eyes with Mrs. Shipwick's proffered handkerchief.

"Care t'tell me who 'e was, miss?"

Jacinda shook her head.

"Maybe someday, then," the cook replied as she rose from the side of the bed. "I think your parents would like t'see you, now that you're feelin' more yourself. Let me brush your 'air, miss, and then I'll call them for you." She went to the dresser and came back with the brush. With gentle strokes, she smoothed the flame-red tresses, talking as she did so. "It's been a terrible time for us, miss. Not knowin' what'd become o' you. The viscount was in a fury. 'E thought you'd run off, and 'e demanded your father repay 'im the money 'e'd put out. The master 'ad t'sell the new 'orses and 'ounds t'keep us goin' or we'd 'ave 'ad nary t'eat. The master, 'e searched 'igh and low for you. It's not been a pleasant place t'live, 'ere at Bonclere, since your goin', I can tell you. Findin' poor Jake with 'is 'ead stove in an' not knowin' what 'ad become o' you."

"Jake? Is he . . . is he all right?"

Mrs. Shipwick paused, then shook her head. "I'm sorry, miss." Then, wiping the mournful look from her face, she patted Jacinda's head a couple of times. "There now. You look as pretty as ever. A mite thin, but we'll 'ave you fattened up in no time." She fussed with the collar of Jacinda's nightgown, then left the room in search of Lord and Lady Sunderland.

Jacinda waited nervously. Her gaze moved around the bedroom. Everything looked the same as when she'd last seen it, yet it seemed so strange. It wasn't really her room anymore. Her room was smaller and sparsely furnished. Her room rocked gently with the roll of the sea, and the air was spiced with a salty tang. She shook her head. No. That room was gone.

She turned her tawny gaze back toward the door, straightening her shoulders as she waited for her parents to appear. What should she tell them? How much did they already know? What was it Mrs. Shipwick had said? Her father had had to sell the horses and dogs again? Had he been gambling? No, she'd said he'd given it back to Blackstoke. And Blackstoke. What of him? Mrs. Shipwick had said he was in a fury when she was discovered missing. He'd thought she'd run away rather than marry him.

Jacinda rubbed her temples as her head began to ache. There were too many things to think about. She felt confused and tired. How was she to deal with it?

And then she thought of the duke. He'd have to be told about Tristan and Ella. No one knew but Jacinda. She would have to be the one who told him. It would break his heart. Unchecked tears began to fall from her eyes. The duke would know and understand what she was feeling. Only the duke could know.

The door opened slowly, admitting her parents. Lady Sunderland eyed her warily, as if she had some contagious disease. Lord Sunderland left his wife near the entrance and walked over to sit at the bedside. He took Jacinda's hand in his own. His hazel eyes glittered with tears.

"Daughter," he said softly. "Thank God you've been returned to us."

Hearing his voice jogged her memory. He'd been there at the cottage. It was he who had found her. "How did you know where to find me?"

"Blackstoke. He paid the ransom."

"So he did ask a ransom. I thought they'd left me to die."

Lady Sunderland stepped closer. "You can be glad the viscount prizes you so highly, Jacinda. If he hadn't paid the ransom, you most surely *would* have died. *We* couldn't have paid it." She looked accusingly at Lord Sunderland.

"It's true," her father admitted. "You owe your life to Blackstoke. He's eager to see you when you're well enough."

"Yes. Of course." Her mind was feeling fuzzy again. She felt tired. She owed her life to Blackstoke. She would have to thank him. Yes. She would thank him.

"As soon as you're strong enough," her mother added, "we'll have a quiet wedding for the two of you. Blackstoke agrees it would be for the best."

"Wedding?" She felt stupid. She didn't understand. What were these people talking about?

"Come along, Gwendolyn," Lord Sunderland said. "She's tired. Can't you see she's nearly falling asleep while we're talking?" He bent forward and kissed her cheek. "We'll be back when you're feeling stronger, Jacinda."

"The duke. I'd like to see the duke," she whispered, but they were already gone.

Penneywaite had been a fool. Had he really thought he could blackmail him? But now the fat fool was dead. Now everyone who had known him as the Englishman was dead.

Everyone but White, and he had been well-paid to keep his silence. The danger was past. It was time to move on to other interests.

Blackstoke sat back in his chair and stared at the fireplace, watching the orange flames licking hungrily at the logs. The burning *Gabrielle* must have looked much like that before it sank. What luck that it had perished at sea, the entire crew lost. At least Penneywaite had had the good sense to save Jacinda.

Jacinda. What a shock it had been when he saw her in that cottage! If he hadn't already silenced Penneywaite for good, he would have done it after that. She'd looked nearly starved to death, her beautiful hair hanging limply over her shoulders, the fiery mane dull and dirty. Her tawny-gold eyes had looked at them without seeing, the sparkle gone from their depths. But her beauty would return, and when it did, he would make her his wife. He would have her at last. She would never be free of him again.

He swirled the golden brandy in his glass, then sipped it slowly. Yes, he would have her at last. At least Penneywaite had assured him that she'd never been sold on the auction block. He would still be the man to know her pleasures first. During the months she was missing, he'd been tormented by the thought that she might be with another man. At least he could be thankful to Dancing for having the wisdom to bring her back to him. Now she would be his, and his alone. How he savored the thought.

Once they were married, he would take her away. He would take her to one of his more secluded estates. That way they wouldn't be troubled by outsiders, nor would he be hounded by that money-grubbing woman, Lady Sunderland. He chuckled to himself. Wait until they discovered there would be no more financial help forthcoming. They would continue their descent into ruin. And, with a little help from Blackstoke, the earl might even end up in debtor's prison, just as he'd threatened the old fool. How satisfying that would be.

He drained his glass. Yes, as soon as she was able, they would marry and he would take her away from here. Perhaps they would go to Viridian. It was small and secluded; the perfect place for him to play the country squire. The perfect place for a groom and his shy bride.

27

There was a bird singing outside her window. Jacinda leaned her chin on her arms on the window sill, then closed her eyes. The song was joyous and full of hope, a song pronouncing the coming of spring, a time of new birth, a time for renewal of life.

Oh, Tristan, it would have been such a beautiful spring for us. Perhaps we could have started a new life of our own. Your baby. Our baby. A son with your black hair and eyes. A son to grow tall and strong, just like his father. Or perhaps she would have been a daughter. Oh, Tris . . .

She could think about him more often now without crying. She still refused to talk about the months she'd been gone from England, and no one pushed her to do so. She couldn't bear to talk about Tristan. She couldn't tell anyone she had married him. It hurt too deeply. It would remain her secret, a memory to cling to and share with no one. Only Mrs. Shipwick knew Jacinda had been in love with a man called Tris, and she was the soul of discretion. Until the Lady Jacinda wanted to talk about it, no one else would know.

Besides her parents, Jacinda saw only the household servants (and they were fewer than ever before). Well-meaning friends were allowed to leave their cards, along with their wishes for her return to good health, then sent on their way. Jacinda was grateful. She didn't want to see anyone. Except for the Duke of Locksworth. She longed to see him. She would be able to tell him everything, and he would understand. But he didn't come. Although she longed to know, she didn't ask why.

" 'Scuse me, miss."

Jacinda opened her eyes and looked toward the door. She hadn't heard it opening.

Bridey, the downstairs maid and Mrs. Shipwick's daughter, was peeking into the room. "Lord Fanshawe is 'ere t'see you, miss."

Roger. Here at last. She'd known he would come, and she'd dreaded knowing it. Everyone expected her to marry him, to docilely proceed as if nothing had changed. But everything had changed. She had changed. She wasn't the girl she'd been before Tristan arrived to turn her world upside down.

"Show him into the parlor, Bridey, and tell him I'll be down directly."

"Yes, miss."

Jacinda rose from her window seat and went to the mirror. She smoothed her hair and checked her dress. She was still thin and pale, but her strength was returning. She was strong enough to face him. She would have to be. He was here.

She walked slowly down the stairs, pausing just outside the parlor door. She drew a deep breath to calm her nerves, then stepped inside.

Blackstoke was standing with his back to the window, his hands clasped behind him. He was dressed in a red frock coat that accentuated his broad shoulders and narrow waist. His dark blue eyes met and held hers for a lengthy moment.

She was the first to break the silence. "Roger. You look well."

"I haven't changed." He came toward her, taking her fingers lightly in his hand and bringing them to his lips. "But you are looking better, my dear."

"Yes. I'm getting stronger every day."

Blackstoke led her toward the settee. "I'm glad to hear it."

"Roger," she said as they sat down, "I must thank you for paying the ransom. I owe you my life."

"Not at all, dear lady. Any man would do the same for his bride." He smiled, but it never reached his eyes. "Besides, in the end I got my money back. The scurvy thieves weren't very bright. Still, I would have given my entire fortune to have you returned to me."

His eyes, his smile, left her feeling cold. She must tell him she couldn't marry him, but she was afraid to. "Roger . . . I . . . I've been through a very trying time. I . . . don't think I'm ready to marry yet."

"But of course it's been a difficult time, my dear, and I will be a paragon of patience. Once we're wed, you'll be able to lean on me." The speech was lovely, but his gaze had hardened.

Jacinda pulled her hand away from him and rose to walk to the window. She pushed it open, allowing the crisp air to sting her cheeks. "Roger—" she began softly. Then she stopped, stiffening her resolve as she turned to face him, a stubborn set to her chin. "Roger, I *can't* marry you."

"Can't?"

Whatever she might have expected his reaction to be, it was much worse. Blackstoke got up from the settee. His handsome face darkened, and his eyes narrowed. There was an unmerciful twist on his lips that caused her to shiver involuntarily. He walked slowly toward her, his gaze never wavering from hers. Any sign of conciliation, any hint of tenderness was gone from him. This was the man she dreaded.

"*Can't* marry me?" He stopped before her, taking her hand once again, this time harshly. "You not only can marry me, my dear, you *must*."

"Roger—"

His grip tightened even more. "You see, if you refuse to marry me, I will destroy your parents. You think I can't? Your father has mortgaged this place to the hilt. I'll see you and your parents in debtor's prison. You know what it's like in prison, dear Jacinda? Remember the cottage? Remember being hungry? It's worse. Much worse, I promise."

"I would hate you," she whispered.

He laughed. "I don't care if you hate me or love me, Jacinda. But you *will* be my wife."

She had the horrible, sinking sensation that he was right. She *would* be his wife. There was no way out. What could she do? No matter what

342

her parents had done, no matter how little affection they had shown her, she couldn't send them to prison.

But there was still a ray of hope. The duke. He would help her. She could go to him. She could tell him that Tristan had married her before he died. He would help her. Surely he wouldn't let this happen to Tristan's widow.

"Please go, Roger. I can't think. You're confusing me. I . . . I'll give you my answer soon."

His grin was closer to a leer. "I have given you your answer, my dear lady. But if it will make you feel better, I'll go. For now. But be assured, we *will* be married. And soon." With another laugh, he turned and left her alone.

It was the first time she had left Bonclere since her return. With the help of Mrs. Shipwick, she slipped out of the house without being seen by her parents. In the stables, she was greeted by Pegasus's friendly nicker.

"You've missed me, girl?" Jacinda whispered in the mare's ear, and the horse gave a hearty nod of her head.

"Should you be doin' this, miss?" Giles asked as he led the white mare from her stall and prepared to saddle her.

"I'm feeling quite myself, Giles. I promise I'll be fine."

"Just the same, I think I'd best be comin' with you."

Jacinda nodded and let out a deep sigh. "All right. If it will make you feel better, you may come along."

"Thanks, miss." He grinned his relief.

Despite her protests to the contrary,

Jacinda was feeling tired by the time she and Giles came in sight of Locksworth House. She would be glad to sit down in the drawing room and rest.

As they jogged up the drive, she wondered again why Locksworth hadn't come to see her during her illness. If so many others hadn't called, leaving their cards, she would have suspected that no one knew she was home again. She couldn't imagine what would keep him from visiting her. For the first time, it occurred to her that something might have kept him from it.

Sims greeted her at the door. "Lady Jacinda, what a sight you are to these old eyes. Glad to have you home, milady."

"Thank you, Sims. Is the duke receiving?" she asked as she entered.

Sims was silent.

She turned and looked at him expectantly, a growing apprehension in her chest.

"Could it be you don't know, milady?" The butler's face was stiff with sorrow.

"Know what?" Jacinda whispered.

"His lordship, miss. He's had a seizure."

Jacinda sank into a nearby chair. She wrung her hands, staring at them as if absorbed by the twisting motion. Though her heart cried, she was too stunned even for tears.

"Milady?" Sims had stepped to her side. "Would you like to see him? I think he'd like you to visit."

She glanced up, a glimmer of hope in her eyes. "I can see him?"

"Yes, miss. He can't talk, but he understands. He's paralyzed on his right side, and can't do much with his left either, if truth be told. He hates being bedridden, I can tell you. I can see it in his eyes. We've got a nurse in to help us care for him, but Mrs. Charring's come up from Fernwood and she'd just as soon do it all herself." He took Jacinda's elbow and pulled her from her chair. "Come along now. It'll lift his lordship's spirits to see you and know you're doing so well."

The duke's room on the second floor was large and airy, yet it still had the odor of a sickroom. Jacinda paused just inside the door, needing a moment to gather her emotions and put them under strict rein. Then she walked toward the bed where the old man was hidden beneath several blankets. The nurse watched her approach, and when Jacinda glanced at her, she nodded and rose from her chair, leaving it for Jacinda. Sims followed the nurse from the room, closing the door gently behind them.

Jacinda stopped at the bedside and looked down at the white haired, old man. His eyes were closed, his breathing slow and steady. His face was much thinner than she remembered and heavily lined with wrinkles. One hand lay outside the blankets, and she reached out and gently touched it. His eyes opened. They seemed sightless at first, and then she saw recognition in them.

"Hello, your grace," she whispered. "I've missed you." She kissed his wrinkled cheek, then sat down, still holding his hand. His eyes followed her.

For a long time, she just sat there, reading his feelings in his faded brown eyes. She saw there the pain and the frustration and the anger and the futility. She felt as if her own heart were breaking all over again. Finally, she laid her head down on the bed beside him, unable to stop the tears from slipping from beneath her closed eyelids.

After a long time, she heard the gurgled groan and raised her head. Tears glittered in his eyes, unshed. She reached out to brush them away, able to talk at last.

"We found Ella, your grace. She was living in an elegant home and was cherished by her husband. All the terrible things you'd imagined never came to pass. She was so fond of her husband. I think she even loved him. But she was homesick. I don't know what she would have done if he'd lived, but he died while we were there, and so she came with us. She was so happy to be with Tristan again. I've never seen two people closer than they were." The story, half truth and half lies, flowed easily past her lips as she sought to comfort her old friend.

"I loved him so much, your grace. Desperately loved him, and we were happy together. We were married in Constantinople. I always hoped loving a man could be like that. I'm so glad I belonged to him, even if it was only for a little while."

She fell silent as she remembered . . . Tristan on the beach in Madeira . . . Tristan standing at the wheel, the wind whipping his shirt against his chest . . . Tristan in his pirate costume at the ball at Bonclere . . . Tristan . . .

"He was so special, your grace," she whispered. "I hoped that I would have his baby. I wish I could tell you there would be a great-grandchild soon, but I can't."

Again she paused, this time to compose herself once more. The duke was watching her. Although he couldn't speak, she knew Sims was right. His mind was active. He understood everything she was saying.

"You know he's gone, don't you?" She couldn't ask how he had learned of it, but he knew. Or perhaps he understood that if Tristan were alive, he would be with Jacinda now. Jacinda choked back an unwanted sob as she continued. "He would have wanted you to know how much he loved and respected you, and I know you would have been proud of him. He died bravely. And I promise you, your grace, I will find the man who caused his death. I will find the man who stole Ella from you and Tris, and he'll pay for all he's done." Her voice had deepened with repressed rage. "If I'm alive for only that reason, it will be enough. Penneywaite escaped my wrath, but the Englishman won't."

Jacinda fell silent as the terrible haunting memory of the burning ship flashed before her eyes.

A hand touched her shoulder. "I believe his lordship is tired, miss." Sims had returned without her notice. "Perhaps you could come back another day."

Jacinda glanced behind her, then nodded. "Of course, Sims." She rose from her chair as she turned her gaze back on the Duke of Locksworth. "I'll come again, your grace. I have so much I want to tell you about Tristan." She leaned down and kissed him, whispering, "I'm so glad you shared him with me. No matter what else happens to me, I'll always have this happiness to remember."

She walked across the room, pausing at the door to look back at her friend. She wanted to run back and throw herself across him and plead with him to help her. She wanted to tell him she was being forced to marry Blackstoke and she needed him to stand with her against the viscount and her parents. Instead, she turned and left the room.

28

Gulls screamed overhead as they circled, then swooped earthward in search of food. The wharf was alive with activity, the docks crowded with crates of squawking chickens and barrels of salted meat. Tall masts, bare of white canvas, rocked gently in the harbor as the ships were loaded and unloaded of their cargoes.

Tristan stood at the window of his room, watching the frenzy and wishing he were a part of it.

"Patience, Tris. We'll sail tomorrow."

He turned to face Spar. "It's not soon enough."

Spar shook his head. "One day will make little difference after all this time."

All this time. The weeks and months. She believed him dead, of course. She'd have to after all this time. All this time . . .

He closed his eyes as he turned back toward the window, unconsciously rubbing his shoulder. It still pained him, but he was lucky he had his arm and that it was still useful. If it hadn't been for Spar, he wouldn't have it.

"What do you suppose he did with her?" he asked softly.

"Don't torture yourself, Tris. At least we've learned his ship was bound for England. She's probably been home, safe in her own bed, all this time."

All this time . . .

He tried not to remember the agonizing days and nights that had followed the sinking of the *Dancing Gabrielle*. So few made it to shore. It was Whip who managed to drag Tristan onto the beach before swimming back to save others. His body washed ashore the next day.

Tristan was helpless in those first days. His shoulder was on fire and he lived in a fevered hell. It was Spar who tended the sick, found food for the survivors, and kept their hopes up. And it was Ida who worked tirelessly by his side.

He rubbed his eyes, then leaned his forehead against the glass. Looking down upon the street, his gaze fell on Ella and Danny. A tender smile lifted the corners of his mouth. That they, too, were alive was another miracle.

Danny had rescued Ella from the broiling water and taken her back to land. Both of them half drowned, he had hidden her on the island, staying with her until he knew she would survive. By the time he'd headed for the beach, it was too late. To his horror, he had watched the burning clipper ship sink into the sea. He returned to Ella, believing they were the sole survivors. It was several days later when they learned there were others who had escaped the inferno.

"Sit down, Tris." Spar was standing at his side. A firm hand took hold of Tristan's arm and steered him toward a chair. "Get hold of yourself, man. You'll be no use to her if you kill yourself with worry."

The weeks it had taken before they were rescued and reached Gibraltar. The hell they had had to survive. The hunger. The cold. The thirst.

All this time . . .

What had happened to Jacinda?

She dressed with extra care that morning, donning a new dress of burnished brown lawn with a full, tiered skirt. She brushed her hair until it shone with fiery highlights. She pinched her cheeks to bring color to her pale face. Bridey's knock quickened the erratic beating of her heart.

"' E's 'ere, miss," the maid said as she opened the door.

Jacinda drew a deep breath as she rose from her dressing table and turned away from the mirror. "I'll be right down, Bridey. Please bring us some tea."

"Aye, milady."

Jacinda made her way toward the drawing room with measured steps. She had made her decision two days ago, but that didn't make things any easier.

Blackstoke was seated near the fireplace, calmly smoking his pipe. He watched her enter the room, a grin pulling at his mouth as a ribbon of blue-gray smoke trailed upward from the bowl of his pipe. "Good morning, my dear. You look lovely."

"I've asked Bridey to bring us some tea," she responded, not deigning to acknowledge his compliment.

"How nice."

She sat down in another chair near the fire, a twin to the one Blackstoke occupied, a low table between them. She didn't speak again until Bridey had come and gone, then she poured the hot tea into the waiting cups, adding cream and sugar to both before offering one to her guest.

Jacinda sipped the hot liquid before drawing another deep breath. "I suppose you know I didn't ask you here just to share tea with me."

"I presumed not."

"Roger, I've given much thought to your—" She searched for the right words.

"Proposal," he offered.

"Ultimatum."

He grinned again and nodded in acquiescence. "As you wish."

"You've given me little choice. If it were only me, I would choose debtor's prison, but I won't see you put my parents there."

His smile remained but his jaw tightened. "How generous of you, my dear. Especially since they're not worth such a *supreme*—" His voice grated on the word. "—sacrifice, as you well know."

Her hand was shaking. She spilled tea on the table as she set the cup down. She closed her eyes briefly, praying for her nerves to settle. When she opened her eyes again, they flashed with rebellion and a new sense of courage. "I'm not the same girl I was when I agreed to marry you before. I'll marry you, Roger, but you'll never own me."

"Just what changed you, Jacinda? What happened to you in Constantinople?" Blackstoke leaned forward across the table, a wary glint in his dark blue eyes.

"Nothing, Roger." She would never tell him about Tristan. She would never tell anyone. If she must live with this man, at least she would have her memories of those few happy weeks. They would be her memories alone, and they would help her endure whatever life held in store for her.

Blackstoke's hand darted suddenly toward her, grasping her wrist. "Tell me what happened, Jacinda," he demanded.

She didn't allow her fear to show. "I will never speak of it to anyone, Roger. Not you, not anyone. Never."

"Jacinda, I demand to know."

"Demand all you like. I'll not speak of it."

"Then at least let us know the name of the ship's captain. He at least should be brought to justice."

Oh, Tristan. How I loved you. "I . . . I won't tell you that either."

Suspicious, he asked, "Why not?"

"Because he has family and friends in England who could only be hurt by the news if it got out what he had done. Besides, it doesn't matter now. He went down with his ship. Penneywaite had the ship torched, burning it with all the survivors still on board. He killed them all."

For a terrible moment, she saw the outline of a ship within the flames in the fireplace. She gasped and closed her eyes. "I just want to forget it," she whispered. She swallowed as she turned toward him again. "About the wedding—"

He watched her expectantly.

"I will marry you, Roger, but there are conditions."

"Conditions?"

"I want to see the stables and kennels filled again and the mortgages on Bonclere paid. I want to see the servants returned to their posts, every one of them. I want to see all the debts my father has acquired paid in full."

His eyes hardened. "See here—"

"You're buying my hand in marriage, Roger. That's part of the price."

Blackstoke stood and walked over to her. His hand beneath her chin, he forced her to look up at him, meeting his steely glare. "You hold yourself in great worth, Lady Jacinda."

"Yes," she answered simply, her gaze never wavering from his.

"And your other conditions?"

"Only one."

"Which is?"

"You must help me discover the identity of the Englishman."

Roger's face registered surprise. "The Englishman?"

"He's the man behind my kidnapping, mine and all those other women who were on board with me. He's the man responsible for the death of my friends. And they *were* my friends. Good friends."

"But it was Penneywaite who had the ship burned."

"Penneywaite was only his henchman. I want the man who was really responsible. Will you help me or not?"

Roger's mouth twitched with the beginnings of a smile. "If I give you my word I will help you, can we be married soon?"

There was a terrible ache in her chest as she replied, "In two weeks. Here at Bonclere. Our families and a few friends." *Forgive me, Tristan.*

"Then I will do all I can to help you find this scoundrel you call the Englishman, my dear. I give you my word." He began to laugh. He released her chin and turned back toward his chair. He sat down and raised his teacup in her direction. "I'll meet all your demands, Lady Jacinda. To our wedding day." He paused, then added, "And to our wedding night."

She quelled the shudder his words stirred inside her.

A gentle rain, little more than a gray mist, was falling when Blackstoke left Bonclere. It suited Jacinda's dismal spirit. She stood at the window in the drawing room, watching his carriage disappear down the drive.

"How can you do it?" she asked herself aloud. "How can you marry that man?"

But what else could she do? Tristan was dead; the duke was ill, probably dying. There was no other way to stop Blackstoke from destroying her parents. But after Tristan's loving touch, how could she submit herself to Blackstoke? He was an evil, vile man. She knew it more surely now than ever before. Her life would be a constant torture. Perhaps that was what she wanted. Perhaps she wanted to be punished for living when Tristan and Ella and Ida and Spar and all the others were dead.

She heard the rustle of skirts and turned from the window as Lady Sunderland entered the drawing room.

"Was that Blackstoke's carriage?"

"Yes, Mother."

"Why didn't you tell me he was here? I would have come down sooner."

"I wanted to talk to him alone. That's why I asked him to come so early in the day."

Lady Sunderland raised an eyebrow. "You sent for him?"

"Yes." Jacinda's reply was little more than a sigh. Her strength was dwindling rapidly. "We were discussing the wedding."

Her mother sank gracefully into the chair Blackstoke had occupied just a short time before. "But that's wonderful, Jacinda. When is it to be? My, there's so much to be done. We'll need to have your dress refitted—you've grown so thin, Jacinda—and we must notify the guests and—"

Jacinda closed her ears to her mother's chatter. Was she marrying Blackstoke for this woman? She stared at Lady Sunderland, and with sudden perception, saw her mother as she would be in another ten years. Her beauty would fade. Her admirers would vanish. She would have no one but her husband and this drafty manor, neither of which would have any warmth to share with her. It was a sorry picture.

Yes, Jacinda decided. It's partly for her I'm marrying Blackstoke. Or perhaps it's to get away from her.

"Jacinda! Are you listening to me? You're such a dreamer. Really, you must stop it."

"No." Her reply was so abrupt it startled them both. "No, I won't stop dreaming. It's all I've ever had and all I'll ever have."

"Jacinda—"

"Mother, there won't be any guests to invite and we won't need to bother with refitting the wedding gown. Roger and I will be married here at Bonclere with just our families and a few of our chosen friends."

"But, Jacinda, you're marrying the Viscount Blackstoke! You can't—"

Jacinda turned her back on her mother as she headed for the door. "I know all too well who it is I've agreed to marry, Mother, and I'll marry him *my* way."

Tristan paced the decks of the ship, his eyes scanning the sea ahead of them, urging them on toward England. If his yearning could have been changed into wind, the sails would be filled by the force of the gale.

The wondering was driving him crazy. Had Penneywaite harmed her? Had he returned her to her parents? What had happened to her in the weeks since the *Gabrielle* sank in flames? And a new thought had sprung up to nip at his insides. What of Blackstoke? Tristan had never told her that the viscount was the Englishman behind Ella's kidnapping. He'd been wrong not to tell her. He'd thought he had plenty of time. Now it was too late.

What would Blackstoke do to her?

29

A few days after agreeing to marry him, Jacinda took the carriage into London, arriving unexpectedly on Blackstoke's doorstep in early afternoon, Mrs. Shipwick in tow.

"Jacinda, my dear," Blackstoke said as he met her in the entry. "What brings you to town?" He leaned forward to kiss her cheek.

Jacinda steeled herself for his touch. "I want to start looking for the Englishman."

"Now? But wouldn't it be easier after the wedding, once we're living together in London?"

"No."

Blackstoke sighed expansively. "You have become a very determined woman, Lady Jacinda. I'm not sure it's your most endearing trait." He took her arm and led her into his study. After she was seated, he went to his desk and took up a pipe. As he reached for his tobacco pouch, he said, "I imagine you came here with an idea. What is it?"

"Most of the women came from the slums

of London. That must mean the Englishman had help in the slums. Thugs, thieves, someone. There must be someone who he paid to find and take his women."

"And if you find that someone? Surely this man wasn't so careless that he would tell anyone his name."

Jacinda's look was hopeful. "I don't know, but there must be a lead. This Englishman must have made a mistake, one time or another."

Blackstoke shook his head at her. "So you intend to go wandering through the streets of London, asking about him?" He gave her an indulgent grin. "My dear, it just won't do."

"Maybe not," she replied, standing, "but it *is* what I mean to do. With or without your help." She started toward the door.

Blackstoke caught her by the arm, swinging her around. He glowered his disapproval, but she didn't cower before him. She met his glare with one of her own, her tawny eyes daring him to challenge her further. His urge was to strike her, to force her into submission, but there was something about her that warned him against it. He released her, telling himself that there would be time enough to tame her newly rebellious spirit.

"My dear Jacinda, I haven't said I *won't* help you. Please. Sit down. We'll have tea and then we'll begin."

She studied him a moment longer, then nodded and returned to her chair. Inwardly fuming, Blackstoke left the study to call for tea.

Jacinda's insides were quivering like jelly. She couldn't believe she had stood up to him that way. It was so unlike her. No, it was unlike the person she used to be. She quelled her jitters as she straightened in her chair. She wouldn't be afraid. Not of anyone or anything. No matter what happened to her. She had only one purpose left in life. To find and punish the Englishman. And if she had to marry Blackstoke to reach that goal, so be it.

For six days they tramped through the undesirable streets of London. Fearlessly, Jacinda talked to beggars and prostitutes and thieves alike, asking them about the ships that had taken so many attractive young girls from London, asking about the man known as the Englishman. All she received were shaking heads and sly glances. A time or two, she wondered if she were about to be stabbed and robbed. She knew Blackstoke was always behind her, his pistol hidden but ready, but it wasn't he who gave her courage. It was knowing she was doing what Tristan would have done.

But, at last, she wearied. She was getting nowhere. No one seemed to know anything. She was failing.

She walked with Blackstoke to his carriage, her head hanging forward in resignation. She allowed him to help her in, then waited as he entered the vehicle himself.

"It's useless, my dear," Blackstoke told her. "Haven't you discovered that yet?"

She turned her face away from him to stare out the window at the wretched buildings surrounding them in the narrow street. She listened to the sounds of futile existence, and it saddened her even more.

"This may not have worked, Roger, but I'm

not giving up."

"Of course not. I wasn't expecting you to. But let's not come back to these streets again. It isn't safe."

Jacinda glanced at him. "Are you afraid?" she challenged.

He laughed sharply. "No. I've chanced much worse than this in my life, my dear girl. No, I am not afraid."

They fell silent during the ride back to Langley House, each pondering secret thoughts. When they arrived, Blackstoke helped her from the carriage, but she didn't move toward the house.

"Have my own carriage brought around, Roger. We're going back to Bonclere."

"Now? But it's late."

"I don't care," Jacinda answered. "Mrs. Shipwick and I are going home." Bitterly, she added, "I have a wedding to prepare for."

At that, Blackstoke smiled and went to do her bidding.

Jacinda waited outside, bracing herself against the cool spring breeze that swirled around and beneath her skirts. Her gaze moved up the quiet street, so different from the ones from which they had just returned. These were the homes of the affluent, the homes of the privileged. How very differently these people lived their lives.

In the distance, standing on the street corner, was a woman. She seemed to be watching Jacinda.

You're being silly, she told herself.

But there was something about the way the woman was standing, her long, chestnut hair blowing in the wind. Something familiar . . .

Jacinda started walking, slowly at first, then faster. Suddenly, the woman turned and disappeared down a side street. Jacinda lifted her skirts and began running. She wasn't mistaken. The woman had come to see her and something had frightened her. Jacinda couldn't let her get away. She knew something. She must know something, or why else would she have come?

"Wait!" Jacinda cried, even though there was no one in sight to call after.

She turned the corner, still hopeful, but the street was empty. The woman was gone. Disappointment welled within her. So close. She had been so close to discovery. She was certain of it.

The wedding was nearly upon them. Despite it being supposedly a quiet affair, Lady Sunderland was busily decorating Bonclere as if the queen herself would be in attendance. She paid little notice to the unhappiness of the bride. But her father had noticed.

Lord Sunderland found his daughter in the stables one morning. She was grooming Pegasus and whispering senseless words of affection into the mare's ear. He stood just inside the stables, feeling the warmth, breathing deeply, enjoying the mixture of smells that filled his nostrils—the tang of horse manure, the sweet scent of hay. The stalls were full once again. Filled with the best of their breed. Better horses than had ever graced Bonclere's stables before, and it was this girl who had done it for him.

"Good morning, Jacinda," he said at last, drawing her attention.

"Good morning, Father. I didn't know you were standing there."

"I was enjoying watching you with Pegasus. You have a special hand with a horse." He entered the stall and looked at her over the mare's white back. "You're a better daughter than your mother and I deserve. Don't think I don't know that, Jacinda."

It was the closest thing she'd ever heard to an "I love you" from her father and she warmed to the unexpected affection. Tears came suddenly to her eyes as she continued brushing Pegasus's shiny coat.

Lord Sunderland reached across the horse to place his hand over Jacinda's, stilling the gentle stroking motion of the brush. "Don't marry him if you'd rather not, my child. We'll send the horses back. We'll sell the manor. It's time I took care of my own. Time I did what's right for my family. Your mother and I would manage somehow. You don't have to do this."

"No, Father. I'll marry Roger. I've given my word on it." She raised her eyes once more, blinking back the stubborn tears. "But thank you for telling me," she finished in a mere whisper.

Lord Sunderland's ruddy complexion had deepened and his eyes had a suspicious gleam of their own as he squeezed her fingers, then turned away. He paused at the stall door, glancing back at her as if he would speak again, then with a remorseful shake of his head, he departed.

Jacinda stared at the empty doorway for a

long time, her surprise lingering. After all these years . . . Tears rose again, this time to spill unchecked down her cheeks. She leaned her face against Pegasus and allowed herself a good cry.

Finally, when her tears were spent, she dried her face with her fingers, then reached for her saddle. She had an errand to do today. One she had put off as long as possible. One that was sure to bring more tears to streak her cheeks. She had to tell the Duke of Locksworth that she was marrying Blackstoke. She knew he wouldn't approve. She knew he would have provided a safe haven for her had he been well. He probably would even have paid her father's debts, rescuing them all from the viscount's clutches. But he wasn't well and she couldn't ask him. She'd made her decision. Still, she had to tell him what she was doing. She would have to tell him, and see her own anguish mirrored in his eyes.

She didn't rush Pegasus toward Locksworth House. Instead, she allowed the mare to take the shortcut, taking her first by the forest pool. The newness of spring had splashed a verdant tint over the trees and bushes and grasses. Even the air smelled fresh with the promise of new life.

Jacinda slid from the saddle, dropping the reins to allow Pegasus to graze while she sat beside the still pool. It had been six months since she last visited this spot, six months since she had gazed into the crystal surface and seen Tristan watching her from the edge of the woods.

She closed her eyes and leaned back against

an old stump, willing him to appear before her.

"I love you, Cinda." His ebony eyes traced over her face, caressing with his glance her lips, her throat, even her breasts. A familiar longing sparked in her stomach, the warmth spreading into her loins until she burned with desire for his touch. He kissed her, nibbling playfully at her lower lip, teasing her earlobes, trailing a feathery-light path down her neck. Her arms wrapped around him, enfolding him, capturing him to her. She would never let him go. She loved him, she needed him, she wanted him . . . "Oh, Tristan," she whispered, though it was more of a moan than his name. He lifted his head to smile at her, a smile that tugged at the strings of her heart, that brought an ache to her chest, as if her heart were breaking. He covered her body with his own, and they rose and fell in the timeless rhythm of love. "Tristan," she whispered, but suddenly he was gone.

"Oh, Tristan."

Jacinda opened her eyes. She was flushed with wanting him. Had she fallen asleep or had her imagination taken to new flights of fancy even while awake? She brought her knees up to her chest and clutched them tightly, hiding her face against them.

"Tristan," she repeated with a sigh. "If only I could have had your baby."

She rocked gently, waiting out the hurt as it cut through to her very soul, waiting for that thin shred of peace to return, the slender ribbon of hope that kept her sane as she faced the world without him.

The duke's condition was a little improved.

When Jacinda arrived, he was propped up in his bed, holding a cup of tea with his left hand, albeit shakily so. He tried to smile at her, but only the left side of his mouth curved upward, making the attempt only a mockery of what he meant it to be. The nurse took the cup from him and, with a curt nod to Jacinda, left the bedroom.

Before going over to his bedside, Jacinda walked to the windows and pulled back the heavy draperies, allowing the golden morning sunshine to come pouring into the room. She threw open the windows and took a deep breath of the fresh spring air before turning to face him.

"There. That's better," she said with satisfaction.

She walked toward the duke, smiling cheerily. Sims had told her that the duke still couldn't speak but that he was regaining his strength a little each day. Still, she could see he was far from recovered, and the doctors held out only a slim hope that he would regain use of his right side or his ability to speak.

"You're looking so much better, your grace," she said before placing a gentle kiss on his wrinkled cheek. "Now that spring is here, I expect to see you out driving your carriage to visit all your friends." She sat down in the chair beside his bed and took his hand in hers. She could read a thousand questions in his eyes, all of them bearing Tristan's name . . . and so she began to answer them without delay.

"I first knew he loved me on the island of Madeira. He took me there because I was ill. He and Spar and Ida, they all took such good care of me. I might have died if it weren't for them. And it was a lovely little island with the prettiest village. The weather was so warm, even the nights. When we left, I knew we were going to Constantinople, but I didn't know why. There were times I was so afraid. I didn't know what was going on, or why he'd taken all those women. I just knew that I loved him, and since he'd asked me to trust him, I trusted him.''

She paused, fighting the growing ache in her heart. The duke pressed her fingers with his own.

"We were married in Constantinople with just a few of his shipmates as witnesses. There was never a happier bride, your grace. Never. I . . . I haven't told anyone we were married . . . except you. I knew you would understand, but no one else would. It's too precious, too special to be marred by their questions. If I . . . if I can't have Tristan, I can at least have my memories undisturbed.'' Jacinda lifted the duke's hand to her cheek and pressed it tightly against her face, closing her eyes for a moment. "You do understand, don't you?'' she whispered.

She opened her eyes to see him nod slowly in reply.

"I love you, your grace.''

Again he tried to squeeze her hand, tears glittering before his pale brown eyes.

Jacinda sniffed back her own persistent tears, stiffening her backbone in preparation. She still hadn't told him why she'd come. She reached out and smoothed the coverlet, then brushed aside the white hair falling over his forehead. She knew he was watching her, knew he understood there was more.

Finally, she stopped her fussing. She folded her hands in her lap, clenching them tightly. "I've hated telling you this, your grace, but I must. You have been like a grandfather to me. You have loved me when no one else seemed to care if I lived or died. I fell in love with and married your only grandson. I watched him be murdered and I've vowed to find and destroy the man who killed him. And I will." She stared at her clenched hands. "Viscount Blackstoke still wants to marry me. If I don't, my parents will end up paupers, perhaps even in prison because of their debts. I couldn't let that happen. Roger has cleared those debts and now I must honor my promise to him. I must marry him."

She fell silent. She couldn't bear to look up. She couldn't bear to see what his eyes must be saying to her now. She felt the cold dread seeping through her at the thought of what being Blackstoke's wife would mean. She was frightened and repelled.

More softly, more slowly this time, she spoke again. "I made him promise one more thing before I agreed to marry him. I made him promise he would help me find the Englishman. If I must search until I die, I will find him. Roger is a powerful man. He'll have ways of searching for this man that I would never have. With his help, I'll find Tristan's killer."

The duke groaned, and she glanced up. He was struggling to form a word, fighting to speak. Slowly, he shook his head from side to side. The agonizing sound was torn from grotesque lips. "Nnnnnnnnn . . . ooooooooo."

Jacinda was crying again. "I'm sorry, your grace," she whispered. "I have no choice. Honestly, I haven't any. I will always love Tristan. Until the day I die, I'll love him. But I must do this. I must."

"Nnnnnnnnnn . . . oooooooooo." His complexion was turning red with his effort to speak. The right side of his face seemed to droop even more.

She was frightened by the strain written in his eyes.

"Nnnnnnnnn . . . ooooooooo . . ."

Jacinda jumped up from her chair and ran to the door. "Nurse! Quickly!"

She stayed by the door as the nurse bustled into the room.

"Be still, your grace," the nurse commanded, her hands on his shoulders, but he continued to stare after Jacinda, groaning his painful refusal. The nurse turned around. "Please leave, milady. He must be calmed."

Tears blinding her, Jacinda nodded and left, feeling her way down the hall toward the stairs. It was worse than she'd expected. Now she had lost the duke, too. She was truly alone.

30

It was her wedding day. Black, thunderhead clouds blanketed the heavens and wept, drenching the earth. Bonclere was gripped by an icy chill which remained even with fires in every fireplace in the manse.

Despite Jacinda's instructions to the contrary, Lady Sunderland had invited a large number of guests. For a long time that morning, Jacinda sat in the window seat in her bedroom, watching the carriages arriving, the merry, curious masses spilling out from the black vehicles and hurrying into the manor. They had come to see her wed the Viscount Blackstoke. They had come to envy her good fortune in marrying so well. They had come to pry about her months of captivity, to learn what awful and dire things had been done to her by evil men, and to whisper what a fool Blackstoke was to still marry her, soiled as she certainly must be. Jacinda hated them all at this moment.

Her door opened and closed, but she didn't turn around to see who had entered.

"Milady?"

"What is it, Bridey?"

"The Lady Sunderland says it's time you were dressin', miss. His lordship has arrived."

Jacinda leaned her forehead against the glass. "Just a little longer, Bridey."

"I'll draw your bath, miss." The maid left on tiptoe, as if leaving a house of mourning.

What would he do if she suddenly refused to marry him in front of all these people? Or what if she opened the window and threw herself to the ground? She sighed as she turned around, knowing she would do neither. With resignation, she followed after Bridey.

Minutes later, clouds of steam floated around her head. She reclined in the hot bath water, her eyes closed. For once she managed to rid her mind of any thoughts at all, allowing her consciousness to float idly, mindlessly, just like the steam that filled the small bathing room. But eventually the water cooled, and Bridey stood waiting with a thick bath towel.

There was no avoiding the inevitable.

The horse's hooves flung mud into the air, spattering breeches that were already soaked through from the drenching rain. Water poured off his hat into his eyes, blinding him, but he wouldn't relent. He pushed the tired gelding mercilessly onward, eating up the miles between London and Locksworth House.

He was as tired as his mount. The muscles in his neck were knotted tightly and screamed for a moment to relax. His fingers were numb from the cold. His sodden clothes clung to his skin. There wasn't a dry spot on his body.

Spar had tried to stop him from leaving in the midst of this sudden spring storm, but Tristan wouldn't be delayed. He had to find out if Jacinda was in England. He had to lay all his fears to rest . . . or, God forbid, confirm them. Anything would be better than the unknown. At least that's what he told himself as he galloped through the gray day.

Lady Sunderland may have invited a house full of guests over her daughter's objections, but her cries of indignation had been unable to change her daughter's mind when it came to the wedding gown. The elaborate white gown of satin, lace and pearls lay across the bed, discarded for a simpler gown of lavender silk.

"What will they say?" Lady Sunderland moaned. "I'll be disgraced. They'll say you were unfit to wear white. You know there are rumors about your kidnappers. You are admitting they're right. Please, Jacinda. Don't shame me this way."

"And if they *are* right, Mother, is it your shame or is it mine?" Jacinda turned stiffly away from the mirror, impaling her mother with a frigid glare. "This is my wedding and I will wear what I choose. It will not be that hateful gown."

"Hateful!" Lady Sunderland sank onto the bed. "But the hours we spent at Madame Roget's. The hours of planning for this wedding and planning how you would look."

"*You* were planning, Mother. I was merely enduring." She touched her forehead, rubbing the spot where a persistent pain was promising to grow more noticeable.

Lady Sunderland sniffed indignantly. "The viscount will not be pleased," she warned as she headed for the door.

"The devil take the viscount," Jacinda muttered.

Bridey approached her carefully, holding a string of pearls in her hands. Jacinda looked at them, then waved the girl away.

"Leave me alone, Bridey. I need a moment to myself."

"Yes, milady. I'll be outside your door should you be needin' me."

Jacinda continued to stare at her reflection in the mirror, and slowly, her longing began to change the image. In the glass, she was wearing an emerald green riding gown. Her hair was curled atop her head instead of hanging down her back. In her hands she held a simple spray of flowers. Beyond the door she could see in the mirror, Tristan would be awaiting her, clad in his captain's uniform. Tristan with his black hair and sparkling ebony eyes. Tristan . . .

She reached out and touched the mirror, but the vision was gone. She was wearing the lavender dress and beyond her bedroom door waited her groom, the Viscount Blackstoke. No black hair. No laughing eyes. No suntanned skin and work-roughened hands. Only Blackstoke.

Soon she would descend the stairs. He would take her hand and they would stand before the reverend and pledge themselves to the other for life. She would become his. She would make her home where he chose and live her life as he willed. He would take her to his bed and . . .

Jacinda chased the thought from her mind. She wouldn't think of it. She wouldn't.

"Bridey!" she called. "Come fix my hair."

Tristan vaulted from the stumbling mount, splashing more mud onto his clothes. He dropped the reins as he dashed toward the entrance to Locksworth House. He pushed the door open before him, bringing an alarmed Sims rushing from the back of the house.

"Sir, just what . . . Captain Dancing, is it you, sir?"

"The duke. Where is he?"

"Captain Dancing, we thought you were dead."

"Sims, where is my grandfather? I must see him at once."

"I'm sorry, sir. You can't see him."

Tristan started for the stairs.

"You don't understand, Captain. The duke is ill."

He stopped and looked around at the butler. "Ill? What's wrong?"

"He's had a stroke, sir. He can't speak and he's mostly paralyzed. But he's improving, sir. We have hope for his recovery."

"I must see him anyway, Sims. Will you take me to him?"

"Would you care to clean up first, sir?" Sims asked, eyeing the drenched and muddied condition of the captain.

Tristan looked down at his attire, then shook his head. "I need to see him, Sims."

"Very well, sir. I'll take you up."

As they climbed the stairs, Tristan asked, "Sims, can you tell me anything about the Lady

Jacinda of Bonclere? Is she in England?"

"Oh, yes. That's a story, sir, and a long one, though I've heard more gossip than fact. She was here just two days ago to visit his grace."

Tristan released an internal sigh. She was all right. She was safe in England. She had come to visit the duke. He allowed some of the tension to drain from within.

Sims opened the bedroom door. The heavy curtains had been drawn against the damp chill of the English storm. A nurse looked up from her post at the duke's bedside. Surprise and disapproval registered on her prim face as she saw the mud-spattered captain approaching her charge.

Tristan's eyes were locked on the sick man in his bed. His grandfather was sleeping, but the coverlet barely seemed to move with his shallow breathing. Tristan glanced at the woman and motioned her out. She began to refuse, then thought better of it as she read the command in his ebony glare.

Tristan took hold of Locksworth's frail hand. "Grandfather?"

Eyes fluttered open. He gazed at Tristan for a long moment, then closed his eyes once again.

"Grandfather, it's Tristan. I'm really here."

The duke opened his eyes at his prodding. There was disbelief written there. His mouth tried to work.

"I know everyone thought me dead, but I'm alive and I've returned. Ella's in London. She'll be here in a day or two." He squeezed the duke's hand. "Don't try to talk, Grandfather. We've lots of time to see that you get well."

"Nnnnn . . . oooo," Locksworth managed.

"Of course you're going to get well. Sims tells me you're improving every day."

"Nnnn . . . ooo t . . . iii . . . mmme."

Tristan could see his grandfather was greatly agitated and tried to calm him. "Ella will come soon and we'll be a family. You and Ella and me and Jacinda."

Locksworth squeezed his eyes shut as he twisted his mouth to force out the words. "Bllla . . . ck . . . ssss . . . toooo . . . ke—"

"I know, Grandfather. I plan to take care of him myself."

"Sssimmmmms," the duke said, his eyes pleading with Tristan.

Tristan went to the door and opened it. The nurse was waiting in the hall. "Get Sims," Tristan told her, then returned to his grand-father's beside.

Sims arrived in short order. "What is it, sir?"

"He asked for you."

Sims looked incredulous. "Asked for me, sir?"

"Jjjjjaaaa . . . cccc—"

"By heavens!" the butler cried, hastening nearer to stare at his master.

"Jjjjaaaa . . . ccccc . . . innnn—"

Tristan glanced across the bed at the butler. "He's saying Jacinda. What about Jacinda?"

Sims shrugged. "I don't know, sir."

"Has something happened to her? Tell me, man."

"Nothing's happened to her, Captain, I promise you. In fact, she's marrying that viscount today."

Tristan felt as if he'd been slugged. "Marrying?"

"Yes, sir. Today at Bonclere."

Tristan looked back at the duke. His struggles to speak and be understood had drained him of what little strength he'd possessed, but his eyes begged Tristan to go, to hurry.

"I'll be back, Grandfather. And I'll bring Cinda with me."

Blackstoke sought solitude in the library while he awaited word of Jacinda's readiness. He felt alternately jubilant and fiercely frustrated. He was within minutes of obtaining what he had sought for months. She would be his. He would be her master and she would defy him no more. Yet, he knew she would continue to hold herself aloof from him. She had said he would never own her. Damn the woman! He *would* own her. She would submit to him or he would break her.

Ah, but the taming of the fiery beauty would be pleasurable. He had held his desire for her in check for an eternity. Soon he would not have to contain himself. Soon he would pluck the flower that so many others had lusted after. He, Blackstoke, would be the first.

He drew a deep breath, seeking to control his growing ardor, lest the entire assemblage waiting in the drawing room be aware of his thoughts.

Patience, Blackstoke, he told himself. Tonight will come soon enough.

Seeking to distract his amorous thoughts, he pulled a note from his coat pocket. Written in flowing script, its words were intriguing.

Tell the Lady Jacinda that I know the identity of the Englishman.

You can find me at the Lion's Paw. Ask for Loralie.

Blackstoke wondered who this Loralie was and how she had known to send this note to Langley House. And if she knew he was the Englishman, why warn him in this manner? Once he and Jacinda were married, he would look up this Loralie and find the answer to these and other questions.

"Milord?"

Blackstoke turned toward the library door. "Yes?"

"Lady Jacinda is about to come down."

The time was here. Blackstoke smiled to himself. He had teased himself with this moment for a long time, like a fat woman setting her favorite bonbon on the table hours before she allows herself to eat it. Now the time for indulging was upon him. Soon it would be his turn to devour the tender delicacy.

Jacinda descended the stairs alone, her chin held high, her golden eyes impassive. Her cheeks were alabaster pale. Her mouth held no hint of a smile as her lower lip trembled with repressed emotions. If ever she'd needed her ability to escape into a fantasy world, now was the time. But she could see the waiting, expectant faces all too clearly. The voices stilled as she neared the bottom step. She hooked her hand through his elbow.

"You look beautiful, Jacinda," Lord Sunderland whispered.

She attemped a smile.

"It's not too late, my dear. Say the word, and I'll take you back upstairs myself."

Jacinda turned her head to look at her father. She could see the fear in his eyes. He was afraid she would do just as he suggested. But even fearing it, he offered. This time her smile succeeded as she paused long enough to lean over and kiss his cheek. "Thank you, Father. I'll never forget." She turned to face the waiting crowd. "I think it's time for the wedding to begin."

The Most Reverend Halverson was waiting near an arbor of flowers set near the far wall of the ballroom. Roger was with him. Although Bonclere was not the cathedral they were to have married in, the walk toward her groom seemed miles long. Even so, she arrived much sooner than she wished.

Blackstoke's handsome face was alight with glee. It proclaimed his pride of ownership. His blue eyes never left hers. She shivered as she saw his mouth part ever so slightly and his tongue moisten his lips.

Like a dog eyeing a bone, she thought, and cringed when she imagined how he meant to enjoy her.

"You notice her dress isn't white."

The catty feminine voice was just loud enough to reach her ears. She saw Blackstoke's jaw stiffen, his face growing red as storm clouds gathered in his eyes. He had heard it too. She felt a spark of satisfaction, though she knew she would regret it later.

Lord Sunderland paused, patted her hand, then stepped back from her side as Blackstoke came to claim her. His gaze swept over her, chilling her with his anger.

The Reverend cleared his throat. "Beloved friends . . ." he began, and a hush fell over the room.

Jacinda closed her ears, just as she had closed her heart, to all around her. If she could survive losing Tristan, she could survive this. She was made of stronger stuff than even she had ever known. Blackstoke could not harm her for she wasn't his. He might call her wife, but it was only a shell he was taking for a bride. Jacinda—the real Jacinda—would never belong to another man. Everything she was, everything she had ever been, belonged to Tristan.

Tristan! her heart cried his name.

31

Tristan burst through the doorway, sodden and muddy. "Where is my wife?" he bellowed at the surprised crowd that turned to gaze at him in amazement.

"See here, sir," the butler sputtered, looking askance at the intruder's appearance. "This is a private affair."

"I've come for my wife, the Lady Jacinda."

"What insanity is this?" Lord Sunderland asked as he stepped into the entry hall.

Tristan removed his hat. He took a deep breath, temporarily bringing his anxiety under control. In a calm, low voice, he replied, "It's not insanity, Lord Sunderland. Your daughter and I were married in Constantinople."

"Married, but—" His jaw dropped open.

Loudly again, he repeated his words. "Jacinda and I were married in Constantinople. She thought I was drowned when my ship went down. Now I ask you again. Where is my wife?"

There was a ripple of startled voices at the other end of the room as Lady Sunderland sank to the floor in a dead faint.

"Captain Dancing," Jacinda's father said, ignoring his wife, "Jacinda has married Viscount Blackstoke and has gone with him to his house in London for their—" He paused again, glancing about him as if for help. "For their wedding night," he finished reluctantly.

Tristan grabbed Lord Sunderland by his coat collar. "How long ago did they leave?"

"Not . . . not long. Perhaps a half an hour, maybe a little more."

Tristan released him and left as abruptly as he had arrived.

Jacinda still felt chilled, despite the fire burning on the hearth. Blackstoke had left her alone to change, but she knew he would return soon. Her mouth felt dry and she was shaking again. She hated her own cowardice. The door opened, and she whirled around, feeling the blood draining from her face as one hand gripped the fireplace mantle to steady her.

"But you haven't changed, my dear," Blackstoke said with some surprise as he entered the room, carrying a tray with a bottle of wine and some cheese. He placed the tray on a table and sliced himself a thick piece of cheese with a knife. He settled into a nearby chair while he nibbled the morsel. "Would you care for a bite to eat? I'd guess you haven't had a thing all day."

"No. Thank you, Roger. I'm not hungry."

Suddenly, he dropped the cheese onto the tray and pushed himself up from his chair, crossing the room to stand before her. He reached out to touch her hair. "It's the color of the fire." He pulled out the pins, setting the curly mass of hair free to cascade down her back. "You're so beautiful," he whispered. "And you're mine."

His mouth caught hers, pressing, insisting, demanding. She stood rigidly for a long time, as long as she could endure, then shoved at him, pushing him away.

In the firelight, his face looked sinister as he frowned at her. "My shy bride. Is that it, Jacinda? It's all right, my dear. It's normal for a virgin to be a little frightened on her wedding night."

The words popped out of her mouth before she had time to think. "But I'm not a virgin, Roger."

He took a step backward, as if she'd physically struck him. "What are you saying? Of course you're a virgin."

"No, Roger, I'm not." There was no going back now. She lifted her chin defiantly. "I was married in Constantinople."

"You're lying!"

"I'm not lying, Roger."

"You're lying!" he exclaimed again, lunging forward, his arm raised.

His slap caught her by surprise, knocking her across the room. She steadied herself before she could tumble to the floor and turned around to see him approaching with a menacing gleam in his eye.

"Who was it you married?" he demanded.

"I married the captain of the ship that took me to Constantinople. He's dead now. My marriage to you, unfortunately, is entirely legal."

"You married Captain Dancing?"

"How did you know it was Tristan?" she whispered, sidling around the chair away from him.

He ignored her question. "You gave yourself to that man? He was nothing. You were engaged to me, yet you gave him what was rightfully mine. How dared you do it?"

"I loved him. I still love him. What difference does it make now? He's dead and I'm your wife."

His face turned dark with repressed rage. "Oh, it makes a difference, my dear," he said in a low, threatening tone. Suddenly he smiled. "But I have a secret of my own, Jacinda. Would you like to know my secret?"

She moved farther away from him, shaking her head.

"Well, I'm going to tell you anyway. I know who your Englishman is!"

Neptune's hooves clattered down the London streets. The rain had stopped, but Tristan wasn't aware of it. He was nearly blinded by his own fears. If only he'd told her who Blackstoke was. If only he'd arrived one day sooner. If only . . .

"You know? You know who the Englishman is?" She stopped backing away. "Tell me, Roger. Who is he?"

His smile broadened. "*I* am the Englishman." And then he began to laugh.

"You!" she whispered. *Dear Lord, what have I done? I've married Tristan's killer.*

She thought for a moment that his laughter would drive her insane. She grabbed the sides of her head, trying to drown out the sound. But no, she wouldn't go insane. She had promised to do one thing and only one thing. She had promised she would kill the Englishman. The knife lay on the tray beside the cheese. She reached out and picked it up, turning toward him in a slow, calm manner.

His laughter faded. "What do you think you're going to do with that?" he mocked her.

"I'm going to kill the Englishman."

"Don't be silly, Jacinda. You can't kill me."

"Oh, but I can kill you, Roger. Did you know I've already killed one man? On board Penneywaite's ship. He tried to rape me, and I stabbed him in the back. But I won't stab you in the back, Roger. I want to see your face."

She took a step toward him, warily, watching his every move. He wouldn't deny her this pleasure. He wouldn't live when Tristan had died. She might hang tomorrow for his murder, but he wouldn't survive this night if she could help it.

They both heard the crash of splintering wood coming from downstairs. Jacinda stopped and listened, but she didn't take her eyes off of Blackstoke.

"Jacinda!" a voice called.

She *was* insane. It sounded like Tristan.

"Jacinda!"

"Tristan," she whispered, unable to resist the voice. She turned and ran toward the door. "Tristan!" she cried, throwing the door open.

He looked so real, so alive, standing midway up the stairs, his clothes dripping wet.

And then he smiled at her, and her dark world exploded in a burst of warm colors. He was alive!

"Cinda, I'm here."

And then she was hurtling herself into his waiting arms.

"Tris . . . oh, Tris—" She pressed herself against his rain-soaked chest. She raised her face to look into his eyes, still half-afraid that he would disappear and the nightmare of reality would begin again.

"My lovely lady," he said softly. "My lovely pirate's lady."

"I thought you were dead. I thought—"

"I know, Cinda, but I'm here now." His mouth lowered to claim hers, warm, tender, demanding. Her lips parted as she drowned in the delight of his kiss. Slowly, he held her apart from him. "Where is Blackstoke?" he asked.

She turned and pointed toward the bedroom. "In there." Her hand caught his sleeve. "Tris, he's the Englishman."

"I know." He stepped past her.

The room was empty. While they had embraced on the stairs, Blackstoke had slipped away.

"We'll find him," Tristan promised grimly.

But for now, Jacinda wanted only to forget. "Take me away from here, Tris. Please."

His anger vanished, replaced by the tender look that made her heart flutter. He swept her into his arms and carried her out of the house, placing her on the saddle before he swung up behind her.

"We'll be home soon," he whispered in her ear as his arms wrapped around her.

* * *

Jacinda sat across from Tristan as he told his grandfather all that had happened since the sinking of the *Gabrielle*. She was still wondering if this were all just a wonderful dream, but if it were, she hoped she would never awaken again.

"We were lucky it was a friendly ship that found us. We'd have stood no chance against another shipload of pirates," he finished. Unconsciously, he rubbed his arm.

As she watched him kneading the soreness, she remembered how he'd looked as she was dragged off the *Gabrielle*. That he was alive, that he was here, was a miracle. Especially when so many others had died. If it hadn't been for Whip... She closed her eyes as she swallowed the lump that rose in her throat.

"Jacinda?"

She looked over at Tristan.

"I think the duke is tired. We'd better let him rest." They had decided to ride back to Locksworth House after leaving London, and it was now past midnight.

Jacinda rose from her chair and placed a tender kiss on the old man's cheek. "Sleep well, Grandfather," she whispered, feeling a special joy at her right to call him that.

Tristan wrapped an arm around her waist and guided her from the duke's bed chamber. She snuggled against his side, laying her head on his shoulder as they walked. They made their way in silence down the long hallway, stopping at last before another door. Tristan opened it with his free hand, then drew Jacinda into his full embrace. His dark eyes searched her face, drinking in the adoration that beamed from deep in her golden eyes.

"There's still so much I want to know," she whispered huskily. "So much I need to tell you."

His mouth silenced her, tenderly molding her lips to his, his gentleness more powerful than force. When he lifted his head again, his black eyes smoldered with love and desire. "It will be a simple matter to have your marriage to Blackstoke annulled. Then there'll be plenty of time for talk, my love. A lifetime." While his mouth captured hers in another kiss, his arms swept her feet from the floor, and he carried her into the bedroom.

A fire burned hot on the hearth, warming the room. The bedcovers had been turned back in invitation. Tristan set her on the bed, but when he would have moved away, her arms remained locked around his neck, drawing him down with her.

"Don't leave me, Tris," she pleaded softly.

"Never, Cinda. Never again."

He knelt on the bed beside her, his eyes glowing with the fires of passion. He kissed her again, his exploring tongue parting her lips. Her fingers stroked his back and wended their way up his neck to tangle in his hair. She could hear the quickened pace of his heartbeat, and her own excitement grew.

He drew back from her, studying her face in the flickering firelight, watching how her hair glowed like the fire itself, reading the desire in her tawny-gold eyes. His fingers moved to the buttons on her gown and began their slow descent, a button at a time, as he sought to free her alabaster breasts from the restraining garment.

"You're so beautiful," he whispered.

"And you, my love," she returned. "You are beautiful to behold."

He lifted her up on the bed and slipped the bodice of her gown from her shoulders, then held himself apart from her as he drank in the sight of her breasts bathed in the golden light. A groan slipped through parted lips as he pressed her back against the mattress and tasted the rosy tips, teasing them into taut peaks.

As his mouth traced its way upward, pausing to nibble at the delicate flesh of her throat, Jacinda closed her eyes, savoring each wonderfully agonizing moment. Every place his fingers touched, every place his lips grazed, a glowing warmth was left behind.

"Tristan, I need you. Love me."

He moved away from her and stood beside the bed, disrobing in the glimmering light from the fire. He moved to rejoin her, but she stopped him.

"No," she whispered. "Don't move."

Jacinda slid to the side of the bed and stood before him. Her gown fell in a silken puddle around her ankles as she reached out and lightly touched the fresh scars on his side and shoulder. Tears glittered in her eyes as she lifted her gaze.

"I thought you were dead."

He smiled tenderly. "But I'm not, Cinda."

She kissed his shoulder, then left a trail of kisses across his chest and down to his wounded side, each touch leaving him shuddering with checked desire. Suddenly she threw her arms around his neck, standing on tiptoe to press her lips against his, holding her body so close to his own that there was no denying his need any longer.

They tumbled onto the bed, their mouths greedily tasting the pleasures the other had to offer. They were starved for each other. They rode high on the tide of passion, giving and receiving equally, taking and surrendering all. Time had no meaning. There was no yesterday, no today, no tomorrow. There was only this room and the ecstasy of their shared bodies, the infinite, timeless rhythm of love until their own little world exploded in a moment of unspeakable rapture.

Jacinda whimpered with joy and relief as a delicious trembling spread through her body, searing every nerve. "Tristan," she cried out.

His body heaved as he crushed her against him. "Cinda," he breathed into her ear, the tension in his body dissipating in one final, earthshaking shudder. "Cinda, my love."

He rolled onto his side, taking her with him. His hand tenderly stroked her hair as she nestled her head against his chest. Their love sated, they slept.

32

She awakened to the smell of hot tea wafting from the bedside table. Tristan was sitting up beside her, spreading marmalade on a flaky biscuit.

"Good morning, sleepyhead. I was wondering when you'd pry those golden eyes open and greet the day."

Jacinda pushed her tumbling tresses away from her face and yawned. "It's not really so late, is it?" she asked, snuggling up against his side.

"It's late enough." He whacked her bare backside. "It's time we talked about it."

She groaned and slid back under the covers. She knew what he meant.

Tristan set his biscuit on the tray, then reached out with strong hands and drew her back into his arms. He kissed the crown of her head. "Cinda? Why did you marry Blackstoke, of all people? I know how you always felt about him. You despised him."

She shivered, hiding her face against his

chest. "He paid the ransom to Penneywaite, or at least he said he did. Besides, he swore he would see my parents in debtor's prison if I didn't. I couldn't allow that to happen, Tris. I just couldn't. I thought you were dead, and nothing much mattered to me. And then he promised to help me find the Englishman. I didn't know that he *was* the Englishman until our wedding night. Until just before you arrived."

He tightened his hold on her, burying his face in her hair. "When I think of the dangers I put you in . . . God forgive me."

They stayed there, locked together in silent communication, for several minutes, each of them sensing again the miracle of their togetherness.

Finally, in a reluctant voice, Jacinda spoke. "What about Blackstoke now?"

"I don't know. Even if we find him, it's only my word against his, and I'm an American and he's an English peer."

She sat up, her gaze meeting his. "But you must have had some plan when you set out on this venture."

"Yes. I planned to kill him, but it won't be so simple now. It's known now that I'm the duke's grandson and that you were with me at sea and that we're married. I can't risk bringing suspicion upon you and Grandfather."

"So he's just going to get away with it?" she asked in a small, incredulous voice.

"I didn't say that. I'll find a way to bring him to justice—"

"*We'll* find a way."

Tristan grinned at her. "As you say, *we'll*

find a way, but this time it will have to be within the limits of the law."

Jacinda nodded, feeling once again the lazy contentment which had warmed her upon awakening. Her world was set aright. She had nothing more to fear from Blackstoke or anyone else, not with Tristan by her side. She snuggled down beneath the covers, resting her head on his muscled thigh, and closed her eyes.

Ella arrived two days later. Jacinda was standing at the window, enjoying the return of spring sunshine when the carriage turned up the drive. She knew at once who it must be and raced from the third-story room and down the stairs. She arrived at the front door just as Ella was alighting from the carriage, helped down by an attentive Danny O'Banyon.

"Ella!"

The dark-haired young woman looked up at the cry, and her face broke into a smile. "Jacinda."

Suddenly they were hugging and laughing and crying, all at the same time. It wasn't until Jacinda was backing away to give them both a chance to breathe that she noticed the generous swell of Ella's abdomen.

"The baby," she said softly. "It's all right?"

Ella laid a hand on her stomach and smiled as she nodded. "And very active."

"Hello, Jacinda."

She turned to greet Danny, giving him an affectionate embrace, just as she had Ella.

"Unhand my wife, you cad."

Jacinda jumped back, startled, and then joined the laughter as Tristan stepped up to greet the new arrivals. He hugged his sister, then shook Danny's hand.

"Welcome to Locksworth House," he told Danny.

Ella's black eyes widened as they swept over the massive structure. "Tristan, it's a castle," she said in awe.

"Just about, dear sister. Come on." He threw his arm around her shoulder, guiding her toward the door. "Grandfather has been waiting anxiously for your arrival."

Ella glanced nervously downward, then sought Tristan's gaze. "Does he know about . . . about the baby?"

"I told him, and he's delighted. There's nothing he wants more than to see that first great-grandchild." He grew somber. "But you should know, Ella, the duke's been very ill. He's improving, but he isn't the strong old gent you remember visiting us in America."

Jacinda followed with Danny, noting how his eyes remained on Ella even as he walked. There was no doubting how Danny felt about her sister-in-law, and she couldn't help but approve the match if Ella returned the feelings.

"Why didn't Spar and Ida come with you?" she asked Danny as they entered the house.

"They're making plans to sail for America. Spar is anxious to return to his doctoring, and Ida doesn't exactly have fond memories of England. Don't worry," he said, his gaze following Ella as she climbed the stairs beside her brother. "They'll come to see you before they leave." When Ella was out of sight, he glanced over at Jacinda. Seeing her observant gaze, he smiled sheepishly.

"Does she feel the same, Danny?"

"Not that she'll admit, but I'm patient. I can wait."

"She has a lot of hurt to get over."

Danny nodded. "I know." He moved across the tiled floor, gazing at the portraits on the walls.

She noticed he was limping. "What happened to your leg, Danny?"

"I took a ball when I was going after Ella." He shrugged without turning to look at her. "It's right enough now, though I won't be running any footraces again in this life."

"I'm sorry."

"Could have been much worse." He'd made his way around the room and had arrived back at her side. "Ella and I sort of took care of each other after the ship sank. She removed the ball and staunched the wound. She's got plenty of spunk, that one."

"The Dancings are very special people."

Danny's arm went around her shoulders. "Including Jacinda Dancing."

She glowed. "That has a very wonderful sound. Jacinda Dancing."

Tristan opened the door to his grandfather's bed chamber. The room was bathed in daylight, and the duke was propped up in bed, anxiously awaiting them. The nurse, having fallen under Tristan's spell, gave him a shy nod and hurried out of the room.

His arm around his sister's shoulders, he urged her forward. "Look who's here, Grandfather. Didn't I promise she'd be here soon?"

"Ell . . . llaaa." The duke raised his left

hand toward her.

Tears teetered on the brink of her eyes. "Oh, Grandfather," she whispered. "It's so good to be here at last."

His gnarled hand stroked her hair and caressed her cheek. His eyes said what his lips could not. *Welcome. I love you. You're home.*

"Grandfather, Tristan and I . . . we've talked it over, and we're going to stay with you until you're well." Ella touched her stomach. "And until the baby's born." She smiled shyly. "Then, we'd like you to come back to America with us, if only for just a visit."

He grinned his misshapen smile and nodded.

"See," Tristan added. "I told you he would agree to come. He couldn't deny you anything from the day he first saw you. Now we'll all be together for a long, long time. Things can't go much better for us than this."

The days ran together in serene harmony. Tristan and Jacinda spent their nights loving each other in their big bed on the second floor of the mansion. Each morning, they snuggled in the safe harbor of each other's arms and talked about the future—about the home they would make in America, about the children they would have, about Ella and Danny, and about the duke. Jacinda shared the life she'd created in dreams, and Tristan shared his love of the sea. Tristan learned the secrets of the lonesome little girl, growing up in a home bereft of love. Jacinda learned about a boy's wish to be just like his father and captain his own ship some day. They were very special hours.

The duke continued to improve. Having his grandchildren and Jacinda with him speeded his recovery. Little by little, his speech returned, much to the doctor's amazement. And he began to use his right hand, too, although his right leg stubbornly refused to budge. When he could not abide confinement in his room any longer, he reluctantly agreed to use a wheelchair, but he hated it, regarding it as a sign of being old.

While the baby grew inside her, Ella's laughter returned. The moments when a pained, heartbroken expression passed over her face became fewer in number. It was obvious to everyone that she was beginning to accept Danny's attentions as more than just an offer of friendship, and Danny acted as if he were a man allowed to commune with the angels.

If a spring could ever have been called idyllic, it was this one. Wild flowers bloomed in abundance. The sun chased away rain clouds to bless Locksworth House in its cheery warmth day after day. New colts on spindly legs raced through the pastures beside their dams. New litters blessed the kennels, and Jacinda delighted in picking up the sightless pups and giving them names, names as filled with joy and promise as her own heart.

She wished this time could last forever.

33

Blackstoke walked around the barren drawing room, his mood growing blacker with each step. For weeks he had resided in this godforsaken house in the middle of nowhere. All because of that damned Dancing fellow.

The rumors had started within days of his annulled wedding. The whispers that he'd been involved in something illegal, the reports that scandal would soon disgrace the house of Highport. And then the marquess had called him into his study and banished him to Viridian until the trouble blew over.

"Make no mistake, Roger," the old man had warned. "Should any of these rumors be proven true, I'll disown you. I'll leave you with nothing."

Viridian. It had been the perfect place to commit murder, and it would have been the perfect place to bring Jacinda. No one around to bother them. Just Blackstoke and his bride. But living here alone, secluded from society, without even a wench to vent his anger on . . .

Soon he would go insane.

Smithens entered the room. "A message, milord."

"What is it?" Blackstoke asked without turning to look at his manservant.

"It's from a Miss Loralie, sir. She sends word that she will come as you requested and asks that you send a carriage for her."

Blackstoke swung around. "When?"

"Tomorrow."

"Very well, Smithens. Arrange it."

"As you wish, milord." Smithens turned and left the drawing room, closing the double doors behind him.

So, he would at last meet this woman who could expose him, the woman who could confirm the rumors and ruin him for good.

"Miss Loralie, you have very few chances of ever leaving Viridian alive," he said under his breath, his blue eyes glaring out the window.

"Your choice . . . my dear," the duke said, watching Jacinda with amused brown eyes.

She was seated on the lawn in front of Locksworth House. Her dress of forest green was spread over her feet, forming an island of cloth. "But how can I choose? They're all so beautiful."

Sable lay nearby, proudly nursing her litter of seven, all of them black with white collars. She nuzzled her closest pup, then looked up at Jacinda as if to say, "How about this one?"

Jacinda laughed and picked him up. He wriggled in her hands, eager to get back to his meal before his siblings left their mother dry.

"How about it? Would you like to live in

America with the Dancing family?" She held him up against her cheek, but he continued to struggle, so she placed him in the grass and watched him scurry back to his dinner. "He's the one, Grandfather. As hungry as he is, he should grow into a fine, big dog. Just right for a big, new country."

"And his . . . name?"

"Hmmm. I'm going to have to think about that."

Sounds of laughter drifted across the lawn, and Jacinda and Locksworth both turned their heads toward the sound. Danny and Ella were walking along the drive, her arm hooked through his. She was carrying a parasol and dipped it coyly to the side as she glanced up at his supreme height.

"I . . . think we . . . 'll have . . . another . . . wedding soon."

Jacinda twisted around so she could lean her arms across the duke's lap. "I think you're right, Grandfather," she replied. There was a special tone in her voice when she called him that, and she liked to say it often. After all the years when she'd longed for something that could never be, now it had come true.

The duke placed his hand on her head. "You're . . . very happy?"

"Oh, yes. I'm very happy."

"Good."

"Hello, you two," Danny called to them as he and Ella approached.

"Good day, Danny," Jacinda returned. "Come see my new pup." She held him up for the couple to admire.

"Where's Tristan? I haven't seen him all

day." Ella sat down on a bench beside her grandfather's wheelchair. As she spoke, she took his hand in hers, squeezing it gently.

Jacinda frowned. "He went into London to meet with Spar."

"Still looking, are they?" Danny asked as he knelt beside Sable and picked up another pup. "He should have taken me with him."

It was the only thing that marred Jacinda's otherwise perfect existence. There wasn't any proof of Blackstoke's wrongdoing, and she sensed Tristan's growing frustration. Sometimes she wished they could just get on a ship and leave for America right away. Forget Blackstoke and what he'd done. Just leave and make their own happiness elsewhere.

"Looks like we have visitors," Ella said, drawing Jacinda's thoughts back to the present.

She recognized the pair of horses pulling the carriage. They were from the Bonclere stables. Her heartbeat quickened, wondering what had brought someone from Bonclere here. She hadn't seen or heard from her parents since the day of the wedding. She put the puppy back beside his mother and got to her feet, nervously smoothing the wrinkles in her dress.

The carriage came to a stop near the front of the house. The driver hopped down and opened the door. Lord Sunderland scrambled to the ground, then turned to hold out his hand. Lady Sunderland took it and descended from the carriage. In unison, they turned to glance at the intimate gathering on the lawn before walking in that direction.

The earl spoke first. "Hello, Jacinda."

"Hello, Father. Mother." She wasn't quite

sure what to do. It was as if she were greeting strangers.

Her father stopped before her. Dropping his wife's arm, he placed his hands on Jacinda's shoulders, then leaned forward and kissed her cheek. "You look radiant, my child. Marriage agrees with you."

"Marriage to Tristan agrees with me."

Lord Sunderland glanced over at Jacinda's mother, his eyes commanding her to speak.

Lady Sunderland drew herself up. "You should have told us you were married to the duke's grandson. It would have saved us a lot of trouble and gossip."

The earl glowered. "What she means to say is, we're very happy for you, Jacinda."

She felt a twinge of sympathy for her father. Certainly he and Lady Sunderland had never shared the happiness that blessed her and Tristan. Her parents' marriage had been arranged, an agreement between their respective parents, an alliance of properties with little concern over how the two people most involved felt about each other. If there had ever been any hope for love between them, it was long since past.

"Thank you," Jacinda whispered, returning her father's kiss. Then she turned and kissed her mother too. It was easy to be generous when she was so happy.

"Please . . . sit . . . down," the duke invited, drawing the visitors' attention.

"Phiney, old man," Lord Sunderland said. "Sorry to hear you've been ill, but it looks like you'll be yourself soon."

Locksworth winced at the hated nickname

and fell silent.

Before her parents could sit down on one of the benches, Jacinda introduced the others present. "Father and Mother, may I introduce Tristan's sister, Ella, and Danny O'Banyon, a dear and very close friend."

Lord Sunderland took Ella's hand and raised it near his lips, though he fell short of kissing it. "It's a pleasure to meet you, Mrs. O'Banyon. If it's not too indelicate of me to say so, I see there'll soon be another O'Banyon. Congratulations."

Ella's eyes grew wide as she quickly glanced toward Danny, but he was grinning. Instead of denying the incorrect assumption, Danny walked over to stand behind Ella, placing a possessive hand on her shoulder. His other hand he held out toward the earl.

"Thank you, Lord Sunderland. Ella and I are looking forward to the babe's arrival."

Jacinda and the duke exchanged an amused look as Ella blushed prettily. Lord and Lady Sunderland sat down on the bench, Jacinda's mother looking more miserable by the moment.

For the next hour and more, Lord Sunderland enjoyed his conversation with his daughter and her friends, smoking his pipe, reminiscing, laughing. Jacinda almost wished she had the time to grow close to her father before leaving for America. Almost but not quite. Her mother had a way of spoiling things, even on this day.

Lady Sunderland remained quiet throughout the visit, but as she and the earl were preparing to leave, she pulled Jacinda aside and inquired into what financial arrangements the duke might be settling upon her and would she be able to loan them a little.

"Although the marquess hasn't asked for so much as a farthing back," she told Jacinda, "he would be entirely in his right to do so. If it weren't for those rumors . . . well, he probably would have done so by this time. It could be disastrous for your father and me if he demands recompense."

"I'm sorry, Mother. To the best of my knowledge, the duke's entire estate will pass elsewhere. Tristan is not his closest living male relative. Besides, he's an American, and that's where we're going to live."

Her lovely face pinched, Lady Sunderland entered her carriage, muttering, "You were always such an ungrateful child."

Jacinda watched the horse-drawn vehicle as it departed down the long drive. She was surprised to find that she didn't feel the hurt she used to feel. Mostly, she just felt sorry for her mother. Lady Sunderland would never understand true happiness.

The woman stood in the doorway to the library, surprising Blackstoke with her earthy beauty. She was not what he had expected.

"You know who I am?" he asked, openly appraising her.

"I know. You're the man they call the Englishman, the man who sends shiploads of women to the east to be sold into slavery."

"Where did you get such a ridiculous notion?" He laughed.

"Because I was one of those women, only I was sent back to England by the kindly gentleman who paid my price. When I shared that fact with a drunken sailor I took to my bed for the price of a meal to keep me from starving, he thought it a great joke. It didn't take much expertise to learn your name from him. His name was White, my lord. I think he worked very closely with you in your secret business." She smiled knowingly.

"Why did you come here? You know that if what they say is true I could easily kill you and dispose of your body? Who would know the difference?"

Loralie moved into the room. Her pace was slow and rhythmic, the sway of her hips drawing his gaze like a magnet. She placed her palms on the desk between them and leaned forward, giving him a generous view of her creamy-skinned breasts. "Wasn't that what you were planning to do anyway?"

Heat moved through his loins. "If you plan on identifying me to the authorities," he asked, his gaze never leaving her cleavage, "why come to me first?"

"Because, my lord," she replied in her husky voice, "I don't plan to identify you to anyone."

Finally, he looked up to meet her sultry gray eyes, noticing for the first time the tiny scar below her left eye. Otherwise, her beauty was flawless. "Then what is it you do want, Miss Loralie?"

She sat on the desk, looking at him over her shoulder, her thick chestnut hair cascading down her back. "Loralie, Lord Blackstoke. You may call me Loralie." Her full mouth hardened. "And I want only one thing. I want revenge."

Blackstoke was intrigued. He felt a kinship

with this woman, an understanding. "Revenge against whom, Loralie?"

"Jacinda Dancing."

Cold rage swept through him at the mention of her name. Her image sprang before him—flaming red hair and ivory skin, golden eyes that sparkled like firelight. Hate and desire mingled strangely in his heart. "What kind of revenge?"

"The thing that would hurt her the most." Her smile widened. "Now that he's returned, I think that would be for her to lose the good captain again."

"And then?"

Loralie shrugged. "Whatever you wish to do with her, my lord. Who am I to tell you what you can do with a woman?" The expression she wore bordered on innocence, yet was utterly seductive.

Blackstoke rose from his chair behind the desk and came around to her side. He stood very close, his head bent down so that their noses were mere inches apart. "I think we could work well together, Loralie."

"I'm sure of it, my lord."

He leaned over and sealed their partnership with a kiss. The fires of lust burned even brighter.

Loralie closed her eyes and drew a deep breath, then looked at him again. Her voice sounded even huskier than before as she said, "Shall we make our plans?"

"Not yet, Loralie. I have other things in mind at the moment."

"I know, my lord." She stood before him and draped her arms around his neck. "And I know just what to do to ease your mind."

Blackstoke smiled wickedly and led her from the room.

34

"Are you certain you feel up to this, Ella? It's not many weeks before your confinement." Jacinda frowned as she watched the expectant mother descending the stairs.

"I wouldn't miss seeing Tristan's birthday gift from Grandfather for anything," she replied. "He's been much too excited about it."

"Do you have any idea what it could be?"

Ella shook her head. "Not even a glimmer, and I've tried to pry it out of the old gentleman many times. His lips are more sealed over this than when he couldn't speak at all."

The two young women reached the front door. As they stepped through the doorway, their eyes fell on the three waiting men. The duke was already seated inside the carriage. Danny was leaning on one of the wheels, stretching his long, stick-thin legs out in front of him. Tristan was stroking the muzzle of one of the flaxen-maned mares in harness. The men were chatting and laughing, unaware that the women had arrived and were perusing them.

Jacinda smiled contentedly, marveling again at the perfection of her life.

"Danny wants us to be married before the baby comes."

Jacinda glanced at her sister-in-law. "Why don't you, Ella? You love him, and he adores you and the ground you walk on. You know he'll make you happy."

"Oh, I wish I could," Ella whispered in a small voice, black eyes misty.

"Why can't you?" Jacinda took Ella's hand and squeezed it tightly.

Ella glanced down at her protruding stomach. "Because of my child. Jacinda, the baby's father was a Turk. What if it looks . . . different? What if Danny looks at it and remembers that I was a concubine and begins to hate me?"

"Gabrielle Jackson," Jacinda scolded, using Ella's full name, "I don't think I've ever heard anything so silly in my entire life. Danny O'Banyon would still be in love with you if that baby was born green with purple eyes and a tail. And he would love the baby too. You're being unfair to him, and you know it."

Ella was taken aback by Jacinda's sharp tone. With rounded, watery eyes she stared in silence at her friend.

More gently, Jacinda said, "Come along. Grandfather must be chafing with impatience." She hooked her arm through Ella's and drew her down the steps.

Tristan and Danny saw their descent and hastened to meet and escort them the remainder of the way to the carriage.

"It's about . . . time," the duke growled in

greeting. "The day is half . . . wasted."

Jacinda kissed his cheek, drawing a smile. She knew his bad humor was all an act. He was incapable of being angry with either of the two women who sat one on each side of him, Jacinda holding his right hand, Ella holding his left.

"Where is it you're taking us, Grandfather?" Ella asked.

"You'll see," was his secretive reply. "Driver!"

The carriage jumped forward and traveled down the drive at a good clip. Tristan and Danny followed behind on horseback. As the miles slid away, Jacinda and Ella tried to coerce a clue from the duke, but he still refused to reveal their final destination.

The borough of Portsmouth was a bustling port city, known chiefly for its shipbuilding industry. It was midafternoon when the Duke of Locksworth and his party arrived, the carriage wending its way through the streets on its way toward the harbor. Danny and Tristan exchanged a questioning glance as they followed along behind, both of them wondering what the duke was doing here. When the carriage stopped, the two men dismounted and hurried to open the door and assist the passengers to the ground.

"Grandfather—" Tristan began.

"Quiet, boy. Don't spoil . . . my surprise. Just get me that . . . confounded chair."

Bemused, Tristan obeyed.

As soon as the duke was settled, he pointed the direction and they started off, Tristan pushing the wheelchair with Jacinda at his side,

Danny and Ella following close behind.

Suddenly, Locksworth raised his hand, stopping them. "Well," he said with satisfaction. "There she is, Tris. What do you think of her?" He pointed down the dock.

Four pairs of eyes turned to look, but it was Tristan who recognized immediately the source of his grandfather's question. Rocking gently against the dock was a near replica of the *Dancing Gabrielle*. On her side, bold letters, surrounded by fine gilded scrollwork, proclaimed her name—the *Dancing Cinda*. Tristan broke away from the others, walking toward the sleek clipper, black eyes tracing her lines, caressing her masts, lingering on the figurehead of a woman with flying red tresses.

Jacinda watched him, her heart in her eyes. She placed a hand on the duke's shoulder. "Your grace," she whispered, "it's a wonderful birthday gift."

"What's this 'your grace'?" His voice was gruff with choked back emotions. "I thought I was . . . *Grandfather* to you."

She dropped a kiss on his white-haired crown. "You're the most wonderful grandfather in the world," she assured him softly. With another squeeze of his shoulder, she left him to follow after Tristan.

He sensed her coming. "Look at her, Cinda," he said in awe. "She's a beauty."

Jacinda slipped her arm around his waist and leaned her head against his shoulder. "Aye, Captain. That she is. Most beautiful in all the seven seas."

He returned her embrace. "And named for the most beautiful of women." He drew her around to face him, holding her tightly in his arms. Tenderly he kissed her. "She'll be the perfect ship to carry us to America."

"When, Tris? How soon do we go home?"

"Soon. Very soon." He held her head against his chest, his eyes returning to the ship.

Danny cleared his throat in an obvious ploy for attention. "Excuse me, Captain Dancing, but you have guests who would like a tour of your fine ship. Could you separate yourself from that beautiful woman in your arms long enough to oblige us?"

Everyone laughed, but Tristan kept his arm around Jacinda's shoulders as he led the way up the plank onto the ship.

After circling the main deck, the duke told them to leave him there and go on without him. He would be fine. "No point struggling with this chair up and down those steps. Besides, I've seen the drawings of the ship. I know where everything is."

"I'll stay with him," Ella volunteered. "I'm a little tired anyway."

Danny was instantly concerned. "I should have seen that. Let me find you something to sit on." He hurried off in search of a bench or a chair.

Tristan hesitated only a moment, then took Jacinda's hand and led her up to the poop deck, hastening toward the wheel. With near reverence, he traced the smooth wood, drawing a deep breath of sea air as he did so. Jacinda felt a sting of jealousy.

"There's nothing quite like it," he whispered. "A man couldn't ask for anything more. A fine ship and a loving wife."

He pulled her to stand in front of him, her back against his chest. Her hands joined his on the wheel as she leaned her head on his shoulder, feeling his breath in her hair. The momentary jealousy vanished. She was not in competition with this ship or with the sea. She could share in his feelings for them because she was a part of him. She remembered her first sight of the unfurled sails, clouds of white, filled with the racing wind, and she felt the overwhelming urge to see them that way again.

"Come along, Cinda. Let's have a look at the cabins."

Beneath the poop were several staterooms. Tristan and Jacinda peeked into each one as they made their way along the corridor toward the back of the ship. At last they reached the door at the end of the passageway. Tristan glanced at his wife briefly, then opened the door before them.

There was little resemblance here to the captain's cabin of the *Dancing Gabrielle*. Where it had been small and sparsely furnished, this cabin was large and airy. Actually, there were two rooms here. The door from the corridor opened onto the sitting and dining room. Beyond it, through a narrow doorway, was the bedroom.

The dining room was filled with heavy, ornately carved furniture. A mahogany table filled the better portion of the room. A matching sideboard lined one wall. The table was surrounded by eight chairs, one at each end and three on each side. It was set with gleaming gold tableware and crystal goblets. Two high-backed chairs were set near a black, potbellied stove.

Tristan raised an eyebrow at the ostentatious setting, but a smile tweaked the corners of his mouth. Still holding Jacinda's hand, he moved through the dining room to the captain's sleeping quarters.

A large bed was set beneath the gallery windows at the stern. It was piled high with warm blankets and veiled in emerald green velvet bed curtains.

Tristan began to laugh.

"What's so funny?" Jacinda inquired. "It's a beautiful room."

Tristan managed to stifle his mirth long enough to reply, "It is, indeed, a beautiful room. But my grandfather has obviously had it decorated with you in mind rather than with a ship's captain." And he returned to his laughter.

"Tristan, really." She frowned at him.

He swept her into his arms and carted her across the room, dropping her without ceremony into the middle of the giant bed. "See here, wench," he growled at her in mock warning. "You'll do as the captain orders or walk the plank." With a dramatic flare, he closed the bed curtains behind him and fell onto the bed beside her.

"Tristan," she protested again, but this time with less fervor.

He gathered her close to him and began kissing her with soft, feathery kisses that left her yearning for more. "What do you say we stay here tonight. It's too late to drive back to Locksworth House, and the inns are always so crowded and noisy."

"I wouldn't be at all surprised to learn that's what the duke had in mind," she purred against his throat.

"Then we won't disappoint him, will we, love."

Candles lit the table. The gold plates and table service reflected the light, throwing a warming glow over the room and the five people seated around the table. Tristan sat at the head and Jacinda at the foot. The duke sat at Tristan's right, Ella and Danny at his left.

Tristan had guessed correctly. The duke had, indeed, planned for them to spend the night aboard ship and had arranged for a chef to prepare an extravagant meal in the galley in celebration of Tristan's birthday. Unbeknownst to any of them, he had smuggled a change of clothes for everyone into the carriage, and tomorrow they would explore the town before returning to Locksworth House.

The meal was eaten amid lively conversation and much laughter. The serving platters went around often, giving the diners their choices of roast beef and pork, steaming vegetables, fresh breads, and potatoes and gravy. Then came the desserts—pies and puddings and cakes.

"Here. Have another piece, Danny," Tristan encouraged, holding up the cake platter.

Danny pushed his chair back from the table. "I couldn't possibly. There's nowhere left to put it."

There was a unanimous sound of agreement.

"You ladies mind . . . if I smoke?" the duke inquired.

"Of course not, Grandfather. I love the smell of your pipe." Jacinda slid the candle toward him so he could make use of it.

"Well, Tris," Danny began, joining the duke in a smoke, "just how soon do you plan to take your new ship out?"

"If I had it my way, we'd leave in a day or two."

"What's to stop you?"

"Blackstoke," Tristan answered.

Jacinda felt herself grow cold. She turned her gaze down the length of the table.

"Blast the devil," he continued. "There's nothing I can do. I can't prove his guilt."

"Tris, why don't we just go anyway?" Jacinda suggested softly.

"And let him start up his filthy pirating again? Do you want other women to go through what Ella went through?" His voice was harsh with anger.

Ella paled and gasped sharply.

Tristan was immediately contrite. "I'm sorry, Ella. I didn't mean to be cruel." His face grew darker. "But I should have followed my first instincts and just killed the man."

"Tristan, really. Can't you see you're upsetting your sister?" Jacinda rose from her chair and started around the table.

Ella looked over at her, her eyes as big as saucers. "Jacinda—"

"It's all right, Ella. Tristan won't do anything so foolish. He's not a cold-blooded killer, no matter what noises he's making at the moment."

"No. You don't understand. I . . . I think it's the baby."

"Good lord," Danny whispered, jumping up from his chair. Without hesitation, he gently pushed Jacinda out of the way and lifted Ella in his arms, carrying her from the dining room and into the stateroom next door.

Jacinda followed on his heels. "The baby. But Ella, it isn't due for a few more weeks."

"I don't think it knows that," Ella whispered in a feeble attempt at humor.

Danny smiled down at Ella, brushing a stray ebony lock of hair away from her face. "You relax, princess. Jacinda will help you get out of that dress and into your nightgown. Before you know it, we'll have a doctor here to help you."

Ella grimaced as a sudden pain wrapped itself around her abdomen. As it faded, she nodded but didn't speak.

Danny kissed her forehead, then left the room, shutting the door behind him. Tristan was waiting with the duke in the captain's dining salon. "Tris, you'd better find a doctor fast. I have a sneaking suspicion that your sister isn't going to wait long to have that baby."

"What makes you think so?"

"I don't know. Just a notion. You learn a thing or two, here and there." He shrugged his shoulders. "Just get going, will you? And find a good one. I don't want some idiot bringing that babe into the world and risking Ella's life in the process."

Sweat beaded Ella's brow as the waves of pain gripped her abdomen. When it had receded again, Jacinda tugged the dress over her head and replaced it with a white nightgown. As she placed a pillow beneath Ella's neck, the girl moaned again and grabbed the sides of the bed.

Jacinda didn't know what to do. She'd

never even heard what to do for a birthing, let alone assisted in one. One thing she did know, Ella was in a lot of pain. She went to the door and opened it. Danny was waiting right outside.

"Danny, I don't know what to do."

The tall man patted her arm as he moved by her. "Bring some blankets and some towels, and see if you can find a pair of scissors." He knelt on the floor beside Ella's bed, taking hold of her hand. "Just squeeze my fingers when it hurts, love. It might help a wee bit."

"I'm frightened, Danny," Ella said.

"Of course you are, princess. All women are frightened the first time around. But when you see the little one's wrinkled face and count all the toes and fingers, you forget the travail they caused while bringing them into the world."

Ella's eyes filled with trust as she gazed up at him. But she hadn't long to enjoy the peace he had given her before another pain enveloped her, this one seeming more intense and twice as long as the last. She gripped Danny's hand and bit her lip, refusing to cry out.

"Easy, love," he soothed.

Jacinda had returned with the blankets and towels. She had even managed to find the scissors he'd requested.

"Jacinda," Danny whispered, drawing her close enough to hear him. "I don't think this babe means to wait for a doctor. We'll have to do it ourselves."

"But Danny—"

"There's not much choice. Bring me some water so we can sponge her forehead, and tell the duke not to worry. We'll be placing his great-grandchild in his arms in a lamb's shake."

Once again Jacinda hurried out of the stateroom. Danny got to his feet, his gaze returning to Ella's drawn features.

"Ella, do you trust me, love?"

"Yes, Danny, I do."

"Good, because I think we're going to have this baby without the help of our good physician, whoever he might be." He smiled at her.

Her paled face felt a rush of heat. "But Danny, you can't...I mean...we're not married. You can't—" Her protest was cut short by a violent contraction.

"I'll be helping you, Ella, whether you like it or not. Now you listen to what I have to tell you and no more arguing with me. We both know I mean to be your husband and this child's father, and I might as well start right now."

Ella couldn't have argued anymore if she'd wanted to. Her body demanded her obedience to its will. There was no time to be afraid. She gripped the sides of the bed and pushed, straining to eject the life within. Danny spoke in a gentle but confident tone, encouraging her efforts.

Jacinda returned to the room with the pitcher of water just in time to witness the baby's head emerging. She froze, mesmerized by the wonder of it.

"One more push," Danny demanded.

A groan tore itself from Ella's lips as the baby slipped into Danny's waiting arms. There was a moment of silence, then the baby's thin wail filled the room, objecting to his difficult passage into life. Danny tied the cord connecting mother and child with a string, then snipped it with the scissors. With the towels Jacinda had brought, he rubbed the baby's skin, then lifted the infant, naked and pink, into his arms and carried the baby toward Ella.

"Look at him," he said in awe. "Look at my son. What a bonny lad he is, Ella."

If ever Ella had doubted how he would feel about her child, that doubt was now forgotten as she looked at Danny's beaming pride. She knew he had called him son without even realizing he had done so. Ella held out her arms to receive her child, her face serene, the pain already a dull memory.

"Have you a name picked out, Mr. O'Banyon?" she asked softly.

"I rather like the name Brandon." He paused. "Brandon O'Banyon. Yes. I like that, I do."

Jacinda slipped out of the room, unnoticed by the happy couple. As much as she wanted to see the baby, she could wait. This special time was theirs alone.

The ship rocked gently, lulling all aboard to sleep. All except Jacinda. She lay beside Tristan, listening to his steady breathing, remembering all she had seen and felt that evening. She'd been terrified, as much by her own helplessness as by the pain she could see in Ella's face. But at that moment of birth, when she had seen that new life emerging into Danny's arms, she had known she would go through anything to share in that same experience, to bear a son for Tristan.

When Tristan had returned with the doctor,

all that was left for the man to do was pronounce mother and child healthy and prescribe a long rest. They would be staying in Portsmouth at least a fortnight before Ella could travel back to Locksworth House.

Later, Jacinda had held little Brandon in her arms and kissed the black fuzz on his head, wondering at the tininess of his hands and feet, each finger and toe so perfect.

Tristan had seen the longing in her look and had come to stand beside her. "We'll have our own," he'd whispered, caressing her hair.

"But I'm so impatient, Tris," she'd confessed, and he smiled at her and nodded.

They'd made love with a special tenderness that night, and long after Tristan had drifted into a satisfied slumber, Jacinda lay awake, praying that she had conceived a child from the seed of their loving.

35

Over a week later, Jacinda and Tristan strolled
arm in arm through the port city, gazing in
windows, admiring hats and gowns and boots,
but mostly just enjoying each other's company.
It was a small infant's gown that drew Jacinda's
special notice.

"Oh, Tris. I'd like to buy that for Brand.
And maybe a few new things for Ella."

He hugged her against him, kissing her
forehead. "Go ahead, love. I'm going to try to
find some of that special tobacco Grandfather
likes so much. I'll meet you here when I'm
finished."

Jacinda watched as he strolled away from
her, enjoying just watching him move, then
turned and entered the shop, a tiny bell tinkling
above her head. She picked up the white baby's
gown and held it against her cheek. Young
Brand would look so handsome in it, his dark
complexion and black hair contrasting with the
white fabric.

Would her own child have black hair or

would it be red? Would he have Tristan's ebony eyes, or would he inherit the golden shade of his mother's eyes? He would be tall like his father; she never had a moment's doubt of that. Would he feel the call of the sea or would he choose a profession that kept him closer to home?

"May I help you, madam?"

Jacinda turned, startled from her day-dreaming, to face the shopkeeper. "I would like this gown." She paused a moment, then asked, "In fact, I would like two of them. Have you another?" *One for Captain Dancing's son*, she thought.

"Yes, madam. I believe we do. Let me look."

Jacinda smiled to herself as she turned toward the dresses hanging against the wall. Ella was so tiny, even after having a baby, it would be hard to find something ready-made. Perhaps she should just look at nightgowns.

The bell tinkled again behind her as she looked at one gown, then another.

"That color would never suit you, Jacinda," a man's voice said at her shoulder.

Jacinda drew in a startled breath and whirled around, backing against the dresses. "Roger!"

His blue eyes were cold and heartless. His mouth was pressed in a thin line, then tipped up in a cruel smile. "So you remember me. How kind of you."

Jacinda glanced quickly toward the door, praying for Tristan's return.

"He won't be along yet. He ran into some old sea dogs like himself and they're discussing old times." He placed a hand on her upper arm and squeezed. "Did you know you've destroyed me, Jacinda? You and the rumors you've caused."

"You destroyed yourself."

His fingers tightened, pinching the flesh on her arm. He leaned closer. "You won't get away with this, Jacinda. I meant to have you and I will."

Jacinda's heart was pounding in her ears. She'd never witnessed so much hate in a person's eyes before. "You're an evil, wicked man, Roger." She would not cower before him. "You deserve no woman, and you shall never have me. Soon Tristan will take me to our home in America, and I shall never have to lay eyes on you again."

"So that's why you're here in Portsmouth. A new ship for the captain."

"Madam—" The shopkeeper stopped when she saw the couple standing so close together.

Jacinda slipped from Blackstoke's reach, taking the infant gowns from the woman's hands. "Thank you, miss. How much for the two of them?" Her voice was shaking. She knew that Blackstoke hadn't moved. She knew his gaze was still fastened on her back, and she shivered involuntarily.

The shopkeeper wrapped her purchases, then handed them to Jacinda. "Thank you, madam. Do come again."

Unable to delay any longer, Jacinda turned.

"Why are you buying such things?" he asked, his voice threatening in its softness.

She would not let him frighten her. She was not alone. He could not harm her here. She lifted her chin in defiance. "Why do you think?"

Blackstoke stepped toward her suddenly,

his stance malevolent, his eyes speaking unthinkable things. "You would have his child?"

She thought he was about to strike her.

"Blackstoke!" The door shut, the bell still tinkling. "Touch her and I'll kill you right here and now. It would be my pleasure."

Blackstoke turned to face Tristan, his face mottled with rage. With great effort, he brought himself under control. "And then you would be hanged and leave this lovely young woman a widow. That would be a shame, Dancing." He smoothed his coat as he walked slowly, evenly, toward the door. He paused near Tristan. "There is no proof against me. You are helpless and you know it, and if you harm me, it is you and your wife who will suffer. Good day, Captain." Over his shoulder, he added, "Good day, Lady Jacinda."

The tiny bell jingled one more time. Tristan's gaze locked with Jacinda's. She was still shivering—shivering violently—her face as pale as a sheet. She thought she might faint. Tristan hurried over to her, placing a protective arm around her back. She dropped her package and grasped his arms, looking up at him with pleading eyes.

"Tristan, I beg you. Let's leave England. Let's leave all of this behind. If you stay, you'll do just as you threatened. You'll kill him and you'll hang and I'll be a widow. I can't bear to lose you. Not again. Not again. Please, God. Not again." Her voice rose hysterically.

Tristan gathered her into strong arms. "All right, Cinda," he whispered into her ear. "All right. We'll go. I promise. I promise. Hush, love.

You'll not lose me. I promise."

Danny stayed in Portsmouth to scout up a crew for the *Dancing Cinda*. Tristan went with the carriage that carried his grandfather, wife, sister, and infant nephew back to Locksworth House. The journey was a slow one; the driver took great care not to jar the new mother. Ella, in fact, was feeling quite hale and hearty, but the doting grandfather and uncle weren't taking any chances.

When they arrived at Locksworth House, they discovered Spar and Ida waiting for them. It was the first time Jacinda had seen Ida since Penneywaite took her from the *Gabrielle*, and their reunion was an emotional one, especially when Ida showed her the wedding band Spar had given her.

"We've given up on finding anything in London," Spar told Tristan, thinking the women couldn't hear over their gleeful chatter. "You know I'd like to avenge my friends as much as you, but there's nothing we can do, short of dragging the man out for a duel or way-laying him in his home. I'm tired, Tris. Ida and I are ready to head for home and a new start. I've booked our passage for next week."

Jacinda moved over to stand beside Tristan, taking hold of his arm. "Spar, we've decided to leave, too. Tris has a new ship and we're preparing to sail in a few weeks. Why don't you wait and sail with us? Ella should have a good doctor on board with her and Brand. Please."

"Is that right, Tris? You're giving up?"

Tristan bristled at the words "giving up" but nodded.

"Glad to hear it, my friend. It's time we all got away from here." Ida had slipped up beside her husband, and Spar put his arm around her shoulders and ruffled her mop of orange curls. "The missus and I are eager to start my practice in America."

A gamine grin on her lips, Jacinda asked, "That means you'll go with us?"

"I've always preferred sailing under the best captain around. If he wants me, I'll join his crew."

Tristan chuckled, his good humor returning. "I'll have you, as long as you promise not to poison us all from the galley."

Jacinda couldn't think of a more perfect start for the *Dancing Cinda*, filled with three loving couples, a beloved grandfather, and a new baby.

Blackstoke was in a foul mood when he returned to Viridian. He was hardly more than in the door when he grabbed Loralie and dragged her up to the bedroom they shared. He ripped the clothes from her body and took her on the floor, his movements violent and vengeful. When his release came, he called her Jacinda. Afterward, he crawled off to the bed to sleep, leaving Loralie to nurse the bruises on her body and the renewed hatred in her heart for Jacinda Dancing.

Tristan and Spar left Locksworth House early the next day to go back to Portsmouth. It would take them some time to find the right men to sail under Tristan's command. He wouldn't take on just any sailor off the docks,

430

especially not when he was carrying such precious cargo as he would have with him this trip. He wanted experienced, trustworthy men.

"I'll send word to let you know how we're doing," Tristan told Jacinda as he kissed her good-bye on the front lawn of Locksworth House. "While I'm gone, you'd better start packing. If there's anything you have at Bonclere—"

"There's nothing at Bonclere I want to take with me. Pegasus is already here. There's nothing else."

"Perhaps you should still say good-bye to your parents," he suggested softly.

"I will, Tris. I'm not angry at them. Honestly I'm not."

"Good." He kissed her again, a long, sweet kiss that left her dizzy. "I'll be back for you and the family just as soon as I can."

"I'll be waiting." Her voice was husky. She was missing him already. "Hurry, Tris. I hate it when you're away."

He kissed her again, then swung up onto Neptune's back. The stallion shook his shaggy mane and pranced sideways, eager to be off. Tristan waved at her as he spun the black barb around and cantered down the drive, Spar riding along beside.

The house seemed empty with him away, more so than at any time in the past few months. It wasn't the first time he had left her for a day or two, but somehow this time felt different. She wandered through the rooms of the mansion, hearing the echo of her shoes on the floor. She sat with Ella, watching the young mother nursing her child at her milk-swollen breasts. She visited with Ida, the two of them planning together for their new lives in America, wondering aloud at what their new homes would be like. Still, she couldn't seem to shake the hollow feeling in her heart. She felt so alone.

By the time she retired to her bedroom, she was near tears. She crawled into the bed, a bed too large without Tristan beside her. She felt cold without his arms around her. She pulled the blankets up over her head and snuggled deep beneath them, surrounding herself with pillows, seeking a place of comfort. Still, it seemed an eternity before sleep took hold.

It was the captain's bedroom on board the Dancing Cinda. *The curtains were drawn around their bed. She could hear the lapping of water against the sides of the new ship and smell the salty freshness of the breeze as it entered through the open windows. She stretched, then turned to curl up against her husband's sleeping form. Her hand touched his back, drawing comfort from his closeness. He turned on his side. "I told you you'd be mine." It wasn't Tristan. It was Blackstoke. She tried to draw away, tried to flee from the bed, but his hands clasped her wrists and held her there. "I warned you, Jacinda. I told you I would have you. You will be mine." "Tris!" she cried. "Tris, help me!" Blackstoke's laughter rang in her ears. "He can't help you, Jacinda. Don't you remember? He went down with the* Dancing Gabrielle. *Don't you remember, Jacinda? He's dead. He's dead."*

"No!" she screamed, bolting upright in bed. "No!"

Her bedroom door flew open, and Ida came rushing in, candle in hand. She set the light on the bedstand and crawled into bed with the weeping Jacinda, cradling her friend in her arms. " 'Ush, now. 'Twas only a dream. Ye're not afraid o' dreams, are ye now?"

"Oh, Ida. It was . . . it was Roger and he . . . he said that Tris was dead.He said he'd gone down with the *Gabrielle*."

"Ye know better, Jacinda. 'E was 'ere just today. 'E's gone t'get a crew for the *Cinda*, and we're all going t'sail t'America."

"But you don't understand, Ida. We saw him. We saw him in Portsmouth."

" 'E can't do ye no 'arm, Jacinda. Ye're with yer family. And Tristan can take care o' 'imself."

The panic began to fade as reason returned. "It was so real, Ida," she whispered.

"Yer dreams always 'ave been, but 'aven't ye learned that life is even more real? I know ye 'ave. Now let's sleep, shall we? We've got packin' and makin' ready t'be done."

Ida lay down beside her, talking soothingly, until Jacinda drifted into a fitful slumber once again.

36

A gentle rain had sweetened the earth during the night, and the flowers in the gardens of Locksworth House had opened their fragile petals in delight. Still seeking comfort after her restless hours in bed, Jacinda sought refuge amid the floral splendor and stayed throughout the morning hours. She was still there when the rider came thundering down the drive, his horse in a lather. A sense of foreboding hastened her exit from the gardens.

Sims opened the door on the echo of the stranger's rapid knock.

"I'm seeking a Mistress Dancing," he gasped. "Wife of the captain."

Jacinda heard him as she entered from the back of the house. "I'm Mrs. Dancing. What is it? What's wrong?"

"There's been an accident at the shipyard, ma'am. The captain's hurt and hurt bad. The doctor sent me for you before—" He stopped. "I think you should come now, ma'am."

"Dear lord," she whispered, her world

teetering precariously. She grabbed for a nearby chair, holding onto its back for dear life. She felt all the blood draining from her head.

"Ma'am?"

She shook herself. She couldn't allow herself the luxury of falling apart. Not now. Not when Tristan needed her.

"Yes. I'm coming. Sims, have Pegasus saddled. I'll throw a few things into a bag and—"

"Never mind that," Ella said from behind her.

Jacinda turned around. By her face, she knew her sister-in-law had heard everything.

"Go with him, Jacinda. Ida and I will bring your things. We'll be there before nightfall. Now go."

Jacinda gave Ella a quick hug and kiss, then raced out to the stables. Pegasus was already waiting for her. The groom lifted her quickly onto the saddle and handed her the reins. Without wasting a breath, she turned the mare down the drive and galloped toward Portsmouth, the messenger riding close behind.

What happened? her mind screamed. Was he dying? Would he die before she reached him? No! No, she wouldn't let him die. He had died once already in her heart. She wouldn't allow him to die again. She wouldn't allow it. He had to live. He had to!

"Wait, ma'am!" a cry came from behind her. "Wait!"

She glanced back over her shoulder, reluctant to slow Pegasus's race toward the seaport.

The man rode up beside her. "There's a

shortcut just up ahead. We can save over an hour that way."

Jacinda nodded eagerly. Anything to get her to Tristan sooner.

"But ma'am, you'll have to ease up or my horse will never make it. He's wore out as it is."

She knew it was true. She wondered if the shortcut could really save them so much time if she had to slow down for him to show her the way. Pegasus was fresh and fast, and if she stayed on the main road, she wouldn't have to slow down at all. But an hour? It was such a precious amount of time.

Jacinda pulled Pegasus in a little more. "Lead the way, sir, but proceed with as much haste as possible."

"Josh is the name, ma'am," he cried over the sound of thundering hooves. Then he motioned for her to follow him, turning his mount abruptly onto a little-used road that was hardly more than a path.

For half an hour or so, Jacinda followed in silence, the cantering hooves of the two horses sounding a steady harmony against the damp earth. It seemed that the further they followed the path the more dense the brush grew, the more unused it appeared. She was opening her mouth to question his guidance when he lifted a hand and drew his horse to an abrupt stop. Caught by surprise, Jacinda jerked back on the reins. Pegasus planted her back hooves and slid to a halt, her head flying up to avoid the lead horse's rump.

"What the devil—" Jacinda began to protest.

Two riders emerged onto the path behind

her. She turned to look at them, recognizing their seamen's garb as they sat, uneasy, on their mounts.

"What is this?" she demanded, quelling her own erratic heartbeat.

"What is this, indeed."

She swung around once more to meet the steely blue gaze she had learned to fear and despise.

Blackstoke's mustache twitched as he grinned at her. "Fancy meeting you in these parts, my lady. Is it trouble that has brought you calling or merely your desire for my company?"

With a sudden swing of her arm, she slapped Pegasus across the rump with the ends of the reins, sending the mare leaping forward. Josh's mount shied sideways into the brush, nearly unseating him. She slipped past Blackstoke before he could react. They raced through the trees, branches slapping her across her cheeks and stinging her hands and arms. She leaned low over the saddle, praying for the appearance of a manor house or a road that would take her to help. Hard on her heels came Blackstoke and his cutthroats. If Pegasus had been fresh, Jacinda would have been confident of her ability to outrun them, but the mare had already come a fair distance.

They emerged into a clearing, causing Jacinda's hope to rise. Surely there must be a farmhouse nearby. In the middle of the meadow was a flock of sheep. Jacinda and pursuers thundered through them, scattering the bleating animals in all directions. Then they were back into the woods again, zigzagging around trees, soaring over bushes, racing on and on.

Jacinda could sense Blackstoke's nearness. His horse was gaining on Pegasus. "Come on, girl," she urged. "Come on. We've got to keep going. We've got to."

Sensing her mistress's anxiety, the mare flattened her ears and stretched out for all she was worth. The ground was a blur beneath her hooves. Jacinda dared to glance back over her shoulder and felt a flutter of relief as she saw them drawing away from Blackstoke.

Suddenly, a tree branch seemed to reach at her from out of nowhere, catching her in the shoulder and nearly tossing her from the saddle. She managed to cling on, but her awkward posture threw off the mare's stride, slowing her down. Jacinda knew Blackstoke would be upon them soon.

And then, once again, her luck changed. The woods gave way to pasture, and at the far end of the field stood a two-story brick house, surrounded by outbuildings. If only they would offer her refuge.

Speaking encouragement into Pegasus's ears, the mare gathered herself for flight, then jumped the pasture fence. Jacinda glanced back long enough to see Blackstoke still in hot pursuit, but his cronies had pulled up at the fence. One more fence to jump. That was all. Just one more fence.

Pegasus carried her masterfully over it and galloped up to the manor house. Jacinda threw herself to the ground, stumbling over flying skirts, then raced toward the door.

"Help me! Please help me!" she cried as she

pounded on the door with her fists.

She glanced behind her. Blackstoke had entered the yard but had slowed his mount to a walk. He was approaching her with a satisfied smile pasted on his mouth.

"Oh, please let me in!"

The door opened. Jacinda swung around, relieved.

"Well, I never would have guessed it would be you coming for a visit. Welcome to Viridian, Lady Jacinda." Loralie grinned and stepped backward, motioning her inside.

Tristan was pleased with all they'd accomplished already. With Danny's help, he had assembled a skeleton crew, men who could be trusted to know what to do in all kinds of weather at sea, seasoned sailors with good reputations. Spar, in the meantime, was gathering provisions for the weeks they would be at sea. If things proceeded at this pace, he would be able to head for Locksworth House by the end of the week.

He closed the log in front of him and got up from his desk, stretching. Then he left his cabin, strolling out onto deck and up to the poop. His gaze was turned out to sea when he heard the excited voices coming from the gangplank and went to investigate. He certainly didn't expect the commotion to be caused by his sister, baby in her arms, and Ida as they pushed their way past one of his new men who was unwittingly blocking their way.

"Out o' our way, ye scurvy bloke," Ida was sputtering angrily.

"Ella! Ida! Whatever are you doing here?"

he called to them.

They both froze in their tracks, gazing at him as if he'd grown two heads. Instantly he sensed trouble. His black eyes shifted down the docks, looking for Jacinda.

"Tristan," Ella said, gathering her wits about her, "we heard . . . we were told . . . we thought you were hurt in an accident."

"An accident?" He touched his fingers to his chest. "As you can see, I'm fine." Again his eyes flicked to the docks. "Where's Jacinda?"

"You mean she isn't here?" Ella glanced over her shoulder at Ida.

Ida frowned. "She left Locksworth an hour before we did. On 'orseback. She should've been 'ere long before now."

Tristan felt icy apprehension tapping out a warning in his brain. "Why did you think I'd had an accident? What made Jacinda leave Locksworth?"

Ella sat down on a keg resting near the main deckhouse. "A man came for her. He said he'd been sent by a doctor here in Portsmouth. He said there'd been an accident and she was to come quickly." She placed a hand over her mouth. "Tris, do you suppose—" Her question was left hanging unfinished in the air.

Tristan swore, striking the wall of the deckhouse with his fist. "I should have killed him when I had the chance."

He turned away from the women and marched toward the companionway at the stern. He went down to his cabin, his thoughts black and filled with dread. He found his pistol and poked it through his belt. His knife he stuck in a sheath on his bootleg. He grabbed a jacket before heading back up on deck.

"Danny! Spar!" he yelled, but it was unnecessary. The men were already waiting for him.

"I've sent for our horses," Spar told him. "Any idea where to look?"

"None, but he must have a place close by. We last saw him here in Portsmouth, and he had to know I'd returned here. We'll have to ask around. Surely, if the Marquess of Highport has land hereabouts, someone will be able to tell us."

Danny and Spar gave their respective women brief kisses, then the three men marched grimly down the gangplank.

Jacinda sat at the supper table, staring bleakly at the food before her. At the far end of the table, Loralie was eating her meal with gusto. At the other end, Blackstoke was merely toying with his food while his eyes devoured Jacinda.

Even without looking at him, she knew what was on his mind. She knew what he intended to do with her. She fingered the knife beside her plate, wondering if she could smuggle it somehow into her gown.

"Don't even think it, my pretty. You tried that once before," Blackstoke said softly. "This is not a night for anger and fighting. It's a night for celebration. It's to be our wedding night, and this time there'll be no knives between us."

She nearly choked.

"Look what you've done, Roger, my dear," Loralie purred sweetly. "You've frightened the chit."

Blackstoke's fist hit the table, causing both Jacinda and Loralie to jump. "I warn you, Loralie. Be careful what you say to the lady or you'll regret it."

Jacinda looked at him then. His mind was unhinged. She was sure of it. There was an unnatural gleam behind his dark blue eyes, an absence of reason. She didn't know what to do, what to say, but she knew she had to get away. She couldn't bear the thought of him touching her.

It never occurred to her to wonder how fate had brought these two together. It almost seemed as if she would have expected it. Blackstoke and Loralie. It didn't surprise her in the least.

Dinner over at last, Blackstoke went in search of his pipe, leaving the two women momentarily alone. Loralie jumped at her opportunity.

"He's planned this night for a long time, Jacinda. I know you'll do your best not to disappoint him."

Jacinda's eyes shot golden daggers at the woman.

"I want you to know something else. I plan to watch as he uses you. I plan to take great pleasure in your degradation. And when he's through with you, I plan to scar your face as you did mine. And then I'll go to the dear captain, and it is I who will heal his heart when he learns his wife has flown into the arms of another lover."

Jacinda's hand flew to cover her mouth. She felt a sickness rising in her throat.

Loralie rose from the table. She crossed the

room, her movements catlike and sensual. She paused at the doorway and looked back over her shoulder. "Enjoy your evening, Jacinda. I know I will."

37

Soft lights flickered in the bedroom, illuminating the four-poster that filled the center of the room. Here, like elsewhere at Viridian, the room was sparsely furnished, making the bed seem all the larger.

It was late when Blackstoke escorted Jacinda to the bedroom. Lying across the bed was a satin negligee, its delicate beauty shimmering in the candlelight.

"Put it on, Jacinda."

Her gaze moved from the nightgown to Blackstoke. She was afraid, but she refused to let him see it. "No, Roger, I won't. It's time you stopped this insanity. Let me go. No one has to know that this has happened."

"But of course people will know, my dearest Jacinda. I mean for them to know that you have left your husband to live with me, with or without the benefit of clergy." His voice hardened. "Now, put on the gown."

"No."

Blackstoke gave her a shove toward the

bed. "Do you think I don't have plans for that husband of yours? Do you think I'll let him live if you continue to refuse me? Even now, his life hangs in the balance."

"Roger, what have you done?" Had there really been an accident? Was Tristan lying injured even now?

He laughed. "Just put on the negligee, my dear one." On those words, he turned on his heel and left her alone in the room.

Jacinda heard the click of the key turning in the lock. She could almost feel the same sound in her heart. She turned away from the door, facing the bed once again. She reached out and picked up the white satin gown.

Tristan, what am I to do? Does your life depend on my cooperation? Must I give my body to him to save you? And if I don't . . .

Her choices were too terrible to imagine. Would she suffer more by submitting to Blackstoke or to learn that Tristan had died because she refused? As horrible as the first choice was, it dimmed beside the second. She would do anything to save Tristan's life. Even this.

With shaking fingers, she undid the buttons on her bodice. And with each one, her mind turned in upon itself. She would not think of what she would endure in the coming hours. She would not allow herself to even feel his hands upon her body. What he planned to do to her, he would be doing to someone else. She would not be there. Not her soul. Not her heart. Not her mind.

When she stood naked, she slipped the elegant gown over her head and let the sheer fabric slide over her chilled skin. It clung to her figure, enhancing each curve of her feminine form.

The key turned again. The latch lifted. The door opened. Jacinda raised her head to face her tormentor.

Panic rode with Tristan. Every lead was a dead end. No one knew where Blackstoke was, or no one was talking.

It was dark out, as black as pitch, yet Tristan combed the countryside, searching for a clue, any sign, that might lead him to Jacinda. Danny rode with him, but they didn't talk. Tristan was trapped in a private hell.

What was Blackstoke doing to her now? Had he harmed her? Had he . . . Tristan choked off the thought, a rage so terrible boiling inside him, he thought he would explode. A groan was torn from his lips.

"Tris, maybe we should stop for the night," Danny suggested. "We're doing no good now."

Tristan turned haunted eyes on his friend. "I can't stop, Danny. He must be near. I'll search every cottage, every barn, every bush if I have to. There's no time to rest."

Blackstoke smiled slowly, a fire lighting in his blue eyes. "You're a goddess, Jacinda Sunderland."

She raised her chin a notch. "Jacinda Dancing."

His jaw tightened and he clenched his fists at his sides. Silently, he turned around and bolted the door. She saw his shoulders rise as he took a deep breath before swinging round to face her again. He came toward her with measured steps, his eyes inching slowly down her body, resting on the generous view of creamy cleavage before slipping further to the gentle swelling of her hips.

"Do you know how long I've waited for this moment, Jacinda? Do you know how I've planned for this night, for the moment I would make you mine?"

"Take me you might, Blackstoke, but I shall never be yours. Know that before you touch me. I belong to Tristan Dancing. You might use this body, but you'll not have me. Not really." A strange strength seemed to flow in her veins as she taunted him. "The moment your hand touches me, I will be thinking of Tristan. If your lips kiss mine, it will be his lips I'm thinking of."

He grabbed her shoulders with a sudden fury, pulling her harshly against him. "You'll not deny me the pleasures I've dreamed about. I'll have them and more."

"I'll give you no pleasure, Viscount Blackstoke."

His lips ground down on hers, probing, demanding. She stood like a cold statue, unmoved by his assault. She withdrew herself from what was happening, stepping into the dreamworld that she had sought so often in the past.

Blackstoke broke his kiss and stared down at her, frustration written clearly in his eyes. With a growl, he pushed her backward onto the bed, his hand catching the top of her negligee and tearing the front of the delicate fabric. A laugh of triumph filled the room as he viewed her nakedness. Quickly, he shucked off his own clothing and joined her on the bed.

"Now I will have what I have promised myself. I will have the beauty that all men wanted. I will have what no other has had."

She looked at him, her expression without emotion. "I have given myself to Tristan Dancing and you cannot take what he was given."

"I will, I tell you. I will!" He rose above her.

Jacinda closed her eyes. This was not happening to her. He could not have what she did not give.

Suddenly the mattress raised beneath her, and she realized she was alone on the bed. A shriek of rage rent the air. She opened her eyes to see Blackstoke throwing something at the mirror across the room.

"You'll not do this to me!" he shouted at her.

She didn't understand what was happening at first. Then slowly it dawned. He'd been unable to finish what he'd begun. His passion had ebbed without release.

Hastily he donned his trousers, returning to the side of the bed as he pulled on his shirt. "I'll be back, Jacinda. Don't think you have escaped me yet."

It was dawn before Tristan agreed to return to the *Dancing Cinda* to rest, but only because he'd nearly fallen asleep in the saddle and only when Danny promised that someone would be sent to Highport Hall to demand to know Blackstoke's whereabouts. In the meantime, more men were sent out to search the countryside.

Exhaustion pulled him into a fitful

slumber, one filled with ugly apparitions and threatening visions without form or names. When he awoke after a few hours of sleep, Ella and Ida forced him to eat before he was allowed to leave the ship.

"Ye'll do 'er no good if ye're weak with 'unger," Ida told him. "Now sit there an' eat or ye'll not be steppin' foot off this ship. I'll see t'it meself."

Tristan gulped down the food set before him without tasting it, without even knowing what it was. His thoughts were fraught with dire imaginings, and he was helpless, just as he'd been when it happened to Ella.

He was on the docks, preparing to leave at last, when a lady approached him. She was wearing a hooded cloak and moved furtively through the busy area. He paid her little heed as he took hold of the pommel and swung into the saddle and only stopped when she called his name.

"Captain Dancing."

His head turned sharply.

"I've word of your wife, Captain. Can we talk in private?"

Her voice sounded familiar but he couldn't place it. Her face was still hidden behind the folds of her hood.

"What do you know of my wife?" he demanded.

"In private, Captain. Or not at all." She turned as if to leave.

"Wait." He hopped down from the saddle. "Come with me."

Tristan led the way up the gangplank and down toward the captain's cabin. The woman followed at a discreet distance, looking neither right nor left as she passed Ella and Ida who stood near the companionway. Tristan opened the door to his cabin and ushered her inside.

"Close the door, Captain."

He did as he was told.

"Sit down, Captain."

Once again, he obeyed, pulling out a chair from the mahogany table. His muscles were tense. He longed to reach out and sweep back the hood that hid her face from view. He wanted to shake the news from her lips that would tell him where to find Jacinda.

"Captain, I have a message for you. Your wife has willingly gone to the bed of her former fiancé. She has chosen to remain with him while she seeks a divorce."

Tristan gripped the edge of the table. "You lie," he said evenly.

"Perhaps I do, Captain. But if it is not true, it soon will be. Give up, sir. You will never find her."

"Who are you? What have you to do with this?" He got to his feet, leaning across the table. "Whatever he's paying you, I'll pay you more."

She laughed, a sultry, self-satisfied sound. "My payment is not in money, Captain. My pleasure is gained in other measures." She turned toward the door. As she opened it, she said, "Think on it, Captain. It will go easier on her if you let her go willingly." She paused. "And, Captain, do not try to follow me. I am much too clever for that."

"Wait!"

She turned again.

"What is it Blackstoke wants from me? What must I do to gain her freedom? I'll clear his name, if need be. I'll see that his father believes him innocent of any ill deeds. We are leaving England. There's no more danger for him."

She laughed. "I don't think he wants any of those things from you, Captain. What he wants can only be had from the lovely lady he beds even now. But I will tell him of your offer, and I'll return here in two days to give you his answer."

Tristan followed her up onto the deck and watched her leave the ship. A slight motion of his hand sent Danny following after her, but he returned several hours later, bitterly angry with himself for losing her inside a busy pub. She had duped him and he knew it, and now he had let down his friend.

38

Blackstoke came to her room twice more. Twice more he brought her delicate nightwear and forced her to put it on, only to tear the satin fabric from her body and gaze upon her beauty with fire in his eyes. Twice more he shed his clothes and sought to claim her for his own. And twice more his body turned traitor.

He stood before her now, impotent and enraged. "As long as he lives, you will do this to me. I won't have it!" He grabbed her by the hair and hauled her off the bed. "You think you have won? Well, you haven't, my dearest. Your precious captain is going to die, and then we'll see what will stop my taking what is rightfully mine." He gave her a shove. "He'll die, and you're going to watch him do it." On those words, Blackstoke stormed from the room.

Jacinda lay quivering on the bed. She had beaten him at this game. But at what cost?

A message arrived for Tristan. The marquess was in France and would not return for another month. No one would reveal the whereabouts of his son. Frustrated at every turn, Tristan continued to search the countryside while awaiting the return of the mysterious woman.

Loralie faced Blackstoke with a haughty smile. "I'll go to Dancing, but we won't return. You may do what you wish with the lady upstairs, Blackstoke, but I mean to have the captain for my own pleasures. I won't have you harming him."

"You'll do as I say, Loralie."

"The devil, I will." She tossed her head and turned away from him. "I'll do as I please, you son of a skunk."

Blackstoke's hand arrested her departure. With a jerk, he turned her around and sent her flying across the room. She hit the wall with a resounding thud.

"I tell you what to do," he said with a menacing leer, "and don't forget it."

Loralie rubbed her shoulder and peered up at him from beneath tousled hair. "Your problem, viscount, is you're not man enough to bed the wench, and you and I both know it."

His face turned purple. His hands clenched into fists at his sides as he approached her.

Loralie scrambled to her feet, her bravado vanishing beneath his maniacal gaze. "I'm sorry, my lord," she whispered, backing away from him. "Of course, I'll do whatever it is you wish. I'll go for the captain and bring him back to you. I'll go at once."

"No!" He stepped closer, his sharp glance pinning her to the floor. "No, you will go nowhere, my lovely Loralie."

"My lord, I—"

His hand came up to tangle his fingers through her chestnut mane. He pulled her roughly against him, jerking her head backwards and lowering his mouth close to hers. "I have other plans for you, Loralie. With you I can find my pleasure."

Even from Jacinda's room on another floor, she could hear Loralie's angry, then pitiful, screams. She covered her head with the pillows on the bed, hoping to shut out the cries that were diminishing her own strength, her own determination to survive. But she couldn't escape the sounds of the brutal rape, nor could she stop wondering if she would be next.

"I won't stay here and let him do this to me," she whispered. "I've got to get out of here."

She dressed quickly, putting on the gown she had been wearing the day Blackstoke took her captive. Many times already she had tried to force open the shutters over the windows, but her attempts had always been silent before. She had no time for silence now. She picked up a wooden chair and, with all her strength, struck the window. The glass shattered. Then she struck at the shutters. Again and again, she pounded wood against wood. The cries and screams continued from below, muffling from Blackstoke's ears her efforts to be free.

There was a sudden creak of wood. Jacinda dropped the chair, letting it clatter to the floor. The outer latch was weakening. She pushed on it and could feel the wood giving beneath her touch. She backed away from the window a few steps, then threw herself against it. Twice more she rammed her shoulder against the shutters, and suddenly, they flew open before her. Daylight streamed into the room. Freedom was within reach.

She leaned out the window. The ground was too far to jump, but there was a ledge leading to the roof of one of the house's single-story wings. If she was careful, she could ease along the edge and reach the roof. She turned her head and listened and was frightened by the sudden stillness that engulfed the house. He was finished with Loralie.

Jacinda lifted her skirts and climbed out the window, gripping the side of the house wherever she could find a finger hold. She didn't allow herself to look down, or she knew she would fall. There was a buzzing in her ears. Or was it just the thunder of her heart?

She eased her way along the ledge, praying her feet wouldn't slip and send her hurtling to the ground below. At last, she reached the roof of the wing. Cautiously, she made her way to the far end, then slid down the side of the roof. She looked over the edge. It still looked a long way down, but she had to jump, like it or not. Gathering her skirts up above her knees, she pushed herself away from the roof.

Jacinda landed with a jarring thump, then rolled end over end away from the house. There was a terrible moment when she wondered if she'd broken a leg or an arm, but as she tried them out, she discovered everything was working. She glanced warily around her. No one was in sight. The yard was quiet. The house was quiet. She slipped away toward the trees and shelter.

What should she do now? How long before he discovered she was missing? Would he be sleeping or was he even now turning the lock on the bedroom door? Should she run or should she try to find Pegasus?

Tears threatened, but she blinked them back angrily. She wouldn't give in to tears. She had no time for them now. She had to think, and think clearly.

She didn't know where she was or how far it was to Portsmouth or even in which direction Portsmouth lay. She had no food and no clothing except what she wore. Her lady's slippers, fine when strolling through the gardens at Locksworth House, would be worthless in flight. She seemed to have little choice. She needed her horse.

Slowly, listening and watching, Jacinda worked her way around toward the stables. Every sound made her heart jump. But the closer she came to the barn, the more certain she felt she was going to escape. Blackstoke hadn't gone to her room. He didn't know she was missing.

Jacinda straightened from her crouched position and sidled along the edge of the stables, her back pressed tightly against the wood. She pressed her ear against the door. Except for the familiar sounds of horses, it was quiet. She slipped inside.

Pegasus seemed to sense her presence. Her ears perked forward and she nickered softly.

Jacinda breathed a sigh of relief and hurried toward the white mare. Her bridle was hanging on a nail right outside the door. She wouldn't bother with a saddle. It had been a long time since she'd ridden bareback, not since she was a little girl, but she didn't have time to saddle the mare.

She pulled open the stall door. "Hello, Pegasus. Come on, girl. We must hurry."

"No need to hurry, my dear. You're not going anywhere."

Jacinda's heart seemed to stop completely as she turned around. Blackstoke stood framed in the doorway. He was wearing only his breeches and his boots. His shirt was in his hand. As he entered the barn and came closer, Jacinda could see scratches on his cheeks and arms.

Now she was crying. She tried to continue to force the bit into Pegasus's mouth, but she knew it was useless. She should have run. She should have gone on foot. What a fool she was! What a fool!

Tristan was waiting for her on the dock beside the ship. Without a word, he ushered her on board and down to the captain's cabin. Once the door was closed behind her, Tristan sat in the same chair he'd used during her previous visit and waited for her to speak.

"He wants to meet with you," she said at last. Her voice sounded different than it had before, softer, almost muffled.

"Where? When?"

"You're to sail your ship around the coastline. I'm to show you where. Just you and me, Captain. There can be no one else on board."

"That's insane!" Tristan protested.

"Can it be done, Captain?"

"Well . . . yes. It's possible, but—"

"Then you have no choice. Not if you want to see her again."

Tristan shifted in his chair, trying to think clearly. "When are we supposed to do this?"

"Today. Now," she answered.

"But I need time."

"Captain," she said softly, "I assure you you have no time. The viscount is insane." With those words, she pushed the hood back from her face.

Tristan's stomach twisted in his belly. The woman's face was hideously swollen, the flesh black and blue. One eye refused to open at all.

"You don't recognize me, do you, Captain?"

"Should I?"

"I'm Loralie. I was with you on your last trip to Constantinople."

"Judas Priest!" Tristan stared at her in horror. "Did Blackstoke do this to you?" He got to his feet and came around the table to stand over her. Now he could see the bruises around her neck.

She nodded.

Tristan knelt beside her chair. "Loralie, you must help me. Tell me where he's got Jacinda. I beg you to tell me."

"I can't," she sobbed. "He's taken her away already. I only know we're to drop anchor and wait for him to come to us." Loralie took hold of Tristan's arm, her nails biting into his flesh. "He'll kill her if he even suspects there's anyone else on board."

"How did you get mixed up in this?" he wondered aloud.

With her single gray eye, she stared at him for a long time before replying, "It doesn't matter now, Captain. I was . . . stupid. But I mean to help you. I swear it on my own mother's grave. I mean to see him pay for this."

Tristan stood back up. He raked his fingers through his hair, then rubbed his forehead. He tried not to think about what Blackstoke might have done to Jacinda. He tried not to think of him beating her as he had Loralie. If he thought of those things, he would go insane himself.

"Wait here," he told Loralie, then strode up on deck.

He called Danny and Spar together and told them what Blackstoke wanted. Both men tried to persuade Tristan to let them stow away below deck.

"How can he know we're even there?" Spar queried.

"I don't know. Maybe he's having us watched. I just can't take the chance."

"Then what are we to do to help, Tris?" Danny asked.

"Follow after us on horseback, but keep out of sight. If he sees you—"

"We'll be careful, Tris," Spar promised, placing a hand on Tristan's shoulder. "God keep you . . . and Jacinda too."

Tristan nodded his thanks.

39

With only the topsails and courses unfurled, the
Dancing Cinda set sail with the captain, no
crew, and one badly beaten passenger. They
crept along the coastline, watching for the sign
that would tell them they had reached their destination. Tristan's eyes burned from staring so
hard at the shore. His hands ached from
gripping the wheel so tightly, but he couldn't
make them relax. Sweat beaded on his forehead, and his shirt was damp with perspiration.
Each minute seemed unending, every mile a
thousand miles long.

The July sun had begun its descent when
Tristan caught sight of a flash of yellow along
the rocky coast. He waited until he was certain
it was a flag, then left the wheel in Loralie's
unsteady hands to furl the sails and drop
anchor. When that was completed, he returned
to the helm. With his glass, he studied the shore,
looking for Blackstoke and, more importantly,
Jacinda. The flag had disappeared. There was
no movement along the waterfront.

461

Impatiently, he waited for Blackstoke's next move.

Dusk was gathering around them, the clouds on the western horizon tinged with pinks and lavenders, when Tristan spied the dinghy being rowed out from a small cove. He touched the gun he had hidden inside his shirt, as if to reassure himself that it was still there.

"Throw down the ladder, Dancing," Blackstoke called up to him.

Tristan obeyed, his eyes seeking Jacinda as the small boat approached. Finally, he could see her. Blackstoke was holding her in front of him, a shield against Tristan should he decide to shoot.

"Now back away, Dancing. You and Loralie stand at the other side of the ship. And don't try anything. There's a rope around Jacinda's neck and it's tied to my wrist. If I fall, she goes with me."

Tristan ground his teeth as he backed away as ordered. It took Blackstoke and Jacinda quite a while to work their way up the ladder, Jacinda leading the way, her wrists tied together and a gag in her mouth. When Tristan saw her head appear over the side of the ship, he started forward, but Loralie's hand on his arm stopped him.

"Don't do it, Captain," she warned.

Tristan glanced over at her, warring with her advice and his urge to free Jacinda. He turned his gaze back to Jacinda. He could see the rope around her throat and felt as if he were strangling himself. Then Blackstoke appeared, and a cold fury swept through Tristan, a deadly rage such as he'd never felt before.

Blackstoke jerked lightly on Jacinda's rope collar, drawing her back against him. In the fading daylight, Tristan saw the glimmer of metal as the viscount placed a knife against Jacinda's throat.

"Glad you could join us, Captain," Blackstoke said pleasantly. "Nice day for sailing, don't you agree?"

"What is it you want from me, Blackstoke?"

The viscount laughed. "But I thought you would have guessed by now, Dancing. I want to see you dead."

Jacinda gasped. Blackstoke jerked again on the rope.

"I want to see you dead, and I want her to see it happen."

Tristan took a step forward, his hand raised in supplication. "Let her go, Blackstoke. This is between you and me."

Again he laughed.

Tristan took another step.

"Stop where you are," Blackstoke warned. "Loralie, I imagine there's a gun inside his shirt. Get it."

Loralie stepped cautiously forward. She felt around, then glanced toward Blackstoke. "There's nothing there."

Tristan said a silent thanks for her falsehood, but he thought it too soon.

"Dancing, tell her to take out the gun and throw it overboard. You and I both know you must have one."

Tristan waited, the night already shrouding them in shadows.

"Tell him, Jacinda," Blackstoke snarled.

"Tell him what I'm doing to you."

He heard her muffled cry of pain and knew that Blackstoke was choking her with the rope. "All right, Blackstoke. I'm giving the gun to Loralie. Just stop what you're doing."

"Throw it overboard."

Loralie took the gun from Tristan. He sensed her reluctance and feared she might try to use it herself. "Throw it over, Loralie," he said, echoing Blackstoke.

There was a barely audible splash as the pistol hit the water and sank.

"That's better. Now, Loralie my dear, take this rope—" He tossed it onto the deck between them. "—and tie the good captain to the mast. And do a good job, because if you don't, I'll slit your throat right now."

"I'm sorry, Captain," Loralie whispered as she followed Blackstoke's instructions.

Although it was too dark to be certain, Tristan thought she was crying.

When the rope was secure, Blackstoke ordered Loralie to back away, and dragging Jacinda with him, he walked over to check the knots. "Bring me a lantern, Loralie." While he was waiting for her to do his bidding, he pushed Jacinda up against Tristan. "Look at her, Captain." He removed the gag. "Look at her. Isn't she beautiful? And she's mine. She will always be mine."

"Tris," she whispered painfully.

Even in the darkness he could read her despair and fear. He wanted to ask what he'd done to her, but he wouldn't let himself. It would only hurt her more to tell him.

"Go ahead, Captain. Kiss her. It's your last

chance."

His lips brushed lightly over hers. He could taste the salt of her tears. "Don't be frightened, Cinda. We'll be all right. I swear it."

"I love you, Tristan," she replied.

"No!" Blackstoke yelled, hearing her words. He jerked her sharply away from Tristan, sending her tumbling across the deck.

Tristan snarled and fought against his bindings like a wild man. "Blackstoke!"

But the viscount wasn't listening. He was bent over Jacinda. "It's me you love. It's me. It's me."

Loralie came up from the cabins, lantern in hand. It was a chance and she took it. As she hurried past Tristan, she slipped a knife into his right hand, then moved on by without hardly a pause, carrying the lantern to Blackstoke.

It was the first time Tristan could see Jacinda's face clearly, and he was relieved to see her face was unmarred. She had suffered no beatings at the hands of this madman. She was pale and her eyes were wide with trepidation, but she seemed for the most part unharmed. Until now, that is. There was a red welt rising on her throat from Blackstoke's snap on the rope when he pulled her away from Tristan.

Blackstoke hauled Jacinda to her feet and drew her over to the side of the ship where he bound her hands to the rail. Then he took the lantern from Loralie's hand, grabbed her arm and escorted her below, leaving Jacinda and Tristan in silence.

Jacinda ached to see Tristan's face more clearly. It seemed an eternity since she'd been with him, since she'd felt his strong arms around her.

"He hasn't hurt me, Tris," she said softly into the darkness, knowing he must be wondering and dreading.

"Cinda—"

"I love you," she whispered again as she saw the light returning from the cabins below.

She didn't doubt that Blackstoke meant to kill them all this night, and it looked as though he would succeed, despite Tristan's promise to the contrary.

"Well," Blackstoke announced as he came into view, "Loralie won't be bothering any of us for a while. I convinced her to take a nice, long nap, and just to make certain, I gave her a light tap on the head."

He chuckled as he stepped over to Jacinda's side. He wrapped her rope leash through his fingers again, then freed her hands from the railing, although he left them bound together at the wrists. He carried the lantern closer to Tristan, setting it on the deck between them.

"Shall I tell you my plans, Captain?"

"By all means," Tristan replied, his words controlled, sounding completely unconcerned.

"I'm going to make love to your wife, Captain. Here. On your ship. So that you know it's happened. I'm going to take her from you like you tried to take her from me." His voice rose in anxious anticipation. "I'm going to savor every inch of her. Do you hear me?"

Jacinda closed her eyes, feeling the cold night air creeping over her skin, then stealing inside her and chilling her heart.

"And then, Captain, I'm going to set fire to this precious ship of yours, and it's going to burn just like your last ship did. Only this time you won't get away. You'll still be tied to that mast, and you'll burn with the ship."

"You can't really think you'll get away with this, Blackstoke."

"Oh, but I do, Dancing. I most certainly do think so." Blackstoke turned toward Jacinda as he spoke. "I most certainly do."

It was like looking into the face of Satan himself. The light flickered up from the lantern on the deck, casting shadows upward on his face. His eyes were alight with a frightening glow. He tugged on the rope, drawing her closer to him.

"You won't mind showing him a little of what we plan to enjoy, do you, my dear? And then we'll go below to that nice big bed I saw in the captain's cabin."

The rope tightened a little more.

"This time will be different, my sweet," he whispered.

She tried to pull away, but she choked as the rope bit into her flesh. She reached up with her bound hands and pulled at the cruel hemp, gasping for air.

Blackstoke pulled the knife from his belt. Once again he pressed the sharp point against her throat, just below her jaw. "Don't fight me, my dear. I'd hate to have to hurt anyone as pretty as you." With a sudden flick of his wrist, he cut several buttons from the bodice of her gown. "Are you watching, Captain? I want you to see this." Still with the point of his knife, he lifted the front of her bodice and pushed it back over her shoulder.

Jacinda shivered as the night air touched

her bare skin. Blackstoke was chuckling to himself as he pushed her dress off her other shoulder as well. The dress clung precariously to her breasts. Jacinda wondered if the rope was tightening around her throat again or if she was simply being suffocated by Blackstoke's slow, torturous perusal.

"Look at her, Captain," the viscount ordered again. "Have you ever seen flesh so tempting, so begging to be touched?" He wrapped the end of the leash several more times around his own wrist as he drew her toward him. "I mean to touch it."

With a sudden growl, Tristan broke free from the mast and hurled himself across the deck, crashing into Blackstoke and dragging him down. The force jerked Jacinda to the deck, cutting off her wind. She clawed at the rope, trying to draw a breath. She tried to stand, only to be pulled down again as the two men rolled in a death grip across the deck.

It all happened too fast to be certain of anything. One moment she was struggling to her feet, the next she was soaring through the air, pulled along by the strangling rope leash that was stealing the very life from her. She hit the water and felt herself being dragged down by a heavy weight. She fought and kicked, pulling at the rope around her throat. Her lungs felt as if they would burst. Colorful auroras flashed behind closed eyelids. She struggled to reach the surface, to draw a breath of air.

She felt arms go around her. She knew they were Tristan's arms. He felt for the rope, drawing her upward while sawing at the leash with his knife. But it was going to be too late. She couldn't bear the pressure in her chest any longer. She was going to drown. But if she had to die, at least it would be in his arms.

She waited for him, leaning out the window of her high-towered room. She could see his approach, his black charger loping slowly, neck proudly arched and thick mane and long tail flowing in the wind. Her pulse quickened. He was coming for her. Her love. Her life. She turned from the window and raced down the stone steps and out of the keep. She couldn't reach him soon enough. She longed to feel his strong arms around her. She yearned for the taste of his sweet kisses. There! There he was. Sitting so tall and straight in the saddle. She could see his coal-black hair and imagined his twinkling black eyes. She held out her arms, urging him to come faster. And he did. As his mighty charger slid to a stop, he vaulted from the saddle, gathering her in his arms. "Cinda, my love. It's over. You're safe. Cinda, I need you. Stay with me, love. Stay."

Jacinda coughed and sputtered, the gulps of air burning her throat and lungs.

"Thank God. Cinda."

She was in his arms. She opened her eyes. Everything was blurred behind salty tears. "Am I still dreaming?" she asked hoarsely.

Tristan held her tightly against his chest, rocking her in his arms. "No, my love. You're not dreaming. You're safe." He kissed her wet hair. "I love you, Jacinda Dancing."

Nestled against his chest, the quickened pace of his heartbeat sounding in her ear, she smiled and closed her eyes again.

40

Loud voices called orders, others answered. The horses pulling the wagons stomped their hooves against the wooden docks and shook their heads, snorting and rattling their harnesses. Gulls swooped and cried overhead, adding their voices to the cacophony of the harbor. In the hold, Neptune and Pegasus whickered to each other in their separate stalls as men carted boxes and crates off the wagons and into the belly of the ship.

"Careful with those paintings," Locksworth barked from his chair on the deck. "I don't want to see them taking a dunking."

"Calm yourself, Grandfather. Nothing's going to happen to your paintings."

The duke glanced over at Ella, standing beside his chair, Brandon in her arms. "Hand over the little nipper. Go see about your own things and quit telling an old man what to do."

Ella laughed as she passed her son into Locksworth's arms.

"And tell that husband of yours he needs to

take a bit of the sass out of you," he scolded.

She kissed his white hair and hurried away from him, still laughing merrily.

Locksworth grinned to himself, glowing with warm satisfaction. "Well, young Brand, we're about to start on a wonderful journey. Your life will probably be filled with many great adventures, living in a new country as you will. You've got a fine mother. And a wonderful father in Danny O'Banyon, too. No one need ever know that you weren't sired by O'Banyon. I'm not sure even he remembers he didn't." He chuckled, then turned his eyes back on the orderly disorder that seemed to be going on all around him. "It's a grand day, Brand. Look at this ship. Your uncle's a fine captain, though I suspect he'll have more of an inclination to stay at home now that he'll have Jacinda there with him."

The old man fell silent for a while, then resumed talking as if he'd never paused. "We're a lucky family, Brand. Could've lost that girl so easy. So many times, we could've lost her. If it hadn't been for that Loralie's quick thinking—"

He'd asked the judge for a measure of leniency in the sentencing of Loralie, as a last favor to him, the departing Duke of Locksworth. It wasn't that he felt much pity for her. She deserved her punishment for the part she'd played in Blackstoke's scheme. But if she hadn't acted when she did, if she hadn't given Tristan that knife . . .

"You know, young Brand, some people are just destined for each other and nothing can keep them apart. Not even the Blackstokes of this world." With an oath he added, "May he rot forever in his watery grave."

Locksworth glanced toward the busy city and beyond. England. He would probably not set eyes on her again. He was old and tired. He was ready to spend the last of his days in the bosom of his family. Let his brother's son take care of Locksworth House and the rest of his inheritance until the old duke died. It would all pass on to him anyway. Aldrich Phineasbury, sixth Duke of Locksworth, was leaving it behind with no regrets. His grandchildren had made a life for themselves in America, and he would join them there. He would spend his sunset years watching his great-grandson growing up. And he didn't doubt there would soon be others to follow.

"What are you smiling about, Grandfather?"

He looked up to meet Jacinda's warm, loving gaze. "I was just thinking about how wonderful life can be."

She held his hand and they exchanged a squeeze, understanding more than words had said.

Jacinda stood at the bow of the ship, watching the painted sky as the sun sank into the sea. The ocean sprayed her cheeks and the wind tugged at her loose hair. Her heart felt close to bursting. Her eyes misted with tears.

Somewhere to the west of here, far to the west of here, lay her new home. She had left behind her parents and Bonclere and her title, but none of that mattered. She had long ago been separated from her parents, emotionally if not physically. Bonclere had never truly been a home, merely a place to live. And her title, the

Lady Jacinda, meant nothing to her, less than nothing when she heard herself called Mrs. Dancing.

She listened to the wind whistling through the sails overhead and glanced up. White canvas clouds billowed westward, seeming to lean anxiously in that direction, as if they too were in a hurry to reach America.

Now her gaze fell to the ocean. The white spray before the bow churned and whirled away, leaving a crooked white line behind them. She wondered that she wasn't afraid of the sea after coming so close to drowning. It could have been her grave if Tristan hadn't cut her free when he did. It had become Blackstoke's grave. Knocked unconscious by Tristan's powerful fist, he had disappeared into the ocean's murky depths.

Blackstoke. His name and the memories it evoked seemed to be only a bad dream now. The nightmare had ended, and she was living the best dream possible.

"I thought I might find you here." Tristan stepped up behind her, wrapping her in his arms. He rested his chin on her shoulder and joined her in watching the fading of day.

"How long will it take us to reach America?" she asked him, not for the first time.

Tristan laughed gently. "So eager to get there, are you? And I thought you'd like spending a few weeks with me in the captain's cabin." He kissed her ear, nibbling on the tender lobe. "About six weeks, love," he said, finally answering her question.

Twilight stole the sky from the sun; darkness quickly followed. One by one, the stars flickered to life overhead until the heavens glimmered with a million tiny lights.

Silently, Tristan turned Jacinda around to face him. With his finger, he tilted her chin and lowered his mouth to brush softly against hers. Her heart fluttered like a captured bird.

"Perhaps, if we trimmed the sails, we could make the journey last even longer," he whispered breathlessly in her ear. "If I steer us just a little off course, we could be many weeks at sea."

Her tawny-gold eyes stared up at him, her love shining clearly in the starlight. "Would you pirate us away, Captain?"

Tristan tightened his arms, molding her against him. "I will, Jacinda," he answered softly, "if you promise to always be the pirate's lady."

"Forever, Tristan. For always."

TEMPTESTUOUS
HISTORICAL ROMANCE
BY ROBIN LEE HATCHER

THE SPRING HAVEN SAGA, VOL. III 2318-0
HEART STORM $3.95 US, $4.95 CAN

THE SPRING HAVEN SAGA, VOL. II 2083-1
HEART'S LANDING $3.75 US, $4.25 CAN

THE SPRING HAVEN SAGA, VOL. I 2073-4
STORMY SURRENDER $3.75 US, $4.25 CAN

THORN OF LOVE 2194-3
$3.95 US, $4.95 CAN

BE SWEPT AWAY
ON A TIDE OF PASSION
BY LEISURE'S THRILLING
HISTORICAL ROMANCES!

Make the Most of Your Leisure Time
with
LEISURE BOOKS

Please send me the following titles:

Quantity	Book Number	Price
_____	_____	_____
_____	_____	_____
_____	_____	_____
_____	_____	_____

If out of stock on any of the above titles, please send me the alternate title(s) listed below:

Postage & Handling _____

Total Enclosed $ _____

☐ Please send me a free catalog.

NAME _____
(please print)

ADDRESS _____

CITY _____ STATE _____ ZIP_____

Please include $1.00 shipping and handling for the first book ordered and 25¢ for each book thereafter in the same order. All orders are shipped within approximately 4 weeks via postal service book rate. PAYMENT MUST ACCOMPANY ALL ORDERS.*

*Canadian orders must be paid in US dollars payable through a New York banking facility.

Mail coupon to: **Dorchester Publishing Co., Inc.**
6 East 39 Street, Suite 900
New York, NY 10016
Att: ORDER DEPT.